continued . . .

"An extremely fast-paced book with some great gallows humor, introspection, and references to both the Nightside and Secret Histories series . . . I found it intriguing and highly enjoyable with some crazy action and twisted characters."

—*The Bibliophilic Book Blog*

GHOST OF A DREAM

"Green once again mixes and matches genres with gleeful abandon . . . Readers who enjoy a roller-coaster ride through a haunted house (well, theater, but I'm mixing metaphors here) will love this novel . . . A terrific continuation of the Ghost Finders' adventures, with loads of horrors, thrills, and shocks."

—*SFRevu*

GHOST OF A SMILE

"Packed with creepy thrills, *Ghost of a Smile* is a mighty strong follow-up in this brand-new series. Ghost hunting has never been quite this exciting. Recommended."

—*SFRevu*

"[With] plenty of action and chills, this book keeps pages turning even as a feeling of dread builds. The dialogue between the three characters is snappy and humorous, as is the chemistry between them."

—NewsandSentinel.com

"*Ghost of a Smile* is a lovely blend of popcorn adventure and atmospheric thriller, and good for a few hours of distraction and entertainment. That's one of the reasons why Green's books always leap right to the top of my reading list."

—*The Green Man Review*

"[Green] gleefully tweaks the natural fear of experimentation (and the inscrutable motivations of the men behind it), bringing some real-world paranoia into his fantasy-laden playground. It's a gamble that pays off nicely . . . With his Nightside series ending soon, the Ghost Finders books are quickly proving to be worthy replacements."

—*Sacramento Book Review*

GHOST OF A CHANCE

FORCES FROM BEYOND

SIMON R. GREEN

ACE BOOKS, NEW YORK

ACE

An imprint of Penguin Random House LLC
375 Hudson Street, New York, New York 10014

FORCES FROM BEYOND

An Ace Book / published by arrangement with the author

ISBN: 978-0-425-25995-5

PUBLISHING HISTORY
Ace mass-market edition / September 2015

PRINTED IN THE UNITED STATES OF AMERICA

10 9 8 7 6 5 4 3 2 1

Cover illustration by Don Sipley.
Cover photo: smoke © Honchar Roman / Shutterstock.
Cover design by Judith Lagerman.
Interior text design by Laura K. Corless.

Penguin
Random
House

What are ghosts, really?

The unquiet dead or merely images imprinted on Time? The world's dreaming or nightmares from the past? Those heart-rending screams in the long reaches of the night . . . are they cries for help or desperate warnings? What are ghosts for, really? If anyone knows, the living or the dead, they're not talking.

There have always been ghosts, and there always will be. Because living takes its toll, and dying even more so.

PREVIOUSLY, IN THE GHOST FINDERS

That very secret organisation, the Carnacki Institute, exists to Do Something about ghosts. Along with anything else that won't lie down when it should, or play nicely with the living. The Ghost Finders are the Institute's field agents, tasked with tracking down supernatural trouble-makers and kicking their arses with existential prejudice. Because the living have enough problems of their own without being troubled by the dead.

The Institute's current top-ranking field team is led by JC Chance. Forces from Outside once intervened to save his life, altering him subtly in the process, and now his eyes glow golden. Though whether that's a sign of grace or a mark of ownership has yet to be determined. The team's hard-headed science geek is Melody Chambers, and Happy Jack Palmer is the team telepath and self-medicating headcase. Kim Sterling is dead, the only actual ghost in the Ghost Finders.

JC and Kim are in love even though there are many good reasons why the living and the dead are never supposed to get together.

Sometime back, an opening appeared in the walls that separate the worlds, and something from a higher reality fell through, into our dimension. A fearsome living god: the Flesh Undying. It has plans for our world, none of them good, and agents everywhere, very definitely including inside the Carnacki Institute. JC and his team don't just deal with ghosts any more; they're fighting to save the world.

And now, it's all about to hit the fan.

ONE

THE PAST ISN'T OVER;
SOMETIMES, IT ISN'T EVEN PAST

It isn't ghosts that make places bad; it's the bad places that make ghosts. And, sometimes, other things.

Ghosts hang around hotels like moths drawn to a light. All those empty rooms aren't nearly as empty as people like to think. Managers understandably don't like to mention the unfortunate fact that not every guest who checks in will check out alive. People die in lonely, characterless rooms all the time, so when entering a hotel room, the question shouldn't be: Has anybody died in that bed? Try instead: How many? Bodies are carried out on stretchers and smuggled down the back stairs in the early hours of the morning, out of sight of paying customers, more often than you'd think. Death from causes natural and unnatural . . . heart attack, erotic misadventure, suicide, and murder . . . Hotels have seen it all. Ghosts linger on in some rooms like a bad smell or a stain that won't wash out. And then it's time to call in the professionals.

ııııııııııııııııııııııı

The Ghost Finders came to the Acropolis Majoris Hotel in the early hours of the evening, in the dying days of autumn. The lowering sky had a bruised, sullen look, the gusting wind muttered bad things under its breath, and the air had a bitter chill. Not a good time to be out and about, even in the bright and cheerful seaside city of Brighton. The Acropolis Hotel was nowhere near the beach, or the famous pier, or any of the things tourists like to see. Instead, it was tucked away in a labyrinth of shadowy back streets, well off the main drag. A spillover hotel, where people reluctantly ended up when there were no rooms left in bigger, better establishments.

The Ghost Finders took their time, standing on the opposite side of the street to study the hotel's grubby facade and less-than-inviting ambience. Not a big building, but more than old enough to be steeped in bad incidents and sad memories. Something had happened here, something was waiting . . . like a troll under a bridge or a land mine under a welcome mat. Ghosts mostly prefer to lie in wait and make the living come to them. After all, they have all the time in the world.

JC Chance stood proud and poised in his exquisitely cut white suit, his head held high and his shoulders squared, hands thrust deep into his pockets. Tall and lean, and perhaps just a little more handsome than was good for him, JC had pale, striking features and a rock star's mane of long jet-black hair. He also had the smile of a man who knew things, and not particularly nice things, at that. As head of this particular field team, he could always be relied on to rush in where angels feared to show their faces, looking eagerly around for some trouble to get into. He wore extremely dark sunglasses at all times, for a very good reason.

Melody Chambers stood slouched at his side, scowling and tapping her foot impatiently. Wherever she was, she always gave the impression she didn't want to be there. Conventionally good-looking in a stern sort of way, Melody wore her auburn hair scraped back in a tight bun and glowered at the world through heavy glasses with very sober frames. Gamine thin, she burned with fierce, nervous energy and wore her bad temper openly as a badge of pride. She tended to look like she was only moments away from attacking people at random, just on general principle. She dressed for comfort rather than style—jacket and jersey, jeans and work boots. Melody had heard of fashion and wanted nothing to do with it. Her scientific equipment lay piled up on a motorised trolley that hummed busily at her side like an eager dog.

Happy Jack Palmer, who'd embraced self-medication as a marginally preferable alternative to self-harming, stood a little to one side. Short and stocky and prematurely balding, he wore scuffed jeans and shoes, a grubby T-shirt, and a battered, black leather jacket held together by heavy staples and patches of duct tape. Normally, he would have been the first to say something cutting and inappropriate about their current location; but not this time. He stood quietly, looking at the world with eyes that had seen too much, for far too long.

"I can't believe the Boss sent us here," JC said finally. "We're only supposed to get the most important and significant cases."

"You mean the most dangerous," said Melody.

"Same thing," JC said easily. "Give me action and excitement, death and glory, every time!"

"I'll settle for the glory," said Melody.

JC ignored her with the ease of long practice. "I mean, look at this place! It's a dump. In fact, it would need a serious upgrade and a major face-lift before it could properly qualify as a dump! You couldn't expect any self-respecting ghost to show up here." He paused, to look down his nose at the various pieces of high tech on Melody's trolley. "Odds are you won't need half of that."

"Hush, babies," Melody said fondly to her equipment. "Nasty man doesn't know what he's talking about."

JC sniffed loudly. "Given the general ambience, you could fend off any ghosts you found here with a balloon on a stick and some harsh language. Oh well: onwards! Wait a minute, hold everything. Where's Happy?"

They both looked around quickly as they realised the telepath wasn't with them any longer.

"Oh bugger, he's wandered off again," said Melody.

She spotted him half-way down the street, ambling aimlessly through pools of street-light and deep, dark shadows with equal disinterest. Melody hurried off after him, took a firm hold on his arm, and hustled him back to the Acropolis Hotel. He didn't seem to care where he was. JC studied him expressionlessly.

"Happy, are you with us?" he said finally. "Ready to go to work and kick some ectoplasmic arse?"

Happy didn't answer. There was nothing in his face to indicate he'd even heard the question. JC looked at Melody.

"I saw him last week, and he wasn't this bad. When did he stop talking?"

"He's been saying less and less for some time now," Melody said reluctantly. "Withdrawing inside himself, away from the pressures of the world. It's not easy being a Class Eleven telepath."

"I thought the pills helped with that," said JC.

"He's been taking them too long," said Melody. "Built up too much of a tolerance. The doses he has to take now would kill anyone else."

"What use is he like this?"

"He knows who he is and who I am," said Melody. "He can still function, still do his job when he has to."

"Dear God . . ." said JC.

"It's not going to be a problem!" Melody said fiercely. "He's still in there!"

"I suppose I shouldn't complain," said JC. "His not speaking might actually be an improvement when it comes to dealing with members of the general public."

He was trying for a lightness of touch but couldn't quite bring it off.

"Where's Kim?" said Melody, just a bit pointedly.

"Around," said JC. "She'll turn up, when she's needed. Come on, let's go talk to the hotel manager and get this show on the road. Shouldn't take us long to deal with whatever's bothering them here; and then we can go for a play on the Pier! I love the Pier."

"Of course you do," said Melody. "It's cheap and tacky, just like you."

JC strode determinedly through the front door. Melody fired up her trolley, and it putt-putted importantly along at her side as she followed JC in, still gripping Happy firmly by the arm. The lobby of the Acropolis turned out to be surprisingly large and airy, and only a bit shabby. JC had no trouble identifying the manager, pacing impatiently up and down with a face so full of troubles there wasn't room for anything else. Stocky and middle-aged, with neatly arranged hair, he wore a suit that had once been too good for him but now looked distinctly hard-worn. The only other staff was a faded, middle-aged woman, at Reception. She took one look at the Ghost Finders and busied herself with some vital paper-work.

The manager rushed forward to grab JC's outstretched hand with both of his, smiling weakly, fixing JC with desperate eyes. The manager looked like he was carrying all the cares of the world and getting really tired of it. He went to shake Melody's hand, then quickly gave that up as a bad idea once he took in her expression. Melody did have people skills; she just mostly couldn't be bothered. The manager looked doubtfully at Happy and turned quickly back to JC.

"You are them? The Ghost Finders?"

"That's us!" said JC. "If it moves and it shouldn't, we have the answer."

"I'm Stefan Garth, owner and manager of the Acropolis. Thank you so much for coming! I'm at my wits' end, trying to cope . . . Excuse me for asking; but is this all of you? I was expecting a more substantial response . . ."

"Trust me," said JC. "We're all you need."

Garth took a deep breath and let it out in a long sigh of qualified relief. Some of the weight seemed to come off his shoulders. "I've been trying to get help for ages," he said tiredly. "No-one would listen when I tried to tell them about the Bad Room. No-one would believe me when I told them one of my rooms was killing people. The authorities didn't want to know; friends and family were sympathetic but unhelpful; and when I went to the media, they just made fun of me. Luckily, only the local news ran the story, or it could have been very bad for business. But, finally, I told someone who knew someone at the Carnacki Institute. I was so happy, so relieved, when they assured me they'd send their very best people to deal with the situation . . . You're sure you can help?"

"Of course!" JC said cheerfully. "We are the Pros from Dover; the A team, only with less guns. We know what we're doing, and when we don't, we fake it."

The manager didn't seem particularly reassured. He looked doubtfully at Melody, who scowled right back at him, and dubiously at Happy, who was smiling serenely at nothing in particular. The manager turned back to JC.

"Don't you need a priest? For an exorcism?"

"That's a more specialised procedure," said JC. "Unless you've got hot and cold blood running down your walls, voices speaking in tongues on your internal phones, and a whole bunch of levitating beds . . . it's unlikely to be a demonic presence. We are more your general practitioners. We make the bad things go away."

"I'll show you the room," said Garth. "While it's still light."

"Let me guess," said JC. "No-one goes there after dark."

"I keep the door locked at all times," said the manager. "So whatever's in there can't get out."

....

He led the way to the single elevator, on the far side of the lobby. Melody sulked at having to leave her precious equipment behind, but it clearly wasn't going to fit in the elevator with them. Garth promised no-one would touch anything and even elicited a quick nod of agreement from the silent presence at Reception. So Melody just stuffed a few useful items into her pockets, said *Stay!* to the trolley, and hauled an unresisting Happy over to the elevator with her. Everyone waited for a while, then waited some more. The manager smiled weakly.

"Sorry . . . We've only the four floors here at the Acropolis, so there's only the one elevator. It's getting old and just a bit unreliable. But perfectly safe! Oh yes! Perfectly . . ."

"Speaking of safe," JC said quietly, "Did you arm the defences on your trolley, Mel?"

"Of course! No-one touches my stuff."

"Tell me you set them to non-lethal."

"More or less."

The manager appeared even more unhappy. Especially when he looked at Happy.

"Is he all right?"

"Sometimes," said Melody.

"He's a specialist," JC said solemnly. "Best not to distract him while he's thinking. About things."

Perhaps fortunately, the elevator doors opened at that moment, and they all filed inside. The ascent to the fourth floor was quiet and uneventful, and the doors finally opened onto a perfectly-ordinary-looking corridor. Garth led the way, occasionally glancing back over his shoulder to reassure himself the others were still with him. All the doors on both sides of the corridor remained firmly closed. There was no-one about, not a sound to be heard. Even their footsteps on the faded carpet sounded flat and dull, oddly muffled.

"Are all the other rooms on this floor occupied?" said JC.

"Of course," said Garth. "We do good business on the whole. Brighton is always very popular with the tourists, even at the end of the Season. It's only the one room that's gone bad."

"Have any of your guests reported seeing or hearing anything unusual?" said JC.

"No," said the manager, firmly. "Everything that's happened has been limited to just this one room. No matter how bad it gets inside the room, whatever it is stays inside."

"How bad does it get?" said Melody.

The manager shuddered, briefly. For a moment, it seemed like he might actually turn around and go back; but he squared his weary shoulders and kept going. He had the look of a man on his way to the dentist, or possibly the hangman.

JC looked thoughtfully around him. There was no dread atmosphere in the corridor, no sense of unease, nothing in the least menacing. The carpet was a bit threadbare in places, and the whole place could have used a lick of paint and a touch-up; but that was it. Nothing to indicate a dangerous setting, nothing to warn about bad things waiting in the room ahead.

The manager finally stopped before Room 418. JC noticed immediately that the numbers added up to thirteen but decided it probably wasn't a good time to point that out.

They all stood together, looking at the blank, coffee-coloured door. It stared right back at them, giving nothing away. JC listened carefully but couldn't hear anything. Melody produced a hand-held scanner and ran it quickly over the door. A few lights flickered on the device, but that was all. Melody scowled and put the scanner away. Happy didn't react to any of it. JC looked at Garth. The manager's face was wet with sweat, and his hand actually shook as he produced a magcard and unlocked the door.

"The room is empty, right now?" said JC.

"Of course," said Garth. He pulled his hand back from the handle, as though glad of an excuse to put off actually opening the door.

"How long since anyone's been in it?" said JC.

"I haven't dared let this room for almost seven months now," said Garth. "None of the staff will go anywhere near it. I have to do the turn-down and clean myself. When I can work up the nerve. I don't like to just leave it . . . that would feel like giving up. Giving in. But I always make sure my wife comes with me, to hold the door open. So it can't close on its own. So I won't get . . . trapped. In there."

"What happened, seven months ago?" said Melody. "What brought this to a head?"

"There were screams," Garth said, reluctantly. "Out here, in the corridor. When guests came running out of their rooms to investigate, they found Mr. Harding staggering out of Room 418. He'd torn his eyes out. When they finally got him to stop screaming, he said the room showed him things."

"Any idea what?" said Melody.

"That was all he had to say," said Garth. "He was still saying it when they strapped him into the strait jacket and took him away." He looked suddenly at JC. "Why are you wearing sunglasses indoors?"

"Style," said JC.

The manager clearly wanted to say a great many things but didn't. He braced himself and opened the door to Room 418. And then he turned and ran, bolting down the corridor as the last of his courage evaporated. He didn't look back once, and he didn't wait for the elevator. He was in such a hurry to get away, he plunged straight through the door marked *Stairs*. JC and Melody looked at each other, then at the door standing open before them. JC reached carefully inside, felt around till he found the light-switch, and turned it on. Dull, flat light revealed an empty, quiet, and completely unremarkable hotel room.

"I hate the sneaky ones," said Melody. "Where they try to pretend nothing's wrong . . ."

"Let us run through the briefing before we venture in," said JC.

"You actually read the briefing file, for once?" said Melody. "I am seriously impressed. What brought that on?"

"A long train journey down," said JC. "And I'd already read this month's *FHM*. I'll hit the high lights, and you can chime in on anything you feel is significant."

"Because you don't want to go into that room just yet," said Melody.

"Got it in one," said JC. "Something in there is sharpening its teeth. I can feel it. Anyway, what we have here . . . is a room where bad things happen. And the bad things are getting worse. No ghosts as such. No poltergeists, no dark shapes walking through walls, no menacing figure standing at the foot of the bed smiling at the occupant . . . Not even a door opening on its own in the middle of the night, or a strange face looking back out of the mirror. None of the usual give-aways. Just a room that really messes up the people who stay in it. Not merely suicides though 418 has racked up far more than its fair share. We're talking really nasty cases of self-harming, screams in the night, and people who had such bad dreams, they wouldn't even wait till morning to check out. And a hell of a lot of heart attacks, strokes, and other less-easily-identifiable medical problems."

"Eighty-seven natural deaths in the past three years," said Melody. "And over a hundred people who needed hospital treatment, for physical or mental distress." She frowned. "That is so off the chart, I can't believe no-one alerted us until now."

"The manager hushed it up for as long as he could," said JC. "Happy, are you with us? Are you sensing anything?"

The telepath gave him a vague, child-like smile. His gaze was far away.

"He's only half-awake, most of the time," said Melody. "Though he has moments of lucidity. He's only fully himself, and properly operational, when he's taking his pills."

"And you keep on dosing him," said JC. "Even though you know those things are killing him."

"Yes," said Melody.

JC shoved the door to Room 418 all the way open, slamming it back against the inside wall. The sudden sound was deafeningly loud, but it didn't carry, and it didn't echo. It was as though there was something wrong with sound itself inside Room 418. Happy's head came up slowly, and he looked into the room.

"Bad place," he said in a perfectly normal voice. "Genius loci. There's someone in there."

"I can't see anyone," said JC. "And I am looking really hard."

"It can see us," said Happy.

"What is it?" said Melody.

But Happy's moment had passed.

"I have to look after him," Melody said bitterly. "Like a carer, for someone with Alzheimer's. He's only thirty-two!"

Even as she said that, she tugged absently at Happy's clothes, smartening him up like a mother with a child. Happy didn't seem to notice.

"Be straight with me," said JC. "How bad is he really? I need the truth, Mel."

"Only the pills make him the man I remember," said Melody. "Pump enough chemicals into him, and he can still do his job."

"For how long?" said JC. "You must know that the Boss is pressing me to stand Happy down, replace him with another telepath. For the good of the team."

"Is that what you want?" Melody said sharply.

"Of course it's not what I want!" said JC. "But he's damaged, now. Broken."

"Whose fault is that?" said Melody. "You were always pushing him to take the damned pills, to make him a better telepath."

"So he could do the job," said JC.

"You must have known what they were doing to him!"

"Yes, I knew. So did Happy. He could have walked away from the team anytime. And maybe he should have. The way he looks now, it might be kinder if we did stand him down."

"No," said Melody. "It wouldn't. At least this way, he still has some purpose in his life. Something to keep him going."

"Is that the real reason?" said JC. "Or do you just want him to take his pills, so he can be the man you remember? The man you love?"

"You bastard . . ."

"I need the truth, Mel. Are the pills killing him?"

"Yes," said Melody. She suddenly sounded very tired. "He's taken them for so long, his tolerance is . . . inhuman. Only the most powerful concoctions have any effect at all."

"What happens when the pills stop working?" JC asked.

Melody didn't have an answer for that. She made a meaningless gesture with one hand. "We were supposed to have a life together. I was so sure I could help him, fix him . . . This wasn't the life I saw for us. I hate this! But the only way I could have my old life back, have my freedom back, would be to let them put Happy in a hospital, or an institution. So they could look after him, for whatever remains of his life. I can't do that. Can't just walk away . . . They wouldn't understand what he's done to himself, or why it was necessary. They wouldn't know what pills to give him when he has one of his crying jags. Or an attack of the horrors from something only he can see. I swore I'd hold him while he was dying. I just didn't know it would take so long."

"First thing you learn in this job," said JC, "is that you can't save everyone."

"Even when it matters?"

"Especially then. All we can do is all we can do. Did you bring his pills?"

"Of course," said Melody.

"Then give him some," said JC. "Give him a whole bunch. Bring him back to us. Because he's no use to anyone like this."

Melody nodded stiffly. She already had the silver pill box in her hand. She flipped open the lid, carefully selected three colour-coded pills, and popped them into Happy's slack mouth one at time. Like a mother feeding sweets to a small child. Her mouth pursed in a tight moue of pain; but her hand was perfectly steady.

Happy dry-swallowed with the ease of long practice. Beads of sweat popped out all over his face, he twitched several times like a dreaming dog . . . and then his eyes snapped back into focus with almost vicious force.

"I feel great!" he said loudly. "Great! Where am I?" He looked at Melody and JC. "Oh yes. I remember. This is the haunted-hotel case, right? Even when I'm not here I'm still listening. Apparently. No, Mel, let it go. I'd rather just get to work." He peered through the open doorway, into Room 418. "That room is quite definitely inhabited."

"What's in there?" said JC.

"Not so much a what . . ." said Happy. "It feels more like a mood piece." He looked around him disdainfully. "If you had to bring me back, did it have to be in such a dump? Next time, choose a really nice restaurant. You're paying."

"Not back five minutes and already complaining," said JC.

He strode into the waiting room, rubbing his hands happily together in anticipation.

Happy slouched in after him, shoulders hunched in anticipation of an ambush. Melody brought up the rear, sticking close to Happy, in case he might need her. JC took up a commanding position in the middle of the room and looked carefully at everything. The bedclothes appeared to have been changed recently; but there was a thin layer of dust over everything else. It would seem there was a limit to how long the manager was prepared to stay in the room. The single window was closed, curtains drawn back to reveal a frankly depressing view. And the light in the room was oddly flat, lifeless.

The room had no character, no warmth, and nothing in the least threatening about it. Just an empty room where a great many people had stayed and left no trace of themselves behind. There wasn't even a shadow worth the mentioning. But there was still something about the room . . . as though the Ghost Finders were only seeing, only being allowed to see, the mask on the face of the monster. JC pushed his sunglasses down his nose, and the golden glow in his eyes leapt out into the room, like a breath of fresh air in a killing ground. But he still couldn't see anything out of the ordinary.

"So," said JC, pushing his sunglasses back into place. "Not exactly welcoming; but not actually worrying, either. Hello, ghosts! Come out, come out, whatever you are!"

Kim appeared out of nowhere, snapping into existence like a jump cut in a film. Tall and shapely, carelessly elegant, with a pretty face and masses of bright red hair, the ghost girl looked like a pre-Raphaelite angel. Because she wasn't real any more, she could make her ectoplasm look like anything, so for now she wore a charming white pant suit, to complement JC's outfit. None of the group jumped at her sudden arrival; they were used to Kim. She blew JC a kiss and smiled dazzlingly.

"Hi, JC! How's my sweetie? Miss me? I've been having a quick look around the other rooms on this floor. You wouldn't believe what that sweet old couple in 402 are getting up to. But . . . I haven't seen a ghost anywhere."

"Odd," said JC. "You'd expect there to be a few. Just bog-standard local spirits, same as in any hotel."

"It could be that whatever's in here is so powerful, it

actually suppresses everything else," said Melody. "I need to go back down and fetch my equipment, so I can run proper scans on the environment."

"Not just yet," said JC. "Let's get a feel for the place first."

"It feels depressing," said Happy.

"Yes . . ." Melody nodded slowly. "I'm getting something. Dark, brooding . . ."

"Lonely," said Kim.

"Are you picking up anything useful yet, Happy?" said JC. He was concerned about how long Happy's current frame of mind would last but didn't like to say anything.

"Nothing specific . . ." said Happy. "Just . . . really dark feelings. The whole room is saturated with them." He looked slowly around him. He seemed calm and centred, but his face was an unhealthy colour, with sweat still running down and dripping off his chin. As though the pills he'd taken had lit a fire inside him, and not in a good way. "I thought at first I was just picking up old emotional echoes . . . but it feels more like whatever happened here is still happening. I'm talking real *long, dark night of the soul* stuff. Deep angst and melancholy; despair on an industrial scale. Nasty! But, I have to say, not linked to any particular person, living or dead."

"Given the sheer number of people who died in this room, we should be seeing some ghosts," said JC. "Even if they're just intense emotions imprinted on the surroundings."

"I don't like it here," said Kim, wrinkling her nose. "I mean, I'm dead, and this room is still spooking the crap out of me."

"Could be an extreme case of Sick Building Syndrome," said Melody.

"No," Kim said immediately. "It's more than that."

"Okay, this is getting seriously weird," said Happy. "And I know from weird. I'm getting abstract, almost conceptual psychic pressure. A spiritual undertow, dragging us down."

"Haunted Building Syndrome?" said Melody.

They were all standing close together now, as though they'd been driven into a defensive circle by unseen forces. JC looked quickly back and forth, his skin crawling. It felt like something was sneaking up on him, from every direction at once. As though the walls were closing in, and the ceiling and floor might slam together at any moment. There was a threat in the room, close and real, but he couldn't seem to pin it down. Part of him wanted to just get the hell out while he still could. Because something was coming straight at him, like a runaway ghost train. To run him down and grind him under its wheels. JC held his head high, and snarled around him. Ghost Finders don't run; they make everything else run.

Kim glanced at a mirror on the wall beside her and made a sudden noise. JC's head snapped around.

"What?" he said.

"I always forget I can't see myself in a mirror," said Kim. "Ghosts don't have a reflection because we're not really here. It's been so long since I could see my face that I'm beginning to forget what I look like."

JC smiled at her. "You look great."

But Kim turned her head away, refusing to be comforted.

"So!" said JC, determined to lighten the mood. "Did I ever tell you I once stayed in a hotel room where there was this long, jagged crack in the ceiling, right over my bed? Every night I had to pull the bed out into the middle of the room because I couldn't sleep with the crack hanging over me. And every morning I had to push the bed back into place again, so the chambermaid wouldn't think I was chicken!"

He looked around; but the story didn't get a response from anyone. JC sighed and nodded to Kim.

"All right, girl, you're up. Give us one of your theatrical anecdotes, about the appalling digs you've stayed in. I want this atmosphere broken."

Kim smiled gamely. "Okay . . . I remember touring a play, and the producers booked us into this really low-rent hotel in Birmingham's Chinatown. I didn't even know Birmingham had a Chinatown . . . My room was a fire exit. Really! A big sign on the outside of my door said Fire Exit, along with a hammer attached to the door by a length of chain. The idea was that in the event of a fire, you ran to my door, smashed in the lock with the hammer, then ran through my room to get to the actual fire exit. I never told anyone, but every night before I went to sleep I jammed a chair up against that door.

No-one was getting into my room without my knowing about it . . ."

She looked hopefully around, but there was no response to her story, either. JC looked like he wanted to smile but couldn't remember how.

"Tough crowd," said Kim.

"Tough room," said Happy.

"I can't do anything without my equipment," said Melody. "I can't even tell you how much of this atmosphere is real and how much is just in our heads."

"All right," said JC. "Go get your precious toys and hit this room with the science stick until it tells us everything we need to know."

Melody hesitated, not wanting to leave Happy, but he shot her a reassuring smile.

"Go," he said. "I'll still be here when you get back."

"Will you be all right?" said Melody.

"Hard to tell," said Happy. "But I've got JC and Kim. All jolly companions together. Go."

Melody headed for the door, then stopped abruptly. Without taking her eyes off it, she said, "JC, did you shut this door?"

They all turned to look. The door to Room 418 was very definitely closed.

"I never touched that door," said JC.

"Me neither," said Happy.

"And I can't," said Kim.

"A door that closes on its own, when no-one is looking," said JC. "Now that's more what I expect from a haunted room."

He strode past Melody, took a firm hold on the door-handle, and yanked the door open. It didn't resist him, but when JC looked through the open doorway, there was no sign of the corridor outside. Instead, he was looking into Room 418. With Melody and Happy and Kim facing him. JC turned slowly, to look over his shoulder; and they were all standing behind him. In Room 418. He braced himself, and strode through the open door. Only to find himself walking back into Room 418, towards Melody and Happy and Kim. There was no sense of being turned around. It all felt perfectly normal until he thought about it, then his head hurt. JC walked back and forth through the open doorway several times, and still couldn't feel anything.

"Will you please stop doing that!" said Melody. "You are seriously messing with my head."

"I like it!" said Happy.

"You would," said Melody. "How the hell are we going to get out of here?"

"Could be an illusion," said JC.

"No," said Kim. "Because I'm seeing it, too, and you can't fool ghost eyes. That . . . is real, in its own twisted way."

"Okay," said Happy. "Not panicking even a little bit here."

"Nobody is to panic," said JC. "We aren't necessarily trapped."

He went over to the window, only to stop and consider it thoughtfully. The curtains were closed. JC was sure they'd been open when he entered the room. He took a firm hold on the curtains, yanked them apart, and looked out. And then made a low sound of pain, in spite of himself. There was no view; instead, the window held a complete absence of everything. A terrifying blankness that hurt the eyes, hurt the mind, just to look at. JC averted his gaze. Look at nothing for too long, and the human mind starts to unravel. He carefully pulled the curtains together again and didn't look back until he was sure the window was completely covered. He turned his back on the window and looked at the others.

"All right, it appears we might be trapped in here after all. Any suggestions that don't involve loud noises of distress and involuntary bowel movements?"

Kim tried to disappear and found she couldn't. She frowned prettily, concentrating, and headed determinedly for the nearest wall, to walk through it. Only to find she couldn't do that, either. She didn't actually bump off the wall; she just couldn't seem to get anywhere near it. She looked back at JC.

"Something very odd is happening here. I mean, I'm not in any way material, but I'm still being affected by whatever's in this room."

"It's all in the mind," said Happy.

"What is?" said JC.

"This room . . ." said Happy. "We won't be allowed to leave until the room is finished with us. Finished its business . . ."

"What business?" said JC, just a bit harshly.

"Life and death," said Happy. "The soul in balance. Truth will out . . ."

JC looked at Melody. "Do you know what he's talking about?"

"I'm just telling you what I'm picking up," Happy said patiently. "What the room is saying to me. Or rather, whatever it is that's in this room with us."

JC grabbed up the telephone on the bedside table, but there was no dial tone.

"Nothing," he said.

"Not even the sea?" said Happy.

JC frowned and pressed the phone to his ear. "Wait a minute . . . I just heard someone crying. Hello? Is anyone there? Can we help you? What's wrong?"

The crying stopped. JC put the phone down. "We're on our own . . ."

"If only that were true," said Happy.

"Really not helping, Happy," said Melody.

She got out her cell phone, but it was just as dead. Melody glared at the phone before putting it away, as though it had let her down. She looked at JC.

"I suppose screaming for help is out of the question?"

"Please," said JC. "I have my pride."

"What makes you think anyone would be allowed to hear us?" said Happy.

"Okay!" said Kim. "You are seriously creeping me out now. And I'm dead! I'm supposed to be above such things."

"The room can't hold us here for long," said JC. "The manager is bound to come up, to check why we haven't reported back. We just have to . . . outwait the room."

"And if we can't?" said Happy.

"Then we use your head as a battering ram to break down the door!" said JC. "It's not as if there's anything left in there to damage."

"I've got a few explosive devices about me, somewhere," Melody said demurely.

Happy smiled. "Never knew you when you didn't, dear."

"I think we'll save the scorched-earth policy for a last resort," said JC. "We came here to help the manager, not destroy his livelihood. We need to be more . . . receptive. Work out what this is, what it wants."

"Or needs," said Happy. "I am getting a strong feeling this has all happened before. We're not the first to be held in this room. I am getting a definite sense of history repeating."

"Ghosts are history," said JC. "The Past refusing to go away, imposing itself on the Present."

"Then where is the ghost?" said Kim. "Why isn't it showing itself, making itself known? Why doesn't it just tell us what it wants?"

"I don't think it's that kind of haunting," said Happy.

"I should have hauled my equipment up the stairs," said Melody. "I'd have had this ghost pinned to a wall by now, interrogating it to within an inch of its death."

She stopped because Happy was shaking his head slowly.

"Ghosts are mostly what remains of people," said Happy. "Tortured individuals, with unfinished business. This . . . is nothing like that."

"Come on, Happy," said JC. "Give me something I can use. What kind of haunting is this?"

"The dangerous kind," said Happy. "We could die here. Many have."

"Then where are their ghosts?" said Kim.

The four Ghost Finders came together in the middle of the room, standing shoulder to shoulder, staring quickly about them. Ready for any attack. But the light remained steady, there were no deep dark menacing shadows anywhere at all, and nothing came out of the woodwork. The room looked entirely empty even though they could all tell it wasn't. JC's hands clenched into fists. He hated not knowing what was going on, not knowing who or what to strike out at.

"Hold it," said Happy. His eyes were huge, unblinking, almost fey. "The spiritual weather in this room just changed."

"What?" said Melody. "What does that even mean?"

"Something is heading our way," said Happy. "Closing in on us."

"Where's it coming from?" said JC.

"It's already here. It's always been here. It's just coming into focus. Concentrating on us."

"Who is it?" said Kim.

"It's not a who," said Happy.

They could all feel a growing force in the room, like an approaching storm pressing in from every direction at once. And then they all cried out and rocked on their feet, as harsh emotions sleeted through their minds, unsettling their thoughts in favour of disturbed instincts. They backed quickly away from each other, glaring suspiciously from side to side, at each of their fellow team-mates in turn. Just like that, they knew they couldn't trust anyone. A terrible psychic pressure built up in all of them, a need to speak out. To say things that had been left unsaid for far too long. A desperate need to say awful, truthful, unforgiveable things to each other. Secret things, which once brought out into the light could never be unsaid or taken back. Kim looked abruptly at JC.

"I have to leave you," she said, unreal tears forming in her unreal eyes. "I have to go because that's the only way you can have a normal life. I love you, JC, so I have to give you up. You deserve a real life, a real love, with a woman who has a future."

"I don't want anyone else," said JC. "I only want you. Don't you want me?"

"You know I do!" said Kim. "But I can't touch you!"

"You're all I've ever wanted," said JC. "Please. Don't go."

"I have to," said Kim. "I want you to be happy; and you can't . . . until you've forgotten me and moved on."

"Kim . . . No . . ."

"I want to hold you. I want to be held. This, what we have, it's isn't love, not really. At least you can still touch the world you walk through! At least you can still touch yourself . . . I don't even have that. I'm not real, JC . . . I'm just something that remembers being human and misses it so much . . ."

She sobbed wildly and lurched forward to beat on his chest with her small fists. Her ghostly hands sank into JC and out again, appearing and disappearing. He didn't even feel a chill. He started to reach out to her, to put his arms around her, and then stopped. He just couldn't pretend any longer. Kim snatched her hands away from him and hugged herself tightly.

"Let me go," she said. "Let me die. Better for me, better for you . . ."

"I haven't felt this lucid in a long time," Happy said suddenly. "Everything's so clear . . . I didn't know how far I'd fallen till you woke me up again. Kim's right, Mel. Half a life . . . is no life. I don't want to go back to the way I was, but I will the moment my system burns through the chemicals. Don't keep me around just because you're used to me. Find me a pill to put an end to this."

"I won't give up on you," said Melody. "I won't give up hope."

"There is no hope," said Happy. "No way back. I'm tired, Mel, so tired . . . worn down and burned-out. And the worst part of it is knowing I did this to myself."

"Happy, you have to hold on," said Melody. "I know how hard this must be for you . . ."

"No you don't!" Happy fixed her with his huge-pupiled, unblinking stare. "You have no idea what it's like inside my head. You never did. I'm just one voice, drowned out by all the other voices that keep intruding. Only the pills give me any peace, and they're killing me by inches."

"Then I'll make myself understand," said Melody. She held up one hand, and showed him the silver pill box.

"No," said Happy. "Don't . . . Mel, you couldn't cope."

"I can handle anything you can," said Melody.

She selected three fat pills, and swallowed them down, grimacing at the effort. The others watched, but none of them moved to stop her.

"That is a really bad idea," said JC.

"I know what I'm doing," said Melody.

"Really don't think so," said JC.

He broke off as something new emerged in Melody's face. She looked startled, then shocked, then terrified. She was seeing the world through Happy's eyes, through Happy's chemical consciousness; and it was destroying her. JC started forward, but Happy got to her first. He stood before Melody and took both her trembling hands in his. She didn't even know he was there.

Chemicals rushed through her mind like a storm of razor blades; slicing up her thoughts and sweeping them away. Melody had always prided herself on her methodical, scientific thinking, but that wasn't enough to cope with the bigger, stranger, more-than-human world she'd been plunged into. She could see Space and Time and other dimensions she didn't even have concepts for—the living and the dead and so many other things that were both and neither, all of them screaming . . . as she experienced first-hand all the horror and despair Happy lived with every day. As he died a little more, every day. The only thing that kept him sane, kept him going, was an almost inhuman act of iron will and self-control. And now he was losing even that, day by day and pill by pill. Happy was going under for the third time, feeling the water fill his throat inch by inch.

Melody had finally found a way to see inside Happy's head; and what she'd found there was killing her, too. Happy saw it happening, saw it eating her alive, so he reached out to her in the only way left to him.

He embraced her telepathically, joined with her on every level there was. He calmed her racing thoughts, taught her how to keep the bad things at bay. How to survive when you're hanging on by your fingernails. He loved her; and that made him strong enough to carry the heavy burden of his life for as long as he had to. Melody held him, and he held her, and they were together. For whatever time they had left.

Happy broke the mental link, and they both fell back into their own heads. They stood facing each other, looking into each other's eyes. Melody was back in control again; and, surprisingly, so was he.

"You're back!" said Melody. "I can feel it. You burned up all your pills helping me; but you're still stable."

"Yes," said Happy. "In saving you, it seems I've saved myself. How about that? Your sanity jump-started mine. It won't last, of course. There's no miracle cure for what I've done to myself. But at least I can be me again, for a while."

"You're still dying," said Melody.

"Everyone needs something to look forward to," said Happy.

"You can't die," said JC. "I can't lose you. You're my team. You're all I've got."

"You've got me," said Kim.

He looked at her with calm, unflinching despair. "I gave up my life to do this job; and what has it got me? What good is it, to be a Ghost Finder solving other people's problems, if I can't solve my own? If I can't help you? If I can't save the one woman who means more to me than anything else. Please don't go, Kim. You're all that keeps me going."

"You're all that keeps me . . . me," said Kim. "When I had to leave you for a time, on the Boss's orders, it almost destroyed me. Being a ghost is like enduring endless sensory deprivation. You're all that keeps me focused. Away from you I became vague, uncertain. You're my anchor, JC, my reason for being. You're the only thing that holds me to this world. But . . . you can't move on as long as I'm still here, holding you back. So because I love you, I have to give you up . . ."

She was already starting to fade.

"No!" said JC. "Don't go, Kim! Don't you dare give up on us!"

"If you love them, let them go," said Kim. Her voice sounded far away. "You deserve better than this, JC."

"Please . . . Kim . . ."

"I'm scared to stay," said the ghost girl. "And scared to go . . ."

"You don't have to be frightened," JC said steadily. "And you don't have to go alone. If you're going, I'm going with you. I'd rather die than live on without you."

And, just like that, Kim snapped back into sharp focus again; smiling tremulously at him.

"There is still hope," said JC. "We give each other hope. That's what love is."

All four of them stopped and looked around the room. Something had changed. They could feel it.

"Okay . . ." said Melody. "Let me be the first to say, *What the hell was that?* What just happened here?"

"I feel like I've just been through a spiritual purge," said Happy. "I feel good. I feel good about myself. I'm not used to that."

"It feels like someone cut me open and let all the poison out," said JC.

"Not someone," said Kim. "The room. The room did it . . ."

The door to Room 418 swung slowly open on its own; and beyond it lay a perfectly ordinary corridor. The room . . . felt like just a room. Nothing more.

"Whatever just hit us, I think it's over," said JC. "The room is finished with us. But you know what . . . I'm not finished with this room."

"Normally, I would be the first to say, let us get the hell out of here while the getting's still good," said Happy. "But I have to admit I'm curious. It feels like we all just passed some kind of test."

"A haunted room as personal therapy?" said Melody. "Weird . . ."

"Something made this room a Bad Place, originally," said Happy. "But it doesn't feel like the work of any individual person. So what's powering this phenomenon? There was a definite sense of direction, of purpose, to everything we were put through."

"Don't say purpose," said Melody. "Say rather programming. This room now exists to perform a specific task . . ."

"I don't think this is a Bad Place," said JC. "I think . . . it's a testing ground."

He walked around the room, looking at everything, his nerve endings almost painfully raw and receptive after everything he'd been through.

"Think of all the people who've stayed here, down the years," he said finally. "So many people, in this room, passing long, dark nights of the soul . . . Lying awake in the early hours of the morning, asking themselves the kind of questions that people only ask themselves in the long reaches of the night. All the things we don't dare think about in daylight but can't hide from in the dark. *Is this it? Is this all there is? Is this what my life has come to? What happened to the life I was going to live? What happened to the person I planned on being? When did I lose all my ideals, give up on my dreams?*

"And somehow . . . all that soul-searching and personal despair rubbed off on the room."

"Imprinted it," said Melody. "Soaked into the surroundings and programmed Room 418 to search for the truth in all of us. No wonder so many people died, or went mad, or hurt themselves . . ."

"Why didn't it affect everyone the same way?" said Happy.

"Not everyone can be honest with themselves," said JC.

"But then . . . why aren't all hotel rooms like this?" said Kim. "People must ask questions like that in every hotel room. What's so special about this one?"

"Something about the location, perhaps?" said JC. "Or perhaps some psychically gifted traveller passed through, and supercharged the room . . . Who knows? The result is a room that tests everyone who stays here. Tests to destruction, if necessary. Forces people to confront their own personal demons . . . who sometimes turn on their owner. I suppose we never hear about the ones who pass the test—just the ones who fail dramatically."

"Did we pass?" said Melody.

"Hard to tell, with us," said Happy. "But I think so. We're all still here and as sane as we ever were."

"We can't leave the room like this," said JC. "It's like an unexploded bomb, waiting to go off over and over again. It plays too roughly with people and breaks too many of them. We have to defuse this room."

"How the hell are we supposed to do that?" said Happy.

"I'm open to suggestions," said JC.

"I could bring my equipment up here, hit the room with a small, localised EMP," said Melody. "That might be enough to wipe the slate clean."

"Bit too scientific and real-world, for a spiritual experience," said Kim. "Didn't you once have an exorcist grenade, JC?"

"The energies that have accumulated in this room have become so powerful, they're probably resistant to open attack," said JC. "No; we need something less direct. Lateral thinking caps on, everyone."

He walked around the room, looking at everything, thinking hard. The others looked at him, then at each other, and shrugged pretty much simultaneously.

"This room is haunted," JC said firmly. "By all the lost hopes and broken dreams of everyone who ever stayed here."

"So what are we supposed to do?" said Happy. "Call them all up and give them a big comforting hug?"

JC turned abruptly to look at him, then smiled slowly. "Well, if you put it that way . . ."

"Why do I give him ideas?" said Happy.

"We can't bring back all the people who stayed in this room," said Kim. "The living and the dead . . ."

"But we might be able to call forth the genius loci, the spirit of this place," said JC. "What all the previous guests left behind, that's still powering the testing ground. A . . . representation, of all those people. And then we comfort them."

"So the manager was right," said Melody. "This is an exorcism, after all. Do we need to bring in a priest? I hate that. They're always so smug about it . . ."

"No," said JC. "This isn't about good and evil, Heaven and Hell. Just people. We know how to deal with people. Come on. We've melded our minds together before, to help others. And isn't that why we got into this job in the first place? To help people?"

"Speak for yourself," said Melody. "I got into it for access to technology I couldn't find anywhere else."

"I got into it for access to arcane and unnatural chemicals," said Happy.

"And I got into it for the glory," said JC. "But that's not how it is now, is it?"

"Not always," said Melody.

"Go team," said Happy.

"Let's do it," said Kim.

She stepped forward, slipping effortlessly inside JC, her ghostly form superimposing itself on his body and disappearing inside it as they joined together. The golden glow from JC's eyes sprang up all around his body, like an all-over halo. A sane, healthy light, it pushed back the flat, ugly illumination of the room. JC reached out to Happy and Melody, and they each took one of his hands. The golden light leapt out to surround them, too. Four good friends; a team joined together on every level there was.

They all concentrated on the same shared thought; and the golden light blasted out from them to fill the whole room. Slowly, a presence stirred. Room 418 was waking up from a long, deep sleep. Another figure was suddenly standing in the room, a basic human shape with no details, no identity . . . It walked slowly forward, and the group opened up to accept and encompass it.

You're not alone, they said. *Someone knows, and understands. Someone gives a damn. And isn't that all any of us really needs to hear?*

Comforted at last, the figure faded away slowly.

The Ghost Finders let go of each other and stepped back. The golden light snapped off. Melody and Happy were still holding hands. Kim stepped out of JC.

"Damn," said Happy. "What were we mainlining there? It felt like . . . raw spiritual power. There isn't a pill in the world that could match that."

"Are you ready to swear off the mother's little helpers now?" said JC.

"No," said Happy. "Sorry, JC. I'm still going to need a chemical crutch to lean on. For what little time I've got left."

JC nodded. He'd been doing this job long enough to know some problems don't have answers. Or at least not one you can easily live with.

"Feel the difference in the room," he said. "Like the calm after a storm has passed. It's over. It's gone."

"I am really not comfortable with all this touchie-feelie hippy crap," said Happy. "You'll be wanting me to hug some trees next."

"I think I preferred it when you weren't talking," said JC. "So much more peaceful."

Happy looked at Melody and grinned. "Go on. You know you want to say it."

Melody struck a pose. "This room . . . is clean."

TWO

....

SOME ANTS AND
ONE HELL OF AN ELEPHANT

It's always hardest on the team after the mission is over. When the danger is past, the adrenaline has stopped pumping, and all the nervous energy has packed its bags and gone home. Going down to the lobby in the elevator, the three Ghost Finders stood slumped together. Heads bowed, staring at nothing, too tired even to make small-talk about how good it felt to be alive. It did feel good, to have another successful mission under their belt, but mostly they were thinking about how much better it would feel to get the hell away from the job and take a nice little vacation. No ghosts, no horrors, no weird shit; just peace and quiet and the comfort of normal things. A secure place to get their heads down, where they wouldn't have to worry about closing their eyes. When every mission is a matter of life and death and sometimes worse . . . it does wear you down.

The elevator doors finally opened, and JC gathered up enough strength to lead his team out into the hotel lobby. The manager hurried forward, his face equal parts hope, concern, and desperation. JC gave him a brief smile and a thumbs-up; and Garth almost collapsed with relief.

"It's over now?" he said. "Really over?"

"Down and dusted," said JC. "Four-eighteen is just another room, now."

The manager actually performed a little jig of happiness, right there in front of them, beaming so widely it was a wonder his face didn't crack in half. Behind the desk at Reception, Garth's wife didn't look like she believed it, and perhaps never would, entirely. Which was understandable. Hauntings leave their mark, on all kinds of levels. The manager made a point of shaking all the Ghost Finders' hands, in turn; and it was a sign of how exhausted Melody was that she let him.

"You're all welcome to stay at my hotel, anytime!" Garth said happily. "Any room, on the house!"

JC hadn't been that impressed by the state of Room 418, even after it had been cleansed, but he smiled and nodded politely. Never know when you might need some goodwill or a bolt-hole to hide out in. Happy pulled a face and started to say something; but Melody dug an elbow into his ribs before he could spoil the mood. JC looked at the manager thoughtfully; the man did seem rather more pleased than he would have expected.

"So," he said. "What are your plans for the future?"

"Well," said Garth, still smiling broadly, "now I know the room is safe, I can advertise it as previously haunted! Oh yes; there is a real market for such things these days. Ghost enthusiasts from all over the world will want to come here, to spend the night in a room that was quite definitely haunted! People will pay really good money, just for the experience. I've been looking it up online . . . A once-in-a-lifetime thrill you can sell over and over again . . . I'm going to be rich!"

JC felt like saying a great many things but didn't. He just smiled and nodded, while the manager rushed off to impart the good news to his wife. Melody reacquired her trolley full of equipment and made a point of checking it was all still there. Happy peered blankly around the lobby as though he'd never seen it before. And possibly he hadn't, given the state he was in when he arrived. JC looked around quietly, but there was no sign of Kim anywhere. She had said she'd take the short cut down, then vanished. JC never knew what to say when she said things like that, so he hadn't said anything. She'd turn up. She always did.

He'd only just started for the door when his cell phone suddenly played the theme from *Ghostbusters*. JC stopped, actually startled, then took his phone out and looked at it. Melody moved in beside him.

"I thought you always kept that turned off when we're out in the field?"

"I do," said JC, still staring at his phone as though he half expected it to bite him. "When I'm out, I'm out, and I don't want to be bothered. I only keep it with me for emergencies. And I am now torn between thinking *This had better be a real emergency* and being concerned that it is."

He checked caller ID and winced. Catherine Latimer was calling: the revered and much feared Boss of the Carnacki Institute. She didn't usually contact him in the field; she knew better. Happy leaned in on JC's other side and glowered at the phone.

"Take my advice and throw the damn thing away," he said. "Hurl it to the floor, stamp on it, and piss on the pieces. You must know this isn't going to be anything good."

"Of course it isn't," said JC. "That's why I have to take the call."

He put the phone to his ear. "I didn't know you could turn my phone on from the other end," he said, accusingly.

"Lot of things you don't know about me," Latimer said briskly. "Which is as it should be, given that I'm in charge, and you're not. I need you and your team to take on another case, immediately; at the new Brighton Conference Centre. It's not far. This case is ranked extremely urgent, and you're the nearest A team."

"Of course we are," said JC. "That's why you sent us down here in the first place, isn't it? To deal with this nothing job! Which, by the way, I am here to tell you turned out to be in no way at all routine. You wouldn't believe what we've been through. But you only sent us here so we'd be on hand for this other mission!"

"Got it in one," said Latimer.

Melody studied JC's face. "Is it really that bad?"

"It's another case," said JC. "Important and urgent, right here in Brighton. Smell the joy."

"She can't expect us to go back to work straightaway!" said Melody, so outraged she didn't even try to lower her voice. "We're entitled to downtime between missions! It says so in our contracts."

"We don't have contracts, as such," said JC. "I've been told there is one, but I've never been allowed to see it. I was assured the conditions are very fair. Which is nice. Have you seen yours?"

"Don't change the subject," said Melody, scowling fiercely, both fists planted on her hips. "We can't do this, JC. Really, we're not up to it. Happy definitely isn't."

"Actually, I am," said Happy, blinking mildly. "For now."

Melody looked at him. "Are you sure?"

"I want to keep busy," said Happy. "Make the most of my life, while I still can. And I think . . . that would be better for you, too."

"You're still fragile," said Melody, looking steadily into Happy's eyes. "The strain of another case could damage your mind. I won't risk that. JC, tell the Boss she can go straight to Hell. I'm not scared of her."

"Yes you are," said JC. "All sane people are. Now please keep the noise levels down while I talk some more to our greatly beloved Boss, who is still on the other end and no doubt listening to every word we say."

"I don't care!" Melody shouted at JC's phone. "Screw you, Catherine bloody Latimer!"

"Are you still there, Boss?" JC said politely into the phone. "You are! Pity . . . Don't worry about Melody, she'll come around. Well, she won't, but I'll talk her into faking it. You have rather taken advantage of us, Boss."

"That's what you're for," said Latimer.

"What is so special and important and horribly urgent about this new case?" said JC. "What's the problem?"

"I'll tell you when you get here," said Latimer.

"Hold everything," said JC. "You're here? In Brighton?" He looked at Melody and Happy. "The Boss is here."

"But . . . she never leaves her office," said Melody.

"Not usually," said JC. He gave the phone his full attention again. "Why have you left your office, Boss?"

"I'll tell you when you join me at the Conference Centre," said Latimer. "Some secure channels aren't as secure as they used to be. Now get moving!"

JC shut his phone down and put it away. "Some days you just shouldn't get out of bed."

....

They took a taxi to the new Brighton Conference Centre. JC and Happy and Melody squeezed into the back seat, along with the dozen or so pieces of jagged-edged high tech that Melody hadn't been able to cram into the taxi's boot with the rest. Kim appeared just as the taxi pulled away and flew happily beside it, moving unseen by everyone except the Ghost Finders. She sailed serenely along, sitting cross-legged in mid air, easily keeping up with the taxi as it bullied its way through the slow-moving traffic. Kim was now wearing a female aviator's outfit from the 1920s, complete with goggles. Her long red hair streamed behind her in the wind even though the wind couldn't actually touch it. Kim liked to get the details right. It helped her pretend she was still real. Happy looked at JC.

"If she can make her ectoplasm look like absolutely anything, do you ever make her dress up in . . . special things? Just for you?"

JC stared him down. "You'll never know."

Happy shrugged easily. "Just curious. You wouldn't believe what Melody sometimes likes me to wear . . ."

"Don't believe a word he says," Melody said immediately. "He's on drugs."

It was night now. Bright festive lights flared in the dark as the taxi made its way through a tourist city open for business. People were out on the prowl everywhere, loudly enjoying themselves. It was summer, and the living was easy. For a week, or two. Men and women, young and old, all of them in hot pursuit of a good time. Enjoying today, so they wouldn't have to think about tomorrow. Gaudy neon advertised bars

and clubs and restaurants. Indian and Italian and Harry
Ramsden's Fish Suppers. Smiling faces lined the streets, out
and about in the night. Melody studied them through the side
window.

"Look at them. Contented little sheep, with no idea of
how many wolves there really are, hiding in the shadows."

"That's part of our job," said JC. "To save them from ever
having to know. It's a kindness."

ꞏꞏꞏꞏꞏꞏꞏꞏꞏꞏꞏꞏꞏꞏꞏꞏꞏꞏꞏꞏꞏꞏꞏꞏꞏ

The taxi finally drew up before Brighton's newest Conference Centre. It had started out as a Regency hotel, but time
and hard use had worn away the polish. Extensive refurbish-
ment had put a new face on the building, to make it look like
a modern meeting place for modern business people, and
anyone else the Centre thought it could make money out of.
But the building still had the air of an old, good-time girl,
well past her prime. The taxi had barely stopped moving before Happy and Melody had thrown open both doors and
bolted, leaving JC to pay the bill. He sighed heavily, paid the
driver, and made sure he got a receipt. The Institute had become very strict over approving expenses, just recently.

JC glared at Happy and Melody, who were pretending to
be very busy hauling Melody's equipment out of the boot and
stacking it on her motorised trolley again. JC looked the Conference Centre over. It all seemed quiet enough, with no-one
going in or out of the main entrance. After a while, Happy
and Melody moved in beside JC.

"I have a bad feeling about this place," said Happy.

"You always do," said Melody.

"Anything in particular?" asked JC.

"I am not a fortune cookie," said Happy, with a certain
dignity. "But if I were, I think I would be saying . . . *Warning!
You are about to meet an old friend.*"

"Why are you warning us?" said Melody. "If it's a friend?"

"*Friend* might not be the exact word," said Happy. "Maybe
ally . . . Fascinating, isn't it?" He bounced up and down on
his heels, smiling unpleasantly in anticipation.

"You seem very . . . up," said JC.

"Oh I am!" said Happy. "Really. You have no idea. Enjoy it while it lasts; I am . . ."

Kim had disappeared again.

They went inside. JC led the way, striding across the wide-open lobby while trying hard to look official and professional and more than a little intimidating. Everything seemed suitably ornate and expensive, with comfortable furnishings and modern art on display, a marble floor and dark-stained wood panelling; but what stopped all three Ghost Finders dead in their tracks was a massive sign hanging over the Reception desk, saying, *The Brighton Conference Centre welcomes the Ghost Finders of the Carnacki Institute to their annual convention!*

Melody was the first to get her breath back.

"You have got to be freaking kidding!"

"Have we wandered into another reality, and I didn't notice?" said Happy. "I hate it when that happens."

"Relax," said JC. "I know what this is. It's the public face of the Institute, the tip of the iceberg we occasionally allow the general public to see . . . so they won't think to look for anything else. Officially, the Carnacki Institute is nothing more than a privately funded think tank, sceptical debunkers, and all that. The kind that puts out regular reports in obscure scientific journals no-one actually reads. We had our own television show for a while, on one of the minor channels. But since it was more concerned with collecting evidence of the paranormal and testing it rather than holding the hands of hysterical celebrities, it only lasted the one season. Got really good reviews in the *Fortean Times*."

"We had our own TV show?" said Happy. He shook his head. "No-one tells me anything."

JC and Melody exchanged a look.

"I did tell you, sweetie," said Melody. "We watched several episodes together. You just don't remember."

"Ah," said Happy. "Can't have been a very memorable show, then. Joke! Come on; if we can't laugh about this shit, we might as well give up."

His face was clear and open, his eyes calm and sane. But JC and Melody could still see the strain.

"I have a question," said Melody. She gestured at the sign. "If we're so very welcome, where is everyone?"

They looked around the wide-open lobby. It was completely deserted—no staff, no guests, not a murmur of sound. As though everyone had just . . . stepped out, for a moment. Not at all what one would expect from a Conference Centre at the height of the Season, and the busiest part of the evening. The Ghost Finders moved a little closer together, anticipating enemy action.

"The Boss is here," said JC, after a while. "Maybe she frightened everyone else off. I wouldn't be here if I didn't have to be. Happy, are you picking up anything with your marvellous mutant mind?"

"No," said Happy, frowning. "Absolutely nothing. Which is odd, not to mention worryingly significant. This whole location should be lousy with trace memories and emotions, from all the people who've passed through, but it feels like the place has been scrubbed clean. Which suggests . . . some really major psychic shields. I wonder why. What could be happening here that someone needs to hide so badly?"

"Could be to do with the convention," said JC. "To ensure the poor innocent enthusiasts don't see anything they're not supposed to."

Melody looked at him suspiciously. "This convention . . . These fans . . . We're not going to have to pose for photos and give autographs, are we?"

"In your dreams," said JC. "The public face of the Institute only exists to spread disinformation and half-truths and defuse any real investigations that might get civilians hurt. These people are all about . . . special interests, conspiracy theories, and convivial get-togethers. No doubt there will be panels, with self-proclaimed experts on the supernatural earnestly discussing weird events and general strange stuff. UFOs and crop circles and alien big cats . . . And a whole bunch of people with new books to push. There will undoubtedly be a dealers room, to sell these books, along with specialist magazines, DVDs, and handcrafted ugly objects . . . And anything else people can be persuaded to hand over hard cash for. I might take a wander through later. See if there's anything I fancy. You have to keep up with what people are thinking, if only to know the right lies to tell them to keep them quiet and contented. Besides, I like to collect weird stuff."

"I could make a comment about Kim here," said Happy. "Only given the way you're looking at me, I don't think I will."

"Very wise," said JC.

"Where is Kim?" said Melody.

"She'll turn up," said JC. "Look, don't expect to find anything . . . genuine, at the convention. That's the point. Baffle them with bullshit so they don't have to worry about the really worrying stuff. This whole thing is a con. A cover story . . ."

"For what?" said Happy, immediately suspicious. "What's actually going on here?"

"Good question," said JC. "Hopefully, the Boss will make an appearance soon and enlighten us as to why we're here."

They waited, then they waited some more, but there was no sign of Catherine Latimer anywhere. JC lost his patience first, but it was a near thing.

"Okay, let's go find someone and ask some pointed questions," he said. "And the best place to find people is the dealers room. There will always be people there, no matter what's officially scheduled."

"How are we supposed to find that?" said Melody.

"Just a wild guess," said Happy, "but we could always follow the directions."

He pointed to a number of carefully placed signs indicating the way to various function rooms. One of which said, *Dealers Room*.

"Trust you to notice that," said Melody.

It took a while before they set off because Melody made one hell of a fuss over having to leave her equipment behind again. But JC was firm; he wasn't having her dragging suspicious-looking high tech through crowds of very curious people. In the end, Melody stowed her trolley behind the Reception desk, turned on all the armed protections, and hoped for the best.

,,,,,,,,,,,,,,,,,,,,,,,,,,

Several empty corridors later, they pushed open a pair of very heavy doors, and were hit in the face by a roar of happy noise. The great open hall was packed full of stalls and tables, heavily laden with all sorts of everything. Targeted merchandise, licensed properties, high-priced collectibles, and batshit-mental come-ons. People coursed up and down the narrow aisles, chatting enthusiastically at the top of their voices, money burning a hole in their pockets. The noise level was actually staggering.

JC and Happy and Melody stayed just inside the doors, looking the scene over. JC was glad to see some people at last and quietly pleased that so many of them had come dressed up in colourful and really quite professional-looking costumes. Dr. Whos ancient and modern, Ghostbusters complete with backpacks, Draculas and Frankensteins and Mummies, and several Buffy the Vampire Slayers.

"I didn't know Buffy was still popular," said Melody.

"Some things are just timeless," Happy said solemnly.

"Over there!" Melody said abruptly. "Isn't that . . . ?"

"Yes it is," said JC. "Don't look at him. Soulhunters don't like to be recognised when they're working undercover."

"But what's he doing here?" said Happy. "Soulhunters don't turn out for the minor stuff."

"No doubt the Boss will inform us in due course," said JC. "As and when she deigns to show herself. In the meantime, see if you can spot anyone who looks like they might know something."

"Doesn't seem very likely, does it?" said Melody. "We have come among geeks and nerds. The horror, the horror . . ."

"Snob," said Happy.

"Show no weakness," said JC. "They can smell fear."

"I never thought of ordinary people being interested in the kind of stuff we have to deal with," said Melody. "I mean, I spend most of my downtime trying not to think about it . . ."

"That's because you know for a fact that it's all real," said JC. "Besides, most things look better from a distance."

"A safe distance," said Happy.

"Well, quite," said JC.

They moved unhurriedly through the crowds in the packed aisles, checking out the various goods on offer with great interest. All the usual suspects were well covered: books and DVDs and magazines, all of them claiming to have the inside deal on Roswell and Rendlesham, Area 52 and the Philadelphia Experiment. This last featured a bunch of elves on the cover, and JC wasn't sure what the hell that was all about. There was even a book on the Crowley Project. JC picked it up and flicked quickly through the pages.

"Gossip and conspiracy theory," he said finally. "A distinct shortage of facts, names, or actual occurrences . . . Which is probably just as well, when you're writing about one of the most openly evil organisations in the world. In fact, that's almost certainly why it was allowed to be published."

"Hey!" said the stall-holder, a sulky-looking individual with long, stringy hair, wearing a T-shirt that said *Information Wants to Be Paid For*. "Are you planning on buying that? I'm not running a lending library here."

JC gave him a long, thoughtful look, and the stall-holder suddenly found a really good reason to go and be busy at the other end of his stall. JC put the book down and moved on. Happy stayed where he was, staring at nothing and humming tunelessly to himself, until Melody took him by the arm and gently urged him along. By which time JC had stopped again, to consider a collection of rather ragged dream catchers, relabelled as ghost-catchers.

"Fakes," he said loudly. "They're not even put together properly. You couldn't hold off a daydream with these."

"People will buy anything," said Melody.

"It's all about comfort and peace of mind," Happy said wisely.

"Oh, you're back with us, are you?" said Melody. "Where did you just go?"

"There are gaps in my thoughts," said Happy. "I wonder if someone's tunnelling . . ."

"Don't ask," Melody said to JC.

"Never even occurred to me," said JC.

There was a poster saying *I Want to Believe*, and another beside it saying *Trust Me, You Don't Want to Know*. Handcrafted bonsai wicker men; corn from a Wiltshire crop circle marked *Not Suitable for Smoking*; and an anatomically correct scarecrow that made JC wince. He browsed through a pile of dog-eared old paperbacks and turned up something claiming to be *An Official History of the Carnacki Institute*. JC paged through it carefully.

"Well?" said Melody.

"Should be in the fiction section," said JC, dropping it back on the pile.

Another stall boasted a wide selection of unusual objects. A somewhat ratty scalp from a yeti; a really big tooth from the Loch Ness monster; and a sealed jam-jar half-full of grey goop, labelled *Extruded Ectoplasm*. Melody looked at JC.

"Any of this real?"

"How would I know?" said JC. "Not my area of expertise. But it seems unlikely; if any of this stuff was even half-way authentic, you can be sure these people would be charging a hell of a lot more for it."

At which point, a tall, brooding presence dressed in black leathers with big steel buckles, heavy Goth makeup, and a whole bunch of painful-looking piercings, planted himself in front of JC to block his way. He looked JC up and down and sneered pointedly at his white suit.

"What are you supposed to be? The ice-cream man?"

"This is my tribute to Ray Bradbury," JC said calmly. "Or possibly Marty Hopkins."

The Goth started to say something cutting, then broke off as Happy stepped suddenly forward to glare at him.

"Piss off, Brian," said Happy. "Your mother's looking for you."

The Goth looked startled, then uneasy. He moved away quickly, losing himself in the crowd.

"How did you know that his name was Brian?" said Melody.

"Not good form, Happy, reading civilian minds," JC said sternly.

"Oh please," said Happy. "Like I'd lower myself. He just looked like a Brian."

And then JC said something really bad under his breath as he saw something displayed on a table that had no business being there. Because it was real. He wandered casually over for a closer look, and Happy and Melody moved in on either side of him.

"Is that . . . what I think it is?" Happy said finally.

"Looks like the real thing," said Melody.

"It is," said JC. "A Hand of Glory. Made from the severed hand of a hanged man, with the fingers turned into candles. Light them up, say the right Words, and the Hand will reveal hidden treasures, open locked doors, and slow down the passing of Time. Very dangerous in the hands of someone who only thinks he knows what he's doing."

"Where the hell did these people acquire something as spiritually toxic as that?" said Melody.

"I did hear of a Russian Hand that turned up loose in London a while back," said JC. "God alone knows how it ended up here. They can't know what it is, what they've got . . . probably think it's just some movie prop. We can't risk its getting out on the open market. Anyone activating the Hand could open doors to . . . anywhere. And let anything in. I really wouldn't want to be on the team that had to clean up after that."

"So what do we do?" said Happy. "Buy it ourselves, to take it off the market?"

"Are you kidding?" said JC. "Have you seen how much they're asking for it? And good luck getting a receipt for expenses . . . No, I've a better idea. Kim, are you with us?"

"Right here, darling," Kim said breathily in JC's ear. Which was actually a pretty good trick for someone who didn't breathe any more. "I thought I'd stay unseen so I could watch your back. I don't like the feel of this place."

"We need a distraction," said JC. "Something big and noisy but essentially harmless, to hold everyone's attention. Think you could oblige?"

"Love to," said Kim.

A sudden hurricane squall rushed through the tables and stalls, rocking them violently back and forth and sending goods flying through the air. People ducked and shouted as heavy objects shot past their heads, and stall-holders clung desperately onto their tables, trying to hold them down. Several supposedly mystical artefacts burst into brightly coloured flames, while other equally impressive things just lay there and did nothing. While everyone's attention was fixed on the weird happenings, JC chose his moment carefully, picked up the Hand of Glory, stuffed it inside his jacket, and casually strolled away. Melody and Happy went with him, trying hard to look innocent.

They'd almost reached the exit doors when they swung suddenly open, and a familiar figure stood facing them. Catherine Latimer beckoned them out of the dealers room with an imperative gesture, and the Ghost Finders hurried into the corridor to join her. The doors shut behind them of their own accord as everything in the hall fell suddenly quiet.

,,,,,,,,,,,,,,,,,,,,,,,,,

Looking professionally calm and immaculate in her usual expensively cut grey suit, the Boss was smoking a black Turkish cigarette in a long ivory holder, in defiance of several prominent *No Smoking* signs. She had to be well into her eighties now, but she still burned with a fierce and almost certainly unnatural energy. Latimer wore her grey hair cropped in a severe bowl cut, and her face was all hard edges, harsh lines, and cold, cold eyes. Since she was hardly ever seen outside of her highly protected office at Institute Headquarters, her presence made it very clear just how important this new case was. JC, Melody, and Happy still made a point of glaring at her rebelliously, just on general principles. The Boss calmly stared them down—like a lion-tamer in a cage full of dangerous animals who just happened to have an automatic weapon about her person.

"Why are we meeting here while there's a convention going on?" JC said bluntly.

"So we can hide in plain sight," said Latimer.

"Hide what?" said Happy. "What are we doing here, and are we in danger? Answer the last question first."

"We're finally going after the Flesh Undying," said Latimer.

There was a pause while the Ghost Finders looked at each other. Uncertain as to whether that was a good thing or not.

"Who are we hiding our presence from, exactly?" said JC. "Agents of the Flesh Undying or traitors inside the Carnacki Institute?"

"Yes," said Latimer.

"Well . . . it's about time we got serious about dealing with the Flesh Undying," said Melody. "What's changed to bring this to the boil at last?"

"Aid, from an unexpected quarter," said Latimer.

And that was when Natasha Chang stepped smartly forward out of the shadows, to stand beside Catherine Latimer. All the Ghost Finders jumped, just a little. They knew Natasha Chang of old. A field agent of the Crowley Project, and a self-made femme fatale, Chang was a beautiful creature in her mid twenties with bobbed black hair, dark, slanted eyes, and a heart darker than the night. Half Chinese gangster, half English rose, all villain, all the time. She was wearing her preferred outfit—a pink leather cat-suit with matching pink pillbox hat. Because she'd never got over seeing Eleanour Bron in the Beatles film *Help* at a formative age. Chang's long, sharp fingernails were painted with real gold leaf, and she had enough heavy rings on both hands to qualify as knuckle-dusters. JC remembered Happy's warning of an old friend, or ally . . .

Natasha Chang smiled easily at JC and his team. "Hello, darlings! Miss me?"

"Only because I didn't aim properly the last time," growled Melody.

"Isn't this a super convention?" said Chang, rising above the general unpleasantness with ease and style. "So many open minds, so many soft targets . . . so little time!"

"We should kill her right now," said Happy. "In self-defence."

"Oh, you forget everything else, but her you remember?" said Melody.

"She made an impression," said Happy.

"I do, don't I?" Chang said cheerfully.

"You say that like it's a good thing," said JC. "You eat ghosts!"

"Don't you look down your nose at me!" said Chang. "Ghost lover! Ectophile! Where is your little ghost girl, anyway?"

"Right behind you," said JC. "Hah! Made you look! She'll turn up when she's ready. And if you even look at her like she's a snack, I will bludgeon you into the ground."

Chang started to say something, then stopped as JC took off his sunglasses. The golden glare leapt out from his eyes, filling the corridor, unbearably bright and otherworldly. Chang took a step back. Catherine Latimer took a step forward.

"That's enough! Ms. Chang is under my protection, for the time being."

JC looked at the Boss thoughtfully, then put his sunglasses back on, cutting off the golden light. Everyone relaxed, just a little.

"Why is she here?" said JC.

"Because the Crowley Project is working with the Institute on this case," Latimer said flatly. "Ms. Chang is on loan to us, as liaison, and I promised she'd be returned undamaged. So play nicely, children. An old enemy can be an ally in the face of a common threat."

"Can't hope to rule the world if the Flesh Undying destroys it first," Chang said cheerfully.

"Where's your unpleasant little mad scientist friend, Erik Grossman?" said JC. "Isn't he your usual partner in the field?"

"Erik fell from favour," said Chang. "So I got to eat his soul. Yummy . . ."

JC and his team looked at each other. They all knew Chang ate ghosts, but this was something new . . . They looked to Latimer, but the Boss just shrugged.

"We are working this together," she said calmly. "And I

don't want to hear any arguments. We're all bringing something to the table."

"We're really doing this?" said Melody. "Going up against something from another dimension, maybe even a higher reality, something that's basically a living god? Or devil? We don't stand a chance, Boss! Unless you've been holding out on the kind of weapons the Institute can call on."

"Where it came from, it might have been some kind of god," said Latimer. "But now it's here, it's limited by the physics of our reality. It's flesh now, with all of flesh's built-in frailties. We can do this."

"How?" JC said bluntly.

"We're working on that," said Latimer.

"We are so screwed," said Happy.

Latimer ignored him with the ease of long practice. "Thanks to the Crowley Project, we now have a fix on the physical location of the Flesh Undying. The exact place it fell to Earth."

Chang nodded proudly. "Our scientists discovered it while looking for something else. Isn't that always the way?"

"You've seen it?" said Happy. "What does it look like?"

"Big," said Chang. "Scary big."

"And we need the Project's help because . . . ?" said JC.

"Because they have more impressive killing tools than we do," said Latimer.

"And because it takes one monster to understand another," said Happy.

"Darling," said Chang. "You say the sweetest things. Now come along with me, and Auntie Natasha will show you wonders and marvels that will blast the sight from your eyes."

"Don't bet on it," said JC.

""""""""""""""""""

Natasha Chang swayed elegantly through the deserted corridors, walking arm in arm with Latimer, the two of them apparently chatting quite easily. JC watched them both closely. He wasn't fooled by all these signs of good fellowship and common cause. The two organisations might cooperate in the face of a common threat, but given a chance to stab an old established enemy in the back, either side would take it. That was understood. Because even the very real possibility of the imminent end of the world couldn't change basic human nature.

There was still no-one around. The corridors remained quiet and empty, and the light seemed to grow dimmer as the shadows grew darker. JC felt like he'd gone walking through the darkest part of the forest and allowed himself to be persuaded off the main path. A long way from home, surrounded by monsters . . . with a Boss he wasn't sure about any more. The further he walked, the more JC worried about where he was going. Just how big was this Conference Centre? After a while, Melody leaned in close to JC so she could murmur in his ear.

"If we really are going after the Flesh Undying, at last, why couldn't it be a mainstream operation? Why all this secrecy?"

"Because we don't know whom we can trust," said JC, just as quietly. "In either organisation."

Melody scowled. "I hate this. Not knowing where I stand, or whom I can trust . . ."

"Welcome to my world," said Happy, on JC's other side. "Spooky, isn't it? I'd like to say you get used to it . . . but that's what drugs are for. Remember, just because I'm paranoid doesn't mean I'm not out to get you."

"You got that off a T-shirt," said JC.

"What makes you say that?" said Happy, then spoiled the effect by giggling.

"Are you picking up anything from Chang?" said JC.

Happy shook his head slowly. "She's got really strong shields in place. I can crack them, given enough time, but not without her noticing. Doesn't matter . . . You know you can always rely on her to follow what she believes are her best interests. Anything else . . . will depend on the situation. Come on, JC, you don't need a drug-addicted telepath to tell you that."

"How are you feeling?" said Melody.

"It comes and goes," said Happy.

"What does?" said JC.

"Everything," said Happy.

They finally came to a halt before a secluded back room, in a particularly gloomy back corridor. Half a dozen armed men from the Crowley Project guarded the door, studiedly anonymous in smart black business suits and designer sunglasses. Though none of them had shades as dark as JC's. They all snapped to attention as Chang approached and handled their automatic weapons like they knew what they were doing. Ex-military, JC decided. Though no telling from which country's armed forces, originally. The Crowley Project spread its net far and wide. Happy took one look at all the guns and hid behind Melody, while she stood her ground and scowled impartially at each guard. Natasha put an arm through JC's, and snuggled up against him.

"Don't worry, boys. He's with me."

"Only in the most technical sense," said JC.

Interestingly, the guards seemed most wary of Catherine Latimer.

The door was locked. Chang had to punch numbers into a keypad, and identify herself through a comm unit, before a great many locks disengaged, and the door swung slowly open. Chang led them in, and the door closed itself the moment they were all inside. The locks slammed home again. JC did his best not to feel trapped or intimidated.

⋅⋅⋅⋅⋅⋅⋅⋅⋅⋅⋅⋅⋅⋅⋅⋅⋅⋅⋅⋅⋅⋅⋅

The room was a fair size, packed full of high-tech equipment that covered all four walls and piled up everywhere else. JC didn't recognise half of it, never mind what it was for. But judging from Melody's squeals of excitement and loud, cooing noises as she rushed back and forth, she knew. The half dozen Project technicians sitting at their work stations in neat white lab coats smiled at each other condescendingly.

JC stayed by the door, looking carefully about him. There were no windows and no other door. Harsh, unrelenting, fluorescent strip-lighting gave everything a stark and brutal look. Happy stuck close to JC, shooting jealous looks at the tech and technicians that had seized Melody's attention. The man in charge came forward to greet Natasha Chang and

Catherine Latimer. François Nimmo was a tall, elegant man with neat silver hair, a charming smile, and the kind of eyes you just knew missed absolutely nothing. He wore a standard teacher's jacket, complete with leather patches on the elbows. Melody barged in on the introductions, pelting Nimmo with all kinds of questions about his high-tech toys.

JC and Happy looked at each other and smiled briefly. They were both already thinking of something annoying to do, just to remind everyone of their presence. Never let people take you for granted or they'll walk all over you. Interestingly, Natasha Chang seemed the most upset at being ignored and upstaged. She hated having to compete for people's attention. Latimer didn't seem that bothered.

It turned out, Melody and Nimmo had already heard of each other. She knew about his part in the Haunted Giaconda Caper; and he knew about her role in the Case of the Shadow Kings. Latimer and Chang both reacted sharply to that; they didn't approve of anyone outside their own organisations knowing about such restricted material. Melody and Nimmo ignored them, happily discussing the nature and uses of the various equipment scattered around them. Melody went into positive ecstasies while Nimmo beamed like a proud father. Happy scowled heavily.

"He doesn't look like much," he said to JC. "I could beat him up."

"Pretty sure you couldn't," said JC. "He might look like your average scientist, but you can bet he's Project-trained, just like Natasha."

"With the right pills in me, I could beat up the Flesh Undying," said Happy. And then he slowly subsided. "But . . . Mel's going to need somebody, after I'm gone. I just need to be sure . . . she ends up with the right someone."

"You mustn't give up, Happy," said JC.

"Why not?" said Happy. "It's strangely comforting. You should try it."

"No," said JC. "I can never give up hope."

They both knew he was talking about Kim. Happy shrugged heavily.

"Far too much death in our lives . . ."

The Project technicians suddenly became very agitated as new information came streaming in. They bent over their computer monitors, working frantically at their keyboards. Nimmo and Melody moved quickly over to see what was happening.

JC looked at Happy. "Do you know what they're doing?"

"Haven't a clue," said Happy. "Why are you asking me?"

"You've been hanging around Mel so long, I was hoping some of the science stuff might have rubbed off on you."

Happy smirked. "No, but I'll tell you what did . . ."

"No thank you," said JC, very firmly. "I don't want to know."

"Very wise," said Happy.

Melody and Nimmo stood together before the massive main viewscreen, raptly intent on images that quietly came and went. JC and Happy, Chang and Latimer moved forward to join them. The technicians were still working furiously at their stations. JC cocked his head to one side, then the other, and still couldn't make out what he was supposed to be looking at. Light and dark came and went on the viewscreen, occasionally illuminating or silhouetting vague shapes that might have been anything. Streams of information flowed across the bottom of the screen, constantly updating; and none of it made a blind bit of sense to JC. Though Melody and Nimmo seemed almost indecently fascinated by it.

"Is this like those Magic Eye posters?" Chang said finally. "Only I'm getting a headache just trying to make sense of this."

"Oh good," said Latimer. "I'm glad it's not just me."

"We're looking at sensor feeds from a Project submersible," said Nimmo. "Currently heading for the bottom of the Atlantic Ocean."

"Where the Flesh Undying ended up after its own kind dumped it in our world," said Melody.

"Oh please tell me this is somewhere inside the Devil's Triangle!" said Happy.

"I loved that old documentary with Vincent Price!"

"Not even close," said Melody, crushingly.

"Besides," said Latimer, "that whole area's been quiet for years. Ever since we dealt with the Inverted Black Pyramid."

"That was you?" said Chang. "We thought it was the Droods."

"They get credit for everything," said Latimer.

Nimmo cleared his throat loudly to draw everyone's attention back to him. "We're not talking about a normal submersible here; this is a remote-controlled drone, packed with specially designed and very powerful sensors. A Project ship on the surface is running the drone, we're just piggy-backing its transmissions as it moves along the sea-bottom in full stealth mode, in the deepest, darkest part of the world. Not as far down as the Mariana Trench, but close."

"Though of course the Mariana Trench is in the Pacific, not the Atlantic," said Melody.

"Teacher's pet," said Happy.

"The pressure at this depth would crush or cripple most submersibles," said Nimmo. "But this . . . is a very special craft."

"Who did you steal it from?" said JC.

"It's on loan," said Chang, just a bit sharply.

"Who from?" said Latimer.

"There are limits to the information we're prepared to share," said Chang.

"She doesn't know," said Happy.

Chang turned sharply to glare at him. "Stay out of my head!"

"Just guessing," Happy said airily.

"We're getting close now," said Nimmo, staring intently at the viewscreen. "Less than half a mile, to the Flesh Undying."

"I still can't see anything," said JC.

"Is your submersible armed?" said Latimer.

"It's a Project craft," said Chang. "Of course it's armed."

"Good," said Latimer. "If you get a shot, take it."

"Damn right," said Chang.

Nimmo looked at her sharply. "I understood this was a reconnaissance mission. Information-gathering only."

"Then you understood wrong," said Chang. "Everything we do now is all about the complete and utter destruction of the Flesh Undying. If all we get out of this approach is new sensor data, well and good. But let us hope for more. Dear Dr. Nimmo."

Nimmo and Melody exchanged a glance—of hard-working scientists bedevilled by ignorant superiors and their unreasonable demands and expectations.

And then everyone concentrated on the viewscreen as a single great shape dominated the image. Even without a recognisable setting to gave it scale and context, there was still something about the shape that suggested colossal size and scale. Old atavistic instincts stirred in the back of JC's mind, telling him to run like hell while he still had the chance. It was like looking at something too big to be understood, too complex for the human mind to comprehend. Even the information feed along the bottom of the screen had slowed, as though the sensors couldn't cope with what they were getting.

Kim's voice murmured suddenly in JC's ear. "I leave you alone for five minutes, and when I catch up with you again, you're in bed with the enemy. What's going on?"

Before JC could reply, a whole bunch of alarms sounded shrilly. One of the technicians stood up abruptly and stared wildly about him.

"We have a spiritual incursion! Rogue ghost in the room! A powerful unlife entity has penetrated our defences!"

"Gosh," said Kim. "Do they mean me?"

She appeared suddenly, standing beside JC in a long white gown, looking more like a pre-Raphaelite painting than ever. She smiled sweetly about her. The technician pointed a trembling finger at her.

"Ghost! Ghost!"

"We know!" said Nimmo. "Now shut those damned sirens off so I can hear myself think!"

The technician turned back to his station and hit a switch. The alarms cut off immediately.

Melody glared at him. "Over-react much? I'm surprised there weren't flashing lights as well."

The technician shrugged sulkily. "The special bulbs are still on order . . ."

Nimmo gave the ghost girl his most charming smile.

"Welcome to the Crowley Project, Kim Sterling. It's good to meet you at last. The only actual ghost in the Ghost Finders!"

"You know me?" said Kim. "If I'd known I was expected, I'd have put on something special."

"I know of you," said Nimmo. "You're in our files."

"The Crowley Project has a file on me?" said Kim. She wasn't smiling any more, and the room suddenly felt a whole lot colder. The technicians stirred uneasily.

"We have files on everyone," said Natasha Chang. "How did you get in here, past all our defences?"

"What defences?" Kim said sweetly.

Nimmo glared at the technicians, who all found good reasons to be very busy at their work stations.

"Kim isn't just any ghost," said JC. "I would have thought you'd have known that. From her file."

"He hasn't read it," said Happy.

Nimmo glared at him. "Damn telepaths . . ."

"Still guessing!" said Happy.

"I should have known you'd turn up uninvited," Chang said to Kim. "You get in the way, and I'll hit the exorcism button. Unnatural thing . . ."

"You can talk," said Kim. "I can see the remains of all the ghosts you've eaten, still rattling around in the back of your head. It's a wonder to me you can still hear your own voice in there."

"What are you doing here, Kim Sterling?" said Nimmo. "This is a purely scientific investigation . . ."

Kim looked at the dark shape on the viewscreen. "You're getting close to the Flesh Undying. Close to seeing what no living eyes have ever seen. Would you care to experience a vision of how it was when the Flesh Undying first appeared in this world?"

"You can do that?" said Nimmo.

"Yes," said Melody. "She can. We've already seen it. Go ahead, Kim."

||||||||||||||||||||||||||

Suddenly they were all seeing the same thing, in the dream theatres of their minds. Miles and miles of open ocean, a choppy surface of blue and green under a brilliant sun in a clear sky. And then a dark, seething mess of roiling energies split the sky, forcing it open—a rent in Time and Space and other things. A break in reality itself. Things came and went on the other side of the opening, huge and terrible things. Bigger than cities and more complex, moving in ways impossible in any sane place. A fierce light shone through the opening, more intense than any light had a right to be. It scorched down through the air, slammed into the ocean, and kept on going, diving down and down into the furthest depths of the ocean. And in that light, something fell. An awful thing, unbelievably large, its shape and nature meaningless to merely human senses. It existed in too many spatial dimensions, its extensions reaching off in directions the human mind couldn't hope to follow. It fell and fell through increasingly dark waters, killing every living thing it passed. Until it slammed into the sea-bottom and couldn't go any further. The surface of the ocean slowly grew calm again, while dead fish floated in their thousands. The opening in the sky slammed shut, and the otherworldly light was gone.

·····························

The vision cut off abruptly. Everyone stood still, shocked speechless. Even JC and his team, who'd seen it all before. The viewscreen was still showing things, but nobody cared. Finally, Nimmo cleared his throat and looked thoughtfully at Kim.

"Can I just ask," he said carefully, "How accurate was that? Did we merely witness a reconstruction of events or what actually occurred at the time?"

"That was a memory I found inside the traitor Patterson's head, when I possessed him," said Kim, just as carefully. "He served the Flesh Undying, in life and in death; and he believed it to be entirely accurate."

While everyone was still getting their heads around that, JC leaned in beside Catherine Latimer for a quiet word in her ear.

"We are way out of our comfort zone, Boss. We're trained to deal with ghosts, demons, and the occasional Beast from the Outer Reaches. Not . . . aliens, monsters, or whatever the Flesh Undying actually is. This is Drood territory! Why not call them in, let them deal with it? They've got the expertise and the weapons."

"We clean up our own messes," said Latimer. "And besides, the one thing we can be sure of is that the Flesh Undying has agents everywhere. We have to stick with people we can . . . Well, I hesitate to use the word trust where the Crowley Project is concerned, but at least we know where we stand, with them. All the other secret organisations, with their special agendas, would only complicate things."

"I'm pretty sure I saw a Soulhunter earlier, hanging around the dealers room," said JC. "You didn't call him in . . . ?"

"No," said Latimer. "Did he see you?"

"I don't think so. Could his people have got word about what's happening here?"

"Who knows what the Soulhunters know?" Latimer frowned, thinking hard. "If he and his kind are sniffing around . . . the sooner we conclude our business and get the hell out of here, the better."

JC chose his words carefully. "Happy did say, sometime back, that he'd heard rumours . . . of certain individuals in high places performing secret forbidden experiments. Weakening the walls of reality . . . and that's how the Flesh Undying was able to enter our world in the first place. Might some of these very important people have been Crowley Project? Or Carnacki Institute? And if the latter, is that why you don't want any of the other secret organisations involved?"

"Why do you think we're doing this so quietly?" said Latimer.

"Do you have any idea who these . . . people, might be?" said JC.

"Almost certainly the same people trying to force me out of my position as Head of the Institute," said Latimer. "But I haven't been able to uncover any solid evidence on any particular individual. Or I'd have done something about them."

They both looked around sharply as the people standing in front of the main viewscreen made shocked and alarmed noises. JC and Latimer hurried over to join them. Nimmo was staring fascinated at information streaming across the bottom of the screen. Melody hugged herself tightly, looking as though she wanted to turn away from the images on the screen but didn't dare. Happy stuck close by her side. Chang was quite obviously angry because she didn't understand what was going on. Scattered around the room, the white-coated technicians argued fiercely with each other, over new theories as to what it all meant. Some looked ready to come to blows until Nimmo shouted at them to shut the hell up without once taking his eyes off the viewscreen. A slow, sullen silence settled over the room.

"We're getting close," said Nimmo. "A hundred feet, maybe less. Creeping in, now."

"Does the Flesh Undying know the submersible is there?" said Latimer. "Does it know we're observing it?"

"Who knows what it knows?" said Nimmo. "It shouldn't, but . . ."

"Look at the new readings!" said Melody. "A shape, a body, but . . . it's like nothing on Earth! And what's that, there . . . That's not radiation, or at least not any form we understand . . ."

"It's giving off some kind of energies," said Nimmo. "Maybe a defence system, or a natural response to its surroundings . . . Who knows what's natural, what's normal, where something like this is concerned? It doesn't belong here . . . Wait! We're losing the signal, it's breaking up! Information's dropping out; we need more power!"

"We're giving it everything we've got!" shouted one of the technicians, frantically working his boards. "These sensors weren't designed to cope with . . . whatever the hell that is!"

Other technicians ran over to work with him, struggling to maintain contact with the submersible as it slowly, cautiously, approached the Flesh Undying. The giant shape all but filled the viewscreen now.

"Slow now, steady . . ." said Nimmo. "We are trying not to be noticed. Just a few ants, crawling around the feet of an elephant. Keep the sensors cracked wide open; but reception only. No scans, no probes, nothing invasive. Nothing that might alert it to our presence. Look at that . . . the sensors are finally giving us exact measurements. No. Wait. That can't be right . . ."

"It's enormous," said Melody. "A living mountain! Miles and miles of it."

"I still can't make out any details," said JC.

"The sensors can't detect any that make any sense," Nimmo said numbly. He looked almost shell-shocked. "It could be a matter of scale, or so alien we simply can't comprehend what it is we're looking at. This is bigger than any living thing on this planet! Bigger than any living thing that has ever been on this planet."

"The Mount Everest of monsters," said Happy.

"Try ten times that big," said Nimmo.

"Okay," said Happy. "Head hurting now."

"Oh . . ." said Melody. "Look at that! If I'm reading the information stream right, what we saw in the vision is confirmed. This thing exists in more than three spatial dimensions at once. It extends . . ."

"How is that even possible?" said Latimer.

"I don't know!" said Nimmo, almost viciously. "Because it's not from around here! Perhaps the laws of reality are different where it came from. It must have brought some of its own natural laws with it, as a localised effect. To preserve it. So it can still be . . . what it is."

"Can we kill it?" said Chang. "If we hit it with everything the submersible has, at close range . . ."

"Are you crazy?" shouted Nimmo. "We couldn't even touch it!"

"Breathe," Chang said coldly. "Calm yourself the fuck down, Dr. Nimmo, or I will hurt you."

"Everyone calm down," said JC. "Let's think this through. If the Flesh Undying was forced into our world from a higher dimension . . . Did it bring its body, its flesh, with it? Or did it take what it found here, to make itself a new form, to give it shape and meaning in our world? Help it survive, under our natural laws?"

"Good question!" said Nimmo. He nodded approvingly to

JC, in a surprised sort of way, as though he hadn't expected such clear thinking from a mere Ghost Finder. JC felt like slapping him. Nimmo made an effort to pull himself back together as he studied the images on the viewscreen.

"What difference does any of that make?" said Chang, her voice rising.

"Flesh from a higher dimension might be impervious to anything from our world," said Melody. "But if it created its body from what it found here . . ."

"We can hurt it," said Latimer.

"Whatever that is, its current shape and nature answer to the physical laws of our reality," said Nimmo. "It may possess certain otherworldly attributes, but . . ."

"Hold it," said Melody. "You're making a lot of assumptions. If the Flesh Undying is still holding some of its old laws around it, to preserve its true nature . . ."

"I think . . . they just enforce its existence," said Nimmo. "Physically, it's just flesh. And anything that's material must have limitations. And weaknesses."

"Am I the only one present who knows whistling in the dark when he hears it?" said Happy.

"What have we got," said JC. "Powerful enough to hurt something that big?"

Latimer looked at Chang, who shrugged.

"Don't look at me," she said. "I didn't anticipate . . . this. How could I? How could anyone?"

"You've got contacts inside the Government, Boss," said JC. "Any chance you could get us a nuke?"

Everything stopped, as everyone looked at Latimer. She took her time, considering the question.

"Possibly," she said finally. "Through certain backdoor channels . . . But I'm not convinced even that would be enough to do the job. We know the size and scale of the problem now, but we still have no idea of the thing's structure. What's going on inside it. An explosion, even a really big one, might simply damage the Flesh Undying. We need to completely destroy it. For that, we'd need a thermonuclear device. A really big one. Or the monster might just put itself back together again."

"And God alone knows what that kind of blast would do to the ocean bottom," said Nimmo.

"We might set off a chain reaction," said Melody. "Blow that thing up, and the energies released might be enough to crack open the whole planet."

"I don't believe a nuclear blast would even touch it," said Nimmo. "Consider the energies it's giving off . . . Looks a lot like a force shield to me."

"Enough to hold off a thermonuclear blast?" said Chang.

"Unknown," said Nimmo. "There's too much we don't know . . ."

He broke off as a fierce light blazed up, filling the viewscreen. Everyone flinched away from the glare, crying out and covering their eyes, until the screen overloaded and went blank.

"Energy discharges are spiking!" yelled one of the technicians. "They're overloading the systems!"

"What kind of energies?" shouted Nimmo.

"Unknown!" All the colour had dropped out of the technician's face, and he snatched his hands back from his work station as though they'd been burned. As though he was afraid to touch anything. "The submersible is down! We've lost it! We're not getting any information at all!"

"Is it damaged?" said Melody. "Any chance the systems might reboot?"

"It's . . . gone!" said the technician. "Just gone!"

The room went very quiet. The technicians stopped working. Nimmo looked at the blank viewscreen, then at the various pieces of equipment surrounding him. He seemed lost, unsure what to do.

"Did we get any real information before the submersible was destroyed?" asked JC. "Anything useful?"

Nimmo and Melody conferred quietly, studying the information streams and checking with the technicians, before reluctantly turning back to the others.

"The drone couldn't get close enough," said Nimmo.

"At least we can be sure that was the Flesh Undying," said Melody. "We can find it again. It's not like anything that big can uproot itself and move to some new location. For the first time, it's vulnerable."

The massive viewscreen exploded. Shattered in a moment by some unknown force, its shrapnel tore through Nimmo, killing him instantly. Blood, flesh, and splintered bone flew across the room. Happy started moving before Melody stopped speaking. Forewarned by some psychic insight, he threw himself at Melody and dragged her to the floor. Shrapnel blasted over their heads as they huddled together. All around the room, computers exploded one after another like a string of firecrackers, destroying the work stations and killing all the technicians. Their mangled bodies were thrown in all directions. Fires broke out, burning fiercely, jumping from surface to surface until the air shimmered from the intense heat. Kim stepped inside JC, and the golden glow leapt out to surround and protect them. Catherine Latimer grabbed Melody Chang and pulled her down to the floor. A tall bank of heavy equipment toppled over and fell on them.

JC produced the Hand of Glory from inside his jacket. He activated it with a Word of command, and eerie blue flames jumped up from each fingertip, rising straight up despite all the disturbances in the air. Everything slammed to a crawl as JC slowed the passage of Time, bringing it to an almost complete halt. He looked quickly around him. Shrapnel hung in the air like so many interrupted bullets, while fires bulged and flared with slow, malignant purpose. Protected by the Hand, JC moved carefully forward, forcing his way through the heavy resistance of the air. He set his shoulder against the falling bank of equipment as it hovered over Latimer and Chang, and threw all his strength against it. He couldn't move it an inch. Weight and inertia kept it frozen in place. The golden glow surrounding JC became even more intense as he concentrated, setting all his strength against the bank of equipment. And slowly, inch by reluctant inch, it moved away from its intended victims.

The moment it was clear, JC stepped back, breathing hard. He was soaked with sweat, from his exertions and the increasing temperature in the room. The flames couldn't reach him, but the heat was everywhere. He held up the Hand of Glory, and forced out several very old Words. Time speeded up just a little, as the Hand's protection leapt out to cover the four people on the floor. JC grabbed Happy and Melody, and hauled them onto their feet. They looked around wildly, saw the Hand in his hand, and quickly understood. Latimer and Chang were already scrambling to their feet. Latimer seemed entirely unflustered. Chang started to say something angry, then bolted for the door. The others went after her.

They had to dodge around slowly moving shrapnel, still hanging in the air, and keep out of the way of the slowly rising and falling flames, while forcing their way through resistance from the heavy air. Time was not on their side. Something exploded behind them, and the pressure wave hit their backs like a hard shove. When they got to the door, it was locked. Chang tried to work the number pad, but the buttons wouldn't depress. They were still stuck in Time. Latimer stepped past Chang and put her shoulder to the door. It jumped right off its hinges and out of its frame, falling heavily into the corridor beyond. Latimer hurried out without looking back, and the others went after her.

꜓꜓꜓꜓꜓꜓꜓꜓꜓꜓꜓꜓꜓꜓

Once they were all out in the corridor, JC blew out the flames on the Hand of Glory, and Time slammed back into its normal progress. More explosions tore through the room behind them, and a vicious blast of heat erupted from the open doorway. Happy and Melody and Chang jumped back from it; JC and Latimer didn't. Thick black smoke filled the room and billowed out into the corridor. JC and Latimer picked the heavy door up off the floor and forced it back into its frame. Jamming it in place, sealing off the heat and smoke. And then everyone looked at everyone else.

"What the hell just happened?" said Natasha Chang.

"We were attacked," said JC. "You must have noticed."

"Not that!" said Chang. "How were you, the two of you, able to do that?"

"Sorry," said Latimer. "There's a limit to the information we're prepared to share. You know how it is."

"Hold it," said Chang. "Where are my security guards?"

There was no sign anywhere of the half dozen armed men. The corridor was empty.

"They wouldn't just abandon their post!" said Chang.

"Unless they knew what was about to happen," said Latimer. "I told you. The Flesh Undying has agents everywhere."

"Bastards!" said Chang. "I'll have their balls for this."

"It knew," said Melody. "The Flesh Undying . . . it knew we were watching. Not just the submersible—us!"

"Presumably why it tried to kill us," said JC. "How powerful must it be, that it could strike at us over such a distance?"

Happy cried out suddenly, grabbing at his head with both hands. Melody was quickly there at his side, supporting him.

"What is it, Happy? What's wrong?"

"Psychic attack," he said sickly. His face was white with shock, but his eyes were very dark. "The Flesh Undying is reaching out, trying to locate us. I'm shielding us as best I can, but . . ."

"What pills do you need?" said Melody.

"It's the drugs that have messed up my abilities," said Happy. "My brain chemistry is wired like a weasel on speed, just to keep me focused. I told you, Mel; I'm damaged goods, now. Chang, can you . . . ?"

"No," Natasha Chang said immediately. "My shields were put in place; I don't control them. And I doubt even they can keep out a monster like the Flesh Undying."

JC looked at Latimer. "You and I, we have certain advantages. We could . . ."

"No we couldn't," said Latimer. "We'd blaze too brightly, give away our position. The Flesh Undying would find us in a moment."

"What are you talking about?" said Chang. "And why is he glowing like that?"

"Isn't it in our files?" said JC, unable to resist.

"We have to hide," said Latimer.

"Where?" said Happy. "If I can't shield you, who can?"

"People," said Latimer. "The convention. We can hide in plain sight, among the convention-goers. That is why I arranged for us to meet here, while the convention is in session.

We dive into the crowd and we're invisible. The Flesh Undying won't be able to pick out a few individual minds among so many. Move!"

"Yes, Boss," said JC.

‖‖‖‖‖‖‖‖‖‖‖‖‖‖‖‖‖‖‖

They ran through the empty corridors of the Conference Centre. Catherine Latimer led the way, showing quite a remarkable turn of speed for a woman of her advanced years. They crashed through the doors of the dealers room, then stumbled to a halt. The great hall was just as packed as the last time they'd seen it, but no-one was moving. The crowds stood motionless and utterly silent in the aisles between the stalls and tables, and not one person looked around at the sudden entrance. The newcomers remained by the doors, huddled together for comfort in the face of something they didn't understand.

"Why is it so quiet?" said Melody. Whispering in spite of herself.

"Quiet as the grave," said JC.

"You had to say that, didn't you?" said Happy. "But you're right. I'm scanning the whole room and I am telling you . . . there's no-one here. Not a single living soul."

"What do you mean?" said Chang. "I can see them! Or is this some kind of illusion?"

"They're dead," said Happy. "Every single one of them. We're looking at a roomful of ghosts."

"Can you sense the Flesh Undying?" said Latimer. "Is it still trying to find us?"

"No," said Happy, frowning. "It's gone. That's odd . . ."

"How can they all be ghosts?" said Melody, peering uneasily about her. "I mean, they all look fine. Except for the whole not moving or speaking thing. No-one looks hurt or damaged. How could this many people have all died at the same time?"

"That's it," said Kim, stepping out of JC. The golden glow died away as she looked steadily around her. "Everyone here died at exactly the same moment. I can tell. They all died so suddenly they haven't realised they're dead yet. They're still caught in the moment, waiting for someone to tell them what's happened and what they're supposed to do. Which means . . . it's up to me."

She walked forward, into the great crowd of ghosts, and heads slowly began to turn as the dead became aware of her presence. Of someone just like them. She smiled reassuringly about her, and the dead men and women moved back, to open up a narrow corridor for her to walk through. And just like that, Kim was moving in a new direction, that the living standing by the doors could see but not understand. A new way, a new path, leading away from the world. A door appeared in the far wall. A very ordinary-looking door, with a glowing sign above it, that said simply *EXIT*.

Happy started to go after Kim, drawn towards the door; and then stopped himself. He looked at Melody and smiled briefly. He wasn't ready to go. Not yet.

The exit door swung silently open as Kim approached it, and an unearthly light shone out. The living people at the entrance doors had to turn their faces away, but the silent dead stared into the light with an almost palpable yearning. It called to them—calling them home, at last. Kim stood before the open door and looked in; and then stepped back to stand beside it. She gestured for the ghosts to go through, and those nearest started forward. One by one, every dead man and woman in the room filed through the door and into the light. Taking their time because they had all the time in the world now. When the very last ghost had passed through, disappearing into the light, the exit door closed itself and disappeared. With the light gone, the living standing by the entrance doors were able to look back into the room again. It was just as silent; but now the aisles between the stalls and tables were full of dead bodies, lying sprawled and motionless on the floor.

Kim came back to join the others, walking on the air a few feet above the bodies. She settled on the floor in front of the small group, most of whom regarded her with a new respect.

"Did you call that door?" said JC.

"No," said Kim. "It came for them."

"You looked through the door, into the light," said Happy. "What did you see?"

"I don't remember," said Kim. "I don't think I'm allowed to."

JC looked about him. "So many dead people . . ."

"What killed them?" said Melody.

"The Flesh Undying," said Happy. "This was the psychic attack I felt. It wasn't aimed at us. It was never aimed at us."

"But why kill all these people?" said Melody. "They didn't know anything about the Flesh Undying! They didn't know anything about anything!"

"To get at us," said Latimer. "It couldn't hurt us, so it hurt those it could. To show what it can do and to punish us for daring to go after it."

"You mean this is all our fault?" said Melody.

"No," Happy said immediately. "This is what it would do to everyone. What it will do unless we stop it."

"Hold up," said JC. "Where's Natasha Chang?"

They all looked around, but she was gone. Slipped away while no-one was looking.

"Gone to report to her people, no doubt," said Latimer.

"What do we do?" said JC.

"I have to report back to Institute Headquarters," said Catherine Latimer. "Because you can be sure there will be repercussions. For a failure this bad."

THREE

....

MEET THE NEW BOSS

The best way to hide a thing is to place it behind something extremely visible. And distracting. Which is why there is an office that doesn't officially exist, down a corridor you can't get to, tucked away at the back of Buckingham Palace. It's been the Head of the Carnacki Institute's very private office for as long as the Palace has been there. Before that, the office was somewhere else. Presumably somebody knows where; but if they do, they aren't telling. The current office is centuries old, not a place where you'd expect to find sudden and unexpected change. But when Catherine Latimer returned to Institute Headquarters, the day after the Brighton debacle, she found the door to her office wouldn't open to her. She had to ask her own secretary, Heather, to buzz her through. Which Heather did with a certain self-satisfied flourish.

Latimer gave her secretary a long, searching look, then strode into what used to be her office. To find someone else sitting in her chair, behind her Hepplewhite desk, already looking very much at home. Latimer scowled. She knew Hillary Allbright: young, ambitious, and an almost entirely political creature. Allbright gestured briefly for Latimer to seat herself on the visitor's chair and busied herself sorting through a huge pile of paper-work. Latimer sat down, slowly and thoughtfully. She knew a palace coup when she saw one. The speed with which Allbright had been put in place made clear to Latimer just how long her enemies had been planning this. All they needed was the opportunity, which Latimer had handed to them on a plate.

Hillary Allbright was a large, heavy-set woman in her late twenties, dressed in the tweeds-and-pearls style of the old country-side set. She had a plain face, a fierce eye, and a predator's smile. Somewhere along the line, someone had persuaded her to dye her hair blonde to soften her image. It hadn't worked. Allbright was all business, with no time for frills and fancies. Because she was the kind of person who saw such things as weaknesses. Latimer sat back in her visitor's chair and took out her long ivory cigarette holder.

"Please don't smoke in my office," said Allbright, without looking up from what she was doing.

"Go to hell," said Latimer. She lit her cigarette with her monogrammed gold lighter, inhaled deeply, and savoured the moment. She looked around her. "There used to be an ash-tray . . ."

"I know," said Allbright. "I got rid of it."

Latimer tapped cigarette ash onto the floor. Allbright winced, despite herself. Latimer did her best to appear calm and relaxed, on the extremely uncomfortable visitor's chair. She'd designed it that way to keep visitors in their place. The irony of the situation was not lost on her. Allbright continued sorting through her papers, giving every appearance of being very busy with something far more important than her visitor. Another old tactic that Latimer had used.

She looked around what used to be her office, taking in the shelves full of old books and files, the familiar comfortable surroundings, and all the assorted souvenirs from days when she'd still been active in the field. She hadn't realised how out-dated most of them seemed now. Antiques and curios, from another age. She wondered if she'd be allowed to take any of her things with her when she finally left. Probably not; the Institute never let go of anything it had put its mark on. Latimer looked at her office and wondered just when it had become so small and confining.

A part of her wanted to fight the regime change; but she knew was there no point. An open attack wouldn't get her anywhere. Her enemies would be ready for that. Allbright must have extensive high-level support or she wouldn't be here. Still . . . Latimer smiled slowly. There were still things she could do. To make clear her . . . extreme displeasure.

Allbright finally assembled her papers neatly, levelling the edges just so with her thumbs, and looked directly at Catherine Latimer. Her voice was calm and even and utterly implacable.

"This is not a meeting to discuss your leaving. That decision has already been made, at a much higher level. We're here to discuss the manner in which you will leave office. It doesn't have to be unpleasant. Cooperate, and you will be allowed to retire in peace and obscurity. You are guaranteed an entirely reasonable pension; you could even write your memoirs. As long as you don't expect anyone to publish them. However, if you cause us even the slightest inconvenience, have no doubt that you will be forcibly removed from this office, taken away in handcuffs, and imprisoned somewhere very secure and highly unpleasant. For whatever remains of your life."

Latimer smiled for the first time. "Take me out of here by force? I really would like to see somebody try that. You don't get to be my age without learning some very nasty ways to defend yourself. But let's take a step back, shall we? You said, decided at a higher level. Which is interesting. Who is there who considers themselves higher than the Head of the Carnacki Institute? We're not a Government Department, after all; we are a Royal Charter. Have been since 1587. Technically speaking, I only answer to the Queen."

"Not any more," said Allbright, and she didn't even try to hide her satisfaction. "Her Majesty has been persuaded to allow the Carnacki Institute to be taken in house, at long last. There's no room left in modern Government for rogue operations. We all have to be answerable to someone."

"Yes," said Latimer. "We do, don't we?" She looked

thoughtfully at Allbright, tilting her cigarette holder at a defiant angle. "So you're my replacement. The new Boss of the Carnacki Institute. Just another civil servant."

"You brought this on yourself!" said Allbright. Two spots of sullen colour had appeared in her cheeks. "You lost grip on things. Took your eyes off what really matters. Ignored the business and politics of running a large operation, so you could pursue your own private interests. And see where that's led you . . . a bloody massacre right in the middle of a celebration of the Institute's public face! Have you any idea how difficult it's going to be, covering up the circumstances of so many innocent deaths?"

"It's not that difficult," said Latimer. "I've had to do it any number of times. There's always some useful terrorist bogeyman to blame it on. It's not even the most unpleasant part of the job. Just logistics."

Allbright snorted loudly. "Under your leadership, possibly."

"I suppose I shouldn't be surprised they chose you," said Latimer. "I have followed your rapid progress, up through the ranks. Naked ambition, red in tooth and claw. Trample on the weakest, glory in their plight, and all that. But this . . . this is quite a jump. Given that you have no actual field experience, I can only assume it's your office skills and political connections that brought you here. Clearly, someone has faith in you. I would have gone with someone more accomplished, more qualified; but, of course, that kind of person wouldn't have been so easy to control. Do you even know who's pulling your strings?"

Allbright smiled coldly. "I suppose I shouldn't be surprised someone your age has grown paranoid and deluded."

She made a point of looking around the office and turning up her nose at all the old trophies from Catherine Latimer's past. The goldfish bowl half-full of murky ectoplasm, in which the ghost of a goldfish swam solemnly backwards, blinking on and off like a faulty light bulb. A lady's elbow-length evening glove, in sheer white silk, nailed firmly to a wooden base under a glass jar. The Haunted Glove of Haversham, responsible for strangling seventeen young debutantes in 1953. The glove's fingers still twitched whenever anyone looked at it. A small silver compact from the 1960s, innocent enough until you raised the cover and looked into its mirror. Where something horrible scrabbled forever against the other side of the glass, fighting to break through, to get out.

"I mean," Allbright said finally. "Is there anything here that isn't ancient history? You live in the past, Latimer, hoarding your old triumphs so you don't have to think about today's problems."

"I see," said Latimer. "It's *what have you done for us recently*, is it?"

"The job is about dealing with what's in front of us," Allbright said sharply. "Things have changed since your day. It's not just ghosts in white sheets, rattling chains in countryhouses. New problems require new ways of thinking, new solutions. Your old-fashioned methods are now officially at an end. I will take us forward, into the twenty-first century."

Latimer sat back in her chair and regarded Allbright thoughtfully, casually allowing her cigarette smoke to drift in Allbright's direction.

"You have no idea what's really going on," she said finally. "Or why you were selected to take over this job. But I know. You have no idea of what you're getting into; but you'll find out."

Allbright stirred uneasily. Latimer thought for a moment she might actually have reached Allbright, made her think . . . but the new Boss just shrugged briefly, eager to move on.

"I've been going through your file," she said. "It makes for fascinating reading."

"You don't want to believe everything you read in official, incomplete, and no doubt heavily redacted files," said Latimer. "There's nothing in my file that matters. I saw to that, long ago."

"I'm frankly amazed you've been allowed to stay in office for so long," said Allbright.

"What makes you think anyone had a choice?" said Latimer.

"You should have been forced to retire years ago!"

"Ah, the arrogance of youth," said Latimer. "I remained in my post because I was good at my job. And because there was no-one else good enough to take my place. God knows I looked hard enough. I thought for a while it might be Patterson . . . but we all know how that turned out."

"Whatever influence you might once have held, it's gone," said Allbright. "You have no friends left. Or at least, not anywhere that matters."

"If you really believed that," said Latimer, "you wouldn't be so nervous."

"I am not nervous!"

Latimer smiled, as Allbright slowly sank back into her chair again.

"You should be grateful you're being allowed to retire," Allbright said finally. "But even that is conditional. I want access to all your secret files, all the reports and information you never deigned to submit to the official archives. I want a full report on what really happened at the Brighton Conference Centre, including what you were really doing there. And, on behalf of the Government, I demand you return all the books you took out of the Secret Libraries, without proper permission! You had no right to remove important and valuable items from such a secure location for your own private business!"

"There are no secret files," Latimer said calmly. "I've said everything about Brighton that I'm going to . . . And I never took any books out of the Secret Libraries."

"You're defying me?" said Allbright, her voice rising despite herself.

"I'm defying the people you represent," said Latimer.

Allbright leaned forward across the desk with a satisfied look on her face. As though she'd expected nothing less.

"You must know this makes you look even more guilty. We know there are secret files; there must be. We know there was a Crowley Project presence at Brighton. We have a witness. And the books were taken out in your name. What makes you think you can stand against the new Head of the Carnacki Institute? Who do you think you are?"

"I'm Catherine Latimer!"

This time, it was Latimer's turn to sink back into her chair. The two women regarded each other silently for some time.

"I could fight you," Latimer said finally. "I do still have friends, contacts, influence."

Allbright just smiled. The cold, secure smile of someone who knows they hold the winning hand. "Not inside the Institute. Even as we speak, a root-and-branch reorganisation is going on, from top to bottom."

"A purge," said Latimer.

"If you like. We prefer to see it as a weeding out of inefficient and disloyal elements. Anyone you might have looked to for help is already gone. You've been here too long, Latimer. Outlived all the people who owed you favours or were frightened by your reputation. You're on your own now. You're the past; and I'm the future."

"Then God help us all," said Latimer.

She pushed back her chair and rose to her feet. Allbright was startled into reaching quickly for a desk drawer, in a way that suggested she had a weapon concealed there. Latimer leaned forward, and calmly stubbed out her cigarette on the Hepplewhite desk. And then she turned away.

"Where do you think you're going?" said Allbright, her voice rising again. "You can't believe you'll just be allowed to walk out of here!"

"I don't answer to jumped-up bureaucrats like you," said Latimer. "Never have and never will."

"You'll answer to my superiors!"

"No," said Latimer. "You'll answer to mine."

And just for a moment, she allowed the golden glow to shine from her eyes. The fierce otherworldly light that showed she'd been touched by Outside forces, long ago. The golden light blazed in the room, then was gone. Allbright's jaw dropped, and she sat slumped in her chair. Looking honestly shocked as well as surprised. Catherine Latimer dropped her a sly wink.

"If I were you . . . I'd be wondering what else they didn't tell you."

She snapped her fingers imperiously, and a Door opened in the wall opposite her, which quite definitely hadn't been there a moment before. Allbright's hand went to the desk drawer again; and this time Latimer had no doubt she meant to use whatever she had there. So she turned to the display case beside her, knocked over the glass jar, ripped the Haunted Glove of Haversham free from the nails that held it to its wooden base, and threw the nasty thing right into All-bright's face. The long silk glove writhed and twisted as it shot through the air, its white fingers twitching hungrily. All-bright had no choice but to put up both hands to protect herself as the Glove went for her throat. And while she was busy with that, Latimer strode across what used to be her office and stepped through the open Door. She paused on the threshold to glance back, just for a moment.

"Be seeing you," she murmured, then she was gone. The Door closed silently behind her and disappeared.

\.

Out in the small airless room that served as a waiting area for all those summoned to see the Boss, JC and Melody and Happy were cooling their heels. Sitting resentfully on very uncomfortable visitors' chairs, while they waited to be invited in. A situation they were all too used to. From time to time, one or the other of them would glare at the heavily reinforced and entirely soundproofed steel door that was the only entrance to the Boss's office. And wonder what was going on behind it.

The constantly recycled air in the small windowless room never failed to give JC a headache. And the frankly depressing décor didn't help. Dozens of head-and-shoulders portraits, covering all four walls, of old agents fallen in the field. Not a smile to be seen on any of them. The oldest portraits were paintings, which gave way to daguerreotypes, then photos—from sepia to black-and-white to colour. Men and women who'd faced off against the worst Heaven and Hell could throw at them because the Carnacki Institute doesn't take any crap from the Hereafter. Field agents who had put their souls on the line, not for medals or money, honour or glory, but just because they believed it was a job that needed doing.

JC made a point of sitting calmly, legs casually crossed, back straight and head held high, as though he didn't have a care in the world. Because you never want the enemy to see you looking vulnerable. He looked around the room, for want of anything better to do. Nothing had changed since his last visit; but then, it wasn't the kind of place where anything really changed. The room had been here before he joined the Institute, and no doubt would still be here long after he was gone. People come and go; but the Ghost Finders of the Carnacki Institute go on forever.

He hadn't been told why he and his team had to report in so urgently, so soon after taking on two cases in a row without proper downtime; but he could guess. When a case goes as badly wrong as Brighton had, with so many innocents dead . . . the need to spread the blame around quickly becomes paramount. Everyone feels the need to pass it on before it can stick. JC did feel guilty, that so many people had died on his watch. That he hadn't been able to pull off one of his famous last-minute miracle solutions and save the day. But one of the first things a field agent learns is that you can't always save everyone. Latimer knew that. JC was pretty sure she'd take responsibility. She knew none of it was his fault, or his team's. The whole thing had been her idea, after all.

Melody was sitting stiff-backed, arms tightly folded, scowling defiantly at the whole damned world. She was never comfortable, making personal reports. She'd always related better to machines than to people. Her usual response to criticism was to go for the throat. She darted the occasional glance at Happy, beside her. Hands folded neatly in his lap, staring at nothing. He'd slept surprisingly well, for a change; but he hadn't said a word since he woke up that morning. He was drawing back inside himself, putting up barriers to keep out an increasingly intrusive world. Until he couldn't see out any more.

Melody hadn't dared give him any pills to try and bring him back—not with the Brighton interview hanging over them. Better he say nothing, and risk giving away the extent of his condition, than say something and confirm it. He seemed . . . tractable enough for the moment. And he did still smile, sometimes, when he looked at her. Melody sat stiffly in her chair, her heart breaking, and hoped someone would be stupid enough to give her a good reason to punch them out.

The Boss's personal secretary, Heather, was typing with great concentration at her brutally efficient desk, ignoring all of them. JC considered her, unobtrusively. Heather wasn't just a secretary; she was also the Boss's last line of defence. No-one got past Heather. Calm, professional, pleasantly pretty in a blonde, curly-haired, sweet-faced sort of way. She dressed smartly rather than fashionably and appeared harmless enough. Unless you knew better. Supposedly, Heather was secretly equipped and armed to such an extent she could stop a whole army of invading terrorists in their tracks. Having seen Heather in action a few times, JC was quite prepared to believe it. She was also scarily efficient, close-mouthed about her Boss and her job, and unpredictably dangerous. Right now, she was pounding away at her keyboard so hard, it actually jumped into the air from time to time.

Which was never a good sign. Something was wrong, something had changed. JC couldn't put his finger on anything specific; it wasn't that Heather had said anything . . . It was more in the way she carefully avoided looking at him or his team, concentrating entirely on her work. Normally, Heather and JC would exchange a little sharp-edged banter, just to make it clear neither of them was too impressed with the other. In fact, JC could usually rely on Heather to help him judge what was in the wind before any interview with the Boss. Such as: how deep in it he was, or the best way to jump . . . But not today. The few times he'd tried to strike up a conversation, Heather had shot him down with a curt monosyllable. Which could only mean . . . something really bad had happened. Or was about to happen. JC scowled and wondered if he could get to the door before Heather could produce a gun.

His first thought was to just go to ground and disappear, until whatever shitstorm it was had blown over. But then, that was his usual first thought whenever he was kept waiting to see the Boss. He knew if he ever did decide it was time to go missing, he'd have to run hard and fast to avoid the kind of hounds the Institute would set on his trail. Give up everything he had, leave it all behind, because he couldn't afford to take anything that might slow him down. And he wasn't ready to do that, just yet. His scowl deepened. Brighton had been bad, a full-on disaster, but he honestly couldn't see how any of the blame could be laid at his door. Even an experienced A team couldn't hope to stand off a direct attack by the Flesh Undying. Unless someone was looking for a scapegoat. A public sacrifice for a very public failure. Would the Boss really throw him and his team to the wolves, to protect herself? JC sat very still, his mind racing as he considered . . . possibilities.

Heather suddenly stopped typing, and swivelled around on her chair to look directly at JC for the first time. Her face was entirely unreadable. JC smiled easily at her, while his heart raced so hard he was sure she could hear it.

"The Boss says you can go in now," said Heather.

"About time," said JC.

He stood up, and his knees cracked loudly from being still for so long. He looked thoughtfully at Heather for a moment. "I didn't hear the Boss call you."

"New arrangement," said Heather. "In you go."

Melody helped Happy up onto his feet and tugged briefly at his dishevelled clothes before giving it up as a bad job. She took him unobtrusively by the arm and urged him towards the steel door. He went along willingly enough. JC moved quickly forward to take the lead, though whether to put himself between his team and any attack, or just demonstrate he was still team leader, even he wasn't sure. The heavy steel door swung silently open before him. JC took a deep breath, squared his shoulders, and strode in to confront the Boss with his head held high.

〃〃〃〃〃〃〃〃〃〃〃〃〃

The Ghost Finders stopped dead just inside the door as they took in the new face sitting behind the Boss's desk. They didn't know her; but they knew trouble when they saw it. The door closed quietly behind them. JC looked vaguely around the office, as though half-expecting Catherine Latimer to be hiding somewhere . . . and then looked reluctantly back at the woman behind the desk. She seemed a little flushed and flustered but was clearly doing her best to look like a cold and forbidding authority figure. Somehow, JC just knew they weren't going to get along. He glanced back at the closed door and tried hard not to feel trapped. Or under threat. So . . . when in doubt, go on the offensive. JC knew a lot about being offensive. He strode forward, planted himself before the desk, and glared right at the new face.

"Who are you? Where's the Boss?"

"I am Hillary Allbright, Head of the Carnacki Institute," she said coldly. "Your new Boss. Don't look for Catherine Latimer, she's gone. She's history. You will not be seeing her again. Sit down, Mr. Chance. You and your team take your orders from me now."

"Oh shit," said Happy.

JC and Melody both turned their heads sharply to look at him; but he had nothing more to say. The three of them sat down on the very uncomfortable visitors' chairs and studied their new Boss with a blatant lack of enthusiasm.

"Where is Latimer?" said JC. "What's happened to her?"

"That needn't concern you," said Allbright. "All that matters is, you answer to me now. And only to me."

"Meet the new Boss, same as the old Boss," said Happy. "Don't get sacrificed again."

"Is he being funny?" said Allbright.

"Hard to tell," said Melody. She glared at Happy. "You choose now to start talking again?"

"Self-preservation instincts kicking in," said Happy. "Better than drugs. Though not as long-lasting."

"So," JC said loudly, to drag the conversation back into touch, "Latimer is out . . . Why weren't we informed of this before?"

"Because you didn't need to know," said Allbright. "Such decisions are made well above your pay grade. A great many changes are taking place within the Institute; security must be preserved."

"A bureaucrat!" said Melody. "Oh dear Lord, we're in trouble now . . ."

JC worried his lower lip between his teeth, thinking hard,

trying to sort out the implications. It was like having not just the carpet but the whole floor whipped out from under his feet. Catherine Latimer had been Boss of the Institute for what seemed like forever. If she was gone, did that mean her enemies inside the Institute had finally got to her? And were they, necessarily, agents of the Flesh Undying? You can't be in charge of an important organisation like the Carnacki Institute for as long as Latimer was and not make all kinds of enemies. For all kinds of reasons. JC looked up and caught Allbright looking at him as though she knew exactly what he was thinking. And she was smiling: the smile of a hunter whose prey has just ambled unsuspecting into the trap. JC wished he'd brought the Hand of Glory with him instead of stowing it away somewhere safe for fear they'd take it away from him. He still had a few useful items and nasty surprises tucked away about his person, but under Latimer, this office had been protected by all kinds of seriously unpleasant defences. JC had no doubt they were still in place, just waiting for an excuse to jump on him with both feet. It was what he would have done.

So he sat back in his chair, looking as calm and relaxed as he could manage, giving Allbright his best *I'm no trouble, I know my place* smile. Even though he was pretty sure he wasn't fooling anybody. Allbright looked coldly back at him, then at Melody, and finally at Happy. Melody stirred dangerously in her chair.

"Why are we here, Boss?" JC said quickly. "Do we have a new assignment?"

"Hardly," said Allbright. "After your unmitigated failure at Brighton, you can no longer consider yourself an A team."

"Wasn't our fault!" said Melody.

"That's enough!" said Allbright. "I will not suffer insubordination in my office! You will speak only when spoken to, and only to present answers to my questions."

"Yeah," said Melody. "That's going to happen . . ."

"This is the kind of attitude I was warned about," said Allbright. "Latimer might have put up with it, but you can be sure I will not. As of now, you are removed from field-work until you have completed an extensive course of retraining."

She glared at Happy. "Except for him. That man is not fit for duty. He is suspended, pending a full medical and psychological exam. And a full inquiry into misuse of experimental pharmaceuticals from the Institute's laboratories."

Melody's hand shot towards something in her pocket. Allbright's hand went to a drawer in her desk. JC clamped a hand down hard on Melody's arm, holding it in place. No-one said anything, but the tension in the room ratcheted up a whole series of notches. Melody glared fiercely at JC, her arm straining against his grasp. His hand didn't budge an inch. After a worryingly long moment, Melody nodded reluctantly. JC let go of her arm, and she took her hand away from her pocket. Allbright took her hand away from the desk drawer. JC let out a breath he hadn't realised he'd been holding and turned his attention back to Allbright. Happy hadn't moved a muscle through any of this, staring straight ahead of him. JC gave Allbright his most confident smile.

"You can't shut us down," he said. "We have the best track record of any field team in the Institute."

"You will not be allowed out into the field again until you've been properly debriefed, and re-educated concerning proper procedure," Allbright said flatly. "I've read your files, and I am not impressed. What successes you may have achieved have been undermined by slipshod work and a marked inability to follow orders. You have possibilities, Mr. Chance. Ms. Chambers has a great many questions to answer; but her remarkable aptitude for advanced technology might yet secure her a useful position in the new order. If she can learn to cultivate the correct attitude." Allbright looked at Happy with open distaste. "However, there is no room in this organisation for a drug-addicted telepath. His very presence here is a disgrace! I still haven't decided whether he should go straight from this office to a holding cell or be sectioned immediately under the Mental Health Act!"

"No," said JC. "I don't think so. One for all, all for one, and to hell with everyone else. That's the Ghost Finders team spirit. An attack on one of us, is an attack on all of us; and our files should have warned you what happens when we start feeling . . . unsafe."

"Threats will get you nowhere," said Allbright.

"I think you'll find they will," said JC.

"You won't be allowed to just quit," said Allbright.

"Try and stop us," said Melody.

And then JC leaned suddenly forward in his chair, to fix Allbright with a hard stare. "A thought has just occurred to me. You need us, Boss."

"What are you talking about?" said Allbright. "What use could I possibly have for such a thoroughly disgraced team?"

"You need us to find Catherine Latimer," said JC. His smile widened as he took in Allbright's involuntary reaction, and he sat back in his chair again. "She didn't just retire, did she? She walked out on you. Catherine Latimer isn't the sort to go quietly; and you're scared witless of what she might do, out in the world on her own. She knows all kinds of subterranean people and organisations, and most of them probably still owe her favours. She's the kind who'd hoard them, for a rainy day.

"You can bet good money that Latimer has her own unofficial support system, assembled on the quiet during decades in office. Because she must have suspected something like this would happen one day. If she has been forced out of the Institute . . . and if you were dumb enough to pressure or threaten her first . . . you know she's going to want revenge. Against the Institute in general and you in particular, New Boss. Just think of all the damage she could do with what she knows and who she knows. You need her found, and quickly, before she arranges a show of strength to make clear her power and displeasure. And the only people with any hope of tracking her down before that happens . . . are sitting right here in front of you. Because we know her better than anyone."

"Of course," said Allbright. "We know you and Latimer were close."

It was meant to sound intimidating, but JC was more intrigued that Allbright had finally slipped and said *we* for the first time. Confirming there was a group behind her, a group opposed to Catherine Latimer.

"That was then, this is now," JC said smoothly. "You need us to locate her; and we're ready and willing to go to work."

"We are?" said Melody.

"Hush," said JC. "I'm negotiating."

"What do you want?" said Allbright. "In return for your services?"

"Reinstatement as an A team, with all privileges," said JC. "Access to all Institute records and intelligence. And guaranteed immunity from prosecution for all of us. All our sins forgiven . . ."

"Agreed," said Allbright.

JC didn't like how quickly she'd given in. Either she'd been ready to offer a lot more . . . Or she had no intention of honouring the deal. JC didn't let any of what he was thinking appear in his face. He just nodded and went along.

"You have forty-eight hours," said Allbright. "Starting now. Either you return with Catherine Latimer, suitably subdued and restrained . . . Or you and your team will be shut down. By force if necessary."

"Agreed," said JC.

Allbright looked at him steadily, ignoring Melody and Happy. "Are you sure you want to do this, Mr. Chance? Go after one of the most dangerous women in the world, with a damaged and compromised team? You could still have a bright future in the new Institute . . . but your technician is suspect, and your telepath is barely functioning. Are you sure you wouldn't rather I supply you with replacements?"

"No," said JC. "They're my team."

"On your own head be it," said Allbright.

"No change there," said JC.

Allbright gestured imperiously with one hand, and the heavy steel door swung open. JC declined to be impressed. Latimer never needed to rely on dramatic gestures. He got to his feet, and so did Melody and Happy. JC noticed out of the corner of his eye that Happy didn't need Melody's help this time. The telepath's face was still worryingly blank, but his gaze seemed sharp enough. JC deliberately turned his back on Allbright and headed for the open door.

He'd almost reached it when Allbright said, "Forty-eight hours. And not a minute more."

"I heard you the first time," said JC, not looking around.

"You never learn, do you? Just for that, you now have thirty-six hours."

JC stopped and looked back at her. "The deal was for forty-eight. Or there's no deal."

"You're in no position to bargain," said Allbright.

"Yes I am," said JC. "Or you wouldn't feel the need to pressure me. Forty-eight hours, as agreed. Or I walk and take my team with me. And maybe we'll trash your office before we leave and set the furniture on fire."

"Right," said Melody.

"Love to," said Happy.

Allbright nodded stiffly. Two rising patches of colour showed in her cheeks. "I won't forget this."

"That's the idea," said JC.

"Forty-eight hours, then I set the hounds on you! As well as Catherine Latimer."

JC turned his back on her again and led his team out of the Boss's office. The steel door closed quietly and very firmly behind them.

....

Out in the waiting room, Melody started to explode, but JC immediately hushed her.

"Not now," he said. "Not in front of Heather."

The busily working secretary made a point of finishing what she was typing before turning to smile brightly at them.

"What's the matter, JC? Don't you trust me?"

"You didn't warn us Catherine Latimer was gone," said JC. "Dismissed by the new order."

Heather shrugged. "I work for the Boss. Whoever she is."

"Don't we all," said JC.

Heather cocked her head to one side, listening to something only she could hear. "Ah, apparently I'm to give you and your team all possible support. So what do you need from me?"

"I'll let you know," said JC. "When I've had time to think."

"Don't take too long," said Heather. "Remember, you only have forty-eight hours. The clock is ticking."

"My," said JC. "You are in the loop these days, aren't you?"

"Some of us have the good sense to make ourselves useful," said Heather. "We all have to serve someone."

"But choosing who makes all the difference," said JC.

Later, JC drove carefully through London, going nowhere in particular, just driving. He kept a watch in the rear-view mirror but didn't see anyone following them. Though he couldn't believe Allbright would send anyone obvious. He scowled at the road ahead, barely noticing the heavy traffic. Thinking hard. In the back seat, Melody and Happy watched him thoughtfully. Waiting for him to say something.

"Are we really going after Catherine Latimer?" Happy said finally. "I mean, she's dangerous, JC. Particularly if she doesn't want to be found. And it's not like we owe this new administration anything."

"After the way they treated us, and threatened you, they can all go straight to Hell by the direct route," said Melody. "I say, if Latimer wants to disappear, let her."

"We can't let anyone else go after her," said JC. "They wouldn't have Latimer's best interests at heart."

"And we do?" said Melody. "When has she ever been on our side?"

"I trust her far more than I do the new Boss," said JC. "At least we always knew where we were, with Latimer. She might regularly send us out on dangerous missions, with far too good a chance of our getting killed; but we could always be sure it was for a good reason, and a good cause. I don't get that feeling at all from the new Boss. Latimer had our backs when we needed it. I had to blackmail Allbright to get what she should have given us by right. And she shouldn't have threatened you. No-one threatens my team and gets away with it."

"All right," said Melody. "Who are you; and what have you done with the real JC?"

He laughed briefly. "Maybe I just don't want the hassle of

breaking in a new team, at my time of life. But don't get me wrong; this is all about enlightened self-interest. Having Allbright as Boss is definitely not in our best interests."

"So . . . we're not hunting Latimer down?" said Happy. "We're on her side?"

"We're going to back her, against the Institute?" said Melody.

"She's the only one in the Institute we know we can trust," said JC. "Anyone else could be working for the Flesh Undying."

"Including Allbright?" said Happy.

"Of course," said JC. "Or, at the very least, whoever put her there. And besides . . . if this new order is so ready to bring the hammer down on Catherine Latimer, with all her decades of service, how long before they'd come after us? Retraining and re-education, my arse. Probably more like reprogramming. Make us over into smiling little drones, following the party line, only too pleased to do whatever we were told by our new lords and masters . . ."

"People . . ." said Happy. "Is it any wonder I prefer small dogs?"

"You're right, JC," said Melody. "Screw the new order. But we're going to need some really big guns."

"Let's hear it one more time, for the Charge of the Light Brigade," said Happy. "Come on. JC, where do we even start looking? Latimer must know a hundred places to go to ground, in London alone. With all kinds of powerful allies. Notice I didn't say friends . . . And don't expect me to track her. She's bound to have really heavy-duty psychic shields in place."

JC smiled suddenly. "Why don't we just ask her where she is?"

Melody and Happy looked at each other, then back at JC.

"Okay," said Happy. "Suddenly feeling several steps behind . . . What's going on here?"

"You have the Boss's private number?" said Melody.

"Better than that," said JC. And then he broke off, peering into the rear-view mirror. "Hold everything; we have a tail."

Happy and Melody twisted around, struggling with each other for room on the narrow seat so they could both look out the back window.

"Are you sure?" said Melody. "I don't see anything . . ."

"And I'm not picking up a damned thing," said Happy. "If anyone out there is thinking about us, they're really well shielded."

"They might not be Institute," said Melody. "A lot of people, and organisations, are going to be very interested in Catherine Latimer's whereabouts, now she's no longer protected. They might believe they can use us to get to her."

"Paranoia!" said Happy. "The game the whole world can play!"

"You're back to yourself," said Melody.

"I know," said Happy. "Depressing, isn't it?"

"Which car is it?" said Melody. "JC?"

"The same car has been behind us for some time," said JC. "Keeping well in the background—sometimes one car back, sometimes two."

"Well spotted," said Happy. "For someone who's not nearly as dangerously deluded as I am, you're really very observant. Soon you'll be able to see things that aren't necessarily there, just like me!"

Kim appeared on the passenger seat beside JC, dressed in a starchy nurse's outfit, smiling brightly. "It wasn't him! It was me!"

Melody and Happy both jumped, just a little, despite themselves, then tried very hard to look as though they hadn't. They glared at the smiling ghost girl.

"How long have you been with us?" said Melody.

"Ever since you left Buck House," said Kim. "I did try to go in with you, but I can't get past their shields. They really are obsessed with keeping ghosts out."

"To be fair," said JC, "with good reason."

"Why didn't you show yourself to us before?" said Melody.

"Because I told her not to," said JC. "No point having an ace up your sleeve if everyone can see it."

"Why a nurse?" said Happy.

"Because JC likes the uniform," said Kim.

"A conversation for another time," JC said quickly. Happy sniggered.

"What are we going to do about these people following us?" asked Melody. "I don't have my machine pistol; I knew they wouldn't let me into the Boss's office armed. But I do have a few others things of a generally destructive nature."

"Never knew you when you didn't," Happy said kindly.

"I think we need to teach these people a lesson," said JC. "Kim, be a dear and go do something seriously annoying to them."

"Love to," said Kim.

She disappeared from the passenger seat, without even a breath of moving air to mark her passing. There was a pause, and then a car some distance back suddenly veered all over the road. There was an angry sounding of horns, and much squealing of brakes, as the other traffic hurried to get out of the car's way; and then it suddenly mounted the sidewalk and slammed into a shop-front. Men spilled out of the car and collapsed onto the pavement. Some of them were crying. Kim reappeared in the passenger seat, smiling smugly.

"I won't ask," said JC.

"Best not," Kim agreed.

"Spooky . . ." said Happy.

****

Sometime later, JC took a sharp left and brought the car to an abrupt halt half-way down a narrow side street. A tall, graffitied, brick wall loomed menacingly on one side, and the rear entrances of a row of ethnic restaurants slouched together on the other. JC turned the engine off. It was all very quiet, with lots of shadows and only a few people out and about, all of them carefully paying no attention to anything but their own business. JC turned around in his seat to look at Melody.

"I need something that will hide us from all forms of surveillance, and won't in itself attract unwanted attention."

"On it," said Melody.

She produced several bits and pieces of intricate high tech

from various pockets and set about assembling something. JC turned to Happy.

"How together are you? Are you feeling strong enough to cover us with a psychic shield, to hide us from the Institute's telepaths?"

"I'm fine," said Happy. "But the more I do for you, the sooner I'll burn out again. So make the most of me while you've got me because it won't last."

"You keep saying that . . ." said JC.

"Because you keep not listening," said Happy. "I'm a dead man walking, JC. Get used to it."

"You don't look like you're dying," said JC.

"Believe it," said Happy. He concentrated, for a moment. "Yes, there . . . I can feel outside attention, like insects crawling all over me. There are eyes on us. Not properly targeted in yet but definitely looking."

"Allbright," said JC. "She doesn't trust us."

"Probably never had any friends at school," Melody said wisely, not looking up from what she was doing.

Happy produced his silver pill box and looked at it thoughtfully. Like a suicide trying to decide between several bad choices.

"You're looking very worn-down, Happy," said Kim. "Don't die. I like being the only ghost in the Ghost Finders."

"I don't know," said Happy. "I could use the rest . . ."

He opened the lid and stirred the contents with a single fingertip before finally selecting two large green pills emblazoned with yellow lightning bolts. He dry-swallowed them quickly, then sat back in his seat. All the colour dropped out of his face, and his eyes saw many things, few of them good. He looked drawn and grey and sick.

"Got them!" he said loudly. "Spiked the bastards! They won't be able to think about anything but that rotten advertising jingle for days! Okay, JC, we are now, for all practical purposes, psychically invisible. Unless Allbright brings in some really big guns. I'm good; but there are better."

"You must be feeling bad if you're ready to admit that," said Melody.

"You look like shit, Happy," said JC.

"Move on," said Happy.

"Happy . . ." said JC.

"We need to move on," said Happy. "Allbright knows our current location. I saw it in their heads before I shut them down."

"All technological surveillance is now blocked," said Melody. She patted the complicated thing she'd made, as though praising a pet that had learned a clever trick. "We're covered, JC. But Happy's right: trouble will be heading our way in the very near future. So whatever it is you're planning on doing, do it now."

JC opened up his glove compartment and took out an old baked-beans tin. Someone had washed it out, but it still had the old label.

Melody shook her head slowly. "You have got to be kidding . . . I could have made you a proper comm unit."

"Not like this," said JC. "According to Catherine Latimer, this can is connected to hers by a length of spiritual string. One-to-one connection, so no-one can listen in."

"The world gets weirder every day," said Happy. "It's all that keeps me going . . ."

"When did Latimer give you that?" said Melody, staring suspiciously at the can. "Did she know this was going to happen?"

"She suspected," said JC. "That woman plans for everything."

He put the tin can to his right ear, cleared his throat, and spoke aloud, just a bit self-consciously.

"Boss, this is JC. We need to get together. Where are you . . . ?"

He paused, listened, and lowered the tin can. He smiled briefly as he put it carefully back in the glove compartment.

"It seems the Boss has made arrangements. We are to meet her, and perhaps a few special friends, at the Wulfshead Club."

"The most dangerous private club in London," said Melody. "Favoured watering hole for the more worrying members of the supernatural and superscience community."

"Oh, this can only go well," said Happy.

"Why do you always have to look on the miserable side?" Melody asked.

And that was when a dark figure reared up before their car and smashed in its bonnet with one blow of its fist. The whole car shook and shuddered, throwing the occupants about.

"Oh, no reason," said Happy.

FOUR

RETURN OF THE FAUST

He stood there, in front of the car, that terrible thing from out of their past. A tall, swaggering figure, arrogant and assured. Horror and violence on the hoof and loving every minute of it. He was dressed exactly the same as before, in a smart coal grey suit, with a waistcoat of many colours. Heavily built, muscle and bulk rather than fat, a huge, overbearing physical presence. Like he was always going to be the most important thing in whatever setting he chose to appear; and it would be a damned fool who looked at anything else. Because this man was dangerous. Because he might do anything.

He had slicked-back jet-black hair, and dark, unblinking eyes as inhuman as a shark's and just as hungry. He had the devil's smile; and he knew it. His face was almost classically handsome, but the effect was spoiled because it held no trace of character. It was just a pleasant mask, worn by something only pretending to be human. When he finally spoke, it was the sound of something that liked to play with its prey.

"Hi, guys! It's me! I'm back!"

"Oh bloody hell," said Melody. "It's the Faust. The Flesh Undying's personal attack dog. Doesn't anyone stay dead these days?"

"Well," said Happy. "Given our line of work, as Ghost Finders . . ."

"Shut up." She glared at the Faust. "Didn't we kill you back at the Haybarn Theatre?"

"You wish," said the Faust. "You can't kill me; nothing can. That's part of what I bought with my service. Unlike the original and rather short-sighted Faust, who sold his soul in return for the pleasures of the flesh, I made a better deal. I sold my flesh in return for a better soul. You can destroy my body as often as you like; the Flesh Undying will just give me a better one."

"Now why would he do that?" said JC. "Given that you failed so miserably to bring us down the last time?"

"Because not even death of the body can free you from service to the Flesh Undying," said the Faust. "Once you've signed on, it's forever."

"You don't sound too pleased about that," said Happy.

The Faust's smile widened. "Oh no. Forever is what I wanted. So, my dear old chums, down to business, eh? Tell me . . . where on Earth is Catherine Latimer? Now she's been dismissed by the new order at the Carnacki Institute, all her old protections have been revoked, and she walks naked and alone in this bad old world."

"I think you'll find she can look after herself," said JC. "Catherine Latimer never needed anyone to protect her. That lady was born dangerous."

The Faust shrugged. "Doesn't matter. The Flesh Undying wants her, so I want her. Give her to me."

"Do you see her inside this car?" said JC. "What you see is what you get."

"I know she isn't here right now," the Faust said patiently. "Or I wouldn't be wasting my time talking with you, would I? I would be indulging myself with some happy time by tearing you apart into bite-sized chunks. But you know where your dear old Boss is. Tell me, and I'll let you walk away."

"He's lying," Happy said immediately. "Don't need to be a mind-reader to know that."

The Faust pouted. "Well of course I'm lying! That goes

without saying. But we have to play the game by the rules, or where's the fun in it?"

"A game?" said JC. "When did this become a game?"

"A game is something you play with friends," said Melody. "And friends don't tear friends into bite-sized chunks."

The Faust flashed his devil's smile again. "You're not going to tell me, are you? Surprise, surprise . . . Oh well, don't say you weren't warned."

He grabbed hold of the car with both hands and tore the front section apart with brutal enthusiasm. Metal squealed loudly as it tore, as though it was in pain. The Faust threw broken bits aside as he forced his way forward, walking through the body of the car to get to its occupants, just for the fun of it. JC turned to Happy and Melody.

"Time to go."

"What?" said Melody.

"Get out of the bloody car and leg it!" said JC. "Look at him; do you have a better idea?"

"No she doesn't," said Happy. "We should run. Running is good."

They threw open the car doors and abandoned the vehicle, as it shook and shuddered under the Faust's assault. They spilled out onto the pavement and backed quickly away, unable to take their eyes off the Faust as he strode hip-deep through mangled metal. He stopped, smiled at them, then ripped the whole car in half. The Faust didn't show the slightest strain in his face, and his bare hands took no damage from the jagged metal. He let the two halves of the car fall away to either side of him, and they made a terribly loud clattering as they settled.

Melody looked up and down the empty street. "Why hasn't anyone come out to see what's happening?"

"Would you?" said Happy.

"He's a lot stronger than I remember," said JC.

"Upgrade," Melody said darkly. "Terminator class."

"Just when you thought the day couldn't get any worse . . ." said Happy.

JC looked at Melody. "Do you have anything that might

stop him? Hell, I'd settle for something that might just slow him down."

"If I had my equipment," said Melody. "Or any of my usual weapons . . ."

"I'm going to take that as a no," said JC. "Happy, can you . . . ?"

"I can't reach him," said Happy. "He's . . . I was going to say shielded, but I don't think that's it. More like he isn't really here. No-one home."

"Get behind me," said Melody. "As soon as he gets close enough, I'm going to kick him in the balls so hard he'll be able to wear them as ear-rings."

"No!" Happy said sharply. "He wouldn't even feel it, Mel. He's not human. He just looks that way because it's how he remembers being. He's made of flesh from somewhere else now, given shape and purpose by the Flesh Undying. You can't fight him, Mel! I mean it! None of us can."

"Then what do we do?" said Melody.

"We run," said JC.

"Sounds like a plan to me," said Happy.

They all looked at each other, not even trying to hide the dread in their faces. They had gone up against impossible odds and appalling things in their time as Ghost Finders, but nothing as casually violent and murderous as the Faust. JC turned and sprinted down the narrow street, followed closely by Happy and Melody. And the Faust went after them—not hurrying, just sauntering along. Enjoying the chase and smiling his happy smile at the thought of what he would do once he got his hands on them.

There were no lights anywhere, and doors remained firmly closed. Melody wanted to bang on them all and cry out for help or sanctuary; but she knew there was no point. This wasn't the kind of neighbourhood where people got involved. And besides: what could anyone do to help, against something like the Faust? She glared at JC's back.

"Are we running anywhere in particular?"

"Of course," said JC, not even glancing back. "You don't think I just happened to park in this particular street, do you?

I've got an old bolt-hole here, a safe place I set up before I joined the Institute."

"We can't hide from the Faust," said Happy. He was already breathing hard and struggling to keep up.

"No," said JC. "We can't. But I left a few things here that might just help to spoil his day."

Melody looked at Happy. He was stumbling as he ran, gasping for air. He didn't have much left in the way of resources or any strength that didn't come in pill form. She slowed down to be with him, and JC quickly pulled ahead. He didn't notice he was leaving them behind as he counted off doors along the terraced row. He finally stumbled to a halt before a shadowed door with no number on it and fished in his pocket for the keys. He was breathing hard, and not just from the running. Melody had to grab Happy by the arm and half hold him up, the last few yards. She didn't like the way he looked, or sounded. Behind them, the Faust called out cheerfully.

"Yoo-hoo! I see you!"

JC sorted through his keys with unsteady hands, and swore harshly as he almost dropped them. He finally found the right one, slammed it into the lock, and turned it. The door was jammed in place from long disuse and didn't want to open. JC didn't dare look back. He put his shoulder to the door and forced it open, foot by foot. He squeezed through the gap the moment it was big enough, and Happy and Melody quickly followed him into a dark, quiet corridor that smelled strongly of damp and mould. JC forced the door shut again, locked it, hammered home three heavy steel bolts, and only then allowed himself to relax, just a little. He leaned back against the door, drawing strength from its heavy, reassuring presence. He could hear Happy and Melody breathing harshly in the dark with him.

"Nice place you've got here," Melody said finally. "How big is it?"

"Two floors, lots of rooms, and a whole bunch of nasty surprises lying in wait," said JC. "Enough to give any uninvited visitors a really bad day."

"Is there anyone else here?" said Happy. He sounded really bad, far worse than he should have been after such a short run.

"No," said JC. "We have the place to ourselves. I own the whole property."

"Why do you have a secret hiding place, JC?" said Melody.

"Everyone should have a bolt-hole," said JC. "Their very own safe house. Because you never know when you might need somewhere to disappear to if it all goes suddenly and horribly wrong."

"How very sensible," said Happy. His breathing still didn't sound right. "Can we move on, please? Only it sounds like the Faust is catching up with us."

JC found the light-switch, and a single bare electric bulb glowed reluctantly to life. Strings of dusty cobweb hung down from it. Dull light revealed a bare corridor with cracked-plaster walls and dusty, wooden floor-boards littered with far too many rat droppings. Shadows lurked to every side, and the air was close and stale. Melody looked at Happy, and her mouth tightened. His face was unhealthily pale, and he was trembling all over. His eyes were wild. He tried to smile for her, but it wasn't very successful. Melody glared at JC.

"What now?"

"Welcome to my fortress," he said. "Stout and sturdy, but don't expect any comforts. It was never intended to serve as a home away from home."

"Why did you feel the need for a fortress?" said Melody. "Who did you need to hide from so badly? What did you do, before . . . ?"

"Nothing good," said JC. "Let's just leave it at that, shall we? All that matters is, I ran into something seriously scary and unnatural, had an epiphany, and joined the Ghost Finders of the Carnacki Institute for the good of my soul. The usual story. Are you sure you don't have any weapons on you?"

"I learned the hard way not to try to smuggle weapons in when I'm meeting the Boss," said Melody. "Latimer had absolutely no sense of humour about such things. Even the few bits of tech I had on me, I had to break up so they'd pass as harmless."

"Why were you carrying bits of tech on you?" said Happy.

"Because I hate to go out in public naked," said Melody.

"No you don't," said Happy. "You get off on it."

"I mean metaphorically."

"Oh . . ."

"Don't you have anything useful on you, JC?" said Melody.

"Like you," said JC, "I only brought a few things I thought would get past the Boss. The old Boss. I don't have anything on me powerful enough to stop the Faust."

"We're more used to fighting spiritual, than physical, enemies," said Happy. "Things that need exorcising rather than blowing up. And I never expected to see the Faust again. I can't even attack him telepathically; I can see him . . . but his mind, his soul, just isn't there. I think he's running that body by remote control from some other location."

"Extraordinarily lucid, Happy," said JC. "Well done."

"Panic does tend to bring out the best in me."

"Where's Kim?" Melody said suddenly. "I haven't seen her since we left the car."

"She's around," said JC.

"Well, can't she do anything to help?" said Melody.

"Against the Faust?"

"Come on, JC! There must be someone we can contact," said Melody. "We need backup! Preferably from someone who owns a tank!"

"Who is there we can turn to?" said JC. "Allbright won't intervene. She already thinks we're expendable. I've been with the Ghost Finders so long, I don't know anyone outside the Institute. Do you? No, didn't think so. And we daren't contact Catherine Latimer. The Flesh Undying might listen in and work out where she is. Hell, we can't even leave here until we're sure we can throw the Faust off our trail."

"We can't fight him," said Happy. "He's just . . . too much for us. Maybe Kim could . . ."

"No she couldn't," said JC. "Kim! If you're listening, you

stay away from the Faust! I don't want you going anywhere near him. There's no telling what capabilities the Flesh Undying has built into this new body. For all we know, he eats ghosts—like Natasha Chang."

"Yes! Her!" said Melody. "Why can't we call her? She's supposed to be on our side now!"

"You think we should call in the Crowley Project?" said Happy. "Are things really that bad?"

"Yes!" said Melody.

"Have you got her number?" said JC. "Or anyone's in the Project?"

"Ah . . ." said Melody.

"Could we go somewhere, please?" said Happy. "I really don't feel safe, just standing here with the Faust getting closer. I felt better when we were running. It felt like we were achieving something."

"We're safe in here," said JC.

They all looked around sharply as something hammered on the other side of the locked door. The heavy wood jumped and rattled in its frame. JC and Happy and Melody backed slowly away from the door, not taking their eyes off it for a moment. The hammering grew louder and heavier as something with inhuman strength fought to get in. To get at them. The bare light bulb swung back and forth, disturbed by the vibrations, sending shadows dancing all around them.

"That door is solid oak, around a steel-centre plate," said JC.

"You think he cares?" said Happy.

The Faust punched a hole right through the door. The sound of rending wood and metal was horribly brief. The undamaged fist opened slowly, like a dreadful flower, fingers flexing eagerly. The Faust withdrew his hand, leaned forward, and looked through the jagged hole he'd made.

"Peek-a-boo!" he said. "I see you."

He hit the door again; and the heavy wood split from top to bottom.

"What the hell is he made of?" said Melody.

"I think, flesh from the Flesh Undying," said Happy.

"It gave up some of itself to make a weapon it could send after us."

"We angered it when we sent the submersible to look at it," said JC. "It wants to shut us down, before we tell anyone else how to find it."

The jagged crack in the door widened, under the relentless hammering of inhuman fists. Splintered wood bulged inwards, straining away from the door-frame. One of the steel hinges exploded off the door, its screws flying through the air like shrapnel.

"Why isn't the Flesh Undying attacking us directly?" said Melody. "The way it killed all those people at the convention?"

"Because we have protections," said JC. "Things the Institute taught us before we were allowed out in the field. And God alone knows how many layers of protection Catherine Latimer has acquired down the years. No wonder the Flesh Undying can't find her."

"I have to say, I don't feel very protected right now," said Happy.

"Come with me," said JC.

He led them down the corridor and up a narrow stairway at the end. He turned on more lights as they stepped out onto the next floor. More dull yellow illumination, more shadows. JC ran his hands along a bare wall and pushed back a concealed sliding panel, revealing electronic controls set into the wall. He hit a big red button, and smiled briefly as the controls came alive with blinking, coloured lights.

"Good," he said. "The main power supply is still connected. I always meant to install my own generator, just to be on the safe side, but I never found the time . . ."

His hands moved confidently across the controls, and he nodded, satisfied.

"All right," said Happy. "What did you just do?"

"I armed the place," said JC.

"Good," said Happy. "Armed is good. Armed sounds very good. What does that mean?"

"I've activated all my old traps and deadfalls," said JC. "Simple, brutal, and very nasty. The Faust is going to regret invading my fortress."

He did his best to sound positive, but Happy and Melody just looked at him. JC led them to a solid steel door, that opened with a combination lock, and into a great open loft space. The door locked itself behind them, and JC opened another wall panel. More controls, more flashing lights, and a whole wall of monitor viewscreens lit up, displaying scenes throughout the building. There was no sign of the Faust, as yet. Melody walked slowly along the wall of screens, her gaze jumping from one image to another; and then she turned to look sharply at JC.

"Who did you think was coming after you?"

"I added a lot of this after I joined the Institute," said JC. "Because I always suspected a day like this might come."

"We had so much in common," said Happy. "And I never knew."

Melody pointed suddenly at one screen. The Faust had smashed through the outer door and was standing in the entrance corridor.

"Should we be running again?" said Happy.

"Let the booby-traps do their work," said JC.

They watched as the Faust moved forward. A trap-door opened right in front of him. He saw it in time and jumped lightly across the gap, for all his size and bulk. As he approached the stairs at the end of the corridor, machine-gun barrels emerged from both walls and opened fire. The Faust soaked up the bullets and moved on. He took the stairs two steps at a time; and a thick yellow gas pumped out of the walls from hidden vents. The Faust paused to breathe in deeply. And then he smiled and continued on. There was something deeply disturbing, in his refusal to be affected by what should have been deadly threats. Like something out of a nightmare that just keeps coming, something that you only escape from by waking up.

"Whatever he's made of, it definitely isn't from around here," said JC, trying to keep it light, and failing.

"These are all . . . mechanical traps," Melody said slowly.

"No exorcism grenades, no ghost cages; none of the things you'd need to defend yourself from the kind of things the Institute might send after you."

"This was in case people came after me," said JC. "Bad people. I have another fortress, to defend me from more spiritual threats."

"It's like finding out I have a brother I never knew about," said Happy.

"Bad people?" said Melody. "Guns? Poison gas? Who were you, JC, before you joined the Institute? What were you?"

"A conversation for another day," said JC.

He gestured at one of the screens. The Faust had reached the top of the stairs. He stepped onto a metal grille in the floor, and electricity arced through him, lighting up the corridor bright as day. The Faust laughed amidst the lightning, and moved on.

"We're not even slowing him down, never mind stopping him," said Melody.

"I know," said JC.

"Look at the arrogant bastard," said Happy. "He's enjoying himself. He's not even breathing hard."

Melody looked at Happy. "You look like shit. Do you need to sit down?"

"It wouldn't help," said Happy. "Hey, maybe we should let him eat me? There are so many unstable chemicals in my system now, even his flesh wouldn't be able to cope!"

"Let's leave that as a last resort," said JC.

"Well, obviously I didn't mean eat all of me . . . A little of me would go a long way . . ."

Melody glared at JC. "Don't you have any real weapons stored here?"

"Nothing that would affect the Faust," said JC. "He was made to be unstoppable. And this . . . was only supposed to be a hiding place. Where I could hold out, while I called for help."

"Whom were you going to call?" said Melody. "If you were on the outs with the Institute?"

"I hadn't thought that far ahead, all right?" said JC. "I

always thought I'd have more time. Or, at least, more warning; I never thought my world could fall apart so quickly."

"I did," said Happy. "And I was right. Do you have any idea how vindicated I feel?"

"What do you want, a round of applause?" said Melody.

"That would be nice, yes," said Happy.

JC pointed at a screen. The Faust was standing on the other side of the steel door. He looked it up and down and smiled.

"Tell me you remembered to lock the door," said Melody.

"It locks automatically," said JC.

"Of course it does," said Happy. "I love that door. Good door."

"He'll never break through that," said JC. "I don't care what he's made of now. It's solid steel. Cost me a small fortune to install. There's no way the Faust can break through that door . . ."

They watched, as the Faust stepped forward and placed both hands flat against the door. And then he lowered his head and pushed, putting all his strength into it.

"He can't . . ." said JC.

The Faust strained against the door. The solid steel stirred under the steadily increasing pressure, then jumped forward—blasted right out of its frame. It fell onto the floor, unbroken but broken loose, and the deafening sound reverberated through the open loft. The Faust strolled into the room and smiled at the three Ghost Finders.

"Knock knock."

"JC," said Melody. "What else have you got? Tell me you've got something else."

"Nothing," JC said numbly. "That was it."

"You must have something!"

"No! Nothing! That's it!" JC glared at the Faust, standing smiling in the open doorway. "It's not fair. Nothing human can be that strong."

"I told you," said Happy. "He isn't human. He's channelling the power of the Flesh Undying."

"And looking good doing it," said the Faust. "Love what you've done with the place, JC. It's so you."

He looked around him, studying the surroundings with great interest. Just to show he was in no hurry.

"Is there by any chance a back door?" said Happy.

"Several," said JC, fighting to keep his voice steady. "But we can't use them."

"I think you'll find I can," said Happy.

"If we run, he'll follow!" said JC. "We have to figure out a way to stop him here. Or at least throw him off our trail. Because we can't risk leading him to Catherine Latimer."

"Why not?" said Melody. "She might be able to take him. I'd back her against most things."

"If the Faust knows where she is," JC said steadily, "then the Flesh Undying will know where she is. And who knows what it might send, then . . ."

"Oh," said Melody. "Yes. Got it."

"You can't stop me," the Faust said pleasantly. "But please feel free to try. I love to see a victim struggle."

"We can't stop him," said Melody. "No equipment, no weapons . . . we can't stop him!"

"There's nowhere else to go," said JC.

"You know what he'll do if he gets his hands on us," said Melody.

"I'm thinking!" said JC.

The Faust laughed out loud, to see such fun. Happy turned suddenly to Melody.

"Have you still got that tech thing you put together, to shield us from technological surveillance?"

"Of course," said Melody. She produced it from inside her jacket and held it out before her.

Happy studied it carefully. "There's . . . a signal, for want of anything better to call it, moving between the Faust's body and the mind that animates it. I can feel it."

"But that's psychic energy," said Melody. "My device relies on . . ."

"Doesn't matter," said Happy. "It's all just energy. And I think that if I concentrate my telepathy through that tech, I can generate something strong enough to disrupt the animating signal."

"That sounded almost scientific," said Melody.

"Comes from hanging around you so much," said Happy.

"But what would that do to you?" said Melody. "To your . . . weakened system?"

"Nothing good," said Happy. "But nothing compared to what the Faust has in mind for us. Don't need to be a mind-reader to know that."

"I like him," the Faust said cheerfully. "He's funny. I love it when the prey actually thinks it has a chance. Are you planning one of those last-minute miracle solutions? I love it when they go wrong."

"Shut up!" said JC. "Happy, do you really think this will work?"

"Beats the hell out of me," said Happy. "But at the very least, it should buy us some time, so we can get out of here."

"Sounds like a plan to me," said JC. "Go for it."

Happy took out his silver pill box, and carefully selected a red and two purples. Melody winced.

"That's a dangerous combination, Happy. Can your heart handle it?"

"It's a tough old muscle," said Happy. "I'm more concerned about what this will do to my little grey cells. What I have done to my brain chemistry I wouldn't do to a dead dog. Oh well, down the hatch."

He dry-swallowed the pills, and veins stood out prominently all over his face. His eyes bulged, and he breathed deeply. He grabbed the piece of tech from Melody, and concentrated on it.

"Work, you bastard!"

"All right," said the Faust. "Enough is enough. Let's get this show on the road. Now for the fun part—when bones start breaking, the blood flows, and the screaming starts."

"JC," said Happy, without looking up from what he was doing, "I need you to buy me some time."

"Why did I just know you were going to say that?" said JC.

"I don't know," said Happy. "Maybe you're psychic."

They both smiled briefly at the old joke, then JC stepped forward to face the Faust. Melody started forward, but JC waved her back.

"No, Mel. Guard Happy."

She nodded stiffly and stepped back again. JC looked at the Faust, still coming forward with bad intent, smiling his devil's smile. JC looked at the open doorway behind the Faust. He was pretty sure he could dodge past the Faust and make a run for it. But he couldn't do that. He took a deep breath, squared his shoulders, and gave the Faust his best cocky grin as he moved to block the Faust's way; and the Faust was so surprised, he actually stopped and looked thoughtfully at JC.

"You've probably heard this before," said JC. "But size isn't everything. I've always put my faith in low cunning, lateral thinking, and blatant cheating. Like this . . ."

He took out a pair of heavy, brutal brass knuckles, and slipped them on his right hand.

"Blessed," said JC. "And cursed. Just the job, for when you need to be sure nobody escapes the beating they've got coming."

"Is that it?" said the Faust.

JC took off his sunglasses, and the golden light from his altered eyes spilled out into the room. The Faust flinched away from the golden glare but still stood his ground. He made himself turn his head back, to look at JC. He wasn't smiling any more. JC went forward to close with the Faust, moving so lightly across the bare wooden floor it was almost like dancing. He darted in and hit the Faust square in the face with the brass knuckles. Blessed and cursed metal slammed into the handsome face, and the cheek-bone broke and shattered under the impact. The Faust's head snapped around, but he didn't cry out. And when he turned his face back, the broken bone had already repaired itself. JC hit him again and again, in the face and in the sides. Bones and ribs broke, and just as quickly re-formed themselves. The Faust stood there and took it, letting JC wear himself out. And the moment he slowed, the Faust grabbed JC's arm, picked him up, and threw him half-way across the room. JC hit the ground rolling to try and soak up some of the impact, but he still hit hard enough to knock all the breath out of him. The pain was so bad it scrambled his thoughts. He rolled slowly over onto one side, trying to get his feet under him, as the Faust came forward. Smiling again.

Kim appeared out of nowhere, to stand between the Faust and her man. She wore a pure white gown, and her long red hair crackled around her. She looked like a warrior woman out of legend. The Faust stopped, as she glared at him.

"You stay away from my boyfriend!"

The Faust laughed softly, delightedly. "Hello, little ghost girl! I was hoping you'd show up. Look at you—such a tasty treat . . . I could gobble you right up."

JC forced himself up onto one knee, fighting off pain and weakness with desperate stubbornness. "Get away from him, Kim."

"I won't leave you," said the ghost girl.

"You don't have to," said JC. "Come here."

Somehow he made it up onto his feet again, and Kim hurried back to step inside him. New strength flooded JC as the two of them joined together, and the golden glow leapt out to surround his whole body. The Faust winced again, unable to look directly into the golden light. But he still forced himself forward, his great hands reaching out to seize and tear. JC's brass-knuckled fist shot out again and smashed the Faust's nose. And this time, it stayed broken. It didn't bleed, but the bone shattered. The Faust put a hand to his face, amazed. JC hit him again and again, with all the strength Kim could give him, and while he couldn't hurt the Faust, he did hold him where he was. The Faust reached out for JC with his terrible hands, but JC dodged and ducked and kept attacking. Until Happy finally yelled at him.

"JC, get out of the way!"

JC gladly fell back, almost collapsing as his borrowed strength ran out. Happy stepped forward, holding the piece of tech out before him. He'd done something to it, and now it glowed with an eerie light. The Faust sneered at Happy through his damaged features.

"You think you can stop me with a box of tricks?"

"Of course," said Happy. "That's what we do."

He poured the full power of his chemically augmented mind into the tech, found the signal animating the Faust's inhuman body, and broke the connection. And with that interrupted, the Faust's body just fell apart. Dissolved into undifferentiated alien flesh, a bubbling pool of grey goo. It slumped across the floor, and JC and Happy moved quickly back to avoid touching it. Melody put an arm across Happy's shoulders.

"My tech and your mind, an unbeatable combination."

"Better living through unnatural chemistry," said Happy.

"We need to get out of here," said Melody. "The Flesh Undying will find a way to reanimate . . . that. And then the Faust will be back."

"I've got a better idea," said JC. "I'll hit the self-destruct, set the timer, and blow this whole place up. Let's see the Flesh Undying reanimate a pile of ashes."

"Sounds like a plan to me," said Happy.

"We have to get to the Boss," said JC. "Things are getting serious."

FIVE

HOUNDED OUT OF THE CLUB

Just because you've won a battle, it doesn't mean you've won a war.

Back out in the shadowy side street, JC and Happy and Melody looked sadly at the wreckage of what had been their car. Fortunately, there was no-one else about to see it. Despite all the assorted and very noisy mayhem, no-one had come out to see what was going on. The street remained entirely empty. Windows were dark, doors were closed; and no-one showed any interest in walking the dog.

"There is a reason why I chose this area," said JC. "The last thing you need when you're on the run and on the dodge are is nosy neighbours."

Kim appeared out of nowhere to stand beside him. No-one so much as flinched. Kim looked at what used to be their car and sighed.

"I liked that car."

"No you didn't," said JC.

"I liked it a lot more when it was in one piece. You couldn't put that back together with a whole tube of super-glue."

JC nodded glumly. The two parts of what had been a perfectly serviceable car were now lying so far apart, he had to actually turn his head to look from one to the other. He couldn't have done a better job of destruction with a chainsaw and a lifetime's worth of pent-up frustration.

"Good job getting that approved on your expenses," said Happy.

"How are we supposed to get to the Wulfshead Club without transport?" said Melody. "And nobody even mention walking. I do not do the walking thing. It's bad for my feet, never mind my dignity."

"There's always the Underground," Happy said tentatively. The others just looked at him. They all had bad memories of the London Tube System. Involving murder, trains full of dead people, and Forces from Beyond.

"Too public anyway," said JC. "The Flesh Undying must know the Faust has been taken out of the game. Other agents will be on their way."

"You can bet the Institute will have put new people on our trail by now," said Melody. "And let's not forget certain private individuals who'd be only too happy to sell information on us to all the various interested parties. No-one loves you when you're down and out, and the big guns don't have your back any more."

"When there's blood in the water, the sharks will start circling," Happy said wisely.

"I just said that!" said Melody.

"But not as well," said Happy.

Melody smiled briefly. "You always could out-gloom me."

"I've had more practice," said Happy.

"I know a way to get us to the Wulfshead Club," said Kim. "A very private way, that almost no-one else could follow. But . . . you're really not going to like it."

"There hasn't been much about today I have liked," said JC. "Go on, hit me with it. What did you have in mind?"

"I can get us to the Wulfshead with absolutely no chance of our being observed or interrupted," said Kim. "But . . ."

"Oh hell," said Happy. "Nothing good ever follows that kind of but."

"However," said Kim, "it would mean taking the low road. The path the dead walk."

JC and Happy and Melody looked at each other. They wanted to choose their next words very carefully.

"I have heard of the low road," JC said finally. "I thought you had to be dead to be able to use it."

"Can I just point out," said Happy, "that there is a definite limit to how far I'm prepared to go to help the Boss."

"I don't know what you're fussing about," said Melody. "You're half-dead already."

"That half makes all the difference," said Happy.

"I can open a gateway to the low road," said Kim. "And take you with me as my guests. You'd be perfectly safe, as long as you stuck close to me, but it is a hard way to travel. There are . . . spiritual dangers. You'd see things, experience things . . ."

"We've all seen a lot," said JC. "As Ghost Finders."

"Not like this," said Kim.

There was another long pause as the three living members of the team thought about it. Something in Kim's voice, and something in her eyes, made it clear these dangers were very real. They could all feel hackles rising on the backs of their necks. In the end, JC shrugged quickly.

"We're pressed for time," he said. "And we don't seem to have any other options. A short cut sounds good to me. I'm game. Happy? Mel?"

"A chance to see things no living human has ever seen?" said Happy. "Are you kidding? I live for shit like this! The bragging rights alone . . ."

"There are good reasons why the living and the dead are supposed to stay separate," said Melody. "There are things the living aren't meant to see. That's why there are Ghost Finders—to protect the living from things they're not ready to deal with. But . . ."

"Far too many buts in this conversation," muttered Happy.

"Hush, sweetie," said Melody. She looked steadily at Kim. "Any chance the Faust could follow us? Or any of the Flesh Undying's other agents?"

"I don't see how," said Kim. "They're still flesh. Only the dead can see the way to the low road."

"Then let's do it," said Melody. "Before I get a rush of common sense to the head and run screaming for the horizon. Do you need any help or special circumstances?"

"No," said Kim. "The low road is always only a step away." She glanced at Happy. "You should know that."

"Some days it seems closer than others," said Happy.

Melody looked closely at Happy. "Are you sure you're up to this?"

"Trust me," said Happy. "There's nothing that could happen to make me feel any worse that didn't involve major-organ removals." His gaze softened, just a little. "It's sweet that you're worried, Mel. But I'm not. I'm past that."

JC cleared his throat loudly to draw their attention back to him. Some conversations you just know aren't going to go anywhere good.

"So," he said to Kim, "is this going to be like when you opened that Exit door, at the Brighton convention?"

"Sort of," said Kim, in a voice that strongly implied *Not really.* "We won't actually be entering the after-life. Just approaching it." She looked up and down the empty street, as she searched for a direction none of the living could follow or understand. She nodded slowly. "This way. And for your soul's sake, stick close to me, and don't stray off the path."

She headed off down the street at a steady pace. JC moved quickly forward to walk beside her, and Happy and Melody followed on behind. The light ahead slowly changed as the dirty amber glow of street-lamps and the lowering gloom of evening gave way to golden sunshine. Warm and bright and comforting, full of all the remembered joys of childhood summers. Those glorious holidays when school was just a distant memory and it seemed like summer would just go on forever. Almost without realising it, JC and Kim, Happy and Melody left the street behind to walk through a pleasant open wood. Wild and free and wonderfully inviting. A beaten-earth path led them through a narrow corridor of tall trees, with high-reaching branches weighed down by heavy greenery. Birds sang everywhere, sweet and joyous, and the air was rich with the scents of grass and flowers and growing things. It could have been any wood, or every wood. And the path, the corridor, seemed . . . immediately familiar. As though they'd walked it before. Perhaps before they were born.

Other people were walking the low road with them, strolling unhurriedly between the tall trees. The young and the old and everyone in between. They looked straight ahead, faces full of hope and yearning. They all seemed happy to be there. None of them paid any attention to Kim and JC, Happy and Melody.

"Where is this?" said Melody. Because even in such a marvellous place, her scientist's mind still wanted answers.

"This is the wood between the worlds," said Kim.

"It feels like . . . we belong here," said Happy.

"Everyone does," said Kim.

"All these other people," said JC. "They're dead, aren't they? Why are they all so happy?"

"Why shouldn't they be?" said Kim. "The worst thing that could possibly happen to them is over. They're leaving all the cares of the world behind. Going home at last. Can't you feel it?"

"Yes," said Happy. He stared straight ahead, as though he could almost but not quite work out what lay beyond the wood. "It feels like . . . children being called in from playing by their parents because supper's ready. The promise of love and comfort, and an end to all troubles. A feeling like . . . the long day's work is over. Time to lay down your burdens and rest at last. Oh dear God, it feels good."

"But our work isn't finished," said Melody, warningly. "Our lives aren't finished."

Happy didn't look at her.

They moved steadily through the corridor of trees, through a light so bright and clear it warmed their hearts, towards a destination they knew even if they couldn't put a name to it. Their pace quickened in spite of themselves, drawn on by the promise of what lay ahead. Until Kim suddenly stepped out in front of them, blocking their way and bringing them to a halt. JC looked at her almost angrily until he saw the concern in Kim's face.

"You can't go any further," she said. "Beyond a certain point, there's no way back. You have to come with me now."

JC nodded, slowly and reluctantly, and after a moment, Happy and Melody did, too. Kim led them off the path and through the trees. It took a real effort of will to go with her. They were leaving behind something precious; and even if they didn't know what it was, they missed it. The light began to change again, the golden glow of summer giving way to the drab lights and sounds of the city. Melody stopped abruptly.

"We're going back to the world of the living," she said. "And God help me, I don't think I want to go."

"You have to," said Kim. "You don't belong here, not yet."

"I know!" said Melody. "But . . ."

"You could end up trapped here," said Kim. "Unable to move on, or go back. That's the way most ghosts are made."

In the end, Happy took Melody firmly by the arm and urged her forward. "My turn, Mel, to be strong for you."

Kim led them out of the wood between the worlds and back into London. They emerged into a dirty back alley-way, the light of summer just a memory now, replaced by the dull amber glow of street-lamps at the end of the alley and the distant sounds of city traffic.

Happy let go of Melody's arm. "Welcome back to the world."

"I think the correct reaction is, you're welcome to it," said Melody.

"It's not much, but it's home," said Happy.

They shared a brief smile, and that was that. A lot of their relationship went unspoken because it was the only way they could cope.

"I told you it would be a hard road," said Kim. "Life and death both take their toll."

"What we just saw . . ." said JC. "Was it real?"

"Define real," said Kim.

"Have we at least arrived at the right place?" said Happy.

"Yes," said JC. "The entrance to the Wulfshead Club is at the end of this . . . really quite appallingly smelly alley-way."

"How do you know?" said Melody.

"I had to meet someone here once, on the Boss's orders," said JC. "Picking up a package. Don't know what was inside the box, but it really wanted out . . . And no, I wasn't allowed inside the Club."

"About time we got an invite," sniffed Melody. "It should be automatic—save the world and you're entitled to free membership."

"You guys go on," said Kim. "I'm not going anywhere near the Wulfshead."

They all stared at her, and she looked back unflinchingly.

"Why not?" said JC.

"What do you know about the Club that we don't?" said Happy.

"It disturbs me," said Kim. "Bad things happen there."

"What have you got to worry about?" said Melody. "You're already dead!"

"You should know that doesn't necessarily mean anything," said Kim. "Especially where the Wulfshead Club is concerned. There really are fates worse than death."

"Then you stay out here," JC said kindly. "Watch our backs and give us advance warning if anyone unfriendly turns up looking for us."

"Yes," said Kim. "I can do that."

She stood there, on her own, while the others made their way carefully down the dark alley-way. It was filthy dirty, with pools of standing water and piled-up garbage, some of which seemed to be moving. Layer upon layer of overlapping graffiti covered the sweating brickwork on the two facing walls. The most recent was *Dagon Has Risen! Beware the Yellow Sign*, and, most worryingly, *They're Inside Your Head*. The sound of passing city traffic came faintly but insistently from both ends of the alley. To JC, it sounded strangely distant, as though it was much further away than it should have been. As though just by walking down this alley, he and the others had removed themselves from the everyday world. JC couldn't help feeling that had been happening far too often, just recently.

They came at last to the entrance he remembered, a huge, blocky door set flush into the brickwork, on the left-hand side. Moisture ran down the wall as though it were sweating in the heat, but none of it touched the door—a great slab of solid silver, with warning words etched deep into the metal. Messages made with knives and chisels, claws and other things. In all kinds of archaic languages. JC leaned in close for a better look.

"Can you read any of that?" said Melody.

"I'm pretty sure some this is Enochian," said JC. "An artificial language created in Elizabethan times, so men could talk directly with angels. And I think that . . . is demonic script."

"Okay," said Happy. "I am out of here. Have fun, don't talk to any strange things, tell me all about it when you get back."

"There could be free drinks . . ." said JC.

"Damn you, JC," said Happy. "You always know the right things to say."

But still they stood where they were, looking at the door, none of them in any hurry to enter the infamous Wulfshead Club. They all knew its reputation; everyone in their line of work did. But none of them had ever been inside. If asked why they hadn't followed their usual procedure with forbidden venues and just forced their way in on general principles . . . they would probably have said they considered the Wulfshead Club to be just a bit above their pay grade. A club reserved for the celebrities of the hidden world. For Droods and Soulhunters and Paladins of the Golden Dawn. Heroes and monster-hunters and some of the more reputable names from the Nightside. Not the kind of people you'd want to force yourself upon . . . The Ghost Finders thought of themselves more as the working stiffs of the supernatural scene.

"I've heard stories about this place," Happy said finally. "About the sort of people who come here and the kind of things that happen. None of them good stories . . . Some people in our line of work have developed really strange ideas about what constitutes entertainment."

"No wonder the Boss chose the Wulfshead for her meet," said Melody. "Even agents of the Flesh Undying would have a hard time getting in here, uninvited."

"The Boss is probably a lifetime member," said Happy, scowling darkly. "Her kind of place. I don't think I want to meet the kind of people the Boss would mix with, socially."

"Look on the bright side," said JC. "If any of the people on our trail should turn up here, these are just the kind of people you'd want on your side to see the bastards off."

"Because members of the Wulfshead Club would be more frightening than our enemies?" said Happy. "Really not doing a good job of selling this to me, JC."

"Do you want me to tell the Boss you didn't want to meet with her?" said JC.

"Well, no, not as such," said Happy. He glowered at the solid steel door. "I don't like this door. Have either of you noticed there isn't any handle? Or a bell, or a knocker, or . . . anything? And I'm pretty sure . . . there's something living inside the door."

JC and Melody looked at each other sharply. They both wanted to step back but didn't like to in front of the others.

"What kind of something living?" said Melody.

"The bad kind!" said Happy. "The seriously dangerous kind! And it knows we're here."

"Is that good or bad?" said Melody.

"What do you think?" said Happy.

"Man up!" JC said sharply. "Big brave Ghost Finders don't take any crap from night-club doors. Or their built-in bouncers. It stands to reason a club like this would have serious security at their main entrance . . . but that's no reason for us to lose our nerve! We're invited! We're guests! So, everyone play nice and be on their best behaviour, right up to the point where anyone gives us a hard time; and then I expect to see sudden and gratuitous violence from both of you. We are a Carnacki Institute A team, and we don't take any shit from the Hereafter! Never mind a bunch of stuck-up supernatural celebrities!"

"Nice pep talk," said Melody. "Inspirational."

"Yeah, I feel really inspired," growled Happy.

JC sighed. "Look . . . just smile nicely and stand tall, and whenever possible let me do all the talking; and everything will be fine."

"Can I have that in writing?" said Happy.

"How are we supposed to get in?" said Melody, looking the door up and down with the experienced eyes of a part-time burglar. "Did the Boss give you a password?"

"Swordfish!" Happy said loudly, just on the off chance.

"No key, no password, no secret signs," said JC. "Apparently, we're just supposed to announce ourselves."

He looked quickly around, to assure himself they weren't being observed. The alley-way was still empty and eerily quiet; but it seemed to him the shadows were darker than they had been before. And that he couldn't see Kim anywhere. JC turned back and made himself concentrate on the silver door. He spoke his name aloud and gestured sharply for Happy and Melody to do the same. The door swung slowly back before them. No light from inside spilled out into the alley, and not even a whisper of sound. Beyond the open door there was only a great dark hole in the wall. Happy started to back away. JC nodded to Melody, and they both closed in on Happy, took an arm each, and urged him forward. The three of them strode more or less confidently into the Wulfshead Club. Giving the door and its unseen guardian plenty of room.

''''''''''''''''''''''''''''

Inside, the brilliant illumination was almost painfully sharp and distinct; but there was no loud music, no massed, raucous chatter of raised voices. The Club was deserted. The three Ghost Finders stood cautiously where they were, letting their eyes adjust to the glare after the gloom of the alley. They didn't need to look back to know the silver door had already closed itself. The place stank of booze and sweat and several kinds of illegal smoke, as though a whole crowd of people had been partying in the Club not long before. Massive plasma screens covered the walls. According to gossip, these screens normally ran twenty-four/seven, showing secret moments from the lives of the rich and famous, the good, the bad, and the influential. From secret bunkers, hidden back rooms, and, of course, bedrooms. But someone had shut all the screens down.

JC didn't realise how tense he was, until he glanced down and saw that his hands were clenched into fists, ready to defend him against . . . anything. He took a deep breath and made himself relax. Never let the enemy know they're getting to you. He looked down the long, open space before him and saw that the Club wasn't entirely empty after all. Two people were sitting together at the long bar that took up most of the far end of the Club. The bar itself was a nightmarish art deco structure in steel and glass, with no barmen in attendance. The two people had very familiar faces. JC started forward, trying hard to look relaxed and determined at the same time. Happy and Melody hurried after him. Their footsteps sounded very loud in the quiet.

Catherine Latimer sat perched on her bar-stool with a surprising amount of dignity. Sitting very casually beside her was Julien Advent, Victorian adventurer and hero of the British Empire. JC had heard a lot about Julien Advent. Everyone had. There were any number of books and films based on his historical exploits, and at least one television show. Most people didn't know that the real reason Advent had disappeared so mysteriously was that he'd fallen through a Timeslip in Victorian London and reappeared in the Nightside in the 1960s. He quickly made a name for himself all over again, as a hero and a force for the Good to be reckoned with. A fearless investigative reporter, these days, he also edited the Nightside *Times*. And didn't look a day older than the man in his late twenties who'd appeared in the Nightside some fifty years earlier. Tall, dark, and coldly handsome, Julien Advent still dressed in the height of Victorian fashion, complete with a scarlet-lined opera cloak. He made it look natural.

Latimer and Advent sat companionably together, sipping champagne. An opened bottle of a really good vintage stood on the bar top beside them, along with three more glasses.

Latimer nodded coolly to the three Ghost Finders and gestured to the empty glasses; but Happy was already ahead of her. He poured himself a drink, knocked it back, and poured himself another, before Melody could wrestle the bottle away from him. JC shot Latimer an apologetic glance.

"Go ahead," she said. "It's on the house."

"I don't think so," said Melody, putting the bottle down carefully out of Happy's reach. "I feel a distinct need for clear heads all around."

"Right," said JC. He nodded respectfully to Julien Advent. "So how long have you two known each other?"

Latimer and Advent exchanged an amused smile. There was clearly history between them.

"A long time," said Latimer. "We go way back."

"The last time we met was right here," said Advent. "At the wake for the Drood's Armourer. Good chap. Splendid do, I thought."

JC knew he was staring at Advent but couldn't seem to help himself. The man wasn't just a renowned hero and adventurer; he was a living legend. He'd fought in actual wars between the forces of Heaven and Hell. Just by being on such obvious good terms with Julien Advent, JC was immediately that much more impressed with his Boss. And even more impressed that Advent had been willing to come out of the Nightside to help Latimer. Though it was a mark of JC's long experience with the Boss that his first thought was, *What hold could she possibly have on the legendary Julien Advent that would persuade him to set himself against the massed forces of the Carnacki Institute and the agents of the Flesh Undying?* Did she have something on everybody? Well, no, clearly not, or she wouldn't be in the mess she was in now.

JC looked back down the long room. The Wulfshead Club was quite definitely empty. Even though it was famous for never closing. He looked back at Latimer and fixed her with what he hoped was a firm and demanding stare.

"Where is everyone?"

"I asked Julien for help," said Latimer. "And he very kindly arranged for us to have the Club just to ourselves for a while."

"The Club's Management owes me a great many favours," said Advent, quite unselfconsciously.

"Everybody does," said Latimer.

"But why meet here?" said JC.

"Because it's one of the few places we can be sure of not being found, interrupted, or overheard," said Latimer. "The Wulfshead's built-in security is quite staggeringly powerful, efficient, and frightening. No-one will bother us here."

Advent nodded briefly, not particularly approvingly. "The Roaring Boys . . ."

JC swallowed hard. He'd heard of them and the things they did. The last time they were let loose, officials were dragging body parts out of the Thames for weeks.

"Never heard of them," Happy said loudly. He was nursing his second glass of champagne and looking longingly at the bottle on the bar top.

"Be grateful," said JC.

"So," said Catherine Latimer. "You've met the new Boss? Appalling creature, isn't she? A political appointee, of course. A safe pair of hands, who could be relied on not to rock the boat during the process of transition or make trouble for those above her."

"You might have warned us," said JC.

"I didn't get any warning!" said Latimer. "I just turned up this morning as usual, and there she was, already installed behind my desk! Smirking at me!"

"I'm amazed she's still alive," said Melody. "Given your usual track record with people who annoy you. Not mellowing in your old age, are you, Boss?"

Latimer sniffed loudly. "Hardly. Sometimes I'm amazed by my own restraint. There's no point in killing the silly cow; they'd just replace Allbright with someone exactly like her. There's never any shortage of over-ambitious arse-kissing paper-shufflers." She glanced apologetically at Advent for the language, but he just smiled. Latimer shook her head slowly, and when she spoke again, JC could hear an honest hurt in her voice. "A lifetime in service . . . dismissed in a moment. After everything I've done for the Institute! I've kept this whole world safe, never mind just this country.

Never once shirked my duty . . . despite everything that's cost me, down the years."

"Hush, Catherine," said Advent. He held her hand, and she squeezed his hard.

"Did you expect gratitude?" said JC. "A big ceremony and a gold watch?"

"No," said Latimer. "But I didn't expect to be treated with such . . . contempt. I've given the Carnacki Institute my life. All those years . . . I've outlived two husbands and all three of my children." She smiled briefly as she caught Happy and Melody trying to do the maths in their heads, and add up the years." I've been with the Institute ever since I came down from Cambridge in the twenties. I'm a lot older than I appear."

And just for a moment, she let her eyes glow with the same fierce golden light as JC's, the sign that she had also been touched and changed, by forces from Outside. Melody and Happy looked at her wide-eyed and open-mouthed, then looked to JC. He mouthed the word *Later* . . . Happy and Melody glared at him, as they realised he'd known all along and never said anything. Their expressions said *Damn right we'll talk about this later*. Latimer let the golden light fade from her eyes.

"What remains of my family are . . . scattered, and distanced from me. My fault; I admit it. I never had time for them. There was always some emergency going on somewhere that I felt needed my attention more. Now even that's been taken from me. I'm almost ready to give it all up, to just step aside and stand down and let myself die. I think it might be a relief, to escape from the obligations of a job, and a world, that I have grown so very tired of. A world I barely even recognise, some days."

"I know the feeling," said the Victorian adventurer.

"Of course you do," said Latimer. She realised she was still holding his hand and let go. They shared a brief smile and toasted each other with their champagne glasses.

"In my experience," said Advent, "the world changes, but people don't. They are still worth protecting and fighting for. Mostly."

"Besides!" said Latimer, slamming her empty glass down on the bar top. "I'll be damned if I'll let the bad guys win! Not on my watch! It's just not in my nature . . ."

"Exactly," said Julien Advent. "Now I wonder where you got that from . . ." He produced a golden pocket-watch from his waistcoat, flipped back the cover, and checked the time. "I'm afraid I can't stay any longer, Catherine. Too long in London Proper, and I'll be noticed. Far too many people have an interest in me—friends and enemies and everyone in between. Outside the Nightside, I'm a legend, a myth from history. And I think it's best I stay that way. So, time for me to go. The latest edition of the Nightside *Times* won't put itself out. But, of course, call me if you need anything."

"Thank you, Grandfather," said Catherine Latimer.

Julien Advent leaned over and kissed her on the forehead, and she smiled almost bashfully. Advent rose to his feet, nodded politely to the others, and left the Club. JC and Happy and Melody stared after him, sincerely impressed. They met quite a few myths and legends in their line of work, but not many genuine heroes. And then they turned back to stare at their Boss.

"Grandfather?" said JC. "You never said . . ."

"It was none of your business," said Latimer.

"You know, I actually felt safer while he was here," said Happy.

"He has that effect on people," said Latimer." But it wouldn't have been fair to drag him into this."

"Why not?" said Melody. "I'm all for having a really big gun on our side. Why wouldn't he want to be involved? The Flesh Undying is a threat to the whole world. Having an actual legend backing us . . ."

"Would attract far too much attention," Latimer said firmly. "Powerful individuals and groups from all sides would want to get involved, and we'd end up caught in the middle and trampled underfoot. Besides, this isn't the London he knows. He doesn't belong here any longer. And he knows it." She glared at JC as he started to say something. "Change the subject. Now."

"Given that there aren't any bartenders," said Happy,

"does that mean we can help ourselves to drinks? I've heard you can get some really amazing concoctions in this place. Everything from a wolfsbane cocktail with a silver-bullet chaser, to radioactive sparkling water, to Angel's Urine or Old Shoggoth's Irregular. And I'm in a mood to try them all."

"Never knew you when you weren't," said JC.

"I doubt they've got anything in this place that could even touch your consciousness," Melody said kindly. "Not after everything you've done to it."

"True," said Happy. "But I live in hope. And denial."

Latimer looked him over carefully. "He looks terrible. I mean, even more than usual."

"I do, don't I?" said Happy. "It's a gift."

He looked at Latimer challengingly. The Boss shrugged and let it go. She could be kind, on occasion.

"Forget the bar," she said. "We need to talk. We don't have much time. Even my grandfather couldn't arrange for this place to stay shut down for long."

"What's going on, Boss?" said JC. "I mean, really? There's obviously more to this than just the Flesh Undying and its hidden agents. How many fronts are we fighting on?"

"The Carnacki Institute is being threatened with complete reorganisation, top to bottom," Latimer said grimly. "So it can end up as just a subsection of the newly re-formed Department of Uncanny. With much less power and autonomy, and strict limits on what it will be allowed to investigate. Essentially, the Institute would be just a specialised part of a much larger organisation, more answerable to those in power."

"But . . . they can't do that!" said JC. "We don't answer to the secular powers! That's always been the point. We're a Royal Charter, not a Government Department!"

"That doesn't mean as much as it used to," said Latimer. "Especially when there's a cabal inside the Carnacki Institute that wants it to happen."

"You mean apart from the agents of the Flesh Undying?" said Happy.

"Are you sure about this?" said Melody.

"I found evidence," said Latimer. "Though it seems I've

given myself away in gathering it. I was still putting together solid proof when it all went wrong at Brighton. And that gave them all the excuse they needed to shut me down. They need old hands like me removed, so they can pursue their own agenda . . ."

"But why?" said JC, almost desperately. "Why are they doing this? What do they want?"

"To seize power from the after-life," said Latimer. "Enough power to make the world behave. The living and the dead. Make the whole world over into what they think it should be."

"Are we talking politics here?" said Melody. "Or religion?"

"I think it's simpler than that," said Latimer. "They believe they know what's best for everybody."

"Oh, that's bad," said Happy. "They're always the most dangerous kind . . ."

"It was their secret experiments in pursuit of power that broke the walls between the worlds," said Latimer.

"I knew it!" said Happy. "I was right! I was right all along! Damn . . . I'm not used to that. It's a heady feeling."

Melody hushed him.

"Instead of the cabal reaching out through the gap they made," said Latimer, "Something from Outside broke in. The Flesh Undying. Wiser people would have taken that as a warning; but now the cabal sees the Flesh Undying as a potential asset. Something to be seized, controlled, a weapon to make all the masters of this world bow down to them. And I, along with everyone else presumed to be on my side, are just obstacles on their road to power."

"But the Flesh Undying is threatening to destroy the world!" said JC. "Do the cabal really think they can control something that big?"

"There's none so blind, or more properly speaking narrowly focused, as those led by their noses by their own self-interest," said Latimer. "Did I just mix a few metaphors? Don't care. The cabal believe what they want to believe."

"If they are in control the Carnacki Institute," Melody said slowly, "how do we stop them? Just us?"

"We can't," said Latimer. "They have the entire resources of the Institute behind them and a whole army of manpower at their disposal. There's no-one in the Establishment we can turn to. All my usual friends and allies and sources are either out in the cold or keeping their heads well down and hoping not to be noticed until the storm has blown over. They don't realise how bad the situation is. Or how frighteningly high the stakes are. So, when you can't rely on your friends . . . turn to your enemies. You always know where you are with them. I have therefore reached out to a recent ally." She raised her voice. "You can come in now!"

An office door at the far end of the Club banged open as Natasha Chang made her entrance. Still dressed in her pink leather cat-suit finery, complete with pillbox hat. She swayed down the long room to join them, elegant and sensual, smiling brightly, entirely unaffected by the open antagonism in the faces of JC, Happy, and Melody. She finally came to a halt before them, struck a provocative pose, and smiled sweetly.

"Hello again, darlings! Isn't it funny how things turn out?"

"You have got to be kidding!" said JC. He glared at Chang. "We're supposed to trust you? After you ran out on us at Brighton?"

Chang shrugged. "Didn't see any point in hanging around. The authorities would only have wanted answers to questions, and I don't do that. I'm really a very private person. And anyway, I'm here now! That's all that matters, isn't it?"

"Boss," said Happy. "Please let me shoot her."

"You haven't got a gun," said Melody.

"All right, can I club her to death with a bar-stool?"

JC looked at Latimer. "You really think we can work with her?"

"I believe we can trust Ms. Chang to follow her own best interests," Latimer said calmly. "Nothing has changed between us; we still have a common enemy in the Flesh Undying. A world dominated by the Carnacki cabal, or destroyed by the Flesh Undying, would have no room in it for the Crowley Project. And if we can't rely on the Institute's resources, perhaps the Project will have assets we can use."

"Smell the irony!" said Chang. "I love it! It's not every day the Crowley Project gets to save the world."

"If the world ever finds out," said JC, "it will almost certainly die of embarrassment." He fixed Latimer with a cold stare. "I'll say it again, this whole situation is way out of our league. We should turn this over to the heavy players, even if it means having to go cap in hand to the Droods or the London Knights."

"They wouldn't listen to us," Latimer said flatly. "I have been very thoroughly discredited. By the time I could convince anyone to take a closer look at the evidence, it would be far too late. Of all the people I've already reached out to, people I've helped and supported in the past . . . the only one to come forward was Julien Advent. And that's only because he's family. No. We have to do this . . . There's no-one else left."

"There's a depressing thought," said Happy.

Latimer got up from her bar-stool. "Time to go, children."

Happy downed the last of the champagne in his glass, put it down on the bar top, and looked wistfully at the bottle. Melody took him firmly by the arm and steered him away.

"The Club's Management will lock up after us," said Latimer.

"They're here?" said Melody, immediately suspicious. "Could they have been listening in?"

"My Grandfather paid for privacy," said Latimer. She smiled briefly. "Follow me, my gang."

She led the way to the door. Natasha slipped an arm through JC's, batted her heavy eyelashes at him, and snuggled up against his side.

"This could be the start of a beautiful friendship."

"No it couldn't," said JC, very firmly.

                    ııııııııııııııııııııııı

They left the Wulfshead Club and went back out into the deserted alley-way. The shadows seemed darker than ever, the garbage even more foul, and the smell hit them in the face like a flying half-brick. The silver door slammed emphatically shut behind them; and when they turned to look, the door had already disappeared. Nothing remained but an expanse of heavily graffitied brick wall. Happy stopped, and his head came up sharply.

"Pay attention, people; we are not alone . . ."

They all looked quickly around them but couldn't see anything. The shadows were still, and even the garbage piles had stopped moving.

"We're being watched," Happy said quietly. "By something really close at hand. I can feel it, like someone prodding me with a stick."

"Could it be the Club's security?" said Melody.

"The Roaring Boys?" said Latimer. "I don't think so. You never see them coming."

"You said something, at first, Happy," said JC. "Then you said someone. Which is it?"

"Hard to tell," said Happy. His eyes were fey and far away. "I can't seem to get a fix on it . . . I've never encountered anything like this . . ."

"Could it be the Faust, in a new body?" said Melody.

"No," Happy said immediately. "I'd recognise that sack of shit's psychic imprint, whatever body he was hiding in. This is . . . something new. Or perhaps very old . . ."

JC turned to Natasha, still clinging tightly to his arm. "Tell me you've got a car standing by."

"Of course!" said Chang. "There's a limousine waiting at the end of the alley. You'll like it, Happy; it's got a built-in bar. We travel in style at the Crowley Project."

JC looked around for Kim, worried that he couldn't see her anywhere. "Kim! Are you here? It's time we were going!"

The ghost girl stepped elegantly out of the brick wall immediately opposite him; and everyone jumped, just a little. She smiled warmly.

"Hi, guys! I didn't like being here on my own, so I opted for a little personal camouflage . . ." Her smile snapped off as she looked at Natasha Chang. "JC, why is that woman clinging to your arm?"

JC quickly retrieved his arm and stepped away from Chang, trying hard not to look in any way guilty. Kim looked challengingly at Chang, who stared haughtily back at her.

"We're all friends again," Chang said coldly. "Get used to it."

"Friends?" said Kim, dangerously.

"Allies!" JC said quickly. "Kim, Happy says someone, or possibly something, is watching us. And not in a good way. Have you seen anything?"

"No," said Kim, reluctantly turning her attention back to him. "But I have heard something . . . now and again. I thought it was just the local wildlife." She glared at Chang. "What is this woman doing here, exactly? What use is she?"

"I was about to make the same point about you," said Chang. "Everyone knows you can't trust the dead; they always have their own agenda. Even the ones who say they're in love with the living. Perhaps especially those."

"No bickering in the ranks!" Latimer said sharply. "Let's get out of here. Where is this limousine?"

Natasha Chang led the way down the alley, stepping elegantly past puddles and over garbage, leaving the others to follow after her. But when they reached the far end of the alley-way, she stopped abruptly and looked around her, confused.

"Where's my car?"

JC pointed to a great steel cube, just outside the alley. "I have a horrible suspicion that's it. I think someone has crushed and compacted your limousine."

"We're not doing too well with cars today, are we?" said Happy.

"Someone has compacted my limousine?" said Natasha, her voice rising sharply with sheer fury. "I'll have their balls!"

"You might care to consider just how much strength it would take to do that to a car," said JC. "Given that I don't see any sign of a car compacter around here . . . Whoever's watching us did this themselves, just to send a message."

"I would have settled for a singing telegram," said Happy. "Sorry; I always get flippant when I'm wetting myself with fear."

"Can you call for another car?" said Latimer.

"Of course," said Chang. "Might have some trouble getting another chauffeur, though."

"Ouch," said Melody, looking at the steel cube and wincing. "Also, ick."

"Heads up, people!" said Happy, glaring quickly about him. "Someone is definitely here with us! It's on the move!"

They all turned quickly to look back down the alley.

"How close?" said Latimer.

"Really close!" said Happy.

"Then why can't we see them?" said JC.

"Because it doesn't want to be seen," said Happy. "Not yet."

"Make a circle," said Latimer.

They all moved quickly to form a defensive circle, standing close together, shoulder to shoulder, staring out. Standard field manoeuvre. Kim rose into the air above them, turning quickly to look from one end of the alley to the other. But no matter where any of them looked, they couldn't see anything. The alley was still and silent. Chang suddenly had a weapon in her hand, a nasty-looking gold-plated pistol. She slammed off the safety, the sound loud and carrying in the tense silence. Melody looked at the gun enviously. JC looked at the street beyond the steel cube.

"I don't see or hear any traffic," he said. "No signs of any passersby . . . And no-one appears to have noticed a whole limousine being rendered down into the handy take-away size. Which leads me to believe the whole area has been sealed off. Someone doesn't want any witnesses for whatever's about to happen."

"I don't want to be compacted!" said Happy.

"How did they know we're here?" said Melody. "Who knew we'd be meeting the Boss at the Wulfshead?"

Everyone turned their heads to look at Natasha Chang.

"Don't look at me, darlings," she said. "I'm right here in the trap with you."

"And the Management wouldn't talk," said Latimer. Her mouth pulled into a tight grimace as she considered the possibilities. "I must have been followed. By someone very good if I couldn't spot them." Her scowl deepened. "I went to the Nightside for help. Where did the cabal go? Or who did they go to?"

JC looked at Happy. "Aren't you getting anything?"

"I'm not feeling well," said Happy.

"You look like crap," said Chang.

Happy's face was pulled taut by pain and strain, his eyes hot and feverish. He leaned heavily on Melody's supporting arm.

"I've put a lot of pressure on my body, and my mind, and I think they've both had enough," he said quietly. "Everything's breaking down."

"Do you need your pills?" said Melody.

"Always," said Happy. "But I don't think they'd help. You can only stretch something so far before it breaks. Dear God I'm tired. I need some downtime and a nice apple."

"Once we get out of here, I'll see you get all the rest you need," said JC. "But . . ."

"No!" said Happy. "No more buts! I can only work with what I've got. I am worn so thin now . . ."

Melody hugged his arm tightly to her side. "We need you, sweetie."

"I know," said Happy. "That's always been the problem. I'd die for one of my special pills, but I can't risk it. So bite the bullet one more time." A thin runnel of blood popped out of his left nostril and ran down his mouth and chin as he concentrated. Melody found a handkerchief and mopped up the blood. Happy didn't even notice. "I'm getting . . . a name. The Hound."

"Oh shit," said Catherine Latimer.

Everyone turned to look at her, with something like shock. They'd never heard her sound scared before.

"The Hound?" JC said finally. "It's not a name I recognise. And I thought I'd at least heard of all the really dangerous independent operators."

"The Hound works for whoever will meet its price," said Latimer. "It can track anyone, following their psychic scent."

"A tracker for hire?" said JC.

"An assassin for hire," said Latimer. "It eats hearts."

"Should we be running?" said Happy.

"You can't outrun the Hound," said Latimer. "No-one can."

"I'm willing to give it a try," said Happy.

"Thought you weren't feeling well?" said Chang.

"Stark terror is a wonderful motivator," said Happy.

JC looked up at Kim, still standing on the air above them. "Can you see anything?"

"No," said Kim. "And I can see things that aren't even really there."

JC took off his sunglasses and glared up and down the alley-way. Fierce golden light leapt out of his eyes, lighting up the alley bright as day. Everyone except Latimer had to turn their heads away. JC concentrated, and the shadows seemed to wither and disperse before him, giving up their secrets. But there was nothing there that mattered. The graffiti on the walls came alive under his gaze, full of new significance and meaning. He could see layers of information, like palimpsests in ancient manuscripts, one layer adding meaning to another. It was like being in a library where all the books were shouting their contents at him. JC had to look away. Down the alley-way, he could see ghost images, of people coming and going. Crowds of them, stepping in and out of each other, going back years. Not actual spirits, just images imprinted on the surroundings by the sheer presence of the individuals involved. A lot of very special people come to the Wulfshead Club. JC recognised some of them and had a distinct feeling some of them could see him.

He could see more than one door hidden inside the alley's walls, or at least the potential for doors. None of them the kind that would lead him anywhere he'd want to go.

And above it all a strong sense of being watched by cold, inhuman eyes. But no matter where JC looked, he couldn't see anyone or anything. JC put his sunglasses back on, and the golden glow cut off abruptly. It flared briefly around the edges of his sunglasses as he settled them back into place; and that was it. The alley seemed so much smaller, even diminished, in its own cold light. Everyone around JC relaxed, just a little. Except for Catherine Latimer, who didn't seem in the least bit bothered. But then, there wasn't much that bothered the Boss. JC wondered if what he'd just seen was how she saw the world all the time.

"Boss," he said. "The Hound; what is it?"

"I don't think anyone knows for sure," said Latimer. "It's old. Very old. Some say it was found in a long box, buried under an ancient abandoned city of iron pillars, deep in the Abyssinian desert. Some say it was found in a cave during the Crusades, being worshipped by corrupt Coptic priests. Some say Carter found it waiting for him, inside Tutankhamen's tomb. People say a lot of things; but no-one knows anything for sure when it comes to the Hound. It's supposed to be older than Egypt, perhaps even older than Humanity . . . The Hound. The original dog-faced god. No-one can hide from it, or escape from it. You pay for its services in blood and souls and the slaughter of innocents." She shook her head slowly. "I can't believe the cabal would go to such lengths to put it on my trail. So many deaths to pay for mine. The bastards."

"Oh shit!" said Happy.

Suddenly, it was racing down the alley towards them. Bursting out of the deepest and darkest of the shadows. A large dog-headed shape, part human and part hound, long and sleek and deadly. Savage eyes burned blood-red, blazing in the gloom. Its long, grinning muzzle was full of jagged teeth. Powerful muscles bunched and flexed under its dark-furred hide as it sprinted towards them. Clawed hands and feet gouged chunks out of the alley floor. Its stench filled the air, rank and bitter and feral.

Natasha Chang opened fire on the fast-moving creature with her pistol, but even though she was facing the Hound at almost point-blank range, somehow the Hound was never where she was aiming. It darted and dodged with incredible speed, its movements a blur. Chang's bullets chewed up brickwork on both walls and blew apart piles of garbage but never once came close to hitting their intended target.

Happy reached out with his mind, only to immediately cry out in distress, just from touching the thing's thoughts. He fell to his knees and vomited miserably, soiled to his soul just by the briefest of contacts. Melody quickly put herself be-

tween Happy and the approaching Hound, scrabbling through
her pockets, desperately trying to find something she could
use as a weapon.

Kim shot down from above and threw herself at the
Hound. It jumped right through her, and the ghost girl
screamed horribly. She fell out of the air like a wounded bird
and half-disappeared into the alley floor, shaking and shuddering from psychic shock.

JC cried out furiously and went to meet the Hound with
clenched fists; but Catherine Latimer pushed him to one side
and faced the Hound. Her eyes glowed suddenly golden,
blazing bright as the sun, and the Hound slammed to a halt,
well short of her. As though it had crashed into an invisible
wall.

It rose on its spindly hind legs and stood like a man.
Showing itself off, so they could all adore its inhuman per-
fection. It towered over them, a good eight feet tall. Its face
was an awful mixture of canine and human and something
else, something more. The eyes were old, horribly old. It
threw back its long head and laughed like a hyena, and everyone winced at the sound of it. The Hound took a step forward, its ancient eyes glaring unblinkingly into the golden
glow issuing from Catherine Latimer's eyes. Its clawed
hands reached out to her.

Kim appeared beside JC and stepped inside him. The
golden glow burst out all around his body as the two joined
together, the brilliant light leaping out to fill the whole alley-
way. The Hound snarled angrily and fell back, turning its
head away. JC laughed softly and went forward to meet it,
slipping his blessed and cursed knuckle-dusters onto his right
hand. The Hound turned its head slowly back to face him,
grinning its terrible grin. The dog-faced god, older than Humanity, older than history. JC laughed in its face.

It struck at him with its clawed hands, and snapped at him
with its great teeth, and he evaded them easily, drawing on
inhuman levels of strength and speed. He punched the Hound
in the mouth, and the creature fell back a step, startled. It
made a surprised sound, as though it hadn't known it could
be hurt. JC closed with the Hound and hit it in the head again

and again, driving it back down the alley, step by step. Until
JC landed a particularly solid blow and felt as much as heard
the long skull crack and break under his fist.

The Hound howled horribly and fell to one knee. JC
grabbed hold of the Hound and wrestled with it, using all the
strength given him by Outside forces. His eyes were glowing
unbearably now. He and the Hound surged back and forth,
pitting inhuman strength against inhuman strength, until finally JC stuck one leg behind the Hound's, tripped it, and
threw it to the ground. It landed hard, with an ungodly thrash-
ing of limbs. JC followed it down and pinned it in place. He
held it there, even as it struggled desperately, clawing at his
arms and shoulders. JC gritted his teeth as blood blossomed
on his white jacket. He drew back his fist and drove the
blessed and cursed knuckle-dusters into the Hound's head
with all his strength; and the Hound fell back and lay still.

Panting hard, twitching and trembling, but not fighting
any more.

Catherine Latimer went down on one knee beside JC. She
fixed the Hound with her golden gaze; and it couldn't look
away. And while it lay there, held by the sheer force of the
power within her, Latimer drew a silver knife from inside her
jacket sleeve and cut the Hound's throat.

It died surprisingly quickly. Its blood was just blood. It
looked confused at the end. As though it didn't understand
how anything human could be killing it. And then the light
went out of its eyes, its hind legs kicked a few times, and it
lay still and dead on the filthy floor of the alley-way.

Latimer made the knife disappear back up her sleeve and
reached out her hand to JC. At first he didn't want to let go
of the Hound, afraid it might get up again. But Latimer murmured soothing words in his ear until, finally, he pushed the
limp body away and stood up. He was breathing hard, and
not just from his exertions. He put his sunglasses back on,
with a perfectly steady hand, and Kim stepped back out of
him. The golden glow surrounding JC snapped off immediately. Catherine Latimer's eyes were perfectly normal again.
The only light in the alley seeped in from the distant street-
lamps. Natasha Chang looked back and forth between JC

and Latimer, as though trying to work out which of them was the more dangerous. She realised she was still holding her gold-plated pistol and put it away. Happy leaned heavily on Melody.

"Did we really just take down an ancient Egyptian god?"

"Hard core," said Melody. "Let's just hope it didn't have any friends or family that might come to avenge it."

Chang sniffed delicately at the air. "No trace of a departing spirit. Pity. I wonder what a god's soul would have tasted like . . ."

"You are an appalling person," said Kim.

Natasha Chang nodded demurely. "I try."

"What do we do with the body, Boss?" said JC.

"Leave it," said Latimer. "The Club Management will take care of it. They're used to cleaning up after raucous parties."

"Are you sure?" said Chang. "I can't help feeling the Hound would look really cool, stuffed and mounted and on display at Project Headquarters lobby."

"Things like that don't always stay dead," said Latimer.

"Leave it to the Management," said Chang. "Nasty thing."

"Get us another limousine," said JC. "I think we've outstayed our welcome."

SIX

SECRETS WITHIN SECRETS

The dog-faced god lay curled up in the alley-way, as dead as any other dead thing.

Natasha Chang stood just outside the entrance to the alley, her back firmly presented to the steel cube that had once been her limousine, speaking loudly and determinedly into her phone as she ordered a new car. Someone on the other end was trying to give her problems, and Chang was having none of it. She wanted a new car, right now if not sooner, or someone was going to suffer, and it sure as hell wasn't going to be her. JC stood on the other side of the steel cube, listening with one ear while keeping a watchful eye on everyone. Because somebody had to; and no-one else seemed in the mood.

Catherine Latimer was leaning against the alley wall, her face studiedly calm as she smoked another of her black Turkish cigarettes in the long ivory holder. But something in the way she stood suggested she was feeling tired. Or old. Her gaze was far away. JC wondered what she was remembering, from her very long life. It occurred to him that he really didn't know much about his Boss's past, from before she became Head of the Carnacki Institute. He knew she started out as a field agent, just like him. He'd seen the souvenirs she kept from her old cases. But he had no idea what kind of agent, what kind of person, she'd been. Certainly, the knife up her sleeve had come as a complete surprise.

It was obvious she'd killed before. And equally clear that the killing hadn't bothered her in the least. It wasn't that she'd seemed cold-blooded about it—more . . . practical, professional. So JC had to wonder who or what else she'd killed in the field, in her time. And why. Killing wasn't usually part of a Ghost Finder's job. Normally, field agents only turned up after the killing was over, so they could deal with the mess it left behind. JC didn't even consider asking the Boss about any of this; he knew she wouldn't tell him. Catherine Latimer kept her past a mystery, quite deliberately. For reasons of her own. JC had always known she was dangerous, and scary; everyone did. But for the first time, it occurred to him to wonder what had made her that way.

What had turned the grand-daughter of one of England's most legendary heroes into the feared Boss of the Carnacki Institute.

JC decided he'd think about that later. He had more immediate concerns. He looked back down the alley, to where Happy was sitting on the ground, his back propped against the wall for support. The filthy conditions of the alley-way didn't seem to be bothering Happy at all. He looked . . . old. Worn-down, worn-out. He looked like what he was: dying. JC wished he could do something for him, and at the same time wondered just how much of Happy's current condition might be down to him. All the demands he'd put on the telepath in the field. Because he needed Happy's amazing mental powers to help the Ghost Finders win the day. JC looked past Happy, to where Melody was standing alone, and wondered how much she blamed him.

Melody stood stiffly in the middle of the alley-way, her arms tightly folded, back straight, and chin up, glaring sullenly at the whole damned world. She was deliberately not looking at Happy because he'd made her move off a way, so he could be on his own. It was taking everything he had to cope, to hold himself together, and he couldn't do that if he had to worry about her as well. Seeing her suffer, as she watched him suffer. So he sent her away out of kindness, for purely practical reasons; but all Melody could see was that he'd pushed her away. When she was only trying to help.

She still wasn't ready to admit what everyone else knew— that there was nothing useful she could do to help.

Furthest apart of them all, Kim the ghost girl sat cross-legged in mid air, among the darker shadows of the alley. In the dim light, she looked almost transparent, as though she was fading away. JC wanted to go and be with her; but she didn't want him there, for much the same reasons as Happy with Melody. JC and Kim didn't like to talk about it, but they both knew she was finding it increasingly difficult to maintain her presence in the world. The after-life was calling to her, in a voice that could not be denied. And sooner or later, she would have to go.

JC and Kim, Happy and Melody—both couples had been so happy when they had first found each other. They still believed in happy-ever-afters, back then. Before life and death taught them differently. *Love conquers all* only happens in the movies. Life, and death, are more complicated.

JC leaned casually on the compacted steel cube, then winced as the wounds the Hound had given him flared up. He looked up and down the empty city street. No-one about to walk the pavements, no traffic moving on the road for as far as the eye could see. Just empty space and an ominous quiet. Whoever sent the Hound had cleared out the surrounding area very thoroughly. Presumably they were still waiting for the Hound to report back and lay the still-steaming hearts of its victims at their feet. JC frowned; he'd been assuming the Institute cabal had sent the Hound after them; but the Boss had upset a great many people during her long career. Hell, JC and his team had made their own share of enemies, out in the field. If someone had heard that they were on the run, and vulnerable . . . And, of course, there was always the chance that this could be down to agents of the Flesh Undying.

JC smiled briefly as he wondered just when his life had become so very complicated.

As if he didn't have enough to worry about.

A car arrived. A sleek white stretched limousine with tinted windows, complete with handsome liveried chauffeur at the wheel. The car glided to a halt before the entrance to the alley, its engine barely purring, and the chauffeur tipped his peaked cap to Natasha Chang. She nodded briskly back and smiled cheerfully down the alley.

"Get your hats and coats, boys and girls, your ride is here! Time to leave this appallingly aromatic alley for somewhere far more civilised."

ıııııııııııııııııııııııı

It turned out there was space for everyone in the back of the limousine. Gleaming, leather-upholstered seats, and lots of leg room. Chang demonstrated the capabilities of the built-in bar; and it was a sign of how bad Happy was feeling that he didn't give a damn. He was shaking and trembling and biting his lower lip to keep from crying out. Melody put an arm around him, so he could rest his head on her shoulder. Chang leaned in close to JC.

"Is he going to be a problem?"

"No," said JC.

"We could always drop him off somewhere, like a hospital, or a funeral home."

"No we couldn't," said JC. "We're going to need him."

"How can you be so sure?"

"Because we always do."

He accepted a glass of brandy from the bar, to keep Chang company. And so she wouldn't sulk. Catherine Latimer stared quietly out the side window, taking the whole limousine experience in her stride. Presumably, she was used to such luxury.

"Hold it!" Chang said suddenly, looking quickly around. "What happened to ghost girl? She was here just a minute ago."

"She often disappears for a while, about her own business," said JC. "And no, I never ask. Pretty sure I don't want to know. She'll turn up again when she's needed."

Chang looked unconvinced. She turned away to give the

chauffeur his driving orders and so never saw the small smile
JC allowed himself.

|||||||||||||||||||||||||

The limousine carried them smoothly off through the streets
of London, moving at high speed and breaking all the traffic
laws there were with cheerful abandon. Traffic reappeared
the moment they left the alley behind, and they were soon
surrounded by cars and trucks and buses. The chauffeur
treated them all with equal contempt, aiming his car at on-
coming vehicles like a weapon. He never needed to use his
horn to intimidate other drivers. Other vehicles seemed to
take one look at the limousine and decide it was in everyone's best interests to get the hell out of its way.

"Don't worry," Chang said cheerfully. "No-one's going to
stop us. The Crowley Project has connections, in high and
low places. It's like having CD plates, only better. We don't
just have diplomatic immunity; we have Project immunity!
From everything!"

"You wish," said Latimer, not looking around.

JC looked out the window, taking in the bright lights and
tall buildings, and people everywhere. It was hard for him to
see the real world as real any longer, not when he knew what
was really at large in it. He was surprised to suddenly notice
it was night. Already? When did it get to be night? Where did
the day go? Had he been so busy, so menaced, he simply
hadn't noticed the time? He watched crowds of people surging up and down the packed pavements, all intent on squeez-
ing every last bit of enjoyment out of the city's night-life.
Part of him wanted to stop the car and get out, plunge into the
crowds and disappear into them. Lose himself in the mass of
humanity, so he could be forgotten, and safe. Except, of
course, he would never be safe or forgotten as long as the
agents of the Flesh Undying were still out there. With his
name on their list of things to do.

His lacerated arms and shoulders ached fiercely from the
damage the Hound had inflicted. Nothing serious, but enough
for every cut and gouge to shout at him each time he moved.
Now he couldn't distract himself with conspiracy theories

and having to be strong for everyone else. He could feel the weight of the brass knuckles in his jacket pocket, the ones he used to put a hurt on the Hound. He still couldn't believe he'd gone head to head with a living god. He normally had more sense . . . but that was what the Boss did best. Make you more afraid of failing her than what you were facing. He made a mental note to get the brass knuckles recharged. The blessings and curses were gone; all used up getting past the Hound's supernatural defences. He felt suddenly defenceless in the face of an angry and hostile world. He needed an edge. He leaned over to address Natasha Chang.

"We need to make a stop along the way."

"No we don't," Chang said briskly. "My instructions are to deliver you straight to Project Headquarters."

"We need to make a stop," said JC. "It's important."

"Why?" said Chang, immediately suspicious. "What for?"

"I need to pick up a few things," said JC. "From another of my secret bolt-holes."

"Another one?" said Melody, her ears pricking up. "How many have you got?"

"As many as I need," said JC.

"Don't try to be mysterious and enigmatic," said Latimer. "You don't have the experience. I know all of your hiding places, Mr. Chance. I make it a point to know everything that matters about everyone who works for me."

"If that was true," said Melody, "Allbright wouldn't be sitting at your desk as the new Boss, and you wouldn't be on the run with us."

"Saucer of cream for little miss cat," said Chang, grinning.

"You don't know about this particular bolt-hole, Boss," said JC. "Because if you did, and you knew what I keep there, you'd have shut it down ages ago. And if you don't know, I can be pretty sure no-one else does."

He gave the chauffeur directions, and the man looked into the rear-view mirror at Chang for confirmation. She nodded curtly, and the chauffeur swung the car around.

"You're right," said Latimer. "I didn't recognise those directions. What have you been up to, Mr. Chance?"

"I have always believed in putting a little something aside for a rainy day," said JC. "Dangerous, deadly, and downright spiteful somethings. On the grounds that if someone should bring my world crashing down around me, I wanted to be in a position where I could express my extreme displeasure in a truly appalling and destructive way. Which is why you only know about the hiding places I wanted you to know about, Boss. Enough that you'd feel secure and stop looking."

"I like the way you think," said Chang. "You're going to feel really at home at the Crowley Project."

"Now you're just being nasty," said JC.

ıııııııııııııııııııııı

They ended up in a quiet grimy back street, where old buildings slumped and huddled together as though for comfort, holding out stubbornly against the tide of progress. Dirty, soot-stained walls, whitewashed windows, and doors with no numbers on them. And yet again, nobody out and about. At the end of the street, a series of old railway tunnels had been bricked up and made over into lock-ups and garages. The limousine slowed to a halt before the door JC indicated, and everyone got out. The night air had a bitter chill to it, and the sounds of the city seemed far away.

"These lock-ups have been let and sub-let so many times, no-one really knows who owns what or what's inside them," said JC.

"I remember," said Latimer. "Back during the London bombings in the seventies, the police set out to identify all garage owners, so they could check whether places like this were being used for storage by terrorists; but they couldn't even find the keys to half of them."

"Precisely," said JC. "This whole area is distinctly dodgy, every deal border-line illegal, so everyone around here can be relied on to keep their mouths shut."

The sleek white limousine looked very out of place in the grim surroundings. The chauffer, who'd already refused to leave the car, made a point of hitting the central locking. Chang gave JC a hard look.

"Is this stop really necessary? I don't want to come back and find my car stripped and the chauffeur up on bricks."

"Relax," said JC. "No-one will bother us. Everyone minds their own business, for fear of being barred. It's all part of London's long tradition of subterranean economies, where shady entrepreneurs buy and sell the things people aren't supposed to want but do anyway."

"Illegal things?" said Latimer.

"Illegal, immoral, and occasionally unnatural," said JC.

"I feel right at home," said Chang. "I'm not really bothered about the car. It's armed and armoured, and can look after itself. And the chauffeur's just a preprogrammed homunculus, so . . ."

"I am not!" said the chauffeur.

"It's sweet when they think that," said Chang.

"Memories," Happy said dreamily, peering about with heavy-lidded eyes. "Layer upon layer of memories, imprinted on the surroundings, going back generations. All human life is here; and quite a bit of death, too. We're all standing in blood."

"Maybe you should stay in the car, sweetie," said Melody.

"There's blood in the car, too," said Happy.

"No there isn't!" said Chang. "I had the upholstery dry-cleaned."

"Moving on," said JC, determinedly.

He hauled out a heavy key-ring and unlocked his garage. The door looked like all the others, but he opened it with a key made from human bone.

"It's a skeleton key," he said calmly.

"Whose skeleton?" said Latimer.

"No-one you'd know," said JC.

He pushed the door all the way open and ushered them inside. The garage interior turned out to be a stone cavern, with curving walls and ceiling, lit by buzzing, overhead fluorescents. Boxes and crates were piled up everywhere, with only stencilled numbers on the sides to identify their contents. Along with any number of glass display cases, full of interesting items and curios. JC gestured grandly.

"Welcome to my lair. Weapons, devices, and a whole bunch of really weird stuff I've collected down the years."

Melody grinned broadly, spoilt for where to look first. "Your very own Aladdin's Cave! Why did you never mention this before?"

"Because he knew I wouldn't approve!" said Latimer, openly outraged at the size of the collection. "You were supposed to hand over everything of interest you encountered or acquired in the field!"

"Man's entitled to a few souvenirs," said JC. "You kept yours in your office; I'm just a little more private."

"Boys and their toys," said Chang.

Melody helped Happy sit down on a nearby crate, then went scurrying up and down the narrow aisles, looking at everything. JC helped Happy stand up, moved him to a somewhat less dangerous crate, and sat him down again. Happy nodded understandingly. JC made sure he was comfortable, then turned back to Chang and Latimer.

"Please be careful what you touch," he said. "And don't try to open anything without asking me first. Everything here is protected, on all kinds of levels."

He used his skeleton key to open a few of the display cases, to show off their contents. Starting with the Hand of Glory from the Brighton convention.

"How did that get here so quickly?" said Latimer. "You haven't had time to get here and back again."

"I know some useful short cuts," said JC.

"You mean Kim does," said Melody.

"There are some advantages to having a ghost as your girl-friend," said JC.

"You do know that particular Hand of Glory was made from a Drood's hand?" said Latimer.

JC looked at the Hand with new interest before placing it carefully back in its case again.

"Weaponised Drood body parts," he said. "It doesn't bear thinking about. I didn't know they could be hurt like that."

"They like to keep such information quiet," said Latimer.

"But you know," said Chang.

"Of course," said Latimer.

"Perhaps I should send the Hand back to them," said JC. "I could use being owed a favour by the high-and-mighty Drood family. You know, I once had a Hand of Glory made from a monkey's paw. Now that was seriously powerful."

"And utterly forbidden!" said Chang. "Banned by every civilised country and a few that don't even come close! I've always wanted one . . ."

"Gone now," said JC. "I used it up taking down a train full of demons in the London Underground."

"And just like that, the world feels so much safer," said Melody.

JC carefully opened one of the crates. Its contents turned out to be row upon row of glass phials, full of various enigmatic liquids, resting carefully side by side in protective packaging. JC took out one phial and held it up to the light. The colourless liquid glowed serenely.

"The Universal Nostrum," JC said reverently. "The ultimate healing draught. No-one ever talks about what goes into it because if people knew, you couldn't get anyone to drink it. Very good at repairing physical damage."

He unwound the copper wire holding the cork in place, knocked back the liquid, and pulled a face at the taste. He shuddered briefly, then smiled slowly as all the wounds he'd taken from the Hound healed in a moment. He stretched happily and tossed the empty phial back into the crate. He hadn't realised how tired he'd been until he didn't have to fight the pain off any longer. He selected another phial and went over to Happy. Melody quickly came back to join them.

"I don't know if this will help," said JC. "But it's got to be worth a try."

"Of course," said Happy. "You know me; I'll try anything once. And twice if it's free."

His voice was firm, but Melody still had to hold his hand steady so he could drink the stuff. Happy handed the empty phial back to JC and nodded politely.

"Oh yes," he said. "That feels much better."

He wasn't fooling anyone; but they all pretended to believe him. JC put the empty phial back in the crate and closed it again. He didn't want Happy to see how angry he was.

He'd really hoped the Nostrum would work. He'd been counting on it. He was tired of seeing Happy look so bad, tired of having to make allowances for him. He considered leaving Happy behind or sending him home; if only so he wouldn't have to worry about the telepath when he had so many other more important things on his mind. But he couldn't do that. Happy wouldn't be safe anywhere now, away from the group. Any number of interested parties would risk anything to grab him, so they could use him to put pressure on JC and Latimer. And if Happy went, Melody would insist on going with him; and there went the team. Besides . . . JC just knew that at some point he was going to need Happy. To do the things only he could do.

"This is all very interesting," said Latimer, "not to mention incriminating; but what exactly are we doing here?"

"I came here looking for something to give me an advantage," said JC.

He opened another crate with a handy crow-bar, revealing dozens of assorted guns and boxes of ammunition.

"You didn't pick those up on any Ghost Finders case," said Chang, looking the weapons over with an expert eye.

"I wasn't always a Ghost Finder," said JC. He smiled at Melody. "Help yourself."

She was already rummaging through the contents, grinning broadly. "You know how to show a girl a good time, JC!"

He left her to it and used his skeleton key to open a small, black-lacquered box. Inside was another box, made from intricately carved rosewood, that he had to open with a combination code and a muttered password from a language no-one spoke any more. He looked at the contents for a long moment.

"This . . . is what I came here for," he said slowly. "Something really special. You've heard about genetic engineering—where they make goldfish that glow, or a mouse with a human ear on its back. This is the supernatural community's equivalent."

Latimer and Chang leaned in close for a better look. Inside the box, nestled in tissue paper, was a small furry object not much bigger than a man's thumb. They both looked at JC.

"It's a rabbit's foot," said JC. "One that has been crossed with lucky heather and a four-leafed clover. And a few other things, best not described out loud. It might not look like much; but supposedly in a time of troubles, this can change the odds completely in its owner's favour. Just the once. I've never had a good enough reason to use it, until now."

"That's it?" said Chang. "That is what we came all this way for? I thought you wanted a weapon!"

"I wanted something to make me feel safer," said JC. "And this fits the bill nicely."

"How can you be sure it does what it says on the tin?" said Latimer.

"I can't," said JC. "Another reason I haven't relied on it before."

He lifted the rabbit's foot out of its box, hefted it a few times, then tucked it away in an inside pocket.

"Can we go now?" said Latimer.

"Don't you want to help yourself to anything, Boss?" said JC.

"There's nothing here I need," said Latimer. "I'm dangerous enough on my own."

"Never doubted it for a moment," said JC.

"A rabbit's foot," said Chang, shaking her head. "Can't say I ever believed in them. I mean, didn't do the rabbit any good, did it?"

"I don't have anything capable of destroying the Flesh Undying," JC said patiently. "I'm not sure anyone has. So when I do eventually have to go up against it, I want something capable of turning the odds in my favour at just the right moment. Never under-estimate the importance of a lucky break."

"Let's go," said Chang. "Before you decide you need to study your horoscope."

Melody came over to join them. She now had two different handguns holstered on her hips and was stuffing handfuls of grenades, incendiaries, and other useful items into her pockets.

"Guns? Against a living mountain," said Latimer.

"It's a start," said Melody. "And we might need them to use against someone else." She glared pointedly at Chang.

"We have bigger, better weapons at the Project Armoury," said Chang.

"Of course you do," said Latimer. "And I'm sure you'll be happy to share your toys with us, at some point. I have always depended on the kindness of strangers."

"No you bloody haven't," said JC.

"True," said Latimer. "But I am very interested in seeing the Project's Armoury. While they've got a reason to open it to us."

"Good point," said JC.

Chang smiled haughtily. "You wouldn't believe what we've got . . ."

"Yes I would," said Latimer. "I saw last month's inventory."

"You only think you did," said Chang. "We leaked you a fake inventory deliberately, as disinformation."

"You only thought it was a fake," said Latimer. "One of my people inside your organisation substituted the real thing, at the last moment."

"Well," said Chang. "You would think that, wouldn't you?"

"Spy games," said Happy. "Head . . . hurting . . ."

And then they all looked around sharply as they realised Kim had joined them at some point and was standing before one particular crate, studying it thoughtfully.

"How long has she been here, watching us?" demanded Chang.

"Why?" said JC. "What have you been doing that you didn't want anyone to see?"

Kim ignored them, staring at the crate in front of her. "JC . . . Why is this calling to me? Why do I feel it's important?"

JC moved over to join her. "I was wondering when you'd turn up again."

"I had business to attend to," said Kim. "The living can't walk the low road without consequences. But that's all taken care of now."

Melody looked at Happy. "Don't ask."

"Wasn't planning to," said Happy.

"How did you know to find me here?" said JC.

"I always know where you are," said Kim. "All places are the same to the dead."

"What does that even mean?" said Melody.

"You're better off not knowing," said Kim. "Oh, hello, Happy! Your aura's looking a lot better."

"Thank you," said Happy. "I think."

Kim looked to JC, then back at the crate.

"Inside that crate is something I acquired from the Night-side," JC said quietly, giving all his attention to Kim. "A place where you can, after all, find absolutely anything. And somebody ready to sell it to you for an exorbitant price."

"JC," said Kim. "What have you done? What have you bought?"

JC opened the crate, and brought out a dusty old bottle half-full of a murky liquid that seemed to stir and heave with a life all its own.

"Supposedly," he said carefully, "this very special potion makes it possible for a living man to have sex with a ghost. I've been saving it for a special occasion."

Kim looked at him for the first time, her face radiant. "Oh my love . . . How much did this cost you?"

"Cheap at half the price," said JC.

Kim raised a hand and caressed the air as close to his cheek as she dared to get. She couldn't risk her hand passing through his face, that would spoil the illusion.

"Later," said Kim.

In the background, Happy started singing. "Where do I begin, to tell the story . . ."

"Hush, dear," said Melody.

JC put the bottle back in its crate and turned to look thoughtfully at Natasha Chang. "All right, put it back."

"What?" said Chang, innocently.

"Put back what you took," said JC.

"Don't know what you're talking about," said Chang.

She broke off as Melody stepped forward and stuck the barrel of a Smith & Wesson .45 in Chang's left ear.

"If we can't trust you," said Latimer, "you're no use to us. And this alliance is over. Feel free to explain that to your superiors."

"Oh, all right!" said Chang, pouting. "I just wanted a souvenir. Or two."

She emptied out her pockets, and piled up a series of small but interesting pieces on top of a nearby crate. JC looked her over carefully, and so did Kim. Chang sighed heavily and produced two more objects.

"There!" she said loudly. "That's it! Satisfied now?"

JC nodded to Melody, who lowered her gun and holstered it again. Chang glared at her.

"I won't forget this!"

"Neither will I," Melody said cheerfully. "Most fun I've had all day."

Latimer shook her head. "Even in the face of the coming end of the world, I still can't get you kids to play nicely together."

:::::::::::::::::::::::::::::

They left the garage, and JC locked it up carefully. There was still no-one around. Somewhere along the way, Kim disappeared. JC didn't say anything, so everyone else took their cue from him. Apart from Chang, of course.

"What is the matter with her? Why does she have to keep vanishing on us?"

"Maybe it's the company," said Melody.

"I think she gets car-sick," said JC.

They all piled back into the limousine, and the chauffeur drove off at speed, racing through the London streets with even more disregard for the rules of the road than before, as though determined to make up for lost time. Even if he had to drive right over the cars in front of him. Melody produced a flick-knife and carved her initials and Happy's, surrounded by a heart, into the expensive leather upholstery. Chang pretended not to notice. Happy looked out the side window, but JC couldn't tell what he was looking at. Or even if he was looking at something in this world. More and more it seemed to JC that, between his lucid patches, Happy was becoming increasingly distant. JC looked to Latimer, but she was lost in her own thoughts again.

The ride went on for some time, with no-one saying anything to anyone. Eventually, JC realised the car was driving through a far more up-market area. Expensive cars moved elegantly around the limousine, like so many technicolor fish in a murky ocean. Men and women on the street wore the latest fashions, with style and elegance and cold superiority. The limousine finally slowed to a halt outside a blandly anonymous office building, with a small brass name-plate: *Baphomet House*.

"Welcome to the Headquarters of the Crowley Project!" Chang said grandly. "World domination a speciality!"

"Is it too late to inquire about safe words?" said JC.

Catherine Latimer surprised him then with a sharp bark of laughter.

"This can only go well," said Happy.

They all got out of the limousine and gathered together to carefully consider Baphomet House. It seemed pleasant enough, just another place where business was done. Nothing about its benign facade and warmly lit windows to draw the attention. Chang smiled at how unimpressed they all were.

"We can't all live at the back of a Palace."

Happy scowled at the building and shook his head slowly. "I don't like the feel of this place. It's beyond Sick Building Syndrome, more like Really Sick, Border-line Psychotic and Heading for Feral Syndrome. Sorry, JC; I'm going to have to shut down. In my current state, that place would eat me alive."

Melody glared at Chang. "No-one better try anything in there. I have guns. And other things."

"So do I!" Chang said cheerfully. "Girls together!"

"You know," said Melody. "You're even creepier when you're trying to be chummy."

"It's a gift," said Chang. "Now, follow me everybody. Stick close, smile at everyone, while feeling perfectly free to kick the crap out of anybody who gives you a hard time. We all do, here. Helps enforce discipline and contributes to better working conditions."

"Who knew the Project would have so much in common with the Institute?" JC murmured to Latimer.

"Shut up," said Latimer.

Natasha Chang led the way into the building's lobby. Which turned out to be a wide-open space, expensive and luxurious in an only slightly intimidating way. People came and went, looking perfectly ordinary and not at all evil. Most were smiling. Nothing to suggest this was the entrance to the headquarters of one of the most openly evil organisations in the world. Chang seemed even more amused by the Ghost Finders' reactions.

"What did you expect? Armoured storm-troopers, and a big sign saying *This way to the Torture Chambers*?"

"Well, yes," said JC. "I think I'm actually just a bit disappointed. It seems like no-one on the dark side can be bothered to put on a show any more. Whatever happened to scientific bases hidden inside hollowed-out volcanoes?"

"Not cost-effective," said Chang. "The most efficient plan is a business plan. It's all computers and spreadsheets, these days. Which is why I prefer to spend most of my time out in the field. Far more opportunities to do evil, out in the field."

She led them across the lobby to the high-tech reception desk, where the smartly dressed and sweetly smiling receptionist insisted Chang sign in; and write down all the names of the guests she was vouching for. Chang explained that they were expected, and the receptionist explained that rules were rules. Chang gave the receptionist her best put-upon sigh, and started writing. Melody sniffed loudly.

"I don't think I like people here knowing my real name. I don't want anyone knowing I entered a place like this of my own free will."

"Oh please," said Chang, not looking up from what she was doing. "It would only enhance your reputation."

When Chang finally finished, the receptionist smiled brightly at them all, worked briefly at her computer, then waved them through the electronic gates beside her desk. Chang strode through with her nose in the air, and the others hurried after her.

"That's it?" said JC. "No name tags, no security pat downs? Not even a metal detector?"

"Please," said Chang. "Remember where you are. We were all very thoroughly scanned by a dozen surveillance systems the moment we walked through the door."

"Then what was all that signing-in nonsense?" said Melody.

"Rules are rules," said Latimer. "Evil organisations just love rules and regulations."

JC thought of a great many things he could say concerning the Carnacki Institute, but wisely chose not to.

"And no-one's going to give a damn about all the guns and big-bang things I'm carrying?" said Melody.

"Guns are the least dangerous things you'll encounter in this building," said Chang. "Everyone here goes armed. It's expected."

She led them to the rear of the lobby, where they took the express elevator to the top floor. It played music at them all the way up—orchestral covers of Nirvana's greatest hits. When the elevator doors finally opened, they couldn't get out fast enough. JC looked about him and felt an urgent need to hide behind something. He could feel the difference between this floor and the lobby. This was a place where things happened. Bad things. Chang waited patiently while they all had a good look around. Smart business-suited men and women hurried up and down the corridor, with get-ahead looks and purposeful strides. There was something in their cold, professional smiles and sidelong glances, openly competitive and always ready for an unexpected attack, that made JC think of predators forced through circumstances to share the same watering hole. He spotted a small group standing around a water-cooler, talking animatedly. Their faces seemed pleasant enough, but there was nothing pleasant about their laughter. It sounded like they were enjoying, and even savouring, the downfall of a friend.

JC wondered if he was only seeing what he expected to see, but he didn't think so. People here weren't hiding who and what they were; they had no need to, in Baphomet

House. He thought about that as Chang led the way through a series of pleasantly appointed corridors, past open-plan offices and doors left open to show people hard at work. None of whom looked up to watch the group pass. They were all far too busy.

"Everyone's so . . . occupied," Melody said finally.

"I should hope so," said Chang. "I keep telling you: this isn't just an evil organisation, it's a business. Businesses have to be efficient. Hard work and over-achievement are the bedrock of our success."

"If she launches into a motivational speech, or the company song, I will shoot her," said Melody.

"Go ahead," said Latimer.

"You actually see yourselves as evil?" JC said to Chang.

"Oh yes!" said Chang. "It's very liberating. You should try it."

"Words fail me," said Melody.

"If only," said Chang.

JC also couldn't help noticing that everywhere they went, people saw Chang coming and hurried to get out of her way. Happy moved in beside JC, rubbing distractedly at his forehead.

"They've got some major telepathic defences in place here. I can barely hear myself think."

"Is that going to be a problem?" said JC.

"Actually, it's a relief," said Happy.

He was standing straighter and speaking more clearly. Melody stuck close beside him, just in case, and scowled at anyone who even looked like getting too close. The Project people seemed to accept that as normal. Some stared openly at the Ghost Finders, with a certain number of double-takes as they recognised Catherine Latimer. Who just strode along, looking neither to the left nor to the right, while giving every appearance of being entirely unimpressed by everything around her. JC kept looking for security guards, or weapon emplacements hidden in the walls, and was worried he couldn't see any.

"Will you please unclench?" said Chang. "Trust me; no-one here will bother you."

"Because we're guests?" said JC.

"Because it has already been decided we can use you," said Chang. "If you hadn't already been designated as potential allies, you would have been knocked over the head and skinned alive by now. And then made over into toilet-seat covers."

"Lovely image," said JC.

"I thought so," said Chang.

"Who decided this?" said Melody.

"Our Boss," said Chang. "The current Head of the Crowley Project, the one and only because the world isn't ready for two of them: Vivienne MacAbre."

JC carried on looking around him. He couldn't help feeling it was all very impersonal. There was no sense of character anywhere. It was all steel and glass and plastic, with purely functional furnishings, and not even an occasional piece of art on the walls. Chang noticed him noticing this and was quietly amused.

"What were you expecting? Signs saying *You don't have to be evil, wicked, and morally corrupt to work here, but it helps*?"

"Something like that," said JC.

"This is a place where people come to work," said Chang.

They continued on their way. JC quietly observed security cameras everywhere, swivelling silently back and forth to cover everyone and everything. And somehow he just knew they weren't only there to guard against enemies; the Project was an organisation that wanted to know what its own people were doing, all the time.

"Really don't like this place," said Melody. "Or the people. Everything's . . . off, here. It feels like I've wandered into the Mirror Universe from *Star Trek*. Where everyone was an evil version of themselves."

"You don't need to be a telepath to feel the tension on the air," said Happy. "Or to know that competition in this building operates on a Darwinian level. Survival of the fittest and trample on the weak."

"And that's the way we like it," said Chang. "Deliver the goods, or get out of the way of someone who can."

"Survival only for the strong?" said JC.

"And the sneaky," said Chang.

||||||||||||||||||||||||

They ended up in the Head of the Crowley Project's waiting room; but they didn't have to wait. Even though there was a charming, brightly smiling secretary sitting on guard at her desk, who reminded JC very much of Heather. (Blonde, personable, neatly dressed, with a definite air of menace about her.) Chang just breezed right past the secretary, heading straight for the Head's office. The secretary started to rise out of her chair, only to subside again as Chang gave her a hard look.

Chang raised a hand to knock on the door but it swung open on its own before she could even make contact. JC smiled briefly. He appreciated the touch of drama. Of course the Head knew they were coming; that was what the security cameras were for. But it also meant she'd had all this time to work out how best to deal with her guests. JC didn't have a plan; he just hoped Latimer did. He'd never been big on plans, always preferring to wing it when out in the field and trust to his fight-or-flight instincts to get him out of trouble, as necessary.

Chang led the way in. JC stuck close behind her, ready to use her body as a human shield if necessary. The office looked like all the other work-places; except a little more bleak and spartan. No windows, subdued lighting, no obvious luxuries or comforts. No souvenirs, no shelves full of books or files . . . but alone in one corner stood an elegant scarecrow, dressed in an immaculate morning suit, complete with a top hat set at a rakish angle. A monocle had been carefully glued into place over a stitched eye on the cloth face. It should have looked charming; but it didn't. There was a cold, sinister feel to the scarecrow, and the monocle made it feel like it was always watching. JC recognised the scarecrow as a traditional voodoo fetish, Baron Samedi, Lord of Cemeteries. Not a sane or healthy thing to have standing around in a business office. Chang leaned in close beside JC, to murmur in his ear.

"That is our Head's personal bodyguard. Don't upset it, or you're on your own."

Sitting behind a perfectly bare desk was the current Head of the Crowley Project, Vivienne MacAbre. JC had heard of her but never expected to encounter her in person. Except perhaps over the barrel of a gun. Of course, the Carnacki Institute didn't normally assassinate Crowley Project Heads. They didn't need to. Project people usually took care of that for themselves. Beyond a certain point, the only way to rise further in the organisation was to forcibly retire the person in front of you. Each Head was assassinated by their replacement. It was how they proved they were worthy of the position.

Chang struck a careless pose in front of the desk and threw a mocking salute to the woman sitting behind it. "Greetings, Glorious Leader! May I present refugees from the new order at the Carnacki Institute. Refugees, this is Vivienne MacAbre. Abandon all hope."

MacAbre was tall and more than healthily slender, a woman of a certain age with a pleasant enough face, cool eyes, and a calm, business-like smile. Her long hair was jet-black, and might or might not have been dyed. She wore a dark blue business suit over a starched white blouse. Her only concession to glamour was a pair of jade ear-rings, and heavy silver rings on her fingers.

MacAbre made no move to get up to greet her guests, just waved for them to sit down on the visitors' chairs set out before her. Exactly the right number, of course. Latimer sat down as though she were doing MacAbre a favour; and the others followed her example. The chairs were far more comfortable than the visitors' chairs in Latimer's office. JC and Melody looked to their Boss to begin the conversation. Happy was already off in his own world again. Chang sat back and looked on expectantly, happily anticipating fireworks. MacAbre and Latimer looked steadily at each other for a long moment, then nodded coolly to each other.

"Vivienne MacAbre . . ." said Latimer. "What kind of a name is that?"

MacAbre took her time replying, and when she did, it was in a low, thrilling voice that made all the hackles stand up on the back of JC's neck. It was like being suddenly addressed by a black widow spider.

"To know the true name of a person," said MacAbre, "is to have power over them. Or at the very least, to have preconceptions about them. I chose this name to make an impression."

"And not because you're ashamed of your real name?" said Latimer.

"I didn't ask to be burdened with it," said MacAbre. "With the weight it carries, in certain circles."

"You always did disappoint me, Grand-daughter," said Latimer.

"Stick to what you're good at, that's what I always say," said MacAbre.

JC and Melody both sat bolt upright on their chairs, looking from Latimer to MacAbre and back again. Chang grinned broadly.

"Grand-daughter?" said JC. "Damn, Boss, are you related to everybody?"

"Be still, Mr. Chance," said MacAbre. "Pay attention to your betters."

"You find some, I'll listen to them," said JC.

"Hush," said Latimer. "Grown-ups talking." She hadn't looked away from MacAbre for a moment. "You do know what's happened at the Institute? Not just that I'm no longer in charge, but . . ."

"Of course I know," said MacAbre. "We've been observing the cabal's progress inside the Institute for some time. I did think it might be possible for us to do business with them, on certain matters of mutual interest; but when I reached out to them, they just looked down their noses at me as unworthy of their attention. No-one does that to the Crowley Project and gets away with it."

"So we both disapprove of the cabal," said Latimer. "And their plan to try to take control of the Flesh Undying."

"Damned fools," MacAbre said dispassionately. "They must have known we could never accept that. It would upset the balance of power."

"Do you believe they can control the Flesh Undying?" said Latimer.

"Of course not," said MacAbre. "It's beyond them. My scientists are still studying the data we acquired at Brighton. And the only ones who aren't wetting themselves are the ones with limited imaginations. The Flesh Undying is, by its very nature, a threat to us all, to the continued existence of this world. It must be stopped. Destroyed."

"If possible," said Latimer.

MacAbre smiled briefly. "We'll find a way. We know all there is to know about destruction."

"You say that like it's a good thing," said Latimer.

"The point is," said MacAbre, not rising to the bait, "that no-one here wants an open war between the Project and the Institute. If only because it's better to work with the she-devil you know . . ."

JC raised his hand, like a child at school. "Can I ask a question?"

"Depends," said Latimer. "Is it a good question?"

"I don't know about good," said JC. "But it's certainly relevant."

"Then go ahead," said Latimer. "But don't you dare show me up in front of the enemy."

JC looked steadily at MacAbre. "I was just wondering. Since you know so much about the cabal . . . Could they be just another face for the hidden agents of the Flesh Undying?"

"All right," said Latimer. "That is a good question." She looked steadily at MacAbre. "I'd be interested to hear your answer. If you have one."

"Yes; and no," said MacAbre. "The cabal started out on its own, with its own agenda, but there are definite indications it has since been infiltrated and steered in directions that would best serve the Flesh Undying. It's our understanding that some of the cabal know this; some suspect; and most just follow orders like the good little drones they are. Some serve the Flesh Undying, some still believe they can control it. Which must make for very complicated conversations, inside the cabal. However . . . once we destroy the Flesh Undying, that will undermine the cabal's power base, and it should turn upon itself and fall apart. Leaving the Institute in chaos. Allowing you to return to save the day, Grandmother; and put the Carnacki Institute back together again."

"Good answer . . ." said JC. "Though I'm not sure whether I feel better for knowing all that or not."

"If you're feeling better, you didn't understand the answer," said Latimer.

MacAbre brought her hands together and leaned forward across the desk. "We have to move fast, while the new regime is still finding its feet. We have the advantage, in that we know exactly where the Flesh Undying is, and they don't. So we have to strike first, before they can put something in place to stop us."

"Are you saying you're ready to try to destroy it?" said Latimer.

"Definitely ready to try," said MacAbre. "Rather than wait and risk its falling into enemy hands."

Latimer shook her head. "We need more information. About what the Flesh Undying actually is. Its physical nature, its weaknesses and vulnerabilities."

"Can I just point out," said Melody, "that our last attempt to poke it with sticks almost got us killed? And did get a whole bunch of innocent bystanders killed?"

"I haven't forgotten," said Latimer.

"My scientists have come up with a new plan," said MacAbre. "Which they assure me presents far fewer dangers."

"Liking the sound of it already," said Melody.

"It involves you and your team taking a close-up look at the Flesh Undying, in person."

"Gosh, is that the time?" said Melody. "I really must be going."

"Sit down!" said Latimer.

"You're ready to go along with this?" said Melody, reluctantly subsiding again.

"I'm . . . considering it," said Latimer.

JC fixed MacAbre with a thoughtful stare. "And we're supposed to just . . . place ourselves in your hands? Trust you?"

"You came here looking for the Project's assistance, didn't you?" said MacAbre.

"Yes. We did," said Latimer. "An indication of how desperate we are. What, exactly, do you have in mind?"

"We're ready to provide you with transport to a ship of ours out in the Atlantic," said MacAbre. "Its cover is a scientific research vessel, but actually it's maintaining a position directly over the Flesh Undying. The scientists on board work exclusively for us. They ran the drone submersible that took a look at the Flesh Undying."

"The one that was destroyed because it got too close?" said Latimer.

"Hold it," said Melody. "Are we really assuming the Flesh Undying hasn't made the connection, between the drone and the ship above it?"

"I think we can," said MacAbre, "On the grounds that if it did know, it would have destroyed the ship by now."

"What exactly are we supposed to do once we're on board this ship?" said Latimer.

"The scientists assure me they've come up with a whole new way to approach the Flesh Undying," MacAbre said carefully. "One it shouldn't be able to detect. Because you have the greatest experience with, and knowledge of, the Flesh Undying . . . the plan is that you will go down in a new submersible and make the approach yourselves. Study it up close and deliver us the information we need to destroy this monster."

"So we take all the risks," said JC. "And if we succeed, you take all the credit."

"Exactly," said MacAbre. "A plan with no drawbacks."

JC looked at Latimer. "She's your grand-daughter, all right."

"Do you find this proposal acceptable?" MacAbre said to Latimer, ignoring JC.

"In principle," said Latimer. "But none of us are going anywhere until I've had a chance to pick up a few useful items for the journey." She smiled briefly at JC. "You started me thinking. I want to be in a position to defend myself if it all starts going horribly wrong."

"You have something in mind that could do that?" said Melody.

"Possibly," said Latimer. "I need to do some research first."

"I feel I should make it clear that Natasha Chang will continue to accompany you as my liaison," said MacAbre.

"To keep an eye on us," said JC.

"Exactly," said MacAbre.

"I thought we might stop off at the Project Armoury," Chang said brightly. "Pick up a few useful weapons of mass destruction . . ."

"No," said MacAbre.

"Why not?" said Chang.

"Because there are limits to the secrets I'm prepared to share with the Carnacki Institute," said MacAbre.

"I'm not with them any more," said Latimer.

"But you might be again, one day," said MacAbre. "Or at the very least, working with them in some capacity. A lifetime's dedication and service doesn't end with one setback. Our alliance is a strictly temporary thing—until the threat of the Flesh Undying is over."

"So we don't get to visit the Armoury?" said Chang. She pouted prettily. "Damn. I was looking forward to some serious showing off."

MacAbre ignored her, fixing her attention on Latimer. "Where were you thinking of visiting first?"

"I thought I'd start with the Institute's Secret Libraries," said Latimer. "The cabal probably think they can keep me out, but they're wrong."

Natasha Chang clapped her hands together delightedly. "Oh, I've always wanted to visit the Secret Libraries!" And then she stopped, as she took in the expression on MacAbre's face. "What? What do you know that I don't?"

MacAbre looked steadily at Latimer. "You haven't heard."

"Heard what?" said Latimer. "We have been rather out of the loop just recently."

"And just a bit distracted," said JC.

"Yes," said MacAbre. "I heard about the Hound. A most impressive performance, Mr. Chance. It seems there really is more to you than meets the eye."

JC smiled, in spite of himself. Because Kim was concealed inside him and had been ever since they left the lockup. Because he didn't trust Natasha Chang, or the Project, or its Head. Learning to hide the glow that normally surrounded him when he was joined with Kim was one of the first tricks he'd taught himself. Just as Latimer had learned to hide the glow from her eyes.

"What about the Secret Libraries?" said Latimer. "What's happened to them?"

"They're gone," said MacAbre.

"The cabal destroyed them?" said Latimer.

"No," said MacAbre. "They're *gone*. You know the Project has agents inside the Institute, just as you have people working inside the Project . . ."

"We do?" said JC.

"Of course we do," said Latimer. "How else can we be sure of what's really going on?"

"One of my people fairly high up in the cabal has just informed me that its leaders are currently panicking because they've lost all access to the Secret Libraries," said MacAbre. "Getting their hands on the secret knowledge in those books was one of their top priorities, so they could use it to pay off old favours. But apparently none of the ways in work any longer. All entrance points have just . . . disappeared. Nothing left to show they were ever there. My psychics are saying they can't find the Libraries anywhere on this plane, or in any of the adjoining ones. Even the ghost guard Tommy Atkins has disappeared."

The Ghost Finders looked at each other, shocked and shaken. Latimer looked especially grim.

"The Libraries probably removed themselves," she said finally. "Rather than risk being misused by the cabal."

"They can do that?" said JC.

"Apparently," said Latimer.

"How is that even possible?" said Melody.

"The Secret Libraries were founded by the Travelling Doctor," said JC.

"Oh . . ." said Melody.

"Quite," said JC.

"I have to wonder . . ." said Latimer. "What other Institute resources are no longer available, because they don't approve of the new regime. I think I'd better go straight to my old office."

Chang clapped her hands together again. "Oooh! I've always wanted to go there!"

"We're supposed to take a Project agent right into the heart of the Carnacki Institute?" said Melody. "Oh, this can only go well . . ."

"What do you need from your office, Boss?" said JC.

"Hush," said Latimer. "Not in front of the allies."

MacAbre smiled. "The sooner you pick up what you need, the better. So, we will provide you with transportation. Thoroughly shielded, of course, so the Institute psychics won't be able to see you coming."

"Thanks for the offer," said Latimer, "but that won't be necessary. I know a short cut."

She rose unhurriedly from her chair and walked around MacAbre's desk to face the far wall. She produced a shapeless black blob from an inside pocket and rolled it around in her hands for a while, as though to wake it up. She slapped it against the wall, where it immediately flattened itself out to form a Door. JC realised his mouth was hanging open and shut it quickly. He'd never seen a portable Door in action before.

MacAbre was on her feet, glaring at the new Door and pointing a shaking finger at it.

"*A dimensional Door?* That is not supposed to be possible! Not inside Project Headquarters, and especially not inside my office! Security protocols are supposed to block all other-dimensional access!"

"This particular portable Door is just a bit special," said Latimer. "It was a present from the late Drood Armourer."

MacAbre shook her head speechlessly and sank back into her chair. With all the dignity she could muster.

"Oh," she said. "Him. Jack Drood really did get around, didn't he?"

JC fixed Latimer with an accusing gaze. "You've had an

in with the Droods all this time, and you never told us? Were you and he . . . ?"

"Certainly not," Latimer said firmly. "We were just good allies. And only occasionally enemies. That's Droods for you . . ." She looked steadily at JC. "It's always a good idea to have an ace up your sleeve . . . I liked knowing I could never be trapped anywhere, as long as I had my own secret exit."

"And you never told anyone," said Melody. "You didn't tell the Institute; even before this cabal stuff started."

"Always keep your closest eye on your friends," said Latimer. "You know where you are, with your enemies. My three predecessors as Head all died in their office, and none of them peacefully. From the first moment I accepted the position, I was determined not to follow in their footsteps."

"Even if that Door can take us straight to the Institute," said JC, "how are we going to get into your office? I mean; even apart from the standard shields and protections, won't the new Boss have people standing guard? Heavily armed standing guards? Hell, Allbright has probably had people tearing your office apart, looking for hidden treasures, ever since they heard about the Secret Libraries."

"I don't think so," said Latimer. "After I walked out of my office, certain prearranged protocols kicked into place. The moment Allbright leaves the office, the door will scramble its entrance codes and lock itself down. And given all the protections I've added, down the years, the cabal couldn't break that door down with a nuclear battering ram. No; my office is still mine. I have no intention of handing it over to any new Head I haven't personally approved."

"Did you leave something special there?" said Melody.

"It's more what I don't want the cabal to have access to," said Latimer. "But there are a few things lying around that might prove useful where we're going. Not everything in my office is what it appears to be."

"Department of no surprise at all," said Happy.

They all looked at him. He'd been quiet so long, they'd forgotten he was there.

"Welcome back, Mr. Palmer," said Latimer. "Are you ready to be a useful member of the team again?"

"Possibly," said Happy. "I'm still wondering how that Door is going to break through Buckingham-Palace-level security shields."

"It's a Drood Door," said JC.

"Ah," said Happy. "Sorry. I must have been away when that bombshell was dropped."

"There is one item in particular," said Latimer, "that I want to have with me if we're going face-to-face with the Flesh Undying."

"What might that be?" said MacAbre.

"Just a little something," said Latimer, "to end the world, if necessary."

SEVEN

WHO'S THAT KNOCKING AT MY DOOR?

JC followed Catherine Latimer through the new Door she'd made into what used to be her old office; and it didn't feel like going home at all. Everyone else hurried after him, almost treading on his heels. None of them wanted to be left behind, in the Headquarters of Evil Inc. Latimer waited till they were all safely gathered in, then turned and shut the Door firmly in the face of Vivienne MacAbre.

"Sorry, Grand-daughter. There are limits."

JC couldn't help but notice the obvious delight Natasha Chang took in the outrage on MacAbre's face before the Door closed on it. Perhaps because if there were useful secrets and special advantages to be found in the Boss's office, Chang wanted them all to herself. Latimer sank her hand into the Door, and ripped it right off the wall. It quickly shrank back into a shapeless black blob that barely filled her hand, and Latimer tucked it safely away in her jacket pocket. JC was quietly very impressed. No-one knows how the Droods do the things they do or make the things they make; and it isn't considered wise to ask. Because the answers would only upset you. Latimer looked carefully at the wall where the Door had been, then nodded briefly, satisfied.

"Just making sure we won't be followed. Drood biotech is supposed to be unbreakable, but . . ."

"Biotech?" said Melody. "That stuff is alive?"

"Never ask Droods personal questions," said Latimer. She looked steadily at Chang. "No doubt you'll make a full report on everything that happens here when you see MacAbre again. But I would strongly suggest you be . . . circumspect when it comes to Drood things."

"Of course," said Chang. "The Project doesn't want a war with that family. Not yet, anyway."

Rather than think about the implications of that, JC looked around the Boss's office. After so much had happened, he expected it to look somehow different; but nothing had changed. The same Hepplewhite desk and chair, the same books and files on the shelves, the same air of long-established authority. Latimer's old souvenirs were still set out on display, no doubt soon to be replaced by Allbright's. Assuming she had any. It took JC a moment to realise one particular item was missing.

"Boss?" he said. "What's happened to the Haunted Glove?"

"I found a use for it," said Latimer, in a tone that strongly discouraged further questions on the subject. "At least the new order hasn't got around to ransacking my things, just yet. All my records are still in place, undisturbed . . . I really should destroy them rather than risk such dangerous knowledge falling into the cabal's hands; but I don't think I will."

"Why not?" said Melody.

"Because I have every intention of making this my office again, someday," said Latimer.

"It would be a brave man who bet against you," JC said solemnly. And then he stopped and looked at her thoughtfully. "Were you joking, back in MacAbre's office? When you said you wanted to pick up something here that could destroy the world?"

"I am of course famous for my whimsical sense of humour," said Latimer.

"No you're bloody not," said Happy.

Latimer looked down her nose at him. "My, we are feeling brave today, aren't we, Mr. Palmer?"

"I blame the drugs," said Happy.

"You wouldn't actually destroy the entire world, would you?" said Melody.

"I might," said Latimer. "If it looked like the Flesh Undying was winning and was ready to destroy this world during its escape . . . I would destroy the world first. And take the creature down with us. I have always been a very sore loser."

She went walking around her office, picking things up and stuffing them into a large black Gladstone bag she retrieved from under her desk. As far as JC could tell, none of the pieces she chose were particularly important or powerful. If he hadn't known better, he would have said she was just taking things at random. And then he noticed Chang paying very close attention to everything Latimer did; and it occurred to him that quite possibly the Boss only wanted a few things and was hiding them among the others . . .

Happy looked dubiously at the battered Gladstone bag. "That is a seriously old piece of luggage, Boss. How old are you, really?"

"Never ask a lady her age," said Latimer. She looked quickly around to make sure she had everything she wanted, then closed the Gladstone bag with a decisive snap. "This was a present from my grandfather."

"Who?" said Chang, her ears pricking up immediately.

"Ask my grand-daughter," said Latimer. She put the bag on the desk, sank down into what used to be her chair, and seemed lost in thought.

JC waited for her to say something, and when it became clear that wasn't going to happen anytime soon, he moved slowly around the office, just looking at things. Remembering a time when he used to think this one of the scariest places in the world. When he would get chills and shakes just sitting in the waiting room, preparing to meet the Boss and face her disapproval. It had come as something of a shock to find out she was almost human, after all.

"Some of these pieces look pretty valuable, Boss," he said finally. "Are you sure you wouldn't like us all to grab a handful? Or even an armful? We could shift a lot of this, between us."

"No," said Latimer. "I'm only taking what matters. The

rest is just . . . stuff. And you can always get more stuff. I've never been the kind for sentimental attachments. Live long enough, and you realise it's memories that matter, not possessions. Put that down, Chang."

They all turned to look at Natasha Chang, who froze where she was, caught in the act of slipping something into her pocket. She quickly put it back.

"I was just looking! It's only a small carved stone head, with remarkably ugly features. What's so special about it?"

"It's not something you should be touching," said Latimer. "If you plan on surviving the next few moments. That is the Stone Head of Whitby. It corrupts souls."

Chang sniffed loudly. "Like I need the competition."

Latimer considered the Gladstone bag sitting patiently before her on the desk and nodded slowly. "That's it. I'm finished here."

But she didn't move from where she was. Just leaned back in her chair and looked around her office, her face unreadable.

"Good memories, Boss?" JC said tentatively. He wasn't comfortable with seeing her so human, so vulnerable.

"Good and bad," said Latimer. "All the years I sat behind this desk, trapped by responsibilities and obligations. You tell yourself you're doing a hard and difficult job because it matters. Because you're making a difference. But the world goes on and the problems never end and suddenly you look up . . . and find you're old. And not sure anything you've ever done has made a blind bit of difference."

"Things would have been a lot worse if you hadn't been here," said Melody.

"Perhaps," said Latimer. She didn't sound convinced.

"Everyone at the Crowley Project has their conscience removed when they join," Chang said breezily. "It makes life so much simpler."

"Simpler isn't always better," said Latimer.

"I will say this," said Chang. "You scared the Project more than anyone else ever has."

"Thank you," said Latimer.

Happy's head came up suddenly, and he looked quickly about him. "Pay attention, people! Someone knows we're here."

They all looked quickly round the office. The room seemed perfectly calm and quiet. Happy turned slowly to look at the closed door. His face was clear and his eyes were sharp; but he looked at the door as though the Devil himself was on the other side, looking back. Melody moved in close beside him, not saying anything, not wanting to distract him, just support him with her presence.

"Allbright must have installed some new security systems," said Latimer. "Good for her. First thing she's done that I approve of."

"Nice idea, maybe," said JC. "Really bad timing for us. Who's out there, Happy? Can you tell?"

Happy moved slowly forward and didn't stop until he was right in front of the door, so close his face was almost touching it. His gaze was fierce and intent, as though he could look through the solid material.

"They're standing right outside," he said quietly. "Listening to us. And smiling. Because they're planning on killing every single person in this room and enjoying it."

"Well that's just rude," said Chang. "What if I was willing to surrender?"

"Are you?" said Latimer.

"Of course not!" said Chang. "But that's not the point! The Institute are supposed to be the good guys. You're supposed to offer your enemies the chance to surrender and avoid bloodshed, not just wipe everyone out! Like the Project would . . ."

"Things have changed here," said Latimer.

JC moved forward, to stand behind Happy. "Who is it, Happy? Who's out there?"

The telepath frowned, concentrating. And then his face cleared suddenly, into a look of sheer astonishment. "Oh, JC, you're really not going to believe this . . ."

And that was when Kim stepped out of JC, revealing her presence. Everyone jumped, just a little.

"I knew it!" said Chang, stabbing an accusing finger at Kim and JC. "I knew you were hiding inside him all this time!"

"No you didn't," said Kim. She looked steadily at JC, holding his gaze with hers. "It's time for me to tell the truth, JC. About where I was and what I was doing, all the time I was away, working for the Boss."

JC looked at Happy, still staring in amazement at the door, then back at Kim.

"Now? Really?"

"Yes," said Kim. "You need to know this. You all do. When I occupied Patterson's body, outside Chimera House, I caught a brief glimpse of who had been in his head before me, working his body. Using it against us. Remember, JC, the voice said you'd know it if it said its name. That we all would."

"So who was it?" said JC.

"It was Heather," said Kim. "The Boss's personal secretary and last line of defence."

JC, Melody, and Happy all turned immediately to stare at Latimer, who didn't appear in the least surprised. Chang looked on, fascinated.

"That's why I had to stay away for so long," said Kim. "Keep separate from all of you, on the Boss's orders. So Heather wouldn't suspect anyone knew about her."

"Heather?" said Melody. "*The secretary?* That's like saying the butler did it . . ."

"She was always more than just a secretary," said Happy. And he went back to looking at the door.

"You knew," JC said to Latimer. "How long have you known?"

"I had my suspicions," Latimer said evenly. "Heather had access to everything because I gave it to her. And there were things she said . . . things she did, or didn't do . . . I've had a great many secretaries down the years; I can always tell when something's wrong. When Kim came to tell me what she'd discovered, I wasn't surprised. Just terribly disappointed. Just as I'd been disappointed in Patterson. I put years of my life into training those two, raising them up and giving them every advantage because it's a lonely job to do on your own. I really believed I could depend on them."

"When you put Kim to work," said JC, "you put her in danger."

"She volunteered!" said Latimer. "To protect you! And your team. I couldn't send any of my usual people after Heather; what with the Flesh Undying and the cabal, I didn't know whom I could trust. So I chose Kim. A spy who couldn't be detected because she wasn't really there."

"I haunted Heather," said Kim. "Followed her everywhere, unseen and unsuspected, learned all I could and finally reported back. But I still couldn't tell you anything, JC, in case you gave it away. You still thought of Heather as your friend. And you've always been far too honest and open for your own good."

"Goes with the job," said JC. He still felt hurt that she hadn't felt able to confide in him. Even though he knew she was right.

"And now Heather's here," said Kim. "Right outside that door. Come to murder us all in the hottest of hot blood."

"Hold it," said JC. "Hold everything. How does Heather know it's us in here? No-one saw us enter the office."

"She knows," said Happy.

"Allbright must have installed one hell of an alarm system," said Latimer. "And once the cabal knew we were here, Heather was given her orders. Kill us all while she had the chance. No survivors, no excuses. It's what I would have done."

"And I am here to tell you," said Happy, "that Heather is really looking forward to it. Like a predator with the scent of prey in her nostrils and a thirst for blood and suffering."

"Why is she mad at us?" said JC, just a bit plaintively. "The Boss, yes, I get that; but I always thought of Heather as . . . one of us."

"It seems our little Heather has developed a taste for the kill," said Happy. His mouth twisted. "You wouldn't believe what it's like inside her head right now. I could never see before; the Boss's shields kept me out. But now Heather wants me to see, wants me to know. She can feel my disgust. She thinks it's funny."

"Rotten cow," said Melody.

"Can you see Heather through the door?" said Latimer.

"Sort of," said Happy.

"What kind of weapons has she got?" said Latimer.

"The really bad kind," said Happy. His scowl deepened, as though he wanted to look away but wouldn't let himself. "They aren't . . . ordinary weapons. Unnatural things, horribly powerful. Hurts my head just to look at them. I can't believe the cabal gave them to her . . . They must really want us dead. Hold it . . . I'm getting something else. Oh shit . . ."

"Oh come on!" said JC. "How much worse can it be?"

"Heather isn't just working for the cabal," Happy said steadily. "She's also an agent for the Flesh Undying. A personal agent, like the Faust. She has its power within her."

"Okay," said JC. "You're right. That is worse."

"Heather?" said Melody. "Our Heather? I can't believe it . . ."

"We never knew Heather," said Happy. "Not really. All we ever saw was the smiling face she let us see. Someone else was watching, from behind that mask. Now she wants us to see the real her, before we die, screaming in horror."

"You finally start talking again," said JC. "And every word makes me wince."

"It gets worse . . ." said Happy.

"Time we were leaving," said Latimer.

She took the portable door out of her pocket; but the black blob just lay there in her hand, unmoving and unresponsive.

"Has it died?" said JC.

"It's not listening to me," Latimer said steadily. "Something has shut it down."

"Heather," said Happy. "She really is starting to get on my nerves . . ."

"So we can't leave," said Melody. "Not until we take Heather down."

Latimer put the blob away and sat back in her chair, thinking hard.

"We're trapped in here," said Chang. "You've got to do something! I don't do trapped!"

"Could we blast our way out, through the walls?" said JC.

Latimer gave him a pitying look. "This office was designed to be impossible to get into, except through that door. That was the point. For my protection . . ."

"Well, that's worked out wonderfully, hasn't it?" said Melody.

JC strode back to the desk and leaned over it, so he could glare right into Latimer's face. "Haven't you got anything here we can use against Heather?"

She ignored him, still thinking.

"Weapons!" Happy said loudly, not taking his eyes off the door. "We need weapons! Really big weapons!"

"I have weapons!" said Melody, filling her hands with the two heavy pistols from her holsters. Happy glanced briefly back at her.

"Where did you get those from?"

"JC's lockup," said Melody. "Remember?"

"No," Happy said sadly. "I don't." And he went back to staring at the door. "Nothing as simple as guns is going to stop Heather. Not with what she's got and what's been done to her. She's been made over by the Flesh Undying, made strong . . ."

"How strong, exactly?" said JC.

"It's changed her like it did the Faust," said Happy. "I think she's part of its Flesh now. Channelling its unnatural power . . ."

"Dear Lord," said Latimer. "How ambitious was she that she'd agree to that?"

"She's not crazy," said Happy. "Just . . . very driven to succeed. And kill as many people as possible along the way. She likes that. She thinks she's found her true calling."

"I'm not sure any weapon would be enough to help us here," JC said slowly. "But, we used combined spiritual strength against the Faust, back at the Haybarn Theatre. The power of human souls, joined and working together . . ."

"It took a theatre full of ghosts to overcome the Faust!" said Melody. "All we have is us!"

"But there's no-one like us," said JC.

"We need a Soul Gun!" said Happy.

JC looked at Melody. "Either he's taking too many pills or not enough."

"There was a Soul Gun!" said Happy. "There was! Manifest Destiny used one, against the Drood family!"

"The Droods destroyed it," said Latimer. "And anyway, it wasn't what you seem to think it was."

"The world never fails to disappoint me," said Happy. "Don't we have anything like a Soul Gun?"

"No," said Latimer. "And I don't think I'd trust any organisation that did."

She looked meaningfully at Chang, who just smiled and shrugged.

"I wouldn't know, darlings. All a bit above my pay grade. But I think if the Project did have something like that, we'd have used it against the Flesh Undying by now. Rather than agree to work with you people. Though I have to say, a Soul Gun does sound rather fun. A gun that used souls as ammunition . . . I could fire that all day and never get bored!"

"You are seriously weird," said JC.

"Thank you, sweetie," said Chang.

They all jumped and looked back at the door as something hammered fiercely on the other side, slamming into it so hard it shook and shuddered in its frame. Happy slowly retreated back into the office, step by step, never once taking his gaze off the door.

"Your shields and protections are going down, Boss," he said steadily. "Cracking and shattering, falling apart, layer by layer . . . There. That's it. The last shield just went down. I can hear it screaming. All that's left between us and Heather is the door itself. And that won't last long."

"That door is solid steel!" said Latimer.

"Won't mean a damned thing to Heather," said Happy. "Not with what she's been given."

"Well, what has she been given?" asked Melody.

"I don't know," said Happy. "Weapons, but . . . I've never seen anything like them before . . . And I've seen things that don't even necessarily exist. She's been given things from out of this world. Things that shouldn't exist in any world."

"You're right," Latimer said to JC. "The more he speaks, the worse I feel."

Melody trained both her guns on the juddering door, then looked down at the two pistols and seemed to lose confidence in them. She slammed them back into their holsters and produced several explosive devices and incendiaries from various places about her person. She sorted quickly through them, muttering under her breath.

"Can I just point out, in a calm but very emphatic voice, that any explosion in a confined space like this office would be a really bad idea," said JC.

"I know!" said Melody. She clutched the dangerous objects to her with one arm as she pulled odd bits of tech out of her pockets with her free hand. "I'm working on a shaped, directional charge, if I can cobble something together . . . Buy me some time!"

JC turned back to Latimer. "You've got a lifetime's collection of weird shit in here! Are you really telling me there's nothing we can use to defend ourselves?"

"Do you really think I'd keep anything that dangerous on open display?" said Latimer. "I never needed to defend myself; I had Heather for that . . . There are a few things here that might slow her down . . . But even before the cabal adopted her and the Flesh Undying adapted her, Heather still had access to weapons no-one could hope to stand against. That was the whole point of being my secretary."

Chang nodded reluctantly. "Exactly. We knew about Heather at the Project. And all your previous secretaries. One of the reasons why we never launched an open attack against the Institute. Dear God. The irony in here is so thick, you could cut it with a butter knife . . ."

"Is anyone else feeling nervous?" said Happy. "I'm feeling very nervous."

"Take a pill," said Melody.

"Don't think I've got anything that strong," said Happy.

The heavy steel door shuddered violently. The whole office shook. Books and files tumbled from the shelves. The desk and chairs jumped around as though the office had been hit by an earthquake. Several important souvenirs fell from their places of honour, and Latimer had to jump out from behind her desk to catch the goldfish bowl before it could shatter on the floor. She put it down in a corner, out of the way. The ghostly goldfish still swam calmly backwards, entirely untroubled. Great dents rose up on the inside of the steel door as something hit it impossibly hard from the other side. JC stared at the door, breathing hard. The sheer strength such an attack would take had to be much more than human . . .

"What have they done to you, Heather?" said JC.

"Only what she wanted them to," said Happy. "Some people just can't wait to throw away their humanity because they think it's holding them back. And afterwards . . . they don't even recognise what they've lost. If you could see what I'm seeing, JC, you'd weep hot, bitter tears for Heather. Because everything about her that mattered is already dead and gone."

Chang stepped suddenly forward to face the shaking door, smiling unpleasantly. "Open the door! Let the bitch in. And I'll eat the soul right out of her head."

"You can't," said Latimer. "She's protected against things like that. Things like you. Comes with the job."

"You gave her all these privileges and protections!" said JC. "Can't you just take them away? You're her Boss!"

"If they were that easy to take away, anyone might do it," said Latimer. "I set the revocation process in motion the moment I walked out of this office, just on general principles. But that will take hours, maybe even days. And who knows what the cabal and the Flesh Undying have given her. Doubtless things I would never have authorised . . ."

"There must be something in here we can use against her!" JC said desperately. "Think!"

"Against anyone else, I'm sure I could suggest something," said Latimer. "But this is Heather."

"Well, it used to be Heather," said Happy. "What's outside is so much less, and more, now. Did you ever see a nightmare walking . . ."

"Everyone has their Achilles' heel," said Kim. Everyone looked sharply at her. They'd forgotten she was there. People did because she was dead. Kim smiled. "Remember the Faust? Everyone who serves the Flesh Undying is supposed to have some small piece of it inside them, so they can be in permanent contact with it and wield its power. But we dealt with the Faust, didn't we?"

Her smile slowly widened, and there was something in her smile and in her eyes that made all the living turn away and shudder briefly. Even JC. Perhaps especially JC. He sometimes allowed himself to forget that Kim died long ago and had moved beyond human limitations. Until he was forcibly reminded.

"We only thought we knew about Heather," said Kim. "But she only thinks she knows about us. So let her in."

Latimer fished in one of the drawers of her desk and brought out a thick wooden stick, covered in deeply carved runes. She took the stick in both hands, muttered a few Words under her breath, then snapped the stick in half. There was a sudden pause, as everything went quiet outside the office, and the solid steel door swung slowly open on its own. JC and Happy and Melody moved to stand together.

Heather slammed the door all the way open, sending it crashing back against the inner wall, and stormed into the Boss's office. She was carrying weapons in both hands, things so terrible no-one else could stand to look at them. Shimmering, uncertain shapes, vile and malevolent. Chang threw herself at Heather, grabbing at the secretary's soul with psychic claws, to rip it free so she could eat it. Only to find there was nothing left in Heather that Chang could recognise as a soul. The psychic recoil sent Chang staggering backwards, dazed and disorientated.

Melody stepped forward, her hands full of the awkward shape she'd pieced together. A blast of intense heat erupted out of her hands, flying straight at Heather. Only to stop dead at the last moment, unable to reach her. Heather smiled triumphantly. The blast collapsed and was gone. Melody tried again, and the contraption fell apart in her hands. Happy grabbed her by the arm and pulled her back.

Catherine Latimer threw the Stone of Whitby at Heather. The Head grew rapidly in size as it flew through the air, becoming strange and awful, becoming alive. Its crude features contorted as it roared hungrily. *It corrupts souls . . .* Heather pointed one of her shimmering weapons, almost lazily, and the Head just disappeared. Blasted right out of this world. A chill ran through JC as he realised what Heather meant to do to all of them: destroy them not just in this world but the next.

He turned to Kim and nodded sharply, and she stepped inside him. The golden glow burst out all around his body, fierce and unforgiving, filling the whole office with a light so bright even Heather had to turn her face away for a moment. JC smiled reassuringly to Happy and Melody and reached out a hand to both of them. They took his hands in theirs; and all four of them joined together. Physically and spiritually, wielding power bestowed on them by forces from Outside. Latimer's eyes glowed golden too as she looked at the others; but she didn't try to join with them. That had not been allowed her. Chang looked on, fascinated, shaken . . . and scared, though she'd never admit it. The sheer presence of the four joined souls beat on the air like the slow wing-beats of some gigantic bird of prey.

JC's sunglasses slid down to the end of his nose, revealing his glowing eyes. Happy's and Melody's eyes blazed with the same golden light. Together, they turned their gaze on Heather; and she stood fixed to the spot. Unable to move, unable even to look away. Her terrible weapons fell from her hands and disappeared before they hit the floor. Unable to exist in this world without her will to hold them there. She'd been ready and prepared for any physical defence, but nothing could have prepared her for this. From the joined power of four people made into spiritual weapons by Outside forces.

Heather cried out as her power left her. Swept away, in a moment, by something far greater. She collapsed, falling forward onto her knees. She lowered her head and vomited up the piece of Flesh inside her. It fell wetly onto the floor, dark purple and darkly veined, twitching and pulsating. Chang rushed forward, to grab the Flesh up and eat it; but Latimer got there first. She brought her foot down hard and crushed the Flesh into bloody pulp.

Heather scrabbled backwards across the floor, desperate to get away from the glowing eyes of the Ghost Finders. Her back slammed up against the far wall, and she whimpered as she realised there was nowhere left for her to go. She glared wildly about her, like an animal incapable of understanding the trap it had fallen into. Latimer moved cautiously forward, to address the four glowing figures. She'd let the glow in her eyes go out.

"Please," she said. To JC and Kim, Happy and Melody. "Break the link. Come back. Because even I'm finding your presence unbearable. And because . . . I don't think this is good for you. Human beings were never meant to burn this brightly."

JC let go of Happy and Melody's hands; and the glow in their eyes snapped off. Kim stepped out of JC, and the glow surrounding him disappeared. He pushed his sunglasses back up his nose, and the last of the golden light vanished from the office. Everyone relaxed, just a little.

"Wow!" said Happy. "What a rush!"

Melody slapped him around the back of his head. He looked at her, honestly surprised.

"What?"

JC and Kim looked at each other and smiled. "Imagine what we could do if we really put our minds to it," said JC.

"Best not to," said Kim, kindly.

Catherine Latimer slowly approached Heather and crouched before her. The secretary snarled at her old Boss, but there was no strength left in her.

"I will kill you," she said.

"I feel like I failed you," said Latimer. "I should have taught you better. I should have realised . . ."

"I went to a lot of trouble to make sure you didn't," said Heather, pulling what remained of her dignity about her. Trying hard to sound proud and arrogant, and almost bringing it off. "I fooled you. I fooled everyone. Because I knew you'd try to stop me ascending."

"Is that really how you see this?" said Latimer.

"I have what I always wanted!" said Heather. "To be free of all those stupid human weaknesses that kept me back from what I was destined to be!"

"Were you forced to consume the Flesh?" said Latimer. Her voice was unusually soft, even compassionate. "Were you possessed, dominated by the will of the Flesh Undying? If that's the case, I promise I can get you help . . ."

Heather laughed in her face. "I don't want your help! I don't need anything from you. I chose to serve the Flesh Undying, and later the cabal. Because they could give me so much more than you or the Institute ever could."

"I made you strong," said Latimer. "Gave you weapons, taught you . . ."

"You think I wanted to be a secretary all my life?" said Heather, raising her voice to drown out her old Boss. "All the things I knew . . . all the things I could do . . . I should have been running this organisation! Not an old fossil like you. The things I had planned . . . things you would never have dared do! I would have made the whole world bow down and love me. And I still will." She smiled at Latimer, a cold, mocking thing, like a child that thinks it's got a secret. "You can't stop me. Not after everything that's been done to me, and everything that's been promised me. That . . . light, that stupid trick, won't hold me for long. Already I can feel my strength coming back . . . I am the future!"

"What a depressing prospect," said Latimer. "I'm really very disappointed in you, Heather. I thought you had more sense."

She rose slowly to her feet again, her knees cracking loudly. She took a moment to steady herself, then produced a gun from out of nowhere. She set the barrel against Heather's forehead and pulled the trigger. Heather's head snapped back, her bulging eyes wide and startled, as her brains sprayed all over the wall behind her. Latimer sniffed once, made the gun disappear, and looked coldly at her dead secretary.

"You're fired."

JC was so shocked, he couldn't speak. He wasn't sure

what he'd expected Latimer to do, but cold-blooded execution wasn't even on the list. Latimer looked at him challengingly.

"Well? What would you have done?"

"I don't know," he said.

"Exactly."

JC looked at Heather. At the thick blood dripping down through her blonde hair. He'd thought he'd known her, but apparently he hadn't. He'd thought he was starting to understand Catherine Latimer, but it seemed he'd been wrong about that, too. He should have known. Anyone who'd slit the throat of an old Egyptian god wouldn't hesitate to shoot her own secretary.

Latimer took out her portable door again. This time the black blob responded immediately to her thoughts, pulsing and squirming in her hand. She slapped it onto the far wall, and it became another dimensional Door.

"People are on their way," said Latimer. "People we really don't want to meet. Time to go."

"Aren't we forgetting something?" said Natasha Chang.

Latimer looked at her. "I don't think so."

"You said you came here to get something capable of destroying the whole world, if necessary!"

"Yes," said Latimer. "I did say that, didn't I?"

"Well?" said Chang. "Where is it? What is it?"

"How do you know I haven't already got it?" said Latimer. She hefted the Gladstone bag she was holding.

"I didn't see anything," said Chang.

"That was the point," said Latimer. "Perhaps I have it, perhaps I don't. Feel free to worry about it on your own time. Now, I require the exact coordinates for your research ship in the Atlantic."

"We're not going back to Project Headquarters?" said Chang. She smiled dazzlingly. "One in the eye for Vivienne MacAbre! I love it! Fortunately, I have the latitude and longitude for the ship memorised. I thought they might come in handy . . ."

"Don't tell me," said Latimer. "Tell the Door."

Chang addressed the Door, reeling off a series of figures.

The Door swung open, revealing a great expanse of open sea and sky. JC and Happy and Melody moved forward. Kim had disappeared again. Bright sunlight fell into the office, from the other side of the world. JC breathed deeply, drawing in the salt smell of the sea.

"Time for a sea voyage," said Latimer. "I think we could all use a nice holiday."

"I hate ships," said Melody. "I always get sea-sick."

"I've got pills for that," said Happy.

"What about Heather?" said JC, nodding back at the body.

"What about her?" said Latimer. "All aboard."

EIGHT

ALL AT SEA

Through the Door, and straight onto the ship. And JC still found time to wonder at just how quickly he'd got used to such marvels. Admittedly, his working life was packed full of the weird and the wondrous, but he didn't like to think he was getting jaded. From night-time London to broad daylight half a world away was something that should be savoured and appreciated. He looked quickly about him, half-dazzled by the sudden glare, and confirmed he really was on board a ship, somewhere. A light, gusting wind brought him the salt smell of the sea, and he could feel the deck shifting under his feet, hear the waves lapping against the sides of the ship. He smiled the first real smile he'd enjoyed in ages.

"Now this is what I call travelling first class!" he said. "No hanging around in the airport for three hours; no worrying where they're really sending your luggage; no long queues for the toilets . . . I could get used to this."

There was no response; everyone else was too busy examining their new surroundings. JC sighed quietly and tried not to feel underappreciated. He looked around him, taking his time. The ship they'd arrived on was long and sleek and vaguely futuristic, with all the latest options. As though someone had flicked through a glossy catalogue, offering all the newest services and gadgets, and said, *I'll have one of everything.* High tech gleamed brightly to every side, and wooden crates had been piled up in groups the whole length of the deck. As though even more goodies were just waiting to be unpacked. JC thought to look behind him and discovered that the Door was still hanging unsupported in the air, a few inches above the deck. Latimer peeled it briskly off the air, scrunched it back into a black blob, and tucked it away about her person.

JC moved over to the ship's side, wondering vaguely how you could tell whether it was port or starboard when you weren't sure which way the ship was going, and leaned on brightly polished brass railings to enjoy the view. Dark and mysterious, the ocean stretched away to the horizon under a cloudless blue sky. The sun was strong but not unpleasant, and there was enough of a breeze coming off the sea to feel refreshing. No other ships, no sign of land anywhere . . . and only then did it occur to JC that with the Door gone, he and his people were trapped on the ship, with no way home. He always preferred to avoid getting into situations where there was no obvious exit, or exit strategy. It wasn't that he didn't trust Latimer . . . All right, it was that he didn't trust Latimer. Entirely. After some of the things he'd seen her do just recently.

Natasha Chang stepped away from the group, spread her arms wide, and gestured grandly at the ship. "Welcome to the *Moonchilde*! The Crowley Project's very own floating laboratory, think tank for errant geniuses, and mobile headquarters of mass destruction. If necessary."

She broke off at the sound of rapidly approaching feet, and the ship's crew burst out from behind the piled-up crates. They were dressed in smart white uniforms and very heavily armed. Chang turned to introduce herself and her companions, then stopped abruptly as she realised no-one seemed at all pleased to see her.

The crew opened fire without even shouting any warnings or threats. The sound of massed gun-fire was shockingly loud in the quiet. Melody grabbed hold of Happy and dived for cover behind the nearest wooden crates, guarding his body with her own and cursing him when he didn't move fast enough. Bullets slammed into the other side of the crates, sending ragged splinters flying through the air. The crates rocked back and forth under the repeated impacts but didn't fall. Melody checked that Happy was okay, confused but okay, then drew the two guns from her holsters. She peered around the edge of the crates, picked her targets carefully, and returned fire. Two crewmen cried out, and hit the deck hard. The rest of the crew scattered, diving for their own cover. And carried on firing at the newcomers.

JC watched Melody picking off her targets with undisguised satisfaction, and wondered, *When did you get to be such a gun-slinger, Mel?*

He was still standing out in the open, his body surrounded by a golden glow that shone fierce and sharp even in the bright sunlight, revealing that Kim was still inside him. The crew targeted JC again and again, but the bullets couldn't seem to find him. Catherine Latimer moved quickly to stand behind JC's glowing figure, and use his body as a shield. Her gun was in her hand again, a sturdy old Webley .45. She fired steadily and accurately, and more crewmen crashed to the deck as the impact of the heavy old bullets blasted them right off their feet.

JC advanced untouched into the massed fire, picked up the nearest crate and threw it effortlessly at the nearest sheltering crew members. They were thrown back by the impact and crushed helplessly under the weight. Latimer moved steadily along behind JC, still picking off targets. JC could hear Chang screaming at the top of her voice for everyone to stop firing and listen to her, but no-one was paying her any attention.

And then Happy suddenly stood up, and stepped out from behind the cover of the crates. Melody yelled at him to get down, and grabbed for his arm to pull him back, but he avoided her and moved out into the open. The crew immediately turned their guns to target him.

"*Stand down!*" said Happy. And just like that, the crew did.

"Lower your weapons," he said. "And step out where I can see you."

The crewmen stepped out into plain sight, lowering their guns. From the expressions on their faces, it was obvious they didn't know why they were doing what they were doing, only that they had no choice in the matter. Melody and Latimer stepped cautiously out from cover, still aiming their weapons, but it was clear the fire-fight was over. The sudden hush had a tense, ominous quality of unfinished business. A handful of crewmen lay dead on the deck, and as many more lay groaning in their own blood, clutching at wounds. JC looked thoughtfully at Happy. He noticed Chang doing the same. She'd written Happy off, and now she had to reassess his usefulness. And, as a possible future threat.

JC shut down his golden glow, and moved forward to join Happy.

"Hard core," he said. "Really. I am genuinely impressed."

"Make the most of it," the telepath said tiredly. "It won't last."

He sat down suddenly on a nearby crate, as though all the strength had gone out of him. Blood dripped from his nose and welled out from under his eyelids. Melody quickly holstered her guns, produced a handkerchief, and mopped gently at his face.

"You know," she said quietly, "I am getting really tired of this up-and-down crap. Can't you take something to stabilise you?"

"I don't think there's a chemical that powerful in the world," Happy said sadly.

A few of the crew started to raise their guns again. Natasha Chang strode quickly forward to glare at them.

"Don't you dare! Everyone hold their positions! I am Natasha Chang, representing the Crowley Project!"

"Oh hell," said a voice from the back.

Chang looked through the ranks of crewmen and quickly located the owner of the voice. She smiled sweetly at him.

"Captain Katt . . . Please come forward and join us. I suppose it's just possible there is some acceptable explanation for this utter debacle."

The Captain came forward. He turned out to be a large gentleman, barrel-chested and broad-shouldered, in a smart white uniform and a peaked Captain's cap. He looked to be in his late forties, with a heavily lined face and a fierce black beard. He moved with quiet, assured authority, only slightly undermined by his obvious caution where Natasha Chang was concerned. It was also obvious to everyone that there was history between them, and not the good kind.

"Stand down," he said to his crew. "She's Project. And a hell of a lot further up the food chain than me."

"Some of us are dead!" said a voice from among the crew.

"Then you should have defended yourselves better," Katt said bluntly. He stopped before Chang and nodded brusquely to her. "I should have known . . . You always bring trouble with you, Ms. Chang."

"You remember!" said Chang. "How sweet. Now what the hell is going on here? Hmm?"

"You should have warned us before appearing so suddenly," said Katt. "We've been on full alert for days. The *Moonchilde* has been under constant threat from agents of the Flesh Undying. Project orders are very clear; I am to defend the ship from anyone and anything." He stopped to look back at his crew. "Your reaction times, and your shooting, were damned sloppy! I can see we're going to have to run some more drills!"

The crew looked seriously unhappy about that but had enough sense not to say anything. The Captain turned back to Chang.

"Being this close to the Flesh Undying is affecting all of us. Body and mind and soul."

Catherine Latimer stepped forward. "How, exactly, Captain?"

Katt looked to Chang, who nodded briefly. "Tell them everything. They've been cleared for all scientific information. Talk to them as you would to me."

"Don't tempt me," said Katt. "Might I inquire who these people are?"

Chang smiled happily. "Captain Katt, allow me to introduce Catherine Latimer, once Head of the Carnacki Institute, along with JC Chance, Melody Chambers, and Happy Jack Palmer, once agents of the Institute. Now our allies, if not necessarily our friends, in the face of a common enemy."

Katt reacted immediately to Latimer's name and bowed respectfully to her. JC felt a little bit hurt that the Captain hadn't at least heard of him and his team.

"Here on the *Moonchilde*, things have been going straight to hell," Katt said to Latimer. "It started with bad dreams. Night terrors. Men waking up screaming in the early hours. We've all been affected. It's getting so none of us dare go to sleep any more. And, sometimes, we see things. Walking the deck at night, or climbing over the sides, or swimming in the waters round the ship. There's a constant feeling of being besieged . . . that something will swarm all over us the moment we let our guard down."

"You've been having visions?" said Latimer.

"Sometimes," said Katt. "Other times it's Flesh. Parts of the thing below. I don't believe it knows we're here, or feels threatened by what we're doing, or it would have attacked us directly by now. I think it just dreams sometimes, and its dreams take on solid form. Visions wrapped around bits of Flesh that have flaked off from the main body of the thing or been discarded . . . The scientists haven't been much use in explaining what's happening. But strange things have come to this ship, dangerous things, walking the night with bad intent. We've challenged a few but haven't been able to retrieve anything solid for the scientists to examine."

"Have you tried just shooting them?" said Chang.

"Of course," said Katt. "It doesn't help. Just draws their attention. And that's when the really bad things happen. Mostly now, we just hide until they go away."

Chang shook her head disgustedly. "You are seriously letting the side down, Captain."

"Wait till you've been here a while," said Katt, completely unmoved by her scorn. "Wait until you've seen what we've seen."

"A haunted boat," said JC. "We've come to the right place."

"How many people have you lost to these things?" said Latimer.

"Seven," said Katt. "So far."

"If it's all down to being this close to the Flesh Undying, I'm surprised you haven't just sailed away," said JC.

"We're a Project ship," said Katt. "No-one here is going anywhere without orders."

"Damn right," said Chang. "We need to talk, Captain. Have your crew clean up this mess."

The Captain gave a series of quiet orders, and the crew moved quickly to obey, carrying off the half dozen dead and helping the wounded. There were a few resentful glances at the new arrivals, but no-one said anything. One crewman set to work with a mop and bucket, cleaning up the blood before it had a chance to dry.

"I suppose I should be grateful you're not better shots," said Katt.

"I was shooting to wound," said Latimer.

"Speak for yourself," said Melody. She caught JC looking at her and glared back at him. "We are on the run from everybody and under attack from all quarters. Those bastards opened fire on us without even checking who we were! I am way past the point of playing nice and turning the other cheek!"

"I know," said JC. "But when did you start enjoying it so much, Mel?"

Melody glanced at Happy, sitting slumped and exhausted on his crate. Her mouth tightened into a straight line. "I need to have something I can fight . . ."

"Somehow, I knew this would all turn out to be my fault," said Happy, not looking up.

"My apologies for the reception," Katt said stiffly. "We're all on edge. And I am under orders to ensure no harm comes to the scientists on board. I'm told their work is important for Humanity's survival." He smiled, briefly. "Not the kind of work I'm used to in the Project."

"Don't get too used to it, Captain," Chang said briskly. "This is a strictly temporary situation."

"Let us all fervently hope so," said Katt. He glanced at Latimer. "You did well, against such odds. Your people are lucky to be alive."

Kim stepped out of JC and smiled dazzlingly at the Captain. "Luck had nothing to do with it."

The Captain seemed more shocked than startled, then openly appalled. He looked to Chang, who just shrugged.

"She does that. You'll get used to it."

"You've brought the dead on board my ship?" said Katt, his voice rising. "As well as enemy agents from the Institute?"

"Think of us as rogues," said JC.

"You don't want to know what I'm thinking," said Katt.

"Play nicely with our new friends, Captain," said Chang. "They have top-security rating, for now, which means they get to hear everything. These orders come from the top. The very top. We are here to put an end to the Flesh Undying, once and for all."

"You have to admire her ambition," said Melody.

The Captain nodded slowly. "Vivienne MacAbre already contacted us. She thought you might choose to come here directly. Without going through proper channels, or giving me proper warning. So she sent someone ahead of you—to represent her interests."

"Oh joy," said Chang. "Anyone I know?"

"I wouldn't be at all surprised," said Katt.

iiiiiiiiiiiiiiiiiiiiiii

He took them up to the *Moonchilde*'s bridge. Somewhere along the way, Kim quietly disappeared. No-one saw her go, not even JC. He assumed she'd gone off on her own to check out the situation and make sure everything was as it was supposed to be. A ghost can cover a lot of ground, moving unseen and unsuspected, and it's hard to hide anything from the dead. They see so much more clearly than the living because they have less distractions. JC supposed he approved of her caution. Just because they were temporarily allied with the Project didn't mean they should let their guard down. It's always the knife in the back you don't see coming.

When they finally got to the bridge, Vivienne MacAbre's representative was already there waiting for them. The Baron Samedhi scarecrow stood at the rear of the bridge, silent and unmoving, resplendent in its morning suit and top hat. They could all feel the pressure of its gaze, somehow made even worse by the monocle glued to its face. The crew at their stations were doing their best to ignore it. Captain Katt scowled at the scarecrow.

"Unnatural thing . . ."

"I would have thought you were used to things like this," said JC. "Working for the Project."

"I usually prefer to maintain a safe distance from Mac-Abre's personal attack dogs," growled Katt.

JC looked to Chang. "Did you know that thing was going to be here?"

"No," said Chang. "I did not. I really don't like people checking up on me."

Melody walked right up to the scarecrow and glared into its stitched-cloth face. "Why is it here? What does it do?"

"I don't know that, either," said Chang. "MacAbre didn't get to be Head of the Crowley Project by giving away her secrets. But given that this is her personal bodyguard . . . I wouldn't turn my back on it if I were you."

"Have you seen it do anything?" JC said to the Captain.

"No," said Katt. "Not yet. Let's go down to my cabin. We can talk privately there."

"If we can't do that here," said Latimer, "why bring us to the bridge in the first place?"

"Because I wanted you to see what kind of representative MacAbre sent," said Katt. "Just to remind you that even though we're out in the middle of the Atlantic Ocean and miles from everywhere, it doesn't mean we're on our own. Big Sister is always looking over our shoulder."

‖‖‖‖‖‖‖‖‖‖‖‖‖‖‖‖‖‖‖‖‖

The Captain's cabin turned out to be comfortably snug, with everything tucked and tidied away because that was the only way to fit everything in. There was only just room for all of them. Latimer sat on the narrow bed, with Happy and

Melody jammed in beside her. JC and Chang had to stand, leaning against one wall, while Katt took the only chair. JC spotted a family photo on the far wall—of a perfectly ordinary-looking wife and two teenage daughters, smiling in the sun. JC wasn't used to thinking of the Project's agents, the evil opposition, as just . . . people, with families.

Katt produced a bottle of whiskey from his desk and offered it around. Everyone declined. Katt shrugged and poured himself a large drink into a mug marked *World's Best Captain*.

"I never used to, but I do now. Everyone on board does. Stay here long enough, and you will too. In self-defence."

"I know the feeling," said Happy. "Trust me; it never ends well."

"A report on the current situation if you please, Captain," Chang said firmly. "Starting with, how many people do you have on board?"

"Twenty-two crew, now," said Katt. "Used to be thirty-six. Seven killed by forces unknown, one jumped overboard. Presumed drowned if he's lucky. Six that you people shot."

"Moving on because I don't care," Chang said briskly. "What about the scientific contingent?"

"Three," said Katt. "Used to be five."

"Two killed?" said JC.

"Sort of," said Katt. He paused to take a large drink. It didn't seem to help much. "Both suicides. One stabbed himself in the eyes, to stop him seeing things. When that didn't work, he shot himself in the head. Three times. That man really wanted to die . . . The other scientist locked himself in his room and ate himself."

"What? All of him?" said Melody.

"He made a damned good effort," said the Captain. "But he bled out before he got very far."

"And you blame all of this on the Flesh Undying's influence," said Latimer. "Are we talking direct . . . or indirect?"

"Who can say?" said Katt. He finished his drink and poured himself another. His hands were steady; but there was something a little lost about his eyes. The look of a man who'd been hit hard and hit often. And no longer knew how to defend himself.

"What's been happening with the Flesh Undying itself?" said Chang. "Have there been any changes in its situation since it destroyed your drone submersible?"

Katt shrugged. "It hasn't moved. Doesn't appear to be doing anything, physically. But anything that gets too close, just dies. Used to be an area roughly half a mile wide around it, where the local sea life had learned to stay clear. Then the perimeter widened, and things started dying again. The area is over a mile in diameter now and still growing. Every morning, I go up on deck and look over the side, and there are hundreds of dead fish lying belly-up on the surface. All around the ship . . ."

"Why is it doing that?" said Latimer.

"The scientists have their theories," said Katt. "Lots of them. Which I'm sure they'll be only too happy to share with you, till you scream at them to stop. But they don't have any real answers. Who knows why this thing does anything it does?"

"What else do we need to know, about life and death on the good ship *Moonchilde*?" said JC.

"If you're wise, you'll get out now," said Katt. "While you still can."

"Not an option," Chang said immediately.

Katt smiled at her. It wasn't a pleasant smile. "Wait till you've been here a while. Till you've seen what walks this ship at night. Wait till you wake in the early hours of the morning and find something standing at the foot of your bed, watching you."

Chang smiled at him. "I love a midnight feast."

"What are we talking about here, really?" said JC. "Ghosts, demons, monsters? What?"

The Captain looked at him steadily. "It starts with dreams. Then comes the shakes, hysterical fits, crying jags for no reason. Fights over things that don't matter. Then your hair starts falling out, and something that looks like radiation burns, though the Geiger counter swears not. Accidents are always happening—bad ones, stupid ones. By men experienced enough to know better. It's like all the luck on this ship has turned sour. I think . . . people just aren't supposed to live near things like the Flesh Undying."

JC decided to change the subject. Partly because the Captain was starting to freak the hell out of people who were not easily freaked but mostly because he felt the need for a few facts, some hard information about the situation that he could get his teeth into.

"How are your scientists studying the Flesh Undying? More drone submersibles?"

"After what happened to the last one, we do everything from a safe distance now," said the Captain.

"I saw the scientific equipment on deck," said Latimer.

"There's a lot more underwater," said Katt. "Attached to the underside of the ship by Project divers. Mostly sensors, short- and long-range, and state-of-the-art information-gathering apparatus . . . I don't know. I don't understand that stuff. I just run the ship."

"Is there any chance we might be interrupted in our work?" said Chang.

"Hardly," said Katt. "We are way out in the Atlantic, a long way from anywhere. Nearest port is a month's hard sailing; and anywhere half-way civilised would be even further. We are way off the main shipping routes, so we don't have to worry about unexpected company. There's no-one else out here but a whole bunch of fish. Mostly dead fish."

"Any whales?" said Happy. "I like whales."

The Captain shook his head. "They stay well away. They've got more sense."

"What if a spy satellite were to spot this ship and someone decided to investigate what we're doing out here on our own?" said Latimer.

"The scientists assure me the *Moonchilde* is very heavily shielded," said Katt. He was on his third whiskey now, but his voice seemed entirely unaffected. "We are scientifically and psychically invisible."

"That kind of blind spot can attract attention," said Latimer. "There are certain spy satellites specifically tasked to look for just such unnatural conditions and raise the alarm."

"How do you know shit like this?" said JC.

"Hush, boy," said Latimer. "Grown-ups talking."

"Let them look," said the Captain. "No-one's going to find us."

"Still, I think it would be a good idea to get a move on," said Chang. "Don't you?"

....

She went belowdecks, to check on what the scientists were doing. And then probably shout at them a lot. Melody insisted on taking Happy to a private cabin, so she could see he got some rest. No-one argued. He really wasn't looking good. Latimer decided she could do with a rest as well. The Captain sorted them out two cabins, not far from his. And found himself left with JC.

"You don't have the look of someone in need of rest," said Katt.

"I don't think I could sleep right now if you put a gun to my head loaded with industrial-strength tranquillizers," said JC. "I'm still trying to sort out what use I can be here."

"I feel the same way, most of the time," said Katt. "Let me give you the grand tour, such as it is."

They strolled through the ship together. The Captain seemed a little easier in JC's company, now he had a few drinks inside him.

"Are you people really on the run from the Institute?" he said finally.

"Looks like it," said JC. "Hopefully, we'll be able to go back, someday."

"I used to feel that way, a long time ago," said Katt. "You know, the way most Project people talk about Ghost Finder agents, I was expecting you to be a lot . . . spookier."

"We can be," said JC. "Goes with the job. But I know what you mean; we feel the same way about the bad guys of the Crowley Project."

Katt shrugged. "Soldiers in a war are always taught to hate the other side. Makes the killing easier."

"There's a war?" said JC.

"So they tell me," said Katt. "You must understand; I have no interest in ideology. I am in this strictly for the money. Once I have enough, I am out."

"Is there ever enough?" said JC.

"Hell yes," said Katt.

They walked along the open deck, enjoying the view and the cool breeze of falling evening. The sky had darkened to a dull grey, and the waters around the ship seemed even darker, as though they were concealing secrets. Various crew members went about their work, keeping their distance.

"So," said JC. "These scientists . . . are they Project people?"

"They are now," said Katt. "The *Moonchilde* used to be their ship. The Project bought them out when it realised it needed a research ship out here in a hurry. Just threw money at the scientists until they couldn't refuse. Then we replaced their crew with our own people and put the scientists to work for us. By the time they realised they wouldn't be allowed to leave until the job was done, it was a bit late to complain."

"What were they doing, all the way out here?" said JC.

"Mapping the sea bed, fish-migration patterns . . ." said Katt. "And a whole bunch of other stuff they tried to explain to me until I begged them to stop."

"Doesn't sound like the most lucrative research," said JC.

"Probably why they jumped at the deal," said Katt. "Our people installed new tech, and the scientists settled down to study the Flesh Undying. I'm told its true nature came as something of a shock to them." The Captain paused, to smile wryly. "They do love their new toys, though. They'd never had access to sensors as powerful as ours."

"How did they react to the Flesh Undying once they'd had a good look at it?" said JC.

"Fascinated at first, then horrified. Followed by quite a bit of vomiting, fits of the vapours and tears before bedtime. They would have cut and run; but by then I was here to make clear that wasn't an option. Unless they wanted to swim home. Now I think they're scared to stop working in case they miss something important. They spend every hour there is down in their own little bunker, studying every detail of the Flesh Undying. And arguing loudly with each other as to what it all means. Sometimes we have to remind them to stop and eat."

"They sound . . . very dedicated," said JC.

"They keep talking about the important work they're going to publish, once this is all over," said Katt. "They must know they'll never be allowed to talk about any of this, in public or in private. Assuming we survive, of course . . ." He stopped, to look thoughtfully at JC. "Did the Flesh Undying really come here from another reality?"

"Yes," said JC. "I saw it arrive."

"What the hell is there, outside our reality?"

"Trust me," said JC. "Nothing you'd want to see."

"Why did the Flesh Undying come here?" said Katt.

"Put it this way," said JC. "It didn't jump; it was pushed. That's why it's so determined to get home again, even if it has to break this world apart to escape the ties that hold it here."

"What could hold something like that?"

"Being Flesh," said JC.

"Conversations you never thought you'd have . . ." said Katt. "Let me take you down to visit the brains trust. See if they depress you as much as they do me."

....

They went below, through narrow passageways and down steel ladders, until they couldn't go any further. To where the scientists were tucked away in their own private lab, so they wouldn't be interrupted while they were working. A series of locked bulkhead doors led to a long, narrow room packed with all the very latest equipment, and a great many illuminated monitor screens, presenting more constantly updated information than the mind could comfortably deal with. JC didn't even try. Cool and characterless artificial light bathed everything because there were no port-holes this low on the ship.

Chang was striding up and down, berating and bullying the scientists into providing her with the very latest information and not giving a damn when they plaintively complained that she was interrupting their work. She wasn't happy to see JC and the Captain and sat sulkily in a corner as Katt introduced JC to the scientists.

Dr. Darren Goldsmith was a neatly dressed man in his early fifties, with grey hair, grey eyes, and a grey personality. He was fine as long as he was talking about the things that interested him; everything else just sent him into shrugs and mumbles. Professor Bernie Hedley was a fast-talking New Yorker in his late twenties, wearing a Massive Attack T-shirt and shabby jeans. A man with too much personality for his own good. Dr. Ilse Hamilton was tall and stocky and Swedish, a faded blonde in her late thirties. And the only one wearing a white lab coat. They were all polite enough to JC, under the Captain's watchful gaze, but it was clear they just wanted to get back to their work. Every time they finished answering one of JC's questions, one or the other of them would look plaintively to Katt or Chang, hoping to be excused.

"Look, screw the generalities!" Chang said finally, jumping to her feet and glaring about her with both fists planted on her hips. "I am fed up with hearing endless variations on *We're making good progress*. Have you got anything useful to tell us?"

"We've finished mapping the topography of the ocean bed directly below the *Moonchilde*, where the Flesh Undying is located," said Goldsmith, in his soft Southern accent. "And we are constantly uncovering new information about the form and nature of this . . . organism."

"We've never seen anything like it before!" said Hedley. "There's never been a living thing this big in the world. Not even in the time of the dinosaurs."

"Except that massive fungal growth, deep under a US National Park," said Hamilton. "A single mushroom several miles wide, or so they say. Though, of course, that isn't sentient."

"As far as we know," said Goldsmith.

They all stopped to look at him. He didn't seem to be joking.

"The Flesh Undying gives every indication of being a single living organism the size of a mountain," said Hedley.

"A big mountain," said Goldsmith.

"I still say we should be trying to establish some form of communication with it," said Hamilton. She had the air of someone who'd been saying that for some time. "Try to reason with it."

"That is not going to happen," Katt said immediately. "If it ever discovers we're here, it'll destroy us."

"You can't be sure of that," Hamilton said sulkily.

"I've met some of its human agents," said JC. "They weren't interested in being reasonable. The Flesh Undying wants what it wants, and that's all. We don't matter to it. Nothing does, except leaving this world."

Hamilton looked at him, vaguely interested. "What happened to these . . . agents?"

"We killed them," said JC. "Before they could kill us. Though whether they'll stay dead remains to be seen."

She just nodded. "I don't suppose you could get the bodies transferred here? I'm sure we could learn a lot from them."

"The doctor does love a good autopsy," said Hedley.

"I find them informative," said Hamilton.

"We destroyed what was left of the bodies," said JC.

Hamilton sniffed loudly. "Vandals . . ."

A crewman arrived at that point, bearing a lady's shoe on a silver platter. The Captain looked at him.

"Why?"

"Compliments of Catherine Latimer," said the crewman. "She has instructed me to tell you that this is the shoe she used to stamp on the piece of Flesh vomited up by one of its agents. And, no, I don't understand that either, and I don't think I want to. Apparently she believes there might be some Flesh left on the sole of the shoe if you care to scrape it off and examine it. Please take this thing away from me, so I can get the hell out of here and scrub my hands till they bleed."

Hamilton snatched the shoe on its platter away from the crewman, and bore it away to rear of the room, smiling all over her face. The crewman departed at speed.

"The strangest things make some people happy," said JC.

"You should know," said Chang. "Ghost lover!"

"Soul eater!" said JC.

She smiled. "You say that like it's a bad thing."

"Get away from me," said JC. "Weird person." He turned to Goldsmith and Hedley. "The Captain tells me the Flesh Undying dreams; and sometimes its dreams take on Flesh and board the ship. Is that right?"

"It mostly only happens at night," said Katt. "Mostly."

"We don't go up on deck," said Goldsmith. "We prefer to stay down here, with our work. So we haven't observed anything directly . . ."

"Occasionally, our sensors tell us something is coming," said Hedley. "And sometimes they don't."

"Some things are realer than others," said Goldsmith. And then he surprised them with a brief smile. "Something I never thought I'd hear myself saying."

"The . . . phenomena seem real enough," said Hedley. "By all accounts . . . But we have no clear explanation, as yet, for what's happening."

"We're not equipped to deal with a situation like this," said Goldsmith. "With something as big as the Flesh Undying. Because there's never been anything in this world like the Flesh Undying. We have nothing to compare it to. I keep telling the Captain, we need access to more sensitive equipment and more powerful computers . . ."

"You've been given everything you asked for," said Chang.

"Half the time we don't know what to ask for!" said Hedley.

"We're doing the best we can with what we have," said Goldsmith. "When we're not being interrupted . . ."

And they both turned very firmly back to their work stations, shutting out everything except what was in front of them. Chang shrugged.

"They're doing good work, I suppose . . ."

"Really?" said JC. "I haven't heard anything that will help us destroy the Flesh Undying. That is why we're here, isn't it?"

"Information is ammunition," said Chang defensively.

"Very succinct," said JC. "Probably look great on a T-shirt. But not very helpful, is it?"

"We're here now," Chang said confidently. "Things will start moving, now we're here. I'll see to that."

JC gave her a look and moved over to see what Goldsmith and Hedley were working on. The scientists weren't at all keen on having someone peering over their shoulders but clearly didn't feel in any position to tell him to go away. JC looked at the information flowing across their monitor screens and didn't feel any wiser.

"Is there anything new you can tell me about the Flesh Undying?" he said.

Hamilton wandered back to join them, not wanting to be left out of the conversation. The three scientists looked at each other.

"It's more what we've been able to rule out," Hedley said finally. "We have established, beyond any reasonable doubt, that the Flesh Undying isn't any kind of organic matter that we're familiar with. Doesn't belong to any of the recognised phyla. Which is only what you'd expect, I suppose."

"The pressure at the bottom of the ocean doesn't bother it at all," said Goldsmith. "Nothing does . . ."

"Just its presence seems to be enough to alter things around it," said Hamilton. She sounded almost defensive. "As though it brought some of the physical laws of its own reality with it and holds them close."

"It lives in a bubble of its own reality," said Goldsmith. "A re-creation of the conditions it came from. But the bubble is . . . leaking. And changing the world around it."

"Which is almost certainly why creatures from this world die when they get too close," said Hedley.

"That has yet to be confirmed," said Hamilton.

"Only by you," said Hedley.

"If the Flesh Undying stays here long enough," said Goldsmith, "I believe its influence will continue to spread until it covers the entire world. Making this planet over into something more like where it came from."

"You're talking about terraforming," said JC.

"Exactly," said Hedley. "I'm not sure how much of anything we recognise as life would survive the process."

"So if we can't destroy it . . . Whether it stays or whether it goes, we're screwed?" said JC.

"Well . . . yes," said Hamilton. "But I don't think we can expect it to stay much longer. There do seem to be . . . signs that it is preparing to depart. In the near future."

"Signs?" said JC. "What kinds of signs?"

"Nothing you'd understand," said Hamilton.

"Make me understand," said JC. Just a bit dangerously.

"We're talking about changes on the subatomic level," Hedley said quickly. "Other-dimensional energies, discharging into the local environment."

"And," said Goldmsith, "there are the things we see in dreams. When we can't put off sleeping any longer."

The other two scientists nodded, reluctantly. From the expressions of their faces, it was clear to JC that whatever the scientists saw in their dreams, they wished they hadn't.

"I'm convinced these dreams are an attempt at communication," Hamilton said finally.

"You enjoy them," said Hedley.

"I appreciate them," Hamilton said coldly. "It's telling us things even if it doesn't realise."

"I am not convinced of that," said Goldsmith.

"We are dealing with something from a higher dimension!" said Hamilton, two spots of colour burning on her pale cheeks for the first time. "You have to open your mind to new possibilities!"

"We need to keep our minds closed," said Hedley. "So the bad things can't get in."

"Ahoy below!" Melody said cheerfully from the doorway. "Prepare to be boarded, me hearties!"

Everyone looked round as Melody and Happy entered the bunker. Happy nodded apologetically to all present.

"She's never been the same since she watched those Johnny Depp movies."

JC's first thought was that Happy was looking a lot better though there was still a worrying vagueness to the telepath's eyes. Melody sat Happy down in a corner, out of the way, and quickly ingratiated herself with the scientists by asking all the right questions. She could do that because she spoke their language. JC, Chang, and Katt looked on, excluded from a conversation they had no hope of following. Chang lost her patience first and broke in.

"Where's Latimer? Why isn't she with you?"

"She's sleeping," said Melody. "Worn-out. She is very old, after all."

"Good," said Chang. "That woman creeps the hell out of me. How do you stand working for her?"

"How do you stand working for Vivienne MacAbre?" said JC. "At least our Boss didn't murder her predecessor."

"Are you sure?" said Chang.

Melody persuaded Goldsmith to bring up a direct view of the Flesh Undying on the largest of the monitors, and they all gathered together before the screen, fascinated. JC stood uneasily at the back, remembering a similar screen back in Brighton that exploded. He looked for something substantial to hide behind, just in case, but there didn't seem to be anything. JC moved in quietly beside Captain Katt, so he could duck behind the man if necessary. Katt looked big enough to soak up a lot of damage.

As before, all that could be seen of the Flesh Undying was a great dark shape set against an uncertain background. Like the shadow of an old god, from a time before the world settled down.

"What's sending us this image?" said Melody. "Another drone submersible?"

"A simpler model, this time," said Goldsmith. "Little more than a container for the camera. No complicated equipment and no computers for the Flesh Undying to pick up on. It has no idea the camera is there."

"We think," said Hamilton.

"Where's the light coming from?" said JC. "I mean, if that's the bottom of the ocean . . ."

"That's not light, as such," said Hedley, condescendingly. "We're using very sophisticated equipment. It's not putting out anything that can be detected."

"As far as we know," said Hamilton.

"God, you get on my nerves," said Hedley.

Hamilton ignored him, giving all her attention to the

image on the screen. "I wish we could get in closer, get a better idea of its surface . . ."

"We're already closer than is safe, technically speaking," said Goldsmith.

"You don't make important discoveries by being overly cautious," said Hamilton.

"You don't get killed, either," said Hedley.

JC scowled at the image on the screen but couldn't make out much. The dark shape wasn't even remotely triangular, like most mountains. It was more like a huge stone monolith without the clear edges. There were what looked extremities, or perhaps protuberances, stretching away . . . but their shape and purpose made no sense at all to human eyes. Even ones that glowed golden.

"We are increasingly convinced that the Flesh Undying exists in more than three spatial dimensions, simultaneously," said Goldsmith. "We can't see them; we're only able to infer their presence by observing the effects they have on their surroundings."

"And then make educated guesses," said Hedley.

"They're still just guesses," said Hamilton. "I'm not convinced we're capable of understanding anything as far above us as this is."

"You admire it," said Goldsmith.

"Enough to be seriously scared of it," said Hamilton. "You aren't scared enough. You still want to fire probes into it, to get data directly."

"That request has been turned down by Project Headquarters," Katt said quickly. "Repeatedly."

Goldsmith sniffed loudly, not quite sulking. "I still think that would work. And get us information we couldn't hope to acquire any other way."

"Stick to your number-crunching," said Hamilton.

"I still say we should nuke the damned thing," said Hedley.

"You think that would work?" said JC.

"It wouldn't," said Happy.

They all turned to look at him, but he had nothing more to say.

Goldsmith looked at JC. "Is he with you?"

"Sometimes," said JC.

"Look at that thing . . ." said Melody, concentrating on the dark shape on the screen. "A living mountain, bigger than Everest. Does it have any obvious vulnerabilities?"

"None we've been able to detect," said Hamilton. Her voice was dry, almost entirely uninflected. "It doesn't eat, drink, breathe, move, or react to its surroundings. None of the accepted signs of life. As though it's . . . indifferent, to everything in this world. It doesn't need anything from us. It has no obvious limbs, to manipulate its surroundings. No obvious sense organs, to observe them. No electrical activity, to suggest a brain. Nothing to give us a handle on it."

"You said it kills every living thing that gets too close," said JC. "How, exactly?"

"We don't know," said Hedley. "They just die. Maybe it freaks them out."

"Understandable," said Melody.

"Perhaps it's simply so alien, nothing from our world can exist in its proximity," said Hamilton. "It just . . . overwhelms everything else."

"Your bubble at work, Dr. Goldsmith," said Hedley. "It overwrites the rules of our world with its own."

"It's toxic," said Goldsmith. "To everything our world considers life."

"I'd go along with that," said JC.

"We need to get a closer look," said Melody.

"There is a way," said Goldsmith. He paused, for another of his brief smiles. "But you're really not going to like it."

"Why did I just know you were going to say that?" said JC.

"Maybe you're psychic," said Happy.

"Finally," said Chang, smiling sweetly. "We get to the reason we're here. Vivienne MacAbre's master plan. Captain Katt, be so good as to take us back up on deck, so we can look at our latest toy."

....

They went back up through the levels of the ship and onto the open deck, where the Captain led the way to the far end of the *Moonchilde*. JC and Chang stuck close behind him, with Melody and Happy bringing up the rear. Chang bounced along at JC's side, smiling happily. She slipped an arm through his in a companionable sort of way; and JC politely but firmly pushed it away. Melody led Happy along like a child. He came willingly enough but seemed mostly uninterested in his surroundings. JC wondered if perhaps he should send Happy back to his cabin, to get some more rest. But if he did that, Melody would insist on going with him; and JC needed her. She was the only one who could talk to the scientists for him.

"There!" the Captain said proudly, gesturing at the thing before them. They all stopped to look.

"Oh, you have got to be kidding," said JC. "Is that . . ."

"It is!" said Chang, beaming widely. "The only way to get down to the Flesh Undying and get up close and personal, without being spotted. The old-fashioned way. In a bathysphere!"

She gestured expansively at the huge steel ball, a simple pressurised container some thirty feet or so in diameter, hanging above the deck from its winch mechanism. A wonder of early-twentieth-century science, with all kinds of cables and tubes and support tech dangling off it. A huge, air-generating machine stood to one side, firmly bolted to the deck. JC and Melody stared at the bathysphere with something like shock. Katt grinned, enjoying the astonishment and horror growing in their faces.

"It looks very . . . solid," JC said finally.

"Lots of rivets," said Happy. "I like rivets. Something very reassuring about a lot of rivets."

"But can something like that withstand the pressure?" said Melody. "I mean, if we're going all the way down to the Flesh Undying, that means descending about as deep as you can go . . ."

"The scientists assure me it can cope," said Katt. "It has been specially reinforced."

"I've met your scientists," said JC. "And I didn't find them at all reassuring. Where did you get this thing?"

"Bathyspheres are so out-dated, no-one makes them any

longer," said Chang. "And museums won't give them up. The Project had to buy one, and all its support equipment, from a private collector."

"What kind of person collects bathyspheres?" said JC.

"Come on, JC," said Melody. "People collect anything. I once saw an ad for a convention of barbed-wire enthusiasts."

"You can find anything on eBay," said Happy, nodding wisely.

"You should have seen the size of the crane it took, to transfer the bathysphere onto the *Moonchilde*," said Katt. "I was convinced the other ship was going to tip right over."

"*A bathysphere?*" said JC. "Really? Somebody actually thought this was a good idea?"

"According to our pet scientists, we can't risk any kind of standard submersible," said Katt. "The Flesh Undying would detect the computers that are built into everything these days. And we can't risk doing anything that might wake it up . . ."

"How did it destroy the last submersible?" said JC. "I mean, if it just sits there and doesn't move . . ."

"Some kind of energy attack, I'm told," said Katt.

"It didn't just destroy the submersible," said Melody. "It also reached out to attack the scientists associated with it, half a world away in Brighton. The Flesh Undying has powers and abilities beyond our understanding."

"Then why does it need human agents?" said Happy. "Like the Faust and Heather?"

"Good question!" said Melody. "Are you back with us, sweetie?"

"Now and again," said Happy. "I'm still waiting for an answer to my question."

"I think . . . it needs individual agents for individual actions," said JC. "For when subtlety is required. Maybe that's why it killed a whole roomful of people at the convention. Because it can't focus enough to kill specific people."

"Okay," said Melody. "You are reaching now."

"Somebody has to," said JC.

"All right!" Melody said loudly, glaring dangerously at the bathysphere. "What do we do? Pack this thing full of sensors and data collectors, then just . . . lower away?"

"Not quite," said Katt. "We can only use the most basic equipment if we want to get really close to the Flesh Undying. So we need volunteers to go down inside the bathysphere, to oversee the tech and make sure it's pointing in the right direction. The scientists were getting ready to draw lots, to see which of them would go, before we got word you were coming."

"Why is he looking at me?" said Happy. "JC, tell him to stop looking at me!"

"The bathysphere is so old-school it should sneak past the Flesh Undying's radar, so to speak," said Chang.

"Old-school?" said JC. "That thing is practically steampunk!"

"And that's why it will work," said Catherine Latimer.

They all looked around sharply as Latimer emerged from behind the bathysphere. No-one had noticed she was there. She nodded briefly to everyone before returning her attention to the sphere. She seemed to approve of it.

"Thought you were sleeping?" said JC.

"I've slept enough," said Latimer. "You don't need much, at my age."

"Whatever that really is," said Happy.

"I think I preferred him when he wasn't talking," said Latimer.

"Lot of people say that," Happy said sadly.

"Did you know about this in advance, Boss?" said JC.

"You couldn't have!" said Chang. "This was all kept highly classified, at the highest levels! Really high levels!"

"When I thought about the problem, this was the only approach that made sense," said Latimer. "I have seen one of these in action before . . . Not a word out of you, Mr. Palmer, if you like having your organs on the inside . . . This model seems perfectly sound. It should do the job."

"Could we use it to deliver a nuke?" said JC.

"You keep coming back to that," said Happy. "And I keep telling you, a nuke won't work."

"Why not?" said JC. "I know the Flesh Undying is a bit on the big side, but . . ."

"Because apart from its very unpleasant side effects, any atomic device is still really just a big bomb," said Melody. "Something that goes bang. The Flesh Undying isn't a natural object, so we can't expect it to react in natural ways to simple physics. The blast might not reach it, or damage it; or it might just put itself back together again."

"I'm not sure any physical weapon would work," said Latimer. "The Flesh Undying exists in more than three spatial dimensions, remember? You can't hope to destroy something that exists in physical dimensions we can't even detect. Traditional weapons wouldn't even touch it."

"Then we need untraditional weapons!" said Melody. "You have contacts with all sort of groups; somebody must have something!"

"You have to remember I'm rogue now," said Latimer. "By the time I could convince anyone to listen to me . . ."

JC looked at Chang. "Your people don't have anything?"

"At the Crowley Project," Chang said carefully, "in the Armoury I wasn't allowed to show you, we have all kinds of weapons and devices and really nasty surprises. Designed to destroy all manner of things, in and out of this world. The living and the dead and everything in between. But the Flesh Undying is so far beyond our experience, our comprehension . . . We were rather hoping you'd have something."

"Maybe we could exorcise it," said Happy.

They all looked at him.

"Just a thought," said Happy. "Of course, we would need a really big book, bell, and candle."

"That's not for exorcisms," said Melody. "That's for when you want to curse someone."

"I feel like doing some serious cursing," said Happy.

"So do I," said JC.

"We can use the bathysphere to study the Flesh Undying up close, undetected," said Latimer. "Get new data, and just possibly a better idea of what it is we're up against."

"We?" said Happy. "What's this we shit, kemo sabe?"

"Exactly," said JC. "Does anyone here feel like volunteering?"

Everyone looked at everyone else. Hoping someone would raise their hand so they wouldn't have to. Katt shook his head firmly.

"I will not be going, and neither will any member of my crew. We just run the ship."

"There could be a substantial bonus involved," said Chang.

"There isn't that much money in the world," said Katt.

"Don't you trust the sphere?" said JC, innocently.

"I do not like the idea of walking up to the Flesh Undying and banging on its door," said Katt. "Studying it is one thing; disturbing it quite another."

"But you're happy enough for someone else to do it?" said JC.

"Of course," said Katt.

"What about the scientists?" said Melody. "I would have thought they'd jump at the chance."

"It has been decided, at the highest level, that the scientists are needed here," said Chang. "To run their equipment, and sort and study the new data as it comes in. So who does that leave, to volunteer for this highly dangerous and quite possibly suicidal mission?"

"You are enjoying this far too much," said JC.

"I still have my guns," said Melody.

Chang folded her arms and looked smug. "I do not do the volunteer thing."

Catherine Latimer looked suddenly old, and frail.

"Oh stop it," said JC. "You're not fooling anyone." He sighed, loudly. "It has to be me."

Kim appeared suddenly, standing right in front of him. Everyone jumped at the ghost girl's sudden reappearance, especially Katt.

"You do get used to that," said Latimer. "Eventually."

"I will not have ghosts on board my ship!" said Katt.

"Why not?" said Melody. "Because they're unlucky?"

"I thought that was women?" said Happy.

"Depends on the woman," said Latimer.

Kim was still staring at JC. She looked solid and real and

very human. "Why, JC? Why does it have to be you? Why does it always have to be you?"

"Because I was there at the beginning," said JC. "When forces from Outside reached down to save me from a terrible death and mark me as one of their own. I think perhaps they knew, even then, that this was where my life would lead. To this place, this moment, this decision. So I could be their weapon."

"If you go," said Kim, "I go with you."

"And that means Happy and I go, as well," said Melody.

"We do?" said Happy.

"Yes," said Melody.

"Okay," said Happy. "Just checking."

JC looked at them all. "You don't have to do this."

"Of course we do," said Melody. "We're a team."

"Damn right," said Happy.

"Forever and ever," said Kim.

The four Ghost Finders looked at each other.

"We've come a long way together," said JC.

"And it would appear we still have a long way to go," said Melody.

"Straight down," said Happy.

They all laughed, quietly.

"Don't any of you dare die on me," said Kim. "I like being the only ghost in the Ghost Finders."

"I am not going!" Chang said loudly.

"No-one ever thought you would," said JC, not even turning his head to look at her. "And you're not going either, Boss."

"Of course not," said Latimer. "I'm going to be needed here, to keep an eye on everyone. Go get some rest. You're going to need it. You dive at dawn."

"I thought that was for executions?" said Happy.

"Exactly," said JC.

NINE

‖‖‖‖‖‖‖‖‖‖‖‖‖‖‖‖‖‖‖‖‖‖‖‖‖‖‖‖‖‖‖

THINGS PEOPLE SAY BEHIND
CLOSED DOORS

They all decided they'd had enough for one day. Captain Katt
escorted them back below, showed them to their cabins, and
wished them a pleasant good night. Everyone nodded to everyone else and prepared to turn in. It had been a very long
day. JC opened the door to his cabin and looked it over. It had
clearly been occupied before, and by the look of it, quite recently. The narrow bunk bed was still half-made, and there
were personal belongings scattered everywhere. Including a
half-full bottle of Gordon's gin, standing on the pull-out
table. JC looked at Katt.

"Who did these cabins belong to, originally? Why are
they empty now?"

"I told you," said Katt. "People have died on this ship.
They don't need these cabins any longer. What's the matter,
Mr. Chance? Afraid they might be haunted?"

"No," said JC. "I always bring my own ghost with me."

Kim smiled dazzlingly at Katt, who looked away.

"I wouldn't mind if there were a few ghosts still floating
around," said Chang, from further down the corridor. "I could
use a bedtime treat."

"Don't even think of coming visiting," said JC. "I shall be locking my door."

"If you think that'll help . . ." said Chang.

"I have a gun," said Melody.

"So do I!" said Chang.

"I'm not ready to retire, just yet," said Catherine Latimer. "I've already had enough rest for one life. I think . . . I'll go back down and talk with the scientists some more."

JC looked at her thoughtfully. He had no doubt Latimer was keeping something from him. But that was just business as usual where the Boss was concerned.

He ushered Kim into the cabin ahead of him, then went in, locking the door behind him. He stood by the door, listening to Happy and Melody going into their cabin, then Chang entering hers. Followed by the departing footsteps of Katt and Latimer. It promised . . . to be a very long night.

....

JC pulled all the sheets and blankets off the narrow bed and threw them to the back of the cabin before lying down on the bare mattress. It felt less like lying on a dead man's bed, that way. JC could be surprisingly fastidious about such things. He was almost too tall for the bed, his heels resting on the bottom edge. He worried about putting creases in his marvellous white suit but didn't have the energy to get undressed. Besides, he wanted to be ready for . . . anything that might happen. Kim lay down on the air beside the bed, floating horizontally, as close as she could get without actually touching him. For fear of spoiling the illusion. JC smiled.

"I appreciate the thought, Kim, but you're lying on nothing. It's not much of an illusion."

"You always know what I'm thinking," said Kim.

"Not always," said JC. He wriggled a little, settling himself.

"Try and get some sleep, love," said Kim. "It's been a hell of a day, and you've been through a lot. It's all right; you're safe. I'll keep watch. Nothing will get to you while I'm here."

"I'm tired," said JC. "I don't think I've ever felt this tired in my life . . . My body feels like it's made of lead . . . But I'm not sleepy. My head's too full. Too many thoughts, racing at a thousand miles a minute. Far too many questions and not enough answers."

He sat up again, scowling and hugging his knees to his chest. Kim sat up on the air beside him, hovering gracefully on nothing at all. Still keeping as close to JC as she could. She was wearing the memory of a battered old dressing-gown she used to have, back when she was alive. It helped her feel casual.

"I wish I could hold you," she said. But she could tell he wasn't listening, too busy re-running the events of the day. She sighed and fluffed out her long red hair without touching it. He liked it when she wore her hair long.

"I'm not even sure what time it is," said JC. "My watch says one thing, that clock on the wall says another; but it doesn't mean anything. My body clock's not even talking to me after everything we've been through. Especially since we passed through Latimer's dimensional Door."

"Maybe you're suffering from dimensional jet lag?" Kim said brightly.

JC could tell she was trying to cheer him up. It didn't help, but he managed a small smile for her, to show he appreciated the effort.

"I'm not even sure what time-zone we're in," he said. "This far out in the Atlantic. It's day now, when it used to be night; but is it the same day, or the next day . . ."

"It will be dark soon," said Kim. "I can feel it. Do you think bad things will start to move around up on deck once it's night, like the Captain said?"

"I hope so," said JC. "I could use something straightforward to fight."

"What's really worrying you, JC?" said Kim. "You're not usually this . . . tense."

"The bathysphere!" said JC. "The bloody bathysphere! Can you believe that thing? I wasn't sure where the day's events were leading me, but that big steel ball wasn't even on my list of things to be worried about. The last time I saw a bathysphere, it was on a television show, when I was a kid.

The Undersea World of Jacques Cousteau." He looked at Kim, but she just looked back at him. "Don't make me feel old, girl. The point is, they never seemed safe to me. And now I'm supposed to trust my life to one."

"It looks . . . very sturdy," said Kim. "Do you know what it's like, inside? Have you any idea how to operate it?"

"No!" said JC. "Well . . . given the period it comes from, the systems can't be that complicated. I should be able to handle the basics. And once we're down on the sea-bottom, all we have to do is make sure all the equipment they load in with us is functioning properly."

"How safe is a bathysphere, really?" said Kim.

"Normally, very, I would think," said JC. "But these aren't normal conditions. Bad enough that we'll be sitting on the bottom of the ocean, our only link to the ship a bunch of fragile cables . . . surrounded by God knows how many pounds of pressure per square inch . . . But once we get right up close to the Flesh Undying, anything could happen."

"What if it attacks you?" said Kim. "Could you defend yourselves? Does the bathysphere have any weapons?"

"Just a really thick shell," said JC. "And Latimer's right—weapons wouldn't be any use against the Flesh Undying. Our best hope lies in not being noticed. I think that's what's really bugging me . . . How helpless we'll be. I hate being in situations I can't control. Where I can't hit back."

"You don't have to do this, JC," Kim said steadily. "Tell them to go to hell. I'll back you up. Send that Natasha Chang cow down instead. No-one will miss her."

"No," JC said immediately. "We couldn't trust her. Not that close to something so powerful."

"You think she might be an agent of the Flesh Undying?" said Kim.

"No . . ." said JC. "I like to think she's got more sense than that. Or at least, a better sense of self-preservation. I think it's more . . . if there are secrets to be discovered down there, we need to be the ones who do it. And I can't help feeling . . . that this is what everything in our lives has been leading up to. We've been through so much, there has to be a reason." He stopped and looked at her. "Did I die, down in the London

Underground? On that demon train? When the forces from Outside reached down and touched me, altered me; did they bring me back from the dead for their own purposes? Does that make me a ghost?"

"No," Kim said immediately. "I'd know."

JC thought of several things he could say in response to that, but moved on. "And what are these forces from Outside? I've researched everything I could find on the subject, in some pretty unlikely places, and I haven't been able to find a single solid answer. Or at least, nothing I could trust. Given that the supernatural and the uncanny are our business, it's amazing how little we know for sure about the realms that lie beyond our own. The only other person I know has had direct contact with these Forces is Catherine Latimer. And I'm not sure how I feel about her right now. I'd say she's playing both sides against each other, but I'm not even sure how many sides there are . . ."

He rose abruptly from the bed and prowled around the cabin like a caged animal. Kim drifted carefully back out of his way. They both hated it when he sometimes accidentally walked through her. JC strode up and down, his head bowed, lost inside his own racing thoughts. Kim said nothing. At times like this, he needed to work things out for himself. JC stopped, facing a mirror on the cabin wall. He looked at himself for a long moment, then took off his sunglasses. Bright golden light spilled from his eyes. It was hard for him to see anything of himself in the reflection, past the light.

"I don't even remember what my eyes used to look like," he said slowly. "What does it mean, these changes they've made in me? The glowing eyes show they've marked me, but as what? A warrior for the Good? Or their property? Is this a sign of grace, or ownership?"

"Those eyes have saved your life," said Kim. "On more than one occasion. They've scared off some fairly scary things. I can understand that. They creep me out, sometimes. And I'm dead."

"Yes, but . . . saved me for what?" said JC. "For what reason, what purpose? I need answers, Kim! If I'm going down into the dark, all the way to the bottom of the ocean to stare the Flesh Undying in the face . . . If I'm going to my death tomorrow . . . I need to know what's really going on."

Kim came and stood beside him, standing as naturally on the floor as she could manage. "Being dead isn't so bad. It beats the alternatives."

JC looked at her. "There are alternatives?"

"Look!" said Kim. "This is me, changing the subject! The only way you're going to get any straight answers about the forces from Outside is to talk to them directly. Ask them."

"Is that even possible?" said JC. "How can you make contact with something that isn't even a part of our reality?"

"They reached out to you," said Kim. "Maybe you can reach out to them."

JC thought about it. "Yes . . . When they reached down to touch me, they forged a connection. Whether they meant to or not. And I think . . . it's still there."

"Be careful, JC," said Kim. "And very polite. You don't want to risk upsetting them. If nothing else, they made it possible for us to be together."

"That buys them a lot of credit," said JC. "But not a blank cheque. I have to talk to them, Kim. I need answers, something definite to hang on to. Down in the depths, in the dark."

"All right," said Kim. "How do you want to do this?"

"I think we already know how," said JC. "Think hard; think back to the day you and I first met."

"I remember," said Kim. "Though God knows I've tried to forget a lot of it. The demons, the horror, that old monster Fenris Tennebrae. I was never so frightened in my life. Or my death."

"Concentrate," said JC. "On that moment when the Forces found us, and everything changed forever."

They stood facing each other, staring into each other's eyes. The golden glow and the ghostly gaze.

"What did it feel like?" said Kim. "When something from the world above the world touched and altered you?"

JC concentrated, remembering a great force that raced through his body and soul, transforming the way he saw the world . . . and slowly he turned his head to look in a new direction, one he'd never noticed before.

"JC!" said Kim. "Your eyes! They're glowing so brightly!"

She stared directly, unblinkingly, into the fierce light that blazed from his eyes, filling the cabin. She could do that because she wasn't alive, with life's limitations. And she remembered that she could see beyond this world, too. JC and Kim concentrated on the new direction, looking beyond the cabin wall, beyond the boundaries of this reality, beyond the fields we know. Kim began to glow, just like JC. He pointed an accusing finger at the world beyond the wall.

"I can see you!"

"I can see you!" said Kim.

"Took you long enough," said a calm, kind, and not in any way human Voice.

JC and Kim stood close together, feeling very small in the face of something so vast and overwhelming. The cabin wall had disappeared, replaced by a whole new vista. Another place, of perfect shapes and concepts, perfect thoughts and emotions. Existence on a much grander scale. They could no more comprehend its details and significances than a fly crawling over a stained-glass window in a cathedral. All they could grasp were glimpses, impressions. But in a strange sort of way, it reminded them of home. The home they left, to be born. They couldn't see what was speaking to them, or even where the Voice was coming from. Just a sense of being seen and understood by some incomparably vast Presence. Something taking an interest in them for reasons of its own.

"Who are you?" said JC. "Really?"

"Ah," said the Voice. "The difficult ones first, eh? We're you, JC, only more so. What you need to know is, we are the inhabitants of the realm the Flesh Undying came from."

"Why did you dump it here?" said JC.

"We didn't," said the Voice. "It escaped. You can't hope to comprehend what it really is except through the mercy of metaphors. Think of it this way; it isn't a criminal. It's insane. Broken, on a spiritual level. It was running from us, when some very foolish people on your side of the Veil opened up a gap in the walls of the world. And the Flesh Undying plunged through, to get away from us. And because it thought it could be a god in your lesser reality. It didn't realise how much taking on form and shape and Flesh would bind and limit it."

"Why haven't you come to take it back?" said JC.

"We can't," said the Voice. "If we were to force our way into your world, our presence alone would be enough to damage it forever. Our very existence would be too much for your laws of physics to accept. So, like the Flesh Undying, we have to work through agents. Like you and Kim. Happy and Melody. Catherine Latimer. And . . . others."

"Wait a minute!" said JC. "The Boss said you contacted her ages ago, when she was still young, long before the Flesh Undying entered our world!"

"Time doesn't mean the same thing to us as it does to you," said the Voice. "We see it from the other side."

JC desperately wanted to ask what the hell that was supposed to mean but somehow just knew it wouldn't get him anywhere. So he stuck to the questions he most wanted answered.

"Why did you choose me?"

"You were there," said the Voice.

"Really? That's it?"

"You were there, doing the right thing at the right time, for the right reasons. Do you have any idea how rare that is?"

"I just happened to be there!"

"A long chain of events brought you to that place, to that time," said the Voice. "Do you think they all happened by blind chance?"

"You've been running my life all this time?" JC said angrily.

"All the choices you made were yours. We simply provided a context."

"What if I choose not to serve you?"

"What if your world ends?"

"So I don't have any choice."

"Do any of us?" said the Voice. "We all do what we feel we must."

"If the Flesh Undying escaped from you to come here,"

said JC, "why is it so ready to destroy this world in order to leave it?"

"Because it's crazy," said the Voice. "And because it didn't realise how very limited your world, your reality, would make it. What it would have to be, just to survive your harsh local conditions. Bound in Flesh, tied to cause and effect, trapped in linear Time."

"How do we stop it?" said JC.

"Destroy the Flesh," said the Voice. "That's all that holds it in your world."

"You don't mind us destroying it?" said JC.

"Put it out of its misery, and ours," said the Voice. "With our blessing."

"All right," said JC. "Tell me. How do we destroy its Flesh? What kind of weapon do we need?"

"You don't need anything," said the Voice. "You are the weapon. Our weapon. We made you over into what we needed you to be."

"But what am I supposed to do?" said JC, not even trying to hide his desperation.

"You'll know," said the Voice. "When the time comes."

"I hate answers like that," said JC.

"I know," said the Voice.

"Am I ever going to get a straight answer out of you?"

The Voice actually considered the question for a moment. "I tell you what you are capable of understanding. Anything else would be cruel."

"Could you be any more condescending?" said JC.

"If you like."

"Give me this much, at least," said JC. "Did I die, down in the London Underground? Did you bring me back to life, to serve your will?"

"Life and death," said the Voice. "Such small concepts."

And that was all it had to say. The other reality disappeared gone in a moment. JC and Kim were left staring at a perfectly ordinary cabin wall. JC felt even more tired than he had before, as though he'd just fought a duel, or run a marathon. He put his sunglasses back on and wasn't surprised to find that his hands were shaking. The only thing worse than demanding answers from Above is getting them answered.

"What was that place?" he said slowly. "Was it the after-life?"

"No," said Kim.

JC looked at her. "You sounded very certain, there. You're keeping things from me again."

"Only to protect you," said Kim. "I'd tell you if I could. You must believe that, JC."

He nodded. "Why didn't you ask the Voice any questions?"

"I didn't know what to say," said Kim. "Why didn't you ask the Voice for help? For favours; for you and me?"

"I didn't think of that," said JC.

"You didn't think . . ."

"I've got a lot on my mind! All right?"

Kim looked at him and started to fade away.

"No!" said JC. "Please! Don't go! I didn't mean . . ."

Kim snapped back into focus and smiled at him. "You're so easy to tease. I was only thinking, you could have asked the Voice to improve the bathysphere. Make it safe."

"You heard the Voice," said JC. "They don't intervene di-rectly. What do you suppose it was, really?"

"I don't know. I don't believe we can know. It's just . . . something from Outside."

"I'm not sure I trust it," said JC.

Kim grinned. "Just because something is from a higher dimension doesn't mean it can't also be a manipulative, su-percilious little prick."

"Well said," said JC.

॥॥॥॥॥॥॥॥॥॥॥॥॥॥॥

In Happy and Melody's cabin, it was all very quiet, if not particularly peaceful. Happy lay curled up on his narrow bed, hugging himself tightly to keep from flying apart. Shaking and shuddering, soaked with sweat, he'd run out of strength and stamina, energy and certainty. He'd been running on spiritual fumes for far too long, and the tank had run dry. He collapsed pretty much the moment his cabin door closed, and he didn't have to pretend to be strong any longer. Melody had to use all her strength to haul him across the cabin to the bed and lay him down on it.

He'd shut down most of his mental abilities, to keep the world outside his head. His eyes were wild, fey, frightened. He didn't even react when Melody tried to talk to him. As though he couldn't see or hear her. He'd withdrawn all the way inside, hiding from the world that was killing him by inches. Melody sat on a chair beside the bed, sorting carefully through the contents of his pill box, trying to work out the best combination to help him. She kept telling herself it was just chemicals, just science; nothing more than cause and effect. It didn't help. It was like looking at little coloured pieces of death. She finally settled on some medium-strength pills, poured out a glass of water, and persuaded Happy to swallow the first two. After a worryingly long moment, they brought him some of the way back.

His eyes focused on Melody, and he smiled wearily. His face was unnaturally pale and horribly drawn as she mopped sweat from it with a handkerchief. He had the look of someone who was on his last legs and knew it, and didn't have enough strength left to care. Melody knew he was dying but stubbornly refused to accept it. She needed to believe there was still something she could do. She showed Happy the other pills she'd selected, and he sighed and nodded resignedly. He got them down though it took most of the glass of water to help him do it. And then he sat up.

"How are you feeling?" said Melody.

"Hard to tell," said Happy. "Everything feels . . . loose, unconnected. My thoughts are all drifting . . . I can't be sure whether I'm speaking to you now, or if I'm just remembering a conversation I had earlier. I feel so tired, Mel . . . Used up and worn-out."

"Tired of me?" said Melody.

"Tired of living," said Happy, almost casually. "I don't know what day it is, or what time of day . . . Whether I've eaten or slept recently . . . I can't always remember why I'm here. What I'm supposed to be doing. Sometimes I look at you and wonder who you are. And it worries me that it doesn't worry me more . . . I'm scared, Mel. I'm scared all the time, now. And that's no way to live."

He stopped because Melody was crying. She didn't make a sound, but tears rolled jerkily down her cheeks, and she couldn't seem to get her breath. "I don't know what to do," she said finally, forcing the words out. "Tell me what I need to do to help you, Happy!"

"If you love them, let them go."

"No! I can't do that! I won't do that!"

"Sooner or later, we all come to the point where we don't have any choice in the matter," said Happy. "Give me my pills, Mel."

"You've just had some," said Melody.

"I mean the really heavy-duty ones," said Happy. "You know the ones I mean. The baseline bombers. The kamikaze chemicals."

"Are you sure?" said Melody.

"It's time," said Happy. "One last battle against the forces of evil, so let's go out on a high. A real high."

She looked at the pill box in her hand but couldn't bring herself to make the decision. So she handed the box to Happy, and watched numbly as he chose half a dozen of the largest, prettiest pills. She winced with every selection he made but wouldn't let herself say anything. Happy rolled the pills around on the palm of his hand.

"Time to be the best a man can be," he said lightly. "One last time."

He had to struggle to get the pills down, even with another glass of water, then sat looking at nothing for a long moment. Melody took the pill box back from him, and he didn't even notice. And then he jumped up off the bed and stretched widely, like a cat in the sun. Suddenly full of energy, if not life. His face was flushed, his pupils were huge, and when he grinned broadly at Melody, she had to look away. The smile was a death's-head grin.

"Do you want to try a little something?" said Happy. "A little taste of Heaven and Hell, to put a smile on your face?"

"All I have is my mind," Melody said steadily. "I won't put it at risk."

"You always were the practical one," said Happy. "When I'm gone, throw it all away. Flush the pills down the toilet. Though I hate to think what they'll do to the sewer rats . . . Mel? What is it?"

"What will I do?" she said. "What will I do, when you're gone?"

"Be happy for me," said Happy.

Melody put her arms around him and hugged him close. Because she'd promised to hold him while he was dying.

''''''''''''''''''''''''''

Natasha Chang sat alone in her cabin, in full lotus position on her narrow bed. Her face was calm, her thoughts untroubled. She wasn't thinking about the bathysphere, or the descent in the morning, or any of the problems on board ship. She'd always believed in dealing with things as they happened. And she'd already had a good look around the cabin, to assure herself there was no trace of a surviving personality anywhere. Nothing to nibble on. When faced with complicated situations and problems beyond her immediate control, Chang always fell back on her favourite pastime. Plotting how best to kill all the people who'd annoyed her. There were never any shortage of qualified candidates.

As soon as the Flesh Undying had been dealt with, and its threat neutralised, (and Chang never doubted for a moment that it would be,) then Catherine Latimer and her precious Ghost Finders would become irrelevant. And fair game. Chang smiled sweetly, working out the best order in which to finish them off, in the most appalling ways. It never failed to calm her. Something with knives. You can't go far wrong with knives. She'd leave JC till last, of course. Because he would suffer so, watching all his friends die before him. And by then she'd have worked out something really nasty to do to him. She had no doubt his tortured soul would be the tastiest of all.

There was a knock at her cabin door, and it swung open before she could tell her unwanted visitor to get lost. Catherine Latimer entered the cabin as though she had a written invitation and nodded brusquely to Chang, who just looked back at her. Latimer closed the door. Chang was sure she'd locked it.

"How did you . . . ?"

"I'm Catherine Latimer."

"Of course you are, darling. Pull up a chair and park your ego."

Latimer looked at Chang and the snappy little gold-plated pistol Chang was pointing at her.

"I am never unarmed," said Natasha Chang.

Latimer raised both hands, to show they were empty. "I come as a friend."

"Really?" said Chang.

"Well," said Latimer. "As an ally."

Chang shrugged and made the gun disappear. She unfolded gracefully out of her full lotus and sat on the edge of the bed, her long legs elegantly crossed. Latimer pulled up a chair and sat down facing her. Both women gave every appearance of being totally relaxed and at ease; and neither of them fooled the other for a moment.

"Did you have a nice time, chatting with the science nerds?" said Chang. "Learn anything useful?"

"No; and no," said Latimer. "Except . . . there's something wrong with the scientists."

"All of them?"

"Perhaps. They've spent all this time studying the Flesh Undying, but I couldn't get a single straight answer out of any of them."

Chang shrugged. "Scientists . . . I could go down and crack the whip over them, but I sort of get the feeling they'd enjoy it."

"I wouldn't be at all surprised," said Latimer.

"So! What can I do for you, oh hated Boss of a rival organisation?" said Chang.

"I thought it was high time we had a nice little chat," said Latimer. "We have so much in common, after all."

Chang raised an elegant eyebrow. "We do? Gosh . . . News to me."

"We have the same enemies," said Latimer. "If we can just keep from killing each other long enough, I think we could achieve great things together."

Chang considered the point. "What did you have in mind, exactly?"

"Destroying the Flesh Undying, obviously," said Latimer. "And then dismantling the current regime at the Carnacki Institute. Yes, I thought you'd like that. Afterwards, I thought we might overturn the current regime at the Crowley Project."

"The only way to retire a Project Head is in a coffin," said Chang. "Are you really ready to approve your granddaughter's death?"

"She's been dead to me for years," said Latimer. "Ever since she murdered her mother."

Chang made a soft, pleased sound. "I never knew that!"

"Not many do," said Latimer. "And please, don't act like you care."

"Oh, I don't," said Chang. "But it is . . . interesting. You know. You're not part of the Carnacki Institute any longer. They threw you out, set you free. You don't owe them anything. So why not come and join us at the Project? You'd be made very welcome, with your extensive experience . . . You might even end up running things. I understand there could be a vacancy soon."

"I don't think so," said Latimer.

"Think of all the good you could do, with the power and resources of the Project at your command."

"Get thee behind me, Chang."

Chang shrugged easily. "Can't blame a girl for trying. What is it you want from me; exactly?"

"Backup," said Latimer. "If necessary. The situation on this ship is . . . complicated."

"But what do you want me to do?" Chang said patiently. "Eat the Flesh Undying? I hate to admit it, but even my appetite has its limits, darling."

"You will be up here on the ship, with me, while my people go down in the bathysphere," said Latimer. "I wouldn't want anything to interfere with their safety; and I can't be everywhere at once."

"You think there might be . . . interested parties, on board ship?" said Chang. "Maybe even agents of the Flesh Undying?"

"Perhaps," said Latimer. "Keep your eyes open. Darling." She rose to her feet and went over to the door. "We both have a lot to think about, now. See you in the morning."

She let herself out of the cabin, and the door closed and locked itself behind her. Chang frowned, thoughtfully. For the first time Latimer wanted something from her. Something she couldn't take or intimidate out of her. Which meant, finally, Chang had leverage over Catherine Latimer.

Natasha Chang smiled slowly, thinking many things.

TEN

‖‖‖‖‖‖‖‖‖‖‖‖‖‖‖‖‖‖‖‖‖‖‖‖‖

DISTURBANCES IN THE NIGHT

There's nothing worse than waking up suddenly and not knowing where you are.

Well, actually, there are a great many things worse than that, sometimes involving the imminent end of the world, and JC had been through most of them. But still . . . being hauled out of not enough sleep to discover you don't recognise a single damned thing in your surroundings was right there in JC's top ten personal horrors. He hated it.

Kim had finally persuaded JC to lie down on the bed again and try to get some sleep. And JC had felt so exhausted by then that he'd gone along. Partly because he wanted to keep Kim happy but mostly because he didn't have the energy to argue. He didn't believe he'd be able to sleep with so much weighing on his mind, but perhaps just the rest would do him good. Of course, the moment his head hit the mattress, and his eyes closed, he was fast asleep. Only to be roughly jolted awake by loud noises and raised voices.

Someone was banging insistently on the cabin door and calling his name. JC sat bolt upright on the narrow bed and panicked when he realised he didn't have a clue where he was. His heart pounded against his chest, and he had to fight to get his breath. Cold sweat beaded on his face as he looked wildly about him . . . and then he saw Kim, and it all came rushing back.

She was standing between him and the assault on the door, ready to protect him from anything; and that immediately calmed JC down and put courage back in his heart. If only because he was damned if he'd let Kim down by being less than what she expected him to be. He drew in a deep breath, knuckled at his eyes behind his sunglasses, and swung his legs over the side of the bed.

"What time is it, Kim?"

"Just past two in the A.M.," said Kim, not even glancing at the clock on the wall. Ghosts knew things like that.

"Answer me, JC!" said the voice on the other side of the door. "This is Catherine Latimer! Open the door! There's an emergency!"

"Isn't there always," growled JC. He got up from the bed, swayed unsteadily for a moment, and stumbled forward to glare at the closed door. He made no move to unlock it, just on general principles.

"What kind of emergency?" he said loudly, wincing at the rough sound of his voice. "Is the Flesh Undying stirring?"

"Something is," said Latimer. "I think we should go up on deck and find out what. The Captain sounded very concerned."

"Good," said JC. Because if he had to suffer, it made him feel better to know everyone else was having an equally bad time. Made it seem fairer.

"Things walk the ship at night," Kim said quietly to JC. "That's what Captain Katt said."

"Sometimes, the world just won't leave you alone," said JC. "I'd kill for a Red Bull . . . Can you feel anything moving, up on the main deck?"

"Something's happening," said Kim, frowning. "There are forces abroad in the night . . . weird shit is on the prowl. You look awful, JC."

"I'm awake," said JC. "And I'm up. Asking for anything more at this point would be pushing it."

The heavy knocking on the door became even louder, if

possible. JC winced. "All right! I'm coming! Now leave my door alone, or I'll rip it off its hinges and beat you to death with it!"

He tugged vaguely at his crumpled white jacket, trying to get it to hang neatly again. His marvellous suit hadn't responded at all well to being slept in. JC felt like he could use a shower, a complete blood transfusion, and some personal dry-cleaning. He had slept in his clothes before, on stakeout, and felt he should get danger money for what he put his clothes through. And what that did to his image. JC had always taken a certain pride in knowing that whatever supernatural beastie he ended up facing, in whatever situation, he would always be the best dressed one there. He glared at the closed door and still made no move to open it. Because that would commit him to getting involved in whatever was happening.

"JC . . . ?" said Kim. "I really don't think she's going to go away . . ."

"Working on it," said JC. He straightened his back, squared his shoulders, said some very bad things under his breath, and unlocked the door. He hauled it open and glared at Catherine Latimer, standing in the corridor. *"What?"*

She glared right back at him. "You look terrible."

"I know!" said JC. "I wonder whose fault that is? There had better be a very good reason for disturbing me at this time, or I swear I will run amok with the nearest blunt instrument. No jury would convict me."

"Well . . . someone's not a morning person," said Latimer. "But on the other hand, it's not a bad attitude to have when it comes to dealing with things that go walkabout in the night."

JC walked right at her, so that she had no choice but to back away from him. He slammed the cabin door shut behind him and winced at the noise. A moment later, Kim strode through the door and glared at him.

"Don't do that! You know I hate having to walk through things! It makes me feel . . . not real."

"Sorry," said JC. "Blame it on the Boss."

"I do," said Kim, switching her glare to Latimer. "Whenever something bad happens in your life, it's always her fault."

Latimer ignored Kim and moved on down the corridor to Melody and Happy's cabin. JC stepped quickly in between her and the door.

"Maybe we should leave Happy be," he said carefully. "He needs his rest even more than I do."

"Can't help that," said Latimer. "I'm pretty sure we're going to need his particular talents." She waited till JC stepped reluctantly aside, then hammered on the door with her fist. "Mr. Palmer! Ms. Chambers! This is Catherine Latimer; you're needed!"

The door was suddenly pulled open, and Happy bounded out into the corridor. Full of energy, smiling widely, his eyes unbearably bright.

"Is it pirates?" he said cheerfully. "Are we being boarded? I knew I should have packed my cutlass . . ."

His voice trailed away as something further down the corridor caught his attention. There was nothing there that JC could see, but Happy seemed fascinated by it. Melody stepped quietly out into the corridor, closing the door behind her. She looked worn-out. She nodded to JC, and he nodded to her. It was amazing how much information you could pack into a nod.

JC could tell Happy was back on the pills again and didn't know whether to feel sad or relieved. He only had to look at the telepath to see the damage they were doing. But Latimer was right; if there really was something nasty up on the main deck, courtesy of the Flesh Undying, they were going to need Happy at the height of his abilities to deal with it. Melody looked accusingly at Latimer but didn't say anything. She didn't need to.

"Is Happy up to this, Mel?" JC said quietly.

"He's better when he's doing something," she said, just as quietly. "There's nothing more I can do for him."

JC picked up on the loss and feeling of failure in her voice but didn't know what to say.

"I feel fine!" Happy said loudly. "Fine!"

For a long moment, they all just stood there in the corridor, looking at each other, thinking many things but saying nothing.

"I am a telepath," Happy said finally. "So I know what you're all thinking. And you, Boss; you should be ashamed. Just . . . generally."

They all jumped as a cabin door slammed open further down the corridor, and Natasha Chang appeared. Looking immaculate in her pink leather outfit, complete with pink pillbox hat perched on the back of her perfectly arranged hair. JC felt obscurely outraged. She had no right to look that good after only a few hours' sleep. Chang scowled at them all impartially.

"You weren't going to call me, were you? You were planning to go up on deck and leave me behind! I hate being left out of things. I want to play, too!"

"Let her come," JC said to Latimer. "She'll only make a fuss if we don't."

"Loudly and violently and all over the place," said Chang.

"Come on then," said Latimer. "I'm sure we can find a use for you, Ms. Chang."

"If only as something to hide behind when the ectoplasm hits the fan," said Melody.

Happy giggled.

‧‧‧‧‧‧‧‧‧‧‧‧‧‧‧‧‧‧‧‧‧‧‧‧‧

Up on the main deck, the air was cool and fresh, but the night was very dark, beyond the massed lights of the *Moonchilde*. Fierce arc-lights had been strung up on high, illuminating the whole length of the deck with a harsh glare. No-one trusted the shadows; they might be hiding something. The night sky held only the barest sliver of a new moon though the stars seemed sharp and distinct. JC looked quickly around him but couldn't see anything immediately threatening. The night scene gave every indication of being calm and pleasant and entirely undisturbed. JC smiled at Kim.

"You know . . . anywhen else, this would have made a nice romantic getaway. A stroll in the night with my best girl, on a ship out at sea, far from anywhere . . ."

"I always wanted to take a nice cruise somewhere romantic," said Kim, falling in with his mood. "Visit exotic places, with names I only ever heard in films . . . A seat at the Captain's table . . . I always wanted to go for a promenade around the deck; and I don't even know what a promenade is!"

"Concentrate, children," said Latimer.

"You are no fun," Kim said haughtily.

Spotlights from on high lit up the waters all around the ship and moved restlessly back and forth. There were no crewmen in the rigging to direct them, so JC assumed the lights were being operated by remote control, probably by the scientists down in their bunker. An awful lot of the ship's crew had turned out to patrol the main deck, every one of them heavily armed. They stopped frequently to inspect every nook and cranny, and no man went off on his own, even for a moment, clearly something they'd learned the hard way. Their faces were set and grim, and they were all just a bit jumpy, in a highly dangerous and ready to shoot the shit out of everything kind of way. Their guns had moved immediately to cover the Ghost Finders the moment they appeared on deck before reluctantly turning away again. The crew didn't approve of the new visitors; but they were more scared of other things.

JC strode over to the polished brass railings and peered over the side of the ship. The night outside the ship's lights seemed very dark—the kind of night that could conceal anything. Latimer moved in beside him, looked quickly around, sniffed loudly a couple of times, then led her group off in search of Captain Katt. They found him standing beside the bathysphere, staring out at the dark.

"I find its solid presence reassuring," he said, without having to be asked. "And on this ship, you learn to take your reassurances where you can find them."

"Are all your crew up on deck, Captain?" said Latimer.

"All those not needed for essential duties," said Katt.

"Some of them should be guarding the scientists," said Chang.

"My men guard the ship, Ms. Chang," said Katt. "The safety of the ship comes first."

"Your job is to make sure nothing happens to the scientists," Chang said coldly. "Any one of them is more important to the Project than all the ship's crew put together. Including you, Captain. I want those scientists properly guarded!"

Katt looked at her, then quietly detailed half a dozen crewmen to go below and guard all entrances and approaches to the scientists' bunker. Chang smiled briefly, satisfied she'd established who was really in charge on the *Moonchilde*. JC looked up and down the ship's deck. Nothing was happening. The night seemed calm and peaceful. But JC didn't trust it. There was a feeling on the air, of something really bad just waiting to happen. The crew could feel it, too; it was obvious in their darting looks and sudden movements. They had the look of an army patrol that had wandered into enemy-occupied territory.

"Why did you call us up here, Captain?" JC said quietly. "What's the nature of the emergency? I don't see anything . . ."

"My lookouts reported activity in the night," said Katt, not even glancing at JC. "Movements, sounds . . . Things moving in the waters."

"What kinds of things?" said Melody.

"Nothing good," said Katt.

"Could be dolphins . . ." said Chang.

"Nothing lives in these waters any more!" Katt said sharply. "Nothing can live in these cursed waters . . . The scientists say they're picking up something on their short-range scanners, but they can't tell me what. All they could say for sure was that whatever's out there . . . are not in any way natural presences." He snorted briefly. "Like I needed them to tell me that. A fine collection of minds you've burdened me with, Ms. Chang. If I had time, I'm beat them all to death with an albatross."

"You think whatever's happening is linked to the Flesh Undying?" said JC.

"There's nothing else out here," said Katt.

"The Flesh Undying is restless," said Happy. "It's dreaming . . ."

Captain Katt looked dubiously at the telepath. Happy was staring off into the dark, his eyes wide and unblinking.

His voice had been dreamy, almost fey. JC moved in beside him.

"What are you picking up, Happy?"

"Hard to tell . . . Presences, right enough, but there's a strange lack of definition to them. Unfinished, incomplete . . . Not really conscious, as such."

"Living things or ghosts?" JC asked.

"Almost certainly one or the other," said Happy. He looked up and down the main deck, considering. JC could tell Happy was seeing a lot more than was in front of him. JC sometimes wished he could see all the marvels and wonders of the hidden world, too, until he remembered what seeing them had done to the telepath.

"The night is full of information," said Happy. "The aether is saturated with strange intelligence . . . but I can't tell where it's coming from."

"The Flesh Undying?" said JC.

"Wouldn't surprise me at all," said Happy.

"You're not being very helpful," said JC.

"You're lucky I'm standing upright and talking coherently," said Happy, unmoved. "I'm out of my depth here, JC. I've never felt anything like this. I'm not sure anyone has. We are right out on the edges of what's real . . ." He looked thoughtfully at JC. "And there's something different about you. It's like . . . there's more of you. If I didn't know better, I'd say you'd been dipping into my stash. What have you being doing, JC?"

"Communing with the gods and getting some interesting if highly frustrating answers," said JC. "Climbing Mount Olympus isn't all it's cracked up to be."

"And people say I'm weird," said Happy.

"Oh they do," said JC. "Frequently."

The two men shared a small smile. The smile of those who've been through things together no-one else could hope to understand. Or joke about.

"I think our arriving here has changed things," said Happy. "Introduced a new factor into the equation; or more likely, a spanner in the works. It could be . . . that the Flesh Undying was disturbed by the opening and closing of the Drood Door.

Or maybe it just recognised us. We have been a considerable thorn in its side, after all."

"You seem very lucid," said JC.

"Yes," said Happy. "Make the most of it. It cost enough."

Melody came over to join them, shooting JC a hard look. "You ask too much of him, JC."

"Let me feel needed, love," said Happy. "It's all I've got left. Apart from you, obviously. I didn't say that fast enough, did I?"

"You should have said it first," said Melody.

"I don't know why you put up with me," said Happy.

Melody grinned. "Because you're great in the sack. Nothing like being in bed with a mind-reader, to locate those important little places."

"Okay!" said JC. "Far too much information . . ."

A sudden flurry of sound and movement caught their attention, half-way down the deck. Katt headed straight for it, with everyone else right behind. Crewmen were crowding together at the railings, staring at something out on the waters. Spotlights converged on one particular spot, lighting up the dark surface, but didn't reveal anything.

"Is it the Flesh Undying?" said JC.

"Yes," said Happy. "I can feel it. Like thunder in the distance. Is it dreaming? Or waking up? Hard to tell . . ."

"Careful, Happy," said JC. "Don't try to make direct contact."

"I'm not stupid," said Happy, with some dignity. "Direct contact with something that big would have my brains leaking out my ears. I'm just observing. From a distance."

"A safe distance?" said Melody.

"No such thing, here," said Happy. "This whole situation is a spiritual mine-field. And we are tap-dancing our way across it."

"A mental image I could have done without," said JC.

"Can you tell? Does the Flesh Undying know what we're planning?" said Katt. "Does it know about the bathysphere?"

"*Knows* . . . is probably too strong a word," said Happy.

"It sort of knows about this ship, but it doesn't know where we are. I think it just feels threatened."

"Is it waking up?" said Katt.

"It's never been asleep, as we understand it," said Happy. "Just . . . distanced from the world."

"How do you mean, distanced?" said Latimer.

"It's crazy," said JC.

Happy looked at him. "I wouldn't be at all surprised."

They were all standing pressed up against the railings now, looking out over the ocean. All they could see was the surface of the waters. There could have been anything underneath, anything at all. Melody shivered suddenly, perhaps from a cold breeze.

"I wish I had my equipment with me," she said. "So I could make sense of what's happening."

"This close to the Flesh Undying, science as we know it breaks down," said Latimer.

"Horseshit," said Melody. "Science is science. A tool for measuring and understanding things. The Flesh Undying may be seriously weird, but let's not get over-impressed. It's just a big beastie from somewhere else. Prod it with a hard enough stick, and it'll tell us everything we want to know. If you don't believe in a scientific investigation, oh wise and revered Boss, why are we going down in the bathysphere in the morning?"

"Because we've run out of everything else to try," said Captain Katt.

Natasha Chang came sauntering over to join them at the railings. She'd been taking her own quiet tour around the main deck, to see what there was to see and sneer at it. Because she never trusted anything until she'd seen it with her own eyes. And preferably kicked it a few times. She didn't seem nearly as unsettled as everyone else, just irritated at a situation she didn't understand and couldn't control.

"I've had enough of this sneaking around," she said bluntly. "Give me something I can shoot holes in."

"You cannot shoot an apparition, Ms. Chang," said Katt.

"I could always eat it," said Chang.

Katt looked at her, then turned to Latimer. "Really?"

"Apparently," said Latimer.

Katt turned back to Chang, not even trying to hide his disgust. "Unnatural creature . . ."

"You work for the Crowley Project, Captain," said Chang. "And as long as I'm here, I represent the Project. Which means you work for me. So choose your next words very carefully, unless you feel like walking home. With an anchor strapped to each ankle."

"You might eat the ghosts of men, Ms. Chang," Katt said steadily. "But the things that walk my deck at night are nothing so ordinary."

"I'm not ordinary either," said Chang.

"I couldn't agree more," said Katt.

He moved away quickly to give orders to his crew, while Chang was still working out how to take that. The Ghost Finders exchanged looks but said nothing. Though there was a certain amount of smirking. And then JC looked round sharply as he realised Kim was no longer with them. He hadn't seen her go. He looked up and down the deck, but there was no sign of the ghost girl anywhere. He stepped away from the railings and called out to her surreptitiously; but there was no response. He turned to Happy, lowering his voice.

"Kim's gone again. Can you track where she is?"

"No," said Happy. "I can only read the thoughts of the living. I've never been able to read Kim. Sometimes, I can't even see her, even when you're looking right at her."

JC was taken aback. It had never occurred to him that the others might not be able to see Kim as easily as he could.

"So, sometimes it looks like I'm talking to myself?"

"Oh yes," said Happy. "Freaks Mel out, every time. You wouldn't believe how much effort she's put into trying to come up with some kind of tech that would allow her to see Kim all the time, like you. Mel hates being left out of things."

"And you never said anything?"

Happy shrugged. "We got used to it. I always thought it was funny."

Melody saw them talking together and came over to join

them, determined not to be left out. "What is it? What's happening?"

"Kim's gone walkabout. Again," said Happy.

Melody sniffed. "Witness my total lack of surprise. Probably just as well. The mood the crew are in, they're ready to open fire on anything unnatural." She saw that JC was genuinely concerned, and her tone softened. "She's probably just looking around. You know she likes to sneak up on people and listen in on conversations. I wouldn't worry, JC. Really."

"Not when there are so many other far more worrying things to be concerned about," said Happy. "It feels more and more to me, that this ship is surrounded. Under siege. Something doesn't like our being here."

A crewman on the other side of the deck cried out suddenly, pointing over the railings at something in the waters. Everyone rushed across the deck to join him. More spotlights snapped on and swivelled back and forth, their fierce light punching through the dark, but it was still hard to make out anything. The crew crammed together at the railings, training their guns on the dark waters. JC could feel the tension building. Happy stepped back a few paces, disturbed by the presence of so many agitated thoughts.

A soft wind blew in off the surface of the waters, cool and damp. JC could feel it on his face, taste the salt on his lips. Looking out into the dark, it felt like someone was looking back at him. His hands clenched into fists. None of what was happening aboard the *Moonchilde* fitted any of the things he was used to. He didn't know what to do. He really wanted some kind of ghost to show up and start walking the deck. He'd know what to do, how to cope, with something as ordinary as a ghost.

Everyone reacted sharply at a new movement in the waters, some distance from the ship. It looked like something really large had surfaced and rolled over. Big as a whale, maybe even bigger. Except . . . JC couldn't see anything out there. Just the agitated waters, with no sign of what caused it. Several crewmen opened fire anyway, to make their feelings clear. They sprayed the surface of the ocean with heavy bursts until the Captain yelled at them to stop.

"Wait till you've got a target! Preserve your ammunition!"

The firing died raggedly away, its echoes hanging on in the still of the night. Chang pushed in beside Katt, leaning right over the railings for a better look.

"Is this an attack?"

"Possibly. Or something leading up to one," said Katt. He frowned unhappily. "It can't be a coincidence, that all of this started up after we decided to deploy the bathysphere."

"I thought you said things like this happened every night?" said Latimer.

"Not like this," said Katt. "This feels . . . more serious. We can't lower the bathysphere if the Flesh Undying knows it's coming."

"It doesn't," said Happy. "Not specifically."

"Are you sure?" said Katt.

"Yes, and no," said Happy.

"You're really not very helpful," said Katt.

"You noticed!" said Happy. And then he grimaced and shook his head heavily, as though trying to dislodge something. Melody looked at him carefully.

"Do you need a lie-down, Happy?"

"There's too much happening!" Happy said loudly. "Too many people thinking. Everyone stop thinking! So much noise in the night . . . It feels like my head's going to explode!"

"Try not to get any brains on my nice jacket," said JC.

Happy turned on him, then relaxed, just a little. They shared their small smile again.

"Male humour," said Melody. "Male bonding. It's a wonder the species has survived this long."

"Back under control, Happy?" said JC.

"Better," said the telepath.

Katt looked sternly at Happy's flushed, sweaty face and his huge eyes. "Is this man on drugs?"

"Usually," said JC.

"I want this man off my ship!" said Katt. "He's a danger to himself, and to my people. Get him out of here, or I'll have him removed!"

"No you won't," said Melody.

"Why not?" said Katt, rounding on her.

"Well," said Melody, entirely unperturbed by his manner or the loudness of his voice, "First, because I'd kick the crap out of anyone who tried. And second, because we need him. He's the best advance warning system in the business."

"Exactly!" said Happy. "That's me, the canary in the cage. Want to hear a song? I do requests . . ."

"Concentrate," said JC, before Latimer could. "What's going on, Happy? What's here in the night with us?"

The telepath looked up and down the deck, frowning thoughtfully. Seeing the things only he could see. He cocked his head on one side.

"Odd . . ."

"What?" said Katt. "What is?"

"There are things in the water," Happy said slowly. "Swimming around the ship. Circling, but keeping their distance. It's like they can't quite find us. Or maybe . . . they're waiting for something."

"What kind of . . . things?" said Katt, peering out into the dark.

"Unnatural," said Happy. "Unreal. Made things . . . I think you might be right, Captain. The Flesh Undying's dreams, and perhaps even its random thoughts and impulses, are taking on solid form. They're projections, sendings . . . I'm trying hard to sound like I know what I'm talking about, but when it comes to something like the Flesh Undying, all I can really offer are best guesses."

"Are these sendings dangerous?" said JC.

"Of course!" said Happy. "You said it yourself—the Flesh Undying is insane. It doesn't have good thoughts."

"You said . . . it doesn't know we're here," said Latimer.

"If it did, it would have destroyed us by now," said Happy. "We're just . . . an irritant, on the edge of its senses. And it's trying to scratch us."

"I think I felt happier before he started telling me things," said Katt.

"I get that a lot," said Happy.

JC took off his sunglasses, and the nearest crewmen cried out in shock and surprise, as golden light spilled from his eyes. Catherine Latimer moved in beside him, and her eyes glowed golden, too. Several crew members backed away, and Captain Katt looked like he wanted to. But he stood his ground and yelled for his men to hold their position; and most of them did. JC and Latimer leaned out over the railings, turning the full force of the otherworldly light from their eyes onto the dark waters. They still couldn't make out anything. Either because there was nothing out there or because it was determined not to be seen.

"Can you see anything?" JC said to Latimer.

"No," said Latimer. "Can you see anything?"

"No," said JC. "But . . ."

"Yes," said Latimer. "I'd have to go along with that. I can feel something . . . a presence in the night, like a gathering storm."

"What does that make us?" said JC. "The lightning rod?"

Everyone looked around sharply as the *Moonchilde* was hit by poltergeist phenomena. Everything on deck not securely attached or tied down started jumping around, or clattered loudly, or slid along the deck. Things banged together or spun in place, while steel cables thrummed loudly like plucked strings. Chairs overturned and kept on turning, somersaulting along the deck. Tall standing aerials tied themselves in knots. The wooden floor-boards of the deck groaned loudly, as though they'd been subjected to sudden and unbearable weights and pressures. Arc-lights flared and dimmed, and some of the bulbs exploded.

The crew bunched together in small groups, gripping their guns till their knuckles whitened. Most stood back-to-back, so they could cover every direction at once. But none of them ran. They'd been through this before and knew running wouldn't help. And then everything stopped, quite suddenly. Nothing moved. Not a sound anywhere.

"So much for the Overture," said Happy.

Crewmen turned their guns back and forth, desperate for a target. Katt moved slowly out into the middle of the deck, his head held high. His footsteps were loud and carrying on the quiet.

"Is that it?" said Latimer. "Is it over?"

"It hasn't even started yet," said Katt. "It's never over till somebody's died."

A series of loud, booming noises ran along the underside of the ship, heavy and measured, as though something in the waters was banging against the hull. The whole superstructure shook and shuddered from the strength of the blows, starting at one end of the ship and running quickly the whole length of the *Moonchilde*.

"Something wants our attention," said JC.

"Or something wants to get in," said Melody.

Their end of the ship suddenly rose out of the water and into the night sky. It kept on rising, and the deck tilted sharply. Everyone had to grab onto something to keep from tumbling down the steep hill the deck had become. Everything loose skidded down the deck and shot off the far end. The *Moonchilde* groaned loudly as its superstructure flexed in ways it was never meant to. Brass railings bent and snapped under the strain. The bottom end of the ship disappeared beneath the surface of the ocean, lost under a great swell of dark waters. As though something was pulling it down. And then the high end suddenly fell back again, crashing into the ocean. Water splashed up and over both sides of the ship, drenching the crew.

The *Moonchilde* rocked back and forth, settling slowly in the dark waters. Crew members reluctantly released their handholds. Katt moved among them, speaking calmly and reassuringly, even as he looked quickly around for signs of damage. Everything seemed intact though a whole bunch of loose equipment had been lost.

"Oh well," said Happy. "Worse things happen at sea."

"It's like something big pushed up against the bottom of the ship," said Latimer. "I mean . . . really physically big."

"Not the Flesh Undying," Happy said firmly. "It's miles below us, and it doesn't move. I'm not sure it can."

"Then what was it?" said JC. "What are you picking up, Happy?"

"There's nothing here," said Happy. "Nothing real, anyway. It's like trying to grab handfuls of fog . . ."

Lights flared suddenly, all across the night sky. Fierce as

lightning, vivid multi-coloured circles cart-wheeling across the dark. Sharp colours lit up the ship, and shadows danced in a dozen different directions at once. The crew looked on, entranced, until the Captain yelled at them to pay attention to their surroundings.

"Ball lightning?" said Melody, tentatively.

"Maybe," said JC.

The lights suddenly all snapped off at once, as though someone had hit a switch, and the night sky went back to being respectably dark again.

"What was the point of that?" said JC.

Happy shrugged. "What's the point of most dreams?"

"You know," Melody said slowly, "I have had some really bad dreams in my time. The kind of horrors you only escape from by waking up. That's what's walking your ship at night, Captain Katt. Nightmares—given shape and form."

"Okay," said Katt. "I think I like it even less when she tells me things."

The bathysphere reverberated loudly, a slow, solemn sound, ringing on the night like a great steel bell. Everyone turned to look as the sphere's support cables coiled and uncoiled, writhing like snakes. And while everybody was looking at that, something grabbed hold of a crewman and hauled him right over the railings. He cried out in shock and horror, but by the time everyone had turned to look, he was already over the side and gone. No-one could even be sure who or what had taken him. Several crewmen rushed to the side and peered down into the dark waters; but there was no splash, no disturbance, no sign of what had happened to him.

"I've lost another man," said Katt. He glared at Natasha Chang. "Sixteen years working for the Project, and I never lost a single member of my crew until I came here!"

"Do you want to make an official complaint?" said Chang. "Because I can tell you right now, officially no-one in the Project will give a damn. You're here to do a job, Captain. Suck it up and get on with it, or I'll replace you with someone who can."

The Captain shook his head slowly. "We should never

have come here. The Flesh Undying hasn't just poisoned these waters; it's poisoned the world."

JC looked up and down the long deck, but nothing was moving. It was eerily quiet, the only sound in the night the gentle murmur of waves lapping against the sides of the *Moonchilde*. Everyone was standing very still, looking about them. Whatever was happening, it wasn't over yet. They could all feel something bad approaching . . . drawing closer every moment. JC couldn't help noticing that Latimer didn't seem particularly bothered, presumably because she really had seen it all before. At least she'd shut down the glow from her eyes. Which reminded JC to put his sunglasses back on.

A shimmering human form appeared, right in the middle of the deck, screaming and howling. It staggered back and forth as though buffeted by an unseen wind, crying out with rage and horror. It seemed to be made entirely of sizzling light, spitting and sparking, like lightning imprisoned in a human shape. The figure lurched forward, its every movement packed with unbearable suffering, leaving a trail of burning footprints in its wake. Everything it touched burst into flames. Crewmen rushed forward to battle the fires, with extinguishers and heavy blankets. None of them wanted to get too close to the apparition, but it paid them no attention at all, caught up in the horror of its own condition.

Katt grabbed hold of Happy's shoulder. "Talk to me, Mr. Palmer! Is that . . . human? Could it be one of my missing crewmen?"

"No," said Happy. "That is not human. Never was. It's just something trying to look like a man."

"Why?" said Katt. "Why would it want to do that?"

"Because whatever is driving all this, it knows what scares us," said Happy. "Sights and sounds are all very well, but nothing terrifies us more than intimations of our own mortality. Essentially, this is the darker side of the Flesh Undying talking to our darker side. Its subconscious in conversation with ours."

Katt turned his back on the telepath and moved away. JC looked at Happy.

"Are you sure about that?"

"No," said Happy. "I'm just talking off the top of my head. It's not like there's a Spotter's Guide for the Supernatural and Uncanny. Though there really ought to be. All I can tell you for sure is that the thing before us is not and never was human."

"What does it look like, to you?" said JC. "You always see things differently from the rest of us, even when you're not blasted out of your skull."

Happy considered the ghost carefully. "Rage, hatred, and a need to destroy."

Some of the crewmen must have got the same feeling because they opened fire on the shimmering figure. Their bullets passed harmlessly through it and chewed up the ship's woodwork. Until Captain Katt yelled at them to stop firing, before they accidentally hit each other. Most did, but some continued, desperate to feel they were doing something. They only stopped when they ran out of bullets. Katt glared at the Ghost Finders.

"Do something!"

"Does panicking count?" said Happy.

"You're not panicking," said Melody.

"I'm not?" said Happy. "Oh, that is a relief."

"What do you think, Happy?" said JC. "Is it Flesh?"

"No . . ." The telepath frowned thoughtfully. "I can't feel any physical presence. It's not really here."

"Are you sure?" said Melody. "Given how much of this ship is currently on fire, because of it . . . If it's not what it looks like, what is it?"

"A distraction," said Latimer. She looked coldly around her. "It's big and bright and destructive, and it's here to hold our attention while something else is happening. Something important that we're not supposed to notice . . . until it's too late."

"Fine," said JC. "You keep an eye out for that, while the rest of us do something about the threat in front of us. If that thing isn't Flesh, it's just some kind of apparition. A ghost. And we know how to deal with ghosts."

"Damn right," said Natasha Chang. Everyone jumped despite themselves as she stepped out of the shadows. In all the excitement, they'd lost track of her. Chang smiled at the ghost, completely unimpressed or intimidated. She strode down the deck and stepped deliberately into its path, blocking its way. The shimmering figure stopped, as though surprised. The howling and crying broke off as it looked at Chang. The deck beneath it scorched black and caught fire.

"Step right up, Casper," said Chang. "You're just what I need. Momma's feeling peckish."

She reached out to the ghost with both hands, so she could rip its soul out and feed on it . . . and then she snatched her hands back again. She couldn't find anything there—nothing to grab hold of. Nothing she could even recognise as human. Just a terrible, aching void that put her spiritual teeth on edge.

The ghost lashed out at her with a brightly shining arm. Chang dropped to the deck and the arm swept past, just missing her. The back of her pink leather outfit scorched and smoked, burned black in a moment from sheer proximity. Chang must have felt it, but she didn't make a sound. She rolled away to one side, putting some piled-up equipment between her and the ghost, before beating at her smouldering hair with both hands. She yanked off her burned pillbox hat and threw it away, cursing loudly. She produced her gold-plated pistol and fired several shots at the ghost. But even her specially treated ammunition couldn't touch it.

"Stay under cover!" JC yelled to her. "Let us deal with it!"

"He's all yours!" Chang yelled back.

"Do we have a plan?" Happy said to JC. "I'd feel so much happier if I thought we had a plan."

"Stop it, contain it, deal with it," said JC.

"Good plan," said Melody. "I feel so much safer."

The three of them moved forward, and the shining ghost spun around to face them. It was hunched and bent over now, seeming somehow twisted and deformed but still burning everything it touched. The Ghost Finders stopped well short of it. JC took off his sunglasses and fixed the ghost with his golden gaze. It shifted uncertainly, disturbed by the light, but that was all. It took a step towards them.

"Don't let it touch you," JC said to Happy and Melody.

"You think?" said Happy.

"Get me a length of steel cable, and I might be able to ground it," said Melody. "Drain off its energy . . .."

"No," Happy said immediately. "Nice idea, but this isn't a natural phenomenon, Mel. It won't follow natural rules."

"When in doubt," said JC. "Go with what's worked before. I don't believe I believe in this thing. Do you believe in it, Mel?"

"Something that doesn't follow the natural laws of physics?" said Melody. "Hell no."

"And I wouldn't believe in anything that ugly even if I wasn't out of my mind," said Happy.

"Good enough," said JC.

He reached out to them, and their hands clamped down on his. Happy reached out with his mind and locked the three of them together. They hit the shimmering figure with a concentrated blast of telepathic disbelief; and it disappeared, gone in a moment, unable to withstand the pressure of their refusal to accept its existence. The moment it disappeared, so did all its burning footprints, and the flames from all the things it had touched. No sign of any damage remained to show it had ever been there, apart from those parts of the ship the crew had shot up. The deck was perfectly empty, utterly quiet. The crewmen lowered their guns and nodded to the Ghost Finders with new respect.

"That's it?" said Captain Katt. "That's all there is to it? You just give it a hard look, and it goes away?"

"Sometimes," said JC. He put his sunglasses back on.

"Say it," said Melody. "You know you want to."

"This ship . . ." said JC. "Is clean."

"No it isn't," said Happy.

Katt looked at him. "What?"

A crewman at the opposite end of the ship called out, pointing desperately at something he'd spotted out on the ocean. Everyone hurried forward to join him, and the spotlights changed their patterns, to send more light ranging out over the dark waters. Captain Katt yelled orders, and more arc-lights blinked on, converging on the new position. Several crew members fired flares into the night sky, to add even more light. And finally, pressed up together against the brass railings, they were all able to see the new disturbance in the ocean. A great depression had opened up, a massive, circular hollow, with all the water spiralling around and around and falling away, disappearing into the depths.

"What the hell is that?" said Katt.

"The water is draining away," said JC. "Being drawn down into some kind of . . . sink-hole?"

"More like a plug-hole," said Happy. "The Flesh Undying has pulled the plug. It's opened up a hole in our reality, and the ocean is draining away into it."

"I told you we were being distracted," said Latimer.

A terrible roaring sound filled the night, a huge and utterly unnatural sound, too powerful for human ears to bear. It was the sound of an ocean being taken away by a force too great for it to withstand. Everyone flinched back from the railings as the ship lurched suddenly, pulled towards the great depression in the waters.

"We're heading for the sink-hole!" said JC. "Doesn't this ship have an anchor, Captain?"

"It's too deep here!" said Katt.

The *Moonchilde* was pulled remorselessly forward through the water, heading for the depression. Katt ran back to his bridge, shouting for his crew to start up the ship's engines, and steer the *Moonchilde* away from the sink-hole's pull. The engines started up almost immediately, and the ship's movement slowed but didn't stop. The engines strained against the heavy pull, and the ship's superstructure groaned loudly, torn between two forces. The crew ran to their stations, to do what they could. JC and the others stood together, staring out at the disturbance in the waters. One thing JC was sure of—the size of the depression in the surface was growing steadily larger.

"How is the Flesh Undying doing that?" said Melody.

"It's dreaming of how it first arrived in this world," said JC. "Through a hole in reality. It's just made another one."

"It can do that?" said Melody.

"Apparently," said Happy.

"We have to close it," said Latimer.

"How?" said JC. "How could we do that?"

"The scientists!" said Melody. "We need their equipment, their data-mining techniques . . . Something to give us some idea of what might work!"

"I've always admired your optimism," said JC.

,,,,,,,,,,,,,,,,,,,,,,,,,,,

The three Ghost Finders raced down through the ship's decks, to the lab at the bottom of the *Moonchilde*. Where the three scientists were darting agitatedly from one monitor screen to another, while shouting and screaming at each other. New information, new theories, and old grudges were thrown back and forth at full volume. They were so caught up in their increasingly acrimonious arguments, they didn't even notice JC, Happy, and Melody arrive. JC looked from one scientist to another, waiting for them to pause for breath long enough for him to get a word in, but they just kept shouting at each other and not listening to the replies. Latimer finally caught up with the Ghost Finders, pushed past them, and raised her voice, demanding the scientists' attention. They didn't even look round, just shouted that much louder to drown her out.

"This is what gives science a bad name," said Melody.

Happy grabbed JC by the arm and pulled him close so he could shout into JC's ear. "Something's very wrong here, JC. One of those scientists isn't human."

JC looked at Goldsmith, Hedley, and Hamilton. "They all look, and sound, very human to me."

"One of them is Flesh," Happy insisted, "masquerading as human."

"I heard that!" said Melody. "Just what we needed. More complications."

JC looked at Happy. "And you didn't notice this before, because . . . ?"

"It was shielding itself. But with everything that's been going on, the shield has weakened. The Flesh Undying has other things on its mind."

"All right," said Latimer. "Which one is it?"

Happy scowled. "I can't tell. It doesn't know it's not human."

"We have to get their attention," said JC.

"I can do that," said Medley.

She drew one of her pistols and fired several shots into the bunker's low ceiling. The three scientists broke off arguing and dived for cover. There was a pause, then they peered cautiously out from their hiding places with wide, startled eyes. JC stepped forward.

"Sorry about that. But it seems one of you isn't who or even what they appear to be. One of you is an agent for the Flesh Undying."

Interestingly, none of the scientists challenged the claim. They just started shouting again: first denying it was them, then accusing the others. Angry voices quickly gave way to pushing and shoving.

"Isn't there some kind of test we can do?" said JC, raising his voice again to be heard over the din.

"Yes," said Latimer. "Shoot them all and see which one is still talking afterwards."

"Works for me," said Melody.

She took careful aim with her pistol. JC was pretty sure she was bluffing. The three scientists stopped arguing to look at Melody. They didn't seem nearly as sure. And Hedley went wild. His shape slumped, his back rising and rippling as his arms and legs stretched impossibly. His face sloughed away, revealing a demonic visage underneath. Hamilton and Goldsmith dived for cover again, making loud noises of distress. Hedley, or what was left of him, moved quickly to intercept them.

"Shoot it!" Latimer said to Medley.

"I can't!" said Melody. "I might hit one of the real scientists. Or some piece of equipment we might need."

"Work with me, Mr. Chance," said Latimer.

Her eyes blazed golden in the gloom of the bunker, and the thing that had been Hedley made a wounded sound and flinched back. JC whipped off his sunglasses and moved in beside Latimer. The combined golden light from their eyes filled the bunker. The Hedley thing broke down even further, barely human now . . . as though it couldn't maintain its shape in the presence of the golden light. Elongated arms lashed out and snapped around Goldsmith and Hamilton, pinioning them in heaving coils.

"Stay back!" said the Hedley thing. It didn't sound at all human. "I'll kill them both if you don't leave me alone and get out of here!"

"Please!" said Goldsmith, struggling helplessly against the dead white tentacle that held him. "Don't let him kill me!"

"Don't leave me here, with this thing!" said Hamilton.

JC and Latimer paused and looked at each other. JC was pretty sure they were going to need Hamilton and Goldsmith's help to stop the sink-hole. But they couldn't let Hedley escape. There was no telling how much it knew, or how much damage it could cause, if they didn't take it down. Happy eased past JC and Latimer in the confined space, holding both hands up to show he didn't have a weapon. What was left of Hedley's face snapped forward on an elongating neck, fanged jaws opening impossibly wide. Happy tossed one of his pills into the gaping mouth, and hit Hedley with a hard, telepathic shove. The mouth snapped shut, and Hedley swallowed. And then the horrid thing just collapsed, slumping almost liquidly to the floor, as Happy's chemicals went to work. In a few moments, there was nothing left of Hedley but a slowly spreading heap of grey, undifferentiated Flesh.

Happy smiled smugly. "My medicine is stronger than your bad medicine."

Goldsmith and Hamilton moved quickly forward, no longer held by the tentacles. They joined the Ghost Finders and shuddered as the last of Hedley's body fell apart, leaving just a pool of thick grey goo.

"That was our colleague . . ." said Hamilton.

"How did that thing replace Hedley?" said Goldsmith.

"How can we be sure there ever was a real Hedley?" said Hamilton. "When he arrived, did anyone check his credentials? Or did they just assume he must have the right clearances to have got this far? Maybe it's been an agent all along."

"But . . . he did good work!" said Goldsmith. "Useful work!"

"How can we be sure of that, now?" said Hamilton. "Maybe it only gave us small successes, to steer us away from bigger ones, or more useful areas we might have investigated?"

"We're going to have to go back and recheck all our work," said Goldsmith.

"Not right now you're not," said JC.

"You've been close to that man all this time," said Latimer. "Working side by side, in close proximity. Didn't either of you notice anything strange about him?"

Goldsmith and Hamilton looked at each other. The question seemed to confuse them. They looked back at Latimer.

"Well, no," said Goldsmith.

"He did good work," said Hamilton.

"We have a more important problem, people!" said JC. "The sink-hole!"

"Yes!" said Goldsmith. "The dimensional rupture! We've been following its progress on the monitors."

"Fascinating," said Hamilton. "Why are you interrupting us? We need to study this . . ."

"What can we do to shut it down?" said Latimer.

Goldsmith and Hamilton looked at each other.

"We have a possible solution," said Goldsmith.

"Something that might work," said Hamilton.

"The theory is sound!" said Goldsmith, bristling immediately.

"It's still just a theory!" said Hamilton.

"What is?" Latimer said loudly, before they could start shouting at each other again.

"An EMP," said Goldsmith, still glaring at Hamilton. "Electromagnetic pulse. We have the capability to generate a small, localised EMP. Enough to temporarily disrupt the Flesh Undying's energies. Scramble its thoughts—the way that pill did with Hedley. The ship's systems won't be affected. They're shielded."

"Hold it," said Melody, suspiciously. "You can generate a localised EMP? Why would you need to be able to do that?"

Goldsmith shrugged, just a bit guiltily. "Project orders. They supplied the equipment. In case another ship got too close and took too much of an interest in what we were doing. The EMP would wipe their computers, shut down their systems."

"But that would have left the other ship dead in the water!" said Melody. "Stranded all the way out here, miles from the shipping routes!"

"We had our orders," said Hamilton.

"Wouldn't something as powerful as an EMP reveal the ship's location to the Flesh Undying?" said JC.

"We don't think so," said Hamilton.

"It shouldn't be in any condition to think that clearly," said Goldsmith.

"Theoretically," said Hamilton.

"Then do it," said Latimer.

The two scientists looked at each other again. JC was getting really tired of that. It always meant something bad was coming.

"What?" he said loudly. "What's the problem now?"

"We need you to do something to distract the Flesh Undying, hold its attention, while we prepare to generate the EMP," said Goldsmith.

"Otherwise, there's always the chance it could detect what's going to happen and shield itself," said Hamilton. "Our only hope is to catch it by surprise."

JC, Happy, and Melody looked at each other.

"I suppose," said JC, "if we were to link up again and focus our thoughts through Happy, like we did with the ghost . . ."

"If we shout loudly enough, that should grab its attention," said Melody.

"Would that wake it up?" JC asked Happy.

"I keep telling you, it's not really asleep!" Happy scowled, as he thought about it. "If we do get its attention . . . that will make us a target. It will see us as a danger and strike directly at us."

"Well yes," said Hamilton. "Probably."

"Almost certainly," said Goldsmith. "But you only have to hold its attention long enough to buy us the time we need."

"We're bait," said Melody.

"Situation entirely bloody normal, where the Ghost Finders are concerned," said Happy.

....

They went back up on deck, so the scientists could get to work. JC, Melody, and Happy stood together at the bow, staring out into the night. Latimer wanted to stay with them, but JC sent her back to join Captain Katt. Because somebody had to survive this.

"So," said JC. "The last stand of the Three Musketeers."

"I could do this alone," said Happy.

"No you couldn't," Melody said immediately. "You'd burn out too quickly. You need JC and me to stabilise you."

"I always did," said Happy. "Let's do it."

"I wish Kim were here," said JC.

"Who's to say she isn't?" said Melody.

They took hold of each other's hands. No-one mentioned how clammy or unsteady they might be. A cold wind was blowing right into their faces. They linked their minds telepathically and sent their joined thoughts blasting out into the dark. Not as an attack; just a concentrated announcement of their presence. And something heard them. A great tower of light manifested in the dark before them, unbearably brilliant, rising into the heavens. Full of unnatural energies. It advanced slowly on the *Moonchilde*, churning up the waters as it came.

"I think we should back away now," said Happy.

"We have to hold its attention," said JC.

"Trust me!" said Happy. "It knows we're here!"

"What's taking Goldsmith and Hamilton so long?" said Melody. "I could have organised an EMP and a tactical nuclear strike by now! Oh shit . . . That thing is getting way too close."

"What will happen if it reaches us?" said JC.

"What do you think?" said Happy.

"That bad?" said JC.

"Worse," said Happy.

"I always expected to die on some job, out in the field," said Melody. "But to die protecting a Crowley Project operation . . . Smell the irony."

And then Kim appeared out of nowhere, smiled dazzlingly at all of them, and stepped inside JC. Her presence blasted power through all of them, as though she was the missing component in some mighty engine; and all of them glowed a bright golden in the night. The blazing tower stopped its advance. And the whole ship shuddered as the EMP detonated.

The tower of light snapped off, leaving behind just a few after-images in the eyes of the Ghost Finders. There was a huge uproar of water off the ship's port bow, as the sink-hole started to fill itself in again. And the night . . . felt suddenly empty.

Kim stepped back out of JC. He let go of Happy's and Melody's hands, and the glow surrounding them disappeared. As though a spiritual current had been cut off. They all sat down hard on the deck, exhausted. Kim sat cross-legged beside JC, floating just an inch or so above the deck. JC looked at her.

"Where have you been, all this time?"

"Hiding from the Flesh Undying until I was needed," said Kim. "I was your secret weapon! Your trouble, JC, is you have no sense of drama."

"What if we had held the Flesh Undying's attention, and the EMP hadn't worked?" said Melody.

"Then we would have been screwed," said Happy. "Aren't you glad you've got me around to explain the technical stuff to you?"

"I have a gun," said Melody.

"And I think we might need it," said JC. "Look . . ."

"Oh shit," said Happy.

They all scrambled back onto their feet. Where the tower of light had been, a shining figure had appeared, apparently standing knee-deep in the dark waters. It rose up before them, looking a lot like the shimmering ghost, but a hundred feet tall or more, towering over the *Moonchilde*. It advanced slowly towards the ship, ploughing through the dark waters. It looked far more solid, more physical and more real, than it had before.

"Where the hell did that come from?" said JC. "I thought we scrambled the Flesh Undying's thoughts!"

"Obviously, not completely!" said Melody.

"I don't think disbelieving in it is going to work this time," said JC.

"I believe in it," said Happy. "It looks very real to me."

The massive shining figure loomed over the *Moonchilde*. It raised a shimmering fist, big enough to sink the ship.

"What do we do?" said Melody.

"Run," said Happy.

"We're on a ship!" said JC. "There's nowhere to run to!"

"It's still a plan," said Happy.

"Try the telepathic link again," said JC. "Just . . . hit it with everything we've got."

"That could get us all killed," said Happy. "Direct mental contact with something as big as the Flesh Undying . . ."

"But would it work against that figure?" said Melody.

"I don't know! Maybe . . ." said Happy.

"Then we have to try," said JC. "Come on, we're the Ghost Finders. We don't take any crap from the Hereafter."

They clasped hands again. And if any of them felt their hands shaking, none of them said anything.

And that was when Catherine Latimer came forward, and threw her portable Door at the huge shining figure. The black blob turned into a dimensional Door as it shot through the air, growing larger and larger; and then it swallowed up the figure whole. They were both gone in a moment, leaving just a few sparks, dropping harmlessly down the night sky.

"Quite pretty, really," said Happy.

JC glared at Latimer. "Very good. Now how are we going to get home?"

Latimer showed him her hand, with the black blob nestling in it. "It's programmed to return to its owner after use. Droods think of everything."

JC shook his head and looked at Happy. "Are you picking up anything from the Flesh Undying?"

Happy cocked his head on one side. "It's . . . confused. Its mind has turned to other things. Don't ask me what. It's like it's forgotten it ever noticed us."

"How long will that last?" said JC.

"Beats me," said Happy.

"That man is weird," said Goldsmith.

"Seriously weird," said Hamilton.

Everyone looked round. The two scientists had left their bunker to come up on deck and were looking around in a surprised sort of way, as though the view was entirely new to them.

"I don't suppose you'd consider letting us have Mr. Palmer for a while?" said Goldsmith.

"Just to run a few experiments on him," said Hamilton. "Nothing too invasive."

"No," said Melody. "The only one who gets to run scientific experiments on his body is me."

"Your whole relationship never ceases to creep the hell out of me," said JC.

"How do you think I feel?" said Happy.

"Heh heh," said Melody.

"You need to prepare for the bathysphere," said Latimer.

They all turned to look at her.

"What?" said JC.

"Right now?" said Melody.

"We can't afford to wait till morning," Latimer said steadily. "The Flesh Undying could renew its interest in us at any time. We need hard information about its physical form, something we can use as ammunition against it. So you need to go down, right now."

"But . . . it's still night," said JC.

"Where you're going, that won't matter," said Latimer. "It's always night at the bottom of the ocean."

ELEVEN

LIFE AND DEATH AND EVERYTHING ELSE

All through the darkest part of the night, Captain Katt had his crew rig up new lights, to better illuminate the deck around the bathysphere. The grey steel ball gleamed dully under lights so bright they didn't leave a shadow anywhere. Crewmen bustled back and forth, bringing armfuls of the very latest technology to be packed into the waiting sphere. Goldsmith and Hamilton drove themselves on at a fierce pace and yelled at anyone who slowed them down by not being where they were needed with what the scientists wanted. Everyone was busy with something, except for JC and Kim, Happy and Melody. They stood together, well to one side, watching what was happening without feeling any need to get involved. They were thinking about what they were going to have to do once the work was finished.

JC looked more like a rock star than ever, in his white suit, long mane of dark hair, and very dark sunglasses. Kim hovered beside him, dressed once more in a white nurse's outfit to match his suit, glowing faintly. Her feet didn't quite reach the deck. Crew members hurrying past made a point of not looking in her direction. Happy looked like someone had found him curled up in a Dumpster, after a week-long drunk.

Melody just looked tired, worn-out from the weight of her life.

Catherine Latimer came over to join them, looking neat and tidy in her plain grey suit, smoking a black Turkish cigarette in her long ivory holder. She looked like a retired head mistress, off on a cruise and not giving a damn about what was proper any more. She took in all the bustle and excitement on deck and smiled briefly, in a self-satisfied sort of way. As though they were only doing it to keep her happy. She nodded to the Ghost Finders, and they nodded briefly in return.

"I would have given you more time to prepare," she said. "But we seem to have run out."

It was as close as she could get to an apology and was accepted as such.

"More time wouldn't have helped, Boss," said JC. "Just given us longer to worry and wet ourselves."

"And the early-morning wake-up call was nothing new," said Melody. "We're used to working the graveyard shift."

"Often in graveyards," said Happy. "I've had more than enough of sitting on a tombstone with a flask of lukewarm coffee, waiting for something dead to get lively. Ooh! Look at the shooting stars! Aren't they magnificent?"

They all looked up at the night sky. There were no shooting stars. The moon was barely bright enough to make its presence felt, and most of the stars had disappeared behind clouds. A cold wind came blowing in over the side, making them all shiver briefly. Except Kim.

"Excuse me," said Happy. "I have to go take my aura for a walk."

He wandered off down the deck, smiling and nodding cheerfully to nobody at all. The others watched him go.

"What is he on?" said Latimer.

"Everything," said Melody, coldly. "Or at least, everything left that can still affect him. His brain chemistry is so compromised now, it's a wonder he can still see the real world from where he is. I hope he's having a good trip; because he won't be coming back." She glared at Latimer. "He's dying; and it's all your fault!"

"So many things are," said Latimer.

"There's something I need to tell you, Boss," said JC.

The tone in his voice caught her attention, and Latimer looked steadily at JC as he brought her up to date on his recent conversation with the forces from Outside. Melody listened intently, too, nodding now and again as some particular item confirmed her deepest suspicions. When JC finally finished, Latimer smiled soberly.

"I always wondered why I was chosen. All these years, fighting monsters and demons and dead things, wondering every time *Is this it? Is this what I'm here for?* And now I find out I was just a holding pattern, someone to fill a gap until the real living weapons arrived."

"Now you know how it feels to be used," said JC.

"We all have to serve someone," said Latimer.

"Can we be sure these Forces are any better than the Flesh Undying?" said Melody. "I mean, we only have their word for it that the Flesh is crazy, and they're the good guys. What if we're being played?"

Latimer looked down the deck at Happy, ambling amiably along and stepping carefully around things that weren't there.

"Crazy is as crazy does. We can only judge the Flesh Undying by its actions. Through the damage its agents have caused, and the damage it intends to do to our world by leaving it. The Flesh's threat is clear; the Forces' . . . less so."

"We have to accept any help that will allow us to stop the Flesh Undying," said JC. "Afterwards . . ."

"Yes," said Latimer. "There will be time for many things, afterwards." She took the holder out of her mouth and pinched off the end of her cigarette with thumb and forefinger. She looked at JC and Melody with serious, considering eyes. "You do understand . . . this descent is just an information run. Get as close to the Flesh Undying as you can, let the scientific instruments do what they're supposed to, then yell for us to pull you back up. Don't do anything, don't get involved, and, above all, don't try to be heroes."

"I'm not sure what we could do, locked inside a steel ball," said JC.

"I wonder what the Flesh Undying will look like . . . up close," said Melody.

"Happy's probably the only one who could see it clearly," said JC.

"Smell the irony," said Latimer.

They all looked down the deck after the telepath as he talked to people who weren't there and ignored people who were. He was freaking the hell out of the crew, who went out of their way to give him plenty of room. JC almost envied Happy, in being so far gone he probably didn't even realise how dangerous things were about to get. JC looked at Melody.

"Why is he . . . ?"

"Different drugs are kicking in as his system metabolises them," said Melody. "Some . . . are more helpful than others. He can keep a rein on them, when he has to. Right now, he's just enjoying himself. While he can."

She glared at Latimer, and for a moment JC thought the Boss might actually respond with a kind word, or a touch of compassion; but the moment passed. Latimer just looked steadily back at Melody, until Melody looked away.

"He's killing himself for you, Boss," she said. "For the job. Putting his life and his sanity on the line . . ."

"Aren't we all?" said Latimer. "All that matters is, can he still function? We can't risk his cracking up at the bottom of the ocean."

"He's stronger than you think," said Melody. "He's had to be. But you'd better pray he can keep it together; because he's still our best bet for taking down the Flesh Undying. Even after everything you've done to him and asked of him, he's still a Ghost Finder."

"Don't try pushing my guilt button, girl," said Latimer. "I don't have one."

JC remembered Latimer shooting her long-time secretary Heather in the head without the slightest hesitation. Latimer looked at him and smiled briefly, as though she knew what he was thinking.

"We all do what we have to," said the Boss. "To preserve what we believe in."

"But you're not going down in the bathysphere," said JC.

"Yes, exactly!" said Melody. "Why aren't you going down with us, Boss?"

"Partly because there isn't room," said Latimer. "Partly because you need someone up here you can trust, to make sure they bring you back up safely. This is a Project ship and crew, remember. And there's always the chance the Flesh Undying might send more of its agents. The ship will need me, then. But mostly I'm not going because I'm not crazy."

They all managed a small smile.

"We could die down there," said Melody.

"Yes," said Latimer. "You could. Try not to."

JC drew Latimer's attention to where Natasha Chang and Captain Katt were standing together, some distance away. They weren't talking to each other, but they were standing together, keeping a watchful eye on everything that was happening.

"I had a word with Ms. Chang earlier," said Latimer. "Just sounding her out, to see where her true loyalties lie."

"And?" said JC.

"Don't turn your back on her," said Latimer.

"I can honestly say I wasn't planning to," said JC. "Keep a careful eye on her while we're down below. In case she takes it into her mind to tie knots in our oxygen lines, just for the fun of it. We might have common cause, but she is not on our side."

"Of course not," said Latimer. "She's Crowley Project. I will be right beside her, all during your time below."

"Don't turn your back on her," said JC.

"Wouldn't dream of it," said Latimer.

She calmly moved away, so she could just casually bump into Katt and Chang. Melody scowled at JC.

"How much help could she be, realistically? One old lady on her own, surrounded by Project people with guns?"

"Come on," said JC. "This is Catherine Latimer we're talking about."

Happy came back to join them. His mood had changed, or the chemicals had changed it for him. His face was full of shadows. His mouth was a flat line, and he darted suspicious glances at Goldsmith and Hamilton as they oversaw the loading of even more scientific equipment into the bathysphere. Happy moved in close to JC and Melody, dropping his voice to conspiratorial levels.

"Can we really trust those two? How can we be sure they're not putting a bomb in there?"

"As you have already pointed out," JC said patiently, "a bomb wouldn't work against the Flesh Undying."

"It would work against us," Happy said darkly. "If Katt or Chang decided they wanted to get rid of us."

"He may be a brain-damaged paranoid, but he does have a point," said Melody.

"Who's brain-damaged?" said Happy.

"We're too valuable to kill off," said JC. "If you're really worried, Happy, why not listen in on what they're thinking?"

Happy's scowl deepened. "Can't. I've had to batten down the mental hatches, lock all the doors, and throw away the keys. I've suppressed all my abilities, to make sure the Flesh Undying won't be able to see me coming."

"Then what use are you going to be to us, down there?" said JC. "Maybe you should stay up here, after all."

"No," Happy said immediately. "If it should all go wrong, I can wake up in one hell of a hurry. I'm your last best hope. You are looking at me doubtfully, JC, as well you should. If I were you, I'd be very worried. About everything."

"I am," said JC.

"Good!" said Happy. "That makes me feel so much better. I'd hate to be this worried on my own." He stopped and looked around. "Where's Kim?"

She'd gone again, when they weren't looking. And, as usual, no-one had noticed.

"I wish she wouldn't keep disappearing like that," said JC. "It gets on my nerves."

"Women," Happy said wisely. And then winced and looked wounded, as Melody elbowed him in the ribs.

For differing reasons, they all decided to watch the action around the bathysphere for a while. Goldsmith and Hamilton were standing before the open air-lock, consulting a checklist and arguing quietly with each other. They ran carefully through the list, twice, then tossed it aside and marched over to join JC, Happy, and Melody. The two scientists looked very professional, very focused. Exactly the kind of people you'd want to be in charge of your descent into the unknown. And then they went and spoiled it, by looking at each other and waiting for the other to speak first. Up close, they both looked like they'd been awake for far too long.

"It's all in place," Goldsmith said finally. "Everything you'll need for the journey. The equipment is set to run itself, it knows what it's doing, so please don't touch anything."

"We'll be lowering you right on top of the Flesh Undying," said Hamilton, in her most severe Nordic tones. "Which realistically means within twenty to thirty feet. If all goes well."

"There are so many imponderables beyond our control," said Goldsmith, apologetically.

"What happens if you get it right on the nose?" said Melody. "And we end up bumping into the Flesh?"

"Best not to think about things like that," said Goldsmith.

"It's not like you'd waken it," said Hamilton. "One small steel ball, bumping along the side of a mountain?"

"Why would it even notice?" said Goldsmith.

"You're both sweating," Happy said accusingly.

"It's a hot night," said Goldsmith.

"No it isn't," said Happy.

"There's a phone cable connecting the sphere to the *Moonchilde*," said Hamilton. "Use that for all communications. We couldn't risk anything else. But even on a direct line, I would still advise you keep contact to a bare minimum. Just in case."

"How will we know when the work is done?" said JC.

"The machines will know," said Goldsmith. "Don't worry, no computers; it's all simple timers. The equipment will shut itself down once its various tasks are completed; and then all you have to do is phone home, and we'll haul you back up."

"Do we have any weapons, for emergencies?" said Melody. "Any defences?"

Goldsmith and Hamilton looked at each other.

"Stop doing that!" said JC. "Whatever it is, just say it! We can take it!"

"The bathysphere's outer shell is strong enough to protect you from the pressure, and all natural dangers," said Goldsmith. Like a parent assuring a child there isn't really a monster under the bed.

"You can electrify the outer shell if you should happen to encounter any threatening creatures," said Hamilton. "But there shouldn't be any. Nothing lives in the shadow of the Flesh Undying."

"What if there are Flesh creatures on guard duty?" said Happy. "It could happen."

"Try not to be noticed," said Goldsmith.

"But if something really interesting should turn up, the equipment will take photos," said Hamilton.

They nodded and smiled to JC, Happy, and Melody, looked at each other to check whether there was anything else they ought to say, then turned and walked briskly back to the bathysphere. With a definite air of having done all that could reasonably be asked of them. Captain Katt and Natasha Chang let them get out of the way, then came forward to take their place.

"It's time," said Katt. "I feel it is my duty to ask. Are you sure you want to do this?"

"No," said JC. "But it's the job. Besides, after everything we've already been through on this ship, we might actually be safer at the bottom of the ocean."

"Don't stay down there one minute longer than you absolutely have to," said Katt.

"Damn right," said JC.

Chang beamed at them all. "Such an exciting adventure! The things you're going to see . . . I wish I was going with you!"

"No you don't," said Happy.

Chang rounded on him. "Stay out of my head!"

"I wouldn't go in there on a bet," Happy said loftily. "When did you last have it cleaned?"

Chang deliberately turned her back on him, to give JC her

full attention and her biggest smile. "Do find a way for us to kill the Flesh Undying, darling. I would love to have a kill that big on my résumé."

"And, you'll have helped save the world," said JC. "Probably a first for the Crowley Project."

Chang pouted. "You're forgetting; I helped you stop Fenris Tenebrae, down in the London Underground."

"You were there," said Melody. "But I don't remember your actually contributing much. We did all the heavy lifting."

"Speaking of which," Chang said brightly, ignoring Melody so she could concentrate on JC, "isn't it time you were loading yourselves into the big, round suicide machine?"

"It is time," said Katt. "We have to do this. Now."

,,,,,,,,,,,,,,,,,,,,,,,,,

JC and Happy and Melody gathered together in front of the small circular air-lock that was the only entrance to the bathysphere. They looked at each other, more than ready to let someone else go first, and in the end JC took the lead. Because in any dangerous situation, he always liked to be first on the scene. If only so he got to be the first to kick the bad guy in the nads, metaphorically speaking. He stepped up onto the rough wooden platform provided, ducked his head more than was comfortable, and squeezed through the opening.

Inside, the sphere was seriously short of open space. It had been packed full of bulky scientific equipment, piled almost to the curving ceiling. Just enough room had been left in the middle for three chairs. JC stepped over and around various pieces of high tech, chose a chair, and sat down. It seemed to fit him well enough. He started to stretch his legs, then had to stop as he discovered there wasn't enough room. Melody looked in through the air-lock, with Happy peering over her shoulder.

"What's it like in there?" said Melody.

"The belly of the whale," said JC. "After a really big dinner."

"Think I'll go for a little walk," said Happy.

Melody took a firm hold on his arm and bundled him inside, with minimum violence. And then she entered quickly behind him, so he had no room to retreat. Happy struggled past the piled-up equipment, sniffing loudly.

"If they've got all this, what do they need us for?"

"In case it all goes wrong," said JC. "We have no way of knowing what might happen once we get close to the living mountain."

"Let me out of here, right now," said Happy. "There aren't enough drugs in the world to make this seem like a good idea."

"Sit down and shut up," said Melody. "You volunteered for this."

Happy looked at her. "I did? When?"

"When I told you to," said Melody.

"Oh, well, that's all right then," said Happy. He sat down.

Melody looked over the various equipment, taking her time. She didn't appear particularly impressed.

"Recognise anything?" said JC.

"Most of it," said Melody. "It's all top of the range, state-of-the-art, and all that . . . Remind me to steal some of it later. We should be able to discover a lot about the true nature of the Flesh Undying with sensors this powerful."

"But?" said JC. "I take it there is a but?"

"But . . ." said Melody, "Everything here was designed to probe and investigate the natural world. The Flesh is something else entirely."

"We have to try," said JC.

"Yes," said Melody. "We do." She sat down in the remaining chair.

They sat quietly for a while, listening to the crew bustling around outside. JC fidgeted. He would have liked to be doing something, but there was nothing for him to do.

"It smells in here," said Happy.

"That's you," said Melody.

"Oh yes," said Happy. "So it is. Sorry about that, people. It's just the chemicals leaking out through my perspiration. And other things."

"Where's Kim?" said Melody. "Isn't she making the journey with us?"

"I'm right here," said Kim's voice, apparently out of nowhere. "I'm with you in spirit. Like Happy, I think it best I conceal my presence from the Flesh Undying. So I've reduced myself to the barest essentials, hardly pressing down on the world at all. Besides, it's cramped enough in here as it is without me floating around."

"Why not hide inside JC again?" said Melody.

"Because that generates power," said Kim. "Real power. The Flesh Undying couldn't help but notice."

The three Ghost Finders sat in their chairs, keeping their hands and feet to themselves for fear of bumping something. There wasn't room to get up and move about, so they just leaned this way and that and craned their heads back, to get a good look at everything. The ship's light spilled in through two small port-holes on opposite sides of the bathysphere, pushing back the sphere's dim and almost cosy glow. It only possessed one small light, set into the curving ceiling, but various pieces of equipment flickered with glowing readouts, along with several small monitor screens. More tech had been layered over the interior walls and ceiling, like silicon coral.

Captain Katt stuck his head in through the air-lock, careful not to disturb his peaked cap. He looked the equipment over carefully and only then nodded to the Ghost Finders.

"We're ready to go. Last chance to change your minds."

"Oh good!" said Happy. He started to get up. Melody grabbed his arm and slammed him back into his chair.

"You're staying!"

Happy looked at Katt. "I'm staying."

"Send us down, Captain," said JC.

"Good luck," said Katt. "Guard the equipment, and try not to get yourselves killed."

He pulled back, and the air-lock closed. The sound of the heavy door slamming into position and locking sounded very final. The bathysphere rocked from side to side as it was jerked up into the air. JC grabbed onto the arms of his chair and swallowed hard. It felt like someone had just kicked the world out from under his feet. There was the sound of rattling cables and straining machinery, as the sphere was winched up. JC breathed steadily, calming himself. Kim murmured softly in his ear.

"I'm here, JC. I'm always here, with you."

They all hung on tightly, as the bathysphere was put out over the side of the ship and lowered toward the water. Light coming through the port-holes was cut off, replaced by night sky. The sphere swung slowly back and forth, offering brief glimpses of the *Moonchilde*. And then even that disappeared as the bathysphere plunged down into the ocean. All outside light was gone, replaced by complete darkness . . . the only sounds quiet murmurings from various piece of equipment. One monitor screen blazed brightly. JC looked at Melody.

"Is it supposed to be doing that?"

"Probably," said Melody.

"Are we nearly there yet?" said Happy.

And down they went, into the dark, and the deepest part of the world.

::::::::::::::::::::::::::

For a long time, the three of them just sat patiently, waiting for something to happen. The sphere tilted slightly from side to side as it descended, but apart from that, there was nothing to tell them they were moving. No sense of progress, of getting anywhere. Just darkness without and flickering lights within. JC felt hot, then cold, and hoped it was all in his mind. Melody leaned forward in her chair to study the instruments before her and finally got up to lean over the monitor screens. She fiddled with the controls, muttering to herself.

"They said not to touch anything!" said JC, just a bit urgently.

"I know," said Melody, not looking round from what she was doing. "I was there, I heard them. When has that ever stopped me? Okay . . . I've transferred the input from the short-range sensors to these monitor screens. So we'll have some idea of what's happening outside. It won't interfere with reception topside."

She sank back into her chair, and they all stared fixedly at the monitor screens. They showed nothing but the dark.

"That's it?" said Happy.

"No light in the ocean this far down, remember?" said Melody.

"Then what's the point of the screens?" said JC.

"To make us feel better," said Melody.

"Not really working," said Happy.

"There's no telling what local conditions will be like, once we get up close and personal with the Flesh Undying," Melody said patiently. "Or what kind of phenomena we're going to encounter. We might be alone down there; and we might not. Any advance warning has got to be a good thing . . . Assuming this shit works."

"Really not feeling better at all," said Happy.

They sat together in the limited light of the sphere's interior, which felt less cosy and more oppressive the deeper they went. There was a growing feeling of having left the world behind, of moving into unknown and unfriendly territory. The sphere's outer shell made slow, creaking sounds, and JC flinched a little every time. He was pretty sure it was just the metal layers adjusting to the changing pressure, but that didn't help. He didn't like to think about what was going on outside the sphere, about the steadily increasing tons of pressure per square inch, and how it would crush the sphere's contents to the size of a walnut if anything went wrong. He looked at Happy. Sweat was coursing down the telepath's face, his eyes squeezed tightly shut as he struggled to keep everything out. JC hoped that was working. He looked at Melody, focusing all her attention on the monitor screens before her. JC wanted to ask if the information scrolling across the bottom of the screens meant anything important, but didn't like to. He just knew he wouldn't understand the answers.

Down and down they went, into the endless night of the world, until JC lost all track of how far they'd come. He wondered if someone on the *Moonchilde* should have talked to them by now, just to make sure they were all right, and only then remembered that communications were supposed to be

limited to emergencies. He really should have asked someone how long the descent would take, or at the very least
insisted on some kind of depth-gauge. But everything had
happened in such a hurry . . . One of the machines made a
sudden pinging noise.

"What?" JC said immediately. "What was that?"

"Calm down," said Melody, still intent on the screens.
"It's just the sonar. It's picking up movement in the vicinity
of the sphere."

"Something's alive out there?" said JC.

"Could be," said Melody. "Happy, can you . . . ?"

"Don't ask me," said the telepath, not opening his eyes.
"I'm shut down."

"You can look out a port-hole, can't you?" said Melody.

Happy reluctantly opened his eyes and got up out of his
chair. He stepped over and around piled-up equipment to get
to the nearest port-hole and pressed his face up against the
reinforced glass.

"Well?" said JC.

"Can't see a damned thing," said Happy. "Just the dark.
It's like night down here, but a night that never knew a moon
or any stars . . ."

The sonar made new sounds, louder and more urgent, then
closer and closer together.

"That's not good, is it?" said JC.

"Sonar is picking up multiple signals," said Melody,
frowning. "Seems like our arrival is attracting a crowd."

"How many?" said JC.

"Lots," said Melody. "Apparently from all directions."

Happy made a sudden, shocked noise, and jerked his face
back from the port-hole. "We are definitely not alone down
here, people! The welcoming committee is here, and I want
to go back up again, right now."

JC got up out of his chair and struggled over to the other
port-hole. And from out of the endless dark, strange, living
things came surging forward to stare at him. Weird, distorted
shapes, glowing with their own light, came swarming all
around the bathysphere. They had eyes and teeth and some
things that made no sense at all.

"Talk to me, JC," said Melody. "What are you seeing?"

"Nothing I can put a name to," JC said steadily. "And I have seen some pretty odd things on deep-water documentaries. These shapes don't make any sense . . . It's like somebody crammed a dozen different species into a blender and hit shuffle. They're more like . . . dreams and fancies, given shape and form."

He couldn't look away, fascinated by the lengths life could go to, away from the normal restrictions of light and warmth and gravity. Impossibly long eels, with forests of trailing tentacles. Huge squid with massive, unblinking eyes and bodies like exploded flowers. Many-legged things that seemed to scull through the water, so transparent JC could see their inner organs pulsing. Some were the size of goldfish, others looked big enough to swallow the bathysphere whole. None of them seemed to want to get too close to the sphere or interfere with its descent. They were just . . . interested. They circled around and around, as though curious at this strange intruder from above, dropping down into their world.

"These things are seriously ugly," said JC after a while. "I'm surprised simple probability hasn't produced something more . . . aesthetically pleasing."

"Hush," said Happy. "They might read lips."

JC pulled his face back from the port-hole. "I can honestly say that never even occurred to me."

"I'm chemically altered, not stupid," said Happy.

"It is amazing, what the ocean depths can produce in the way of new life," said JC.

"No," said Happy. "There's nothing natural about these creatures. You were right the first time—they were made like this. Separated parts of the Flesh Undying, operating as drones, on sentry duty."

JC looked back at Happy. The telepath was staring out his port-hole at the weird creatures with a calm, thoughtful expression. Without glancing back at JC, Happy smiled briefly.

"Yes, I'm operating again. I can feel their presence, tapping on the locked doors of my mind. There's no point in my trying to hide any longer."

"How do you feel?" said JC.

"Astonishingly sane," said Happy. "For the moment. I can feel the drugs surging back and forth inside me like high tides, and I am surfboarding!"

JC decided he'd let that one pass. "If these things are on sentry duty . . . do any of them feel dangerous? Or ready to sound an alarm?"

"They're not alive," Happy said patiently. "Not even sentient, as we would understand it. They're just . . . flecks of Flesh, shed and given shape and purpose by the Flesh Undying's under-conscious. Its version of an early-warning system. I don't think they're necessarily— *Holy shit!*"

He jerked back his head, retreated quickly from the port-hole, and fell over the equipment. JC scrambled right over him, to stare out of the port-hole the telepath had abandoned. And when JC pressed his face up against the reinforced glass, the Faust stared back at him. That cold, familiar face, not in the least distorted by the incredible water pressure. The Faust floated up and down before the port-hole, staring in with wide, unblinking eyes. There wasn't a trace of personality or even awareness in the Faust's face.

"Is that . . . really him?" said JC, not looking away.

"No," said Happy, getting painfully to his feet. "Or, at least, I doubt it. The Flesh is dreaming; and its dreams are coming out to play."

The Faust beat on the outside of the bathysphere with his empty hands. His movements were odd, unreal, disturbing.

"Don't worry," said Melody. "He can't get in. I don't care what he's made of; Flesh is no match for layers of cold steel."

"Can I have that in writing?" said Happy.

The Faust disappeared from in front of the port-hole and went scrabbling across the outside of the bathysphere, scuttling back and forth like an oversized insect. Looking for a weakness, or a way in. He ended up at the air-lock; and they could all hear him fumbling at the lock's mechanisms with his bare hands.

"Tell me he can't get in," said JC.

"He can't get in," said Melody. "Even if he could somehow get through all the security measures, the water pressure would still hold the air-lock door closed."

But she didn't sound one hundred per cent convinced. The three Ghost Finders stared at the air-lock until the sounds suddenly stopped.

"Happy . . . ?" said JC.

"He's gone," said Happy. "Though don't ask me where . . ."

"Was that the Faust we knew?" said JC. "I mean, it looked just like him, but . . ."

"The Flesh made one, no reason why it couldn't make another," said Happy. "But the man we knew couldn't survive under these conditions . . ."

"I'm getting something," said Melody, and the others turned immediately to look at her. She was crouching before one particular monitor screen, tapping on it thoughtfully with a fingertip. "The Geiger counter is adamant there's no radiation down here, not even expected background levels. But this screen is picking up regular surges of unknown, unnatural energies. And these readings . . . are like nothing I've ever seen before."

"Dangerous?" said JC.

"Unknown," said Melody.

"Is there any way to send this sphere into reverse?" said Happy. "Only I really would like to get the hell out of here. Please. Pretty please."

Even as he said that, something bumped heavily against the outside of the bathysphere, hard enough to send all three of them sprawling. Melody held on to the monitor screens, sheltering them with her body. JC cried out as he jarred his back painfully on an outcropping piece of equipment. Happy crouched down behind his chair. The sounds from the sonar rose to a new pitch of volume and intensity. JC hauled himself forward to stand beside Melody.

"Careful!" said Melody, not looking round. "Don't break anything we might have to depend on later."

JC leaned in beside her, looking at the screen holding her attention. Information scrolling across the bottom seemed to make some sense, to her. He stood up again and fought his way back to his port-hole. But even with his face pressed right up against the glass, he couldn't see anything.

"The creatures have all disappeared!" he said. "There's nothing out there!"

Something hit the sphere again, rocking it from side to side. Loose bits and pieces fell and broke, as the three Ghost Finders reached desperately for something to hang on to.

"Something is very definitely still out there!" said Happy.

"Big enough to scare off everything else," said Melody. "Or convince them they're not needed. I'm not getting any readings on the short-range sensors, JC!"

"What's out there?" said JC. "What is it?"

"Big," said Melody. "And I mean seriously big. We are talking about something big enough to punch a blue whale in the mouth and send it home, crying to its mother."

Something hit the sphere hard from underneath, lifting it up and shaking it violently. The overhead light dimmed for a moment, then came back. The Ghost Finders hung on to whatever was nearest, hands clenched painfully tight. Sounds from the sonar were going crazy.

"Everyone get into their chairs!" said JC. "Before it comes back!"

They scrambled across the equipment to their chairs, then looked quickly about them.

"They should have fitted safety straps," said JC. "Are we under attack, Happy? Happy . . . Talk to me! Are you picking up anything from whatever that is?"

"It's not . . . thinking," said Happy. His eyes were very big, and he was sweating heavily again. Holding his hands together, to keep them from shaking. "It's more like it's been programmed to do certain things."

"Then why is it hitting us?" said JC.

"To see what will happen," said Happy.

"There must be something in here we can use as a weapon," said Melody. "Something to drive it away before it ruptures the outer layers or breaks our support lines!"

"The scientists said we could electrify the outer hull," said JC.

"No!" Happy said immediately. "Don't do anything that

might make us appear a threat! That would activate new programming . . . Remember; our best bet to survive this close encounter with the Flesh Undying is not to be noticed. By the thing itself or any of its offshoots."

"So what should we do?" said Melody.

"Nothing," said Happy. "And very quietly."

They sat still, breathing heavily, their eyes darting around the sphere as they listened for any sign of a new attack. JC was so tense, all his muscles were screaming. His hands ached from clutching the chair's arms so tightly. He turned his head back and forth. He could feel something moving outside the bathysphere, a great presence circling in the dark. Watching them, studying them. Maybe wondering whether it should crack the sphere open to see what was inside. JC's back muscles ached in anticipation of the next hard knock as he wondered whether that would be the one to rupture the sphere's seams and let the water in. And whether it would be the pressure that killed them, or the water that drowned them.

But there was no other attack, no more bangs or nudges from outside. The sphere continued to descend, quite steadily, and the sounds from the sonar slowly calmed down. The pings grew further apart, then quieter, and finally fell silent. JC let out his breath in a long sigh and relaxed, just a little. He let go of the arm-rests and flexed his aching fingers.

"Is it gone?" he asked, whispering, as though it might still hear him.

"Sonar isn't picking up anything," said Melody. "All the short-range sensors are quiet. Nothing on the screens, big or small."

"And I'm not feeling anything," said Happy. "Apart from blind terror, muscle cramps, and an urgent need for a toilet."

"I don't think they got around to installing a chemical toilet," said Melody.

"Too late anyway," said Happy. "Joking! Just . . ."

"So hopefully it's decided we're harmless," said JC.

"Or the Flesh Undying has decided it wants a closer look at us," said Melody.

They sat in silence as the sphere sank ever deeper, watching the monitor screens and waiting for the sonar to ping again.

Nothing happened for a long time. JC relaxed, almost despite himself, because it's just not possible to stay that tense for so long. When the sonar did ping again, they all jumped.

"Just the one signal," said Melody. "Not moving . . . we're descending towards it. One really big signal."

"We're there," said JC.

"There?" said Happy.

"Where we're supposed to be," said Melody.

"The living mountain," said JC. "The Flesh Undying, in the Flesh at last."

"We made it!" said Melody.

"I think I'd feel happier if you didn't sound quite so surprised," said Happy.

"How close are we?" said JC.

"I can't tell from these readings," said Melody. "If I had to guess, which I do, I'd say pretty damned close."

JC and Happy looked at each other, then JC got up out of his chair and went back to his port-hole. And there it was—a single huge shape—glowing with a fierce disturbing illumination that only passed for light because there was nothing else JC could call it. A sick, spoiled kind of light. The sphere was just a tiny object set against the scale of the living mountain; and it was clear there was still a long way to go before the bathysphere would reach the base of the mountain and the ocean floor.

JC stared hungrily at what he'd come such a long way to see. The Flesh Undying, the living mountain . . . it had form and mass and attributes, but none of them made any sense to human eyes. JC quietly asked Melody and Happy to come over and join him, and they squeezed in beside him at the port-hole. They all looked for as long as they could stand, then they had to turn their heads away. It was too much, too complex, for human comprehension. Happy was shaking with reaction just from its proximity. Mankind was not meant to look on the face of the Medusa. Melody went back to her monitor screens.

"The sensors are . . . confused. I think they're saying the Flesh Undying is a whole bunch of different things, all at once. Even contradictory things."

"Something that exists in more than three spatial dimensions . . ." said Happy. "How is that even possible?"

"It's like something impossibly complex has been grafted or superimposed onto our reality," said Melody. "Like a cube, glued to a flat piece of paper. When we look at the living mountain, I don't think we're seeing what's actually there. Just as much of it as our senses can process."

"You should be able to see more of it than us, Happy," said JC.

"Doesn't work that way," said Happy. "Even with my brain chemistry currently running on nitrous-oxide superchargers, I'm still only human. All any of us can see is the tip of the iceberg, if you don't mind a somewhat scrambled metaphor. And I think what we are seeing is the least disturbing part. If we could properly grasp everything the Flesh Undying is . . . I think our souls would puke."

"So the forces from Outside really are the good guys, after all," said JC.

"They'd better be," said Happy. "I'd hate to think there was anything worse than the Flesh Undying."

"Now we're here," said Melody, "what are we supposed to do?"

"You heard the Boss, Mel," said Happy. "We're just an information-gathering expedition. No heroics, by order."

"The instruments are here to observe," said Melody. "They don't need us for that. We're here . . . to decide whether it's possible to actually do something."

"The Voice said I was their weapon," JC said slowly. "You think anyone up on that ship has any idea how to destroy something this big? They've no idea what they're really up against."

"So it's up to us to save the day," said Melody.

"Isn't it always?" said JC.

"But . . . what can we do?" said Happy. "This isn't like mice voting to bell the cat; it's more like three ants deciding to beat up an elephant."

"The Voice said . . . Destroy the Flesh, and the animating force would no longer have any hold on our reality," said JC.

"Okay . . ." said Happy. "So doing that will kill it?"

"Presumably," said JC. "I'd settle for its just being gone and no longer a threat to our world."

"The Flesh . . ." said Melody. "The living mountain itself. I don't think that much living matter came through the hole in reality, from the Other Place. More likely, the Flesh Undying gathered organic matter to itself, from the ocean, when it arrived, to make a living form it could inhabit. To root itself in this world and give it the power to affect things here. And only then discovered it was trapped in the Flesh. Limited by our natural laws. Which is why it's been so desperate to escape again. If we destroy the Flesh, but there's no hole between the worlds for the animating spirit to go back through . . . that should put an end to it! Makes sense. Sort of."

"I would like to drag everyone back to my earlier question," said Happy. "How do we destroy a living mountain?"

"We don't," said JC. "We separate the Flesh from its animating spirit. Drive it out, exorcise it."

"And that will kill it?" said Happy.

"Presumably," said Melody.

"I wish you'd stop saying that," said Happy.

"We need to raise enough spiritual power to drive a wedge between body and soul," said JC. "But how can we gather enough spirit to overpower the Flesh's animating spirit?"

They sat quietly for a while, looking at each other, hoping someone else would come up with the answer. And all the time the sonar pinged loudly and aggressively.

"Remember how we gathered the ghosts in the Haybarn Theatre, to overcome the Faust?" JC said finally. "And the spirits in the Acropolis Hotel room? We called, and they came, to do something that mattered, that needed doing. Ready to defend and heal our world in its time of need."

"But this is a problem on a whole different scale!" said Melody.

"Just means we need a much bigger gathering," said JC. "Time to raise our game, people. We need to call together all the ghosts in the world. To save the world."

"All of them?" Happy said incredulously. "Ten out of ten for ambition, JC, but . . ."

"Humanity's unconscious," said JC. "The world's dreaming. Bring them all back, in one last cause. One last chance for the unquiet dead to defend the living they left behind. We call up an army of angry ghosts . . . and then throw them at the Flesh Undying."

"Okay," said Happy. "That's one hell of an idea . . . a very good idea. But how do we do that?"

"We die," JC said steadily. "And then we go ask them."

There was a long pause.

"How did you get hold of my pills?" said Happy.

"No, no; I get it!" said Melody. "Remember how we got those missing students' spirits back, after their séance went wrong? We sent our souls out to contact them and bring them home. We can do that again . . . We die here, under controlled conditions, leave our bodies and make contact with the world's dead but not departed . . . And use that accumulated power to drive the Flesh Undying out of the mountain! And then, afterwards, we return to our bodies!"

"Oh, of course," said Happy. "Because that worked so well last time. The students' minds ended up in the wrong bodies! It took months to sort them out!"

"Do you have a better idea?" said JC. "Do you have any other idea?"

"Give me time," said Happy. "I'm thinking . . ."

They waited.

"All right," said Happy. "We put together an army of ghosts. What happens then?"

"I don't know," said JC. "I don't believe the living can know things like that. But the Voice from Outside said . . . I would know what to do when I needed to. Kim . . . ?"

"Yes, JC," said Kim's quiet voice.

"Is what I'm proposing actually possible?"

"Yes."

"That's it?" said Happy. "No arguments; no ifs or buts or maybes?"

"We can do this," said Kim. "We're Ghost Finders; we find ghosts. I can lead you right to the edge of the Hereafter, where ghosts can hear you. We've done this before. Remember the low road, and the wood between the worlds?"

"Yes," said Happy. "I didn't like it then, and I'm really not keen on revisiting it again until I have to. This is seriously scary, JC. If we do let ourselves die, what guarantee is there we'll make it safely back?"

Melody smiled at him. "You're dying anyway, sweetie. We both know that. At least this way we can die together, and our deaths will have some meaning, some purpose."

"Well . . . if you put it like that," said Happy.

"It all makes a kind of sense," said Kim. "A ghost, leading the living to the dead, to deliver previously prepared weapons into their proper place, against the Flesh Undying. It's almost like the forces from Outside knew what they were doing all along."

"How about that," said JC.

"You know," said Happy, "we could all die down here and stay dead. And no-one would ever know what we did, or how we died, or why."

"We don't do this job for the glory," said JC.

"We don't?" said Melody.

"I was always in it for the money," said JC.

"For access to powerful chemicals!" said Happy.

"For access to forbidden technology!" said Melody.

"For a chance to do something that mattered," said Kim.

"Yes," said JC.

"Good enough," said Melody.

"I can live with that," said Happy.

"Let's do it," said JC. "Before we all lose our nerve."

JC opened communications with the *Moonchilde*, using the direct phone line. He explained the plan to Captain Katt and told him to cut off the air supply to the bathysphere. There was a long pause.

"Let me hand you over to the scientists," Katt said finally.

"Are you sure about this?" said Goldsmith, almost immediately. "It all sounds very . . . metaphysical."

"It'll work," said JC.

"Look," said Goldsmith. "We're getting really good information about the Flesh Undying, from the equipment. Which is what this descent was all about. You don't need to sacrifice yourselves, in some desperate attempt to take out the Flesh Undying personally."

"Yes we do," said JC.

There was another pause, then Hamilton's voice came over the phone. "Goldsmith's gone for a little walk around the deck. He can't handle this. I'm not sure I can. Have you checked your air mix recently? Are you getting enough oxygen, or too much?"

"We know what we're doing," said JC.

There was another break, then Catherine Latimer came on the line. "Talk me through this plan of yours."

JC spelled it out for her, doing his best to sound confident. When he'd finished, there was barely a pause before Latimer's voice came back to him.

"Sounds good to me. I'll tell them to go ahead. How will we know if your plan succeeds?"

"The living mountain will die," said JC. "The sensors will tell you. As soon as you're sure it's dead and gone, start pumping air back into the bathysphere. Not before."

"Come back safely," said Latimer. "If only so you can tell me all about it."

"Sounds like a plan to me," said JC.

He shut down the phone line. He didn't have anything more to say; and he didn't want to risk someone's talking him out of it. The three Ghost Finders sat quietly in their chairs, waiting. Melody held Happy's hand tightly. Because she'd promised to hold him while he was dying.

"I don't hear anything," said Happy, after a while. "How will we know they've shut the air off?"

"We'll know," said Melody.

"I wonder what it will feel like?" said JC.

"Supposedly, just like falling asleep," said Melody.

"I can do that," said Happy. "I've done it before."

"There are worse ways to die," said Melody. "Than with your friends."

"Kim," said JC. "Please manifest. I want you here with us. I want you to be the last thing I see."

The ghost girl appeared before him, glowing faintly in the dim light of the sphere. She'd altered her appearance again, to how she'd looked when they first met. How she looked when she was murdered in the Underground. A pre-Raphaelite dream of a woman in her late twenties, in a long white dress, with a great mane of red hair and a sharply defined face. She had vivid green eyes and a wide smile. She looked very real.

"I'm here, JC. I'm always here, for you."

"Can you tell me what it's like, now?" JC said steadily. "Being dead?"

"Not in any way you could understand," said Kim. "Be patient. You're about to find out."

"I met a ghost woman in that haunted inn," said Happy. "She said being dead was awful."

"For some, it is," said Kim. "What we do with our life defines our after-life."

JC looked at Happy, then at Melody. "Is he really dying, Mel? No hope, no last chance for a miracle?"

"Given everything he's taken, it's a miracle he's still with us," said Melody.

"I've always thought so," said Happy.

"If there's one thing this job teaches us," said JC. "It's that death is not the end. So whatever happens, I'll see you again."

But when he looked at Happy, the telepath's eyes were already closed. His face was slack, and he was barely breathing. JC looked at Melody, and she had passed out, too. JC was suddenly aware of how laboured his breathing had become, and he looked quickly to Kim. A sudden panic rushed through him, like a drowning man who feels the waters closing over his head. He tried to get up out of his chair and found he couldn't. He struggled for air, trying to say something to Kim. She smiled at him reassuringly. And JC stopped fighting. He looked at Kim's face and held on to that image as the dark swept over him.

And then he died.

::::::::::::::::::::::::

The next thing JC knew, he was standing in the bathysphere, looking down at his body, sitting slumped in the chair. It seemed such a small and fragile thing. Melody and Happy and Kim were standing beside him, all of them glowing with a familiar golden light. And JC's first thought was that he didn't feel any different. He did wonder how all of them were able to stand inside the bathysphere; and the moment he thought that, the walls of the sphere just faded away, and they were all standing in the tree-lined avenue he remembered from the low road. The wood between the worlds. JC looked down the long corridor of trees, to where something was waiting for him. He could feel it. Like a voice calling to him, promising him all the answers to all the questions he'd ever had. It didn't feel frightening; it felt like going home, at last. JC turned away from it. Because he still had work to do.

The trees disappeared, and the four of them were left standing on a great open plain, under a colourless, featureless sky. The setting stretched away in every direction, forever. And all around the four Ghost Finders stood row upon row of dead men and women. Ghosts without number, all the unquiet dead who couldn't let go, wouldn't pass on. Because they weren't at peace with themselves, for any number of reasons. JC called out to them, in a voice that was somehow much more than a voice, offering them one last chance for penance and redemption. One last chance to do the right thing; one last service to pay for all sins. Save themselves by saving the world. The dead listened and agreed, it was what they'd always wanted.

In a moment, they were all standing on the bottom of the ocean floor, forcing back the darkness of the depths with the spiritual light they generated. They stood at the base of the living mountain, facing the Flesh Undying. Row upon row, rank upon rank, of the dedicated dead. The Flesh Undying knew they were there, and it was afraid. JC linked with Kim, then with Happy and Melody, as the forces from Outside had always intended. Four minds so close they touched at all points, four souls who fitted together with no joins showing. They became the focus through which the massed power of the angry dead could manifest and be unleashed. A great cry went up, an untold number of voices speaking all at once, as they lashed out at the Flesh Undying. A single, simple hammer-blow; a righteous effort of will and dedication in defence of the world they'd left behind but still loved. And the spirit from Outside was forced out of the unnatural body it had made for itself. It fought them, and it was horribly powerful, but it was nothing in the face of Humanity's spirit. They exorcised the thing from Outside, drove it out. They saw it leave, and they heard it howl with despair as it realised it had nowhere to go. It faded away, dissipating and disappearing forever. Leaving behind just a mountain of dead flesh, already starting to decay.

JC turned to his army of ghosts, to thank them and tell them how proud he was of them, but they were already gone. He turned to Kim and Happy and Melody; but they were gone, too. JC stood alone at the bottom of the ocean, looking at a dead mountain. He smiled briefly.

He'd saved the world. He couldn't have done it without the forces from Outside, but he took a quiet satisfaction in knowing they couldn't have done it without him.

He let go.

::::::::::::::::::::::::

JC came to himself again, standing inside the bathysphere. Looking down at his dead body. Kim and Happy and Melody were also there with him—as ghosts. The three bodies sitting slumped in their armchairs were still very dead.

"All right," said Happy. "What's gone wrong?"

"I don't understand," said JC. "The scientists must know the Flesh Undying is dead. They should have filled the sphere with air again, by now."

"We're dead," said Happy. "We are so dead . . ."

"The air pumps aren't operating," said Melody. "No new air coming in from the *Moonchilde*."

"What do we do?" said JC. "We can't contact the scientists and tell them to get to work unless someone's got a Ouija board handy."

"You have to stop being so limited in your thinking, JC," said Kim. "We're all ghosts now, and the dead can go anywhere. Follow me."

She floated up to the curving roof of the sphere and passed through it. JC looked at the others, shrugged, and went after her. Happy and Melody followed on behind, holding hands so nothing could separate them. The four glowing spirits shot up through the dark waters, blasting through fathoms in a moment, not feeling the pressure or the cold. They appeared standing on the deck of the *Moonchilde*, to discover Captain Katt and his crew covering Goldsmith and Hamilton with their guns. The scientists gestured desperately at the air pumps, but the crew wouldn't let them get anywhere near the controls.

"You have to let us do this!" yelled Goldsmith. "They'll die down there if you don't let us save them!"

"That's the idea," said Katt. His voice was calm and steady, utterly unmoved by the scientists' rage and horror.

"This is murder!" said Hamilton. "Premeditated, cold-blooded murder!"

"Best kind," said Natasha Chang, lounging carelessly beside the Captain. "I told you, I'm in charge here. I speak for the Crowley Project, and I say: no air! Let the Ghost Finders stay dead. They've served their purpose, and we don't need them any longer." She smiled sweetly at Catherine Latimer, covering her with the gold-plated pistol. "Nothing to say, Boss lady?"

"I'd like to say I'm surprised," said Latimer. "But I'm not. I'd plead for my people's lives if I thought it would do any good, but it wouldn't. And anyway, I wouldn't lower myself to the likes of you."

"We don't need you any more, either," said Chang. "So guess what! I'm going to eat your soul! Rip it right out of your head and wolf it down! I'll bet it's really chewy, and just full of secrets . . ."

Latimer fixed Chang with suddenly glowing golden eyes. "No dear, I'm going to eat your soul. I learned that old trick years ago."

She tore Natasha Chang out of her body, and everyone on the deck of the *Moonchilde* flinched, as Chang's body fell limply to the deck. Still breathing, its eyes staring unseeingly. Catherine Latimer smiled coldly about her.

"Not the first bad thing I've had to stomach."

Captain Katt stepped in behind Latimer and shot her twice in the back of the head. The Boss died without a sound, her brittle old body falling to the deck to lie beside Chang. Katt looked down at the two bodies and nodded stiffly to Latimer.

"I suppose I should thank you, for ridding the world of that unnatural monster. But then, you weren't much better in the end, were you? My orders were always quiet specific— no Ghost Finders could be allowed to survive this mission, whatever the outcome. You'd seen too much, knew too much. And we don't like owing favours to anyone. It's the Project way."

JC and Kim, Happy and Melody went striding down the deck, their glowing golden light blazing brightly in the night. Captain Katt and his crew looked round, then froze where they were. Katt's face was full of shock and horror as he saw the people he'd ordered killed coming for him. And knew at last why the dead had always walked the deck of his ship. Katt stumbled back and yelled for his crew to open fire. Many of them did, but their bullets just passed harmlessly through the advancing ghosts.

The four Ghost Finders moved as one, full of a terrible power, and blasted the life right out of the crew. They collapsed all across the deck, their spirits crying out as they saw what was waiting for them. Goldsmith and Hamilton hid behind a tall pile of crates, their eyes squeezed shut and their hands over their ears. Not wanting to know. Captain Katt looked at the four ghosts heading relentlessly towards him and saw what they had planned for him. He put his gun to his head and pulled the trigger. His body made only a small sound as it crumpled to the deck. His ghost didn't appear. It had always known where it was going.

The four ghosts stood still, on the quiet deck. Goldsmith and Hamilton came slowly out from behind the crates and looked around at all the bodies with wide, shell-shocked eyes.

"Pump air back into the bathysphere, you idiots," said JC. "While there's still time. And then haul us back up here."

The scientists nodded jerkily and rushed to obey. After a while, first Happy and Melody, and then Kim and JC faded away, and were gone.

|||||||||||||||||||||||||||

When the scientists finally brought the bathysphere up out of the waters, and swung it over the side and onto the deck, and opened the air-lock . . . All they found inside were three dead bodies, sitting in their chairs. The sphere was full of perfectly good air, but it had come too late. The Ghost Finders had been without oxygen for too long. Goldsmith and Hamilton took turns hauling the bodies out the air-lock and laying them on the deck, side by side. And then they started CPR. Since there were only two of them, they could only work on two people at a time. They chose JC and Happy because they looked strongest. They didn't know about Happy's condition. Goldsmith and Hamilton pounded on chests, breathed air into mouths, and did chest compressions as best they could remember from the brief first-aid course they'd attended ages ago. They did everything they could; and eventually, JC started breathing again.

Happy didn't.

Goldsmith helped JC sit up. He coughed harshly, struggling for breath, slowly realising where he was. Hamilton gave up on Happy and went to work on Melody. It didn't help. Hamilton sat down hard on the deck beside Melody's body, hugged her knees to her chest, and let her head hang down. Goldsmith went over to her and patted her on the shoulder. He didn't say anything. There wasn't anything to say.

JC slowly got to his feet and wondered why he was still alive when his friends were dead. Was it because of something the forces from Outside did to him? Or just blind chance. It hurt just as much, either way. And then he realised the spirits of Happy and Melody were standing before him.

"I'm sorry," said JC. "So sorry."

"No reason to be," said Happy.

"None of this was your fault," said Melody. "We knew what we were getting into."

Happy smiled easily. "We did the job. Saved the world."

"Not a bad way to bow out," said Melody.

"And now it's time for us to go," said Happy. "We just wanted to say good-bye."

Melody smiled fondly at Happy. "I knew he was dying. I'm glad I got to go with him. He's always hated having to go to strange places on his own."

"Be seeing you, JC," said Happy.

They both disappeared, as though it was the most natural thing in the world.

"I'm alone," said JC. "No-one else left. Just me."

"You don't have to be on your own," said Kim.

JC looked round and saw the ghost girl standing over Natasha Chang. Kim smiled at him.

"We have a chance to be together at last. In the flesh. There's no soul in Chang's body. It's empty. If you want, I could go into it. Take up residence and live a normal human life again, with you."

"Yes," said JC. "That's what I want. For us to be together, finally."

Kim grinned. "I always knew you secretly fancied her."

She disappeared. Natasha Chang jerked spasmodically on the deck a few times, then sat up abruptly. She looked at JC.

"I'm here, sweetie," she said. With Kim's voice.

"Okay . . ." said JC. "This is going to take a lot of getting used to."

TWELVE

MEET THE NEW BOSS, PART TWO

JC Chance sat behind his desk, in what used to be Catherine Latimer's office, at the back of Buck House. With the authority granted him by the destruction of the Flesh Undying and saving the world, and all the information he was able to provide on the inner workings of Crowley Project Headquarters, and because everyone was now frankly more than a bit frightened of him . . . JC had been put in charge of the Carnacki Institute. He routed the cabal, sorted the good guys from the bad guys and the wheat from the chaff, and soon had everything running smoothly again.

Getting rid of the cabal people had proved surprisingly easy. In the short time they'd been in charge, they'd screwed up a lot of operations and made a great many enemies . . . inside and outside the Institute. Everyone was glad to see them go.

JC had been quietly asked whether he wanted to sign a whole bunch of kill orders . . . but he declined. He didn't want to be that sort of Boss.

In the office outside his office, Kim had Heather's old job. As JC's personal secretary and first line of defence. Sometimes people thought she was still Natasha Chang, and sometimes JC let people think that. It helped keep them on their toes.

He took off his sunglasses, and the fierce golden light from his eyes illuminated the office. It looked a bit bare and spartan, without Latimer's old trophies . . . but he'd already started a collection of souvenirs from his own old cases. A small black blob, under a glass case. A scarecrow in a morning suit and top hat, standing in the corner, wrapped in silver chains. Just in case. And a rabbit's foot. That might or might not be the reason he was still alive when so many others had died taking down the Flesh Undying.

JC wondered if he'd live as long as Catherine Latimer, after what the forces from Outside had done to him. He also wondered if they had other plans for him. JC put his sunglasses back on and looked at the paper-work piled up on the desk before him. There was a lot of work to be done.

A lifetime's worth.

Also from *New York Times* bestselling author

SIMON R. GREEN

TALES FROM THE NIGHTSIDE

Including "The Big Game," a never-before-published
Nightside novella, and nine other Nightside
favorites now in one volume

Welcome to the Nightside. It's the secret heart of London,
beating to its own rhythm, pumping lifeblood through the
veins of its streets and alleys hidden in eternal darkness,
where creatures of the night congregate and where the sun
is afraid to shine. It's the place to go if you're looking to
indulge the darker side of your nature—and to hell with
the consequences.

Tales from the Nightside presents ten macabre mysteries that
shine a dim beam into the neighborhood's darkest corners
to reveal things that should *never* come to light.

"A macabre and thoroughly entertaining world."
—Jim Butcher, #1 *New York Times* bestselling
author of the Dresden Files

Available wherever books are sold and at penguin.com